G000123402

DEATH'S
STING

Duplicity and Deceit in the Balkans

Published in the
United Kingdom by Westlake Books

Copyright © 2017 Ewen Southby-Tailyour

ISBN 978-1-54084-935-9

Also available as a Kindle ebook
ISBN 978-1-84396-436-0

A catalogue record of this
book is available from the British Library
and the American Library of Congress

Pre-press production
eBook Versions
27 Old Gloucester Street,
London WC1N 3AX
www.ebookversions.com

The characters and organisations described in this
novel are entirely fictional and figments of the author's
imagination. The presence of names that are
shared by living persons or actual organisations is
the result of unintended coincidence.

O death where is thy sting?
O grave where is thy victory?

1 Corinthians, 15:55

About the author

Ewen Southby-Tailyour, who was educated at the Nautical College Pangbourne and Grenoble University, was commissioned into the Royal Marines in 1960 and served, *inter alia*, with the French *Commando Hubert* in the south of France and Corsica; with the Unites States Marine Corps in the Mediterranean; in the West Indies; in the Dhofar War (where he was awarded the Sultan of Muscat's Bravery Medal) in Northern Ireland; in Hong Kong; on North Sea oil rigs; in Arctic Norway and throughout the Falklands Campaign (following which he was appointed an OBE).

In 1982 he was elected British Yachtsman of the Year.

He retired in 1992 as a Lieutenant-Colonel and the following year joined the Foreign and Commonwealth Office for duties as a monitor with the European Community Monitoring Mission (ECMM) in the Former Republic of Yugoslavia. Here he was tasked informally by the Secret Intelligence Service (MI6) to keep an eye on one or two individuals while reporting on Croatia's preparation for war against the breakaway, so-called Republic of Serbian Krajina.

He resigned from the ECMM in 1994 in protest at being ordered to falsify his daily reports in order to prevent the breaking of United Nations Arms Embargo, 713 being made public.

Death's Sting is a novel based on the author's experiences in the Republic of Serbian Krajina and Croatia.

Apart from the Presidents of Croatia and the United States, and those mentioned in the Author's Notes, all characters are figments of the author's imagination.

Other books

DEATH'S
STING

Duplicity and Deceit in the Balkans

Ewen Southby-Tailyour

WESTLAKE BOOKS

Contents

Prologue

Friday 4th August 1995
Operation Storm
Drniš village, Republic of Serbian Krajina.

The first, hollow-nosed, 9 mm round from Colonel Ante Slavić's, Croatian Special Forces, HS 95 pistol gouged a long trough through the skin, hair and shallow flesh of James Laidlaw's scalp, half an inch above his left ear. Stunned by the shockwave and a violent, stinging pain James staggered sideways, dropping the charred, skeletal body of the tiny Croatian woman he was carrying beneath his right arm. Her husband, his eyeballs partially vaporised by the flames, clutched at James's belt: his only guide to safety away from the inferno that had been their house – their home since marriage, over sixty years before.

Matea Laidlaw, eight and a half-months pregnant, ran forwards screaming, "Mama. Tata! Oh my God. James help them. Oh God please help them!"

…but she was too late to say goodbye.

Turning, with loathing distorting her face, she launched herself at Slavić shouting "My parents!   My parents. You've murdered my parents." The colonel, grinning with a perverse pleasure, was too quick for her flailing arms. Aiming behind the approaching woman, his second, hollow-nosed round slammed into James's left shoulder splintering bone, tearing muscle, exploding soft tissue, snapping tendons. The violent impact spun him round, hastening his fall to the ground as

1

blood began flooding through his shirt and down the white, sleeveless pullover's V-neck. He dragged Matea's father with him.

Carefully following his falling target Slavić's third shot bored straight through the Croatian man's forehead. In a dreadful red mist, brains and blood splattered onto the path behind. He was dead before he collapsed across his wife's already-still figure. Fast losing consciousness himself, James tried to squirm free from the obscene pile but his body had lost its strength and was swiftly losing its blood: some of which was now bubbling from a corner of his mouth.

Ignoring Slavić, Matea knelt by her father and mother but there was nothing she could do for them: now James, her son Dino and the child she was carrying were all she had left. She reached for her husband's near-lifeless hand. He was mouthing something, his lips moving but making little sound. Matea bent lower. "I – love – you," he was struggling to form each word individually. "Name – the – baby – after – your – father – or – mother – and – and…" His eyelids fluttered and closed.

'No time for that,' Matea surprised even herself with her cool and rational assessment, 'I've got to stop the bloody bleeding…'

Looking round for a dressing – anything would do – she watched Slavić standing over the grim tableau, surveying his handiwork. His legs were apart, one hand rested on a hip, the other waved his handgun. "Got what they deserved," he mocked, "Serb-loving traitors…"

"You vile man," Matea spoke slowly, quietly and deliberately while removing the paisley pattern scarf from around her neck to use, for the second time in recent years, as a bandage, "Nothing better than a common murderer, a war criminal, and I promise from the very depths of my heart that one day you

2

will face justice." She was too angry, too shocked to shout or even cry: that would come later.

"And you can sod off this world too," Slavić replied, steadily raising his pistol for the fourth time, pointing it at her stomach and the embryo within. "You'll never catch me. Your parents, your boyfriend," he spat the word, "can't protect you and your unborn bastard anymore."

Taking his time, cruelly dragging out the horror, revelling in Matea's wide-eyed terror, Slavić very slowly tightened his finger on the trigger as an inhuman grimace spread across his face.

Suddenly he turned away.

A United Nations Protection Force Land Rover was decelerating swiftly to a halt behind him; the following dust cloud overtaking the vehicle as it stopped. Blanketed from view for a moment Slavić threw his weapon high into the air towards the blazing bungalow. Even before it landed he was shouting at Matea over his shoulder, "I'll get you too. And that's my promise."

Slavić strode confidently towards his Zastava 'jeep' from where, after squeezing his bulk behind the steering wheel and slamming the door shut, he turned to face the dreadful scene that he had created. With a final laughing sneer, he sped away down the stony, dusty track.

Chapter One

Sunday 7th August 1988
Percuil House, Tredenhum Road,
St Mawes, Cornwall, England.

Commander James Laidlaw disliked the telephone's ring as much as he hated the telephone itself. His eight-months pregnant wife, Caroline, had driven to Perranarworthal, the other side of Truro, for a 'girl's lunch'. Despite having woken with a light headache and feeling a touch more 'puffy' than normal she had insisted.

Bugger, James thought, without irritation, dragging himself away from his 'chart table' where he was polishing plans for their annual cruise to the Biscay coast of France. Each September he and Caroline undertook this escape in their fifteen-ton, gaff cutter. There was little else in his life to occupy his days, apart from the admiral's daughter, the growing baby she was carrying and their boat.

Now, after three years of marriage, the welcome excitement of the child's impending arrival was even eclipsing the expectation of their three-week voyage, the planning for which had now become little more than a paper exercise.

James reached the cordless 'phone. Pressing it to his ear he walked into the sunlit drawing-room with its views through two large bay windows: one facing south-west towards the St Mawes anchorage and Carrick Roads while the other looked across the placid Percuil river to the south-east.

"Yes?" he queried firmly.

"James Laidlaw?" The female voice was precise in its intonation, "It's Maureen Thompson here. Sister in charge of the maternity wing at the Royal Cornwall Hospital, Treliske. Friend of Caroline's."

"Good heavens!" answered the commander more softly, "Has she gone into labour?"

"No, but I'm afraid she has collapsed with pre-eclampsia. We're waiting for the ambulance. Can you meet us at A and E?"

"Is it dangerous?"

"How long will you take?"

Exercising as much control as he could, he stuttered, "Is she all right? Is the baby all right?" His voice, un-accustomed to registering panic was doing so now. "How long have I got?"

"Be there as soon as you can."

"Roger!" He replied breaking into his more familiar naval patois. "On my way." His brain was already calculating whether it was quicker to drive via King Harry Ferry or to take the longer route through Tregony. High summer. Mid-August. Long queues for the ferry.

'Hold on Caroline. For Christ's sake, darling, hold on.' He was shouting to himself as he slammed the car door shut, stabbed the key into the ignition and pressed the Bristol's starter button. 'I'm coming as fast as I can.'

He was ten minutes late. She and the unborn boy were already dead.

The fifth anniversary of Caroline's death, as with those before it, was not going to be easy for James's life had remained in limbo since that terrible scene in Treliske's Accident and Emergency department.

He needed no income: his pension as a retired Royal Navy officer, plus a few savings, were bolstered by his late wife's family legacy, along with Percuil House and its house-keeper, Mrs B. Because of this he believed himself beholden to Caroline, feeling, perhaps subconsciously, that he could never, or should never, use her money or share her house with another woman.

As the years moved very slowly by an underlying frustration had developed caused, James had no doubt, by inaction. He had nothing to aim for; nothing to which he could look forward; nothing to give purpose to his life anymore and little to exercise his brain. He knew he had to say goodbye to Caroline sometime, but he couldn't bring himself to do so quite yet.

This lunchtime, as he did on this day every year, he stuffed a cool-bag with fresh food and set off for his elderly gaff cutter swinging to her Percuil River moorings. The weather was fine and he had no plans except to meander for the weekend, maybe a few days longer: perhaps as far west as the Isles of Scilly if the wind served. He was in no hurry other than to escape human contact.

Eventually he dropped *Sea Vixen*'s anchor in the entrance to the Helford river. Then, with the black-hulled vessel snugged down for the night, he poured a generous tot of whisky, tossed a cushion from the saloon into the cockpit and followed it up clutching two unopened letters.

One was from a 'girlfriend' whom he liked but with whom he did not see, nor want, a long-term future; anyway, her regular 'offer' was still one watershed too far. For the moment.

The second was from a Special Boat Service officer, with whom he had kept in touch, describing life as a monitor with the Foreign Office in the Balkans and encouraging him to consider doing the same 'before it is too late'. Despite knowing nothing of monitoring James read it for a second time then, on the third occasion, he read it very slowly indeed analysing each clause until it dawned on him that he did not feel that monitoring events in a foreign country contained the key to his future emotional stability.

Commander James Laidlaw had spent most of his naval career in submarines, even winning the Distinguished Service Cross as a young lieutenant during a particular hazardous special forces operation off the north-west coast off Donegal Bay when they had intercepted and captured a vessel supplying the IRA with arms and ammunition. James worked hard and played hard, enjoying a party as much as anyone and sometimes more than many. He seldom drank at sea, and certainly not when beneath it in his submarine, but would make up for this professional abstinence when ashore or at anchor.

In 1985 he had married Caroline Lennox: a handsome, leggy, long-haired dinghy sailor and offshore crew from the local sailing club. If this union had surprised his friends it had certainly astonished James, the 'un-confirmed bachelor' – as he was known – who had never found 'affairs' easy to forge. He liked girls, he enjoyed their company but usually as an 'outsider' and he was shyly conscious that his height, she had been two inches taller than him, his devotion to his sailors and his love of a good whisky were not, perhaps, wholly encouraging to a long-term relationship.

Afloat he was disciplined and correct to the point of being fastidious but ashore… Ashore and out of uniform was a different matter with his adored, fun-loving Caroline a more than willing partner. Now, since her death, he had never been alone with a woman of his own age, never kissed a woman of any age. His love of a good party had, too, died.

Four years James's junior, Caroline had swept into his life at the St Mawes Sailing Club's summer dance. They knew each other and had occasionally exchanged small talk about dinghy racing, but nothing more. Then, with a suddenness that was to surprise them both, all that changed when James, contemplating a post-dinner glass of 'malt', felt a hand softly squeezing his shoulder.

He turned and looked up, straight into a pair of steady, hazel-green eyes. "Would you like to dance?" she asked gently. It wasn't a question: it was an incontestable order.

In front of his fellow diners he could not refuse. "How unusual," he muttered then, goaded by cries of, "You can't say no to the club's most beautiful lady member." and "Don't let her down, James!" the retired commander replied as softly and as confidently as she had asked. "How lovely," he said, firmly pushing back his chair. He was not to know for some years that she had won a bet, nor were either of them to know, quite yet, that they had, together in that brief moment, won each other.

A year after their wedding in St Just in Roseland church it was clear to both that the navy, marriage and sailing were not mixing well and so James Laidlaw took early retirement in 1986.

This August the weather was unusually benign and the long weekend went without drama, which was just as well for James did not like dramas on these anniversaries. The following Wednesday, as he humped his kit bag back through his house's front door, the telephone was already ringing. For the second time in recent years it was to alter his life: again, irreversibly.

"James Laidlaw here."

"This is the Foreign and Commonwealth Office's Eastern Adriatic Unit."

There was no reason why the Foreign Office's Eastern Adriatic Unit should be telephoning him. Indeed, he thought, who are they and how do they have my number.

"You may never have heard of the European Community Monitoring Mission but it is looking for monitors and we wondered if you would care to come for an interview?"

James was improbably flattered that the Foreign Office should have contacted him and although he had only recently heard of the monitoring mission through his friend's letter, he had determined that it wasn't for him. He brought the conversation to a polite end yet it had, unlike the letter, sparked a modicum of interest. Monitoring with the Foreign Office might, just, offer something useful, satisfying even, to help him move forward.

Two days later he picked up the telephone.

"We didn't expect to hear from you," the Eastern Adriatic Unit replied.

"I didn't expect you to hear from me either," he teased, "but I would like to know more about this monitoring business."

There was a pause during which he listened to pages being turned and papers ruffled.

"We can offer you an interview on Thursday 30 September. We'll pay your travel expenses and accommodation for one night."

On the agreed date and at the correct time James presented himself at the King Charles Street headquarters of the Foreign and Commonwealth Office. Unsure if he wanted to pass the interview he knew that pride would prevent him from failing it on purpose. Ushered into an ornate, high-ceilinged office James Laidlaw was surprised to be faced by three dark-suited members of the quaintly-named Eastern Adriatic Unit. Less surprising were the questions: he had predicted them and needed only to give the rehearsed answers. However, when asked what he knew of events in the former Republic of Yugoslavia he was on less-safe ground and replied, more flippantly then he meant, "I was rather hoping you would tell me."

As the interview drew to a close James offered a military

résumé of his career rather than the wholly-nautical one that, on the rare occasions he needed it, was the one he had used. "No," was the chairman's quick response, "it is your maritime expertise that we are looking for."

"In that case I should only accept the appointment if I can serve on the coast."

Eventually they all stood, shook hands and, following good wishes for a safe journey back to Cornwall, Commander Laidlaw walked out of King Charles Street and into Whitehall.

He had booked into the Army and Navy Club on St James's Square for the night where, during his occasional journeys to London, he had seldom failed to meet a friend. One was not long in coming.

"James. Don't see you here too often. Did you get my letter?"

James turned from ordering a large pink gin to face Julian Hathaway's stocky, pugnacious, beaming face. In reply he turned back to the barman, "Better make that two, please," then answered, "Yes, you bugger I did get your letter and I guess it was you that told the Foreign Office I was free?"

"Thought it might help."

Julian had often taken passage in the diesel-electric, Oberon Class submarine HMS *Orion* when James had been the Third Hand responsible for the navigation. Then, during one patrol, Julian had persuaded James to apply for the Royal Marines', all-arms commando course. Once proudly qualified to wear the 'commando green beret' he became responsible for coordinating, and sometimes conducting, his boat's maritime special forces operations.

After dinner they moved into the Club's Smoking Room for a glass of port and a rare cigar, where Julian, having recently returned from Zagreb, the capital of Croatia, was keen to share his experiences. James was happy to hear them.

"I promised I would tell you about the ECMM."

"I know but I'm not sure that I want to go."

"The hundred and fifty quid a day might persuade you."

"I'm not looking for money."

"She was a great girl, James, but you can't be in mourning for ever. How old are you now?" Julian did not wait for a reply: he knew the answer. "Thirty-nine. Same as me and high time you re-joined our world. We've missed you. And your sailing invitations!"

They were silent for a minute before James responded, "Thankfully, I enjoy sailing on my own. Not such fun, of course. She was bloody good in a boat, equally efficient with a sextant as a saucepan. Never sea sick..." He trailed off... this was not the way he wanted a rare evening of escape to end. "Go on," he ordered, "Tell me about the ECMM."

"Funny organisation," Julian began, reaching for his glass, "When the Cold War came to an end I didn't see much enjoyment being a Royal Marine anymore. Thought the Falklands was a 'one-off' but how wrong I was. Look what's been happening in the Gulf. Anyway I thought I might try and claw back a bit of excitement somewhere and the ECMM seemed as good a bet as any."

"And did you claw back that excitement?"

"I certainly did but not quite in the way I was hoping. I also found the job rather satisfying. Instead of killing terrorists I was, for once, trying to save civilians from being murdered..." He paused long enough to take a sip before continuing in a near whisper, "...or from being ethnically cleansed."

It seemed to James inconceivable that Julian, of all people, would have found satisfaction in 'saving foreign civilians'.

Julian continued, "I was only in Serbia and Croatia and have to say that they are both as bad as each other. Serbia gets the worst press but, believe me, the Croats with their holier-than-thou attitude, together with their new-found independence that supposedly gives them respectability, are every bit as corrupt. Either way, there are no good guys out there. One has to be impartial but it is not always easy." He paused, then repeated, "It was never easy."

Julian was in full flow, "One moment you might be arranging for decomposed bodies to be collected from the minefields along the confrontation line and returning them to their families. The next you could be monitoring the interminable cease-fire violations." Julian inhaled deeply before adding chillingly, "Incidentally, it will be you that has to walk through the minefields to collect the bodies...

"You will have to prepare yourself for some pretty grizzly experiences that surprised even me after twenty or so years chasing down the world's hooligans."

"Such as?"

"Coming upon the after effects of a bomb is one thing. As you well know, an improvised explosive device, detonated by remote control, is indiscriminate, and the bastard that placed it has usually skedaddled by the time it goes off. He won't see the bits that are left. A leg here. Half a torso and a pool of split-open guts there. The back of a skull and a dollop of brains somewhere else. It's all pretty impersonal. But what one human being can do to another in cold blood when fuelled by so much hatred is altogether something different. It is something very personal."

"Give me an example."

"A few months ago there was a fracas between Serbs and Muslims who were being 'cleansed' from a village called Fojnica in Bosnia Herzegovina. A British army lady monitor..."

"A lady monitor?"

"Rare, but there are some. Anyway, she was called to assess what was going on but by the time she arrived things had got out of hand. Reaching the village square she saw what appeared to be an elderly man and a woman kneeling on the ground facing each other. As there wasn't another soul in sight she knew something wasn't right. Fearing an ambush she left her driver and interpreter behind cover and walked forwards by herself. I talked to her afterwards when she admitted that it was all she could do not to be sick on the spot. Although she was later."

"They had been murdered?"

"Worse. They had been bound and staked to the ground in kneeling positions each with a wooden pole stuffed up their rectums and their arms fastened behind to keep them up-right. The perpetrators, Serbs this time but it could have been any of the other bastards, then cut off the man's genitals in front of his wife and stuffed them in her mouth. They died within minutes of the monitor's arrival."

"Poor bastards." James shuddered, "Brave lass."

"Very. The job is not without its dangers as all the constituent countries think the monitors are spies in disguise. With every good reason, too, for there are certainly enough intelligence agencies rushing all over the place."

"Doing what?"

"Good question," Julian replied, "You'll find that the Dutch *Militaire Inlichtingendienst* operates across the area and, hardly surprisingly the German *Bundesnachrichtendienst* is also pretty active. The French *Direction générale de la sécurité* extérieure seem to be everywhere and, as always, making a bloody nuisance of themselves; not least of all because they have their own internal radio network. And quite why the Danish *Forsvarets Efterretningstjeneste*, is involved beats me… unless they all want to fight over the pieces when it goes tits up."

"Meaning precisely what?"

"I can't speak for the interior such as Bosnia-Herzegovina but I have a sneaking suspicion that one day Croatia will simply march across the Serbian confrontation line."

"Into the Republic of Serbian Krajina?"

"I'll explain but before I do so let me say that I don't admire what the Serbs in Krajina have done but I certainly understand why they have done it."

"Enlighten me?"

"In a moment because I think you should know about the other intelligence agencies. Outside the ECMM, as it were, you will find that Mossad always seems to be around the next corner. It is concerned about the Muslim aspect and employing very clever and very attractive girls for all the obvious reasons. And getting results. The Russian agents are more sophisticated than their European counterparts and are unlikely to show their hand. Inevitably, the Yanks have an entrée, especially as their Defense Attaché in Zagreb is a member of the Defence Intelligence Agency and is believed to be actively anti-Serb. As always America is using the United Nations as a condom…"

"A what?" James was unsure he had heard correctly.

"Something I picked up recently from an Assistant General Secretary in the United Nations. He said that the United States regards, and I quote directly, 'the UN as a mighty great condom with which it can fuck the rest of the world with impunity.'"

James smiled and changed the subject, "Presumably you were working for MI6? Doing what many ex-Special Forces guys get up to on retirement."

Julian shook his head slowly, "No, you see I had done with all that and was happy to be a straightforward monitor. But I did keep my eyes and ears open although everything I passed back was through the British in Zagreb and not direct to Century House."

"Why?"

"SIS asked me to keep an eye on one or two things but, as I said, I'd had enough of that so only agreed providing it was on a rather more open basis. Hence I kept the Head of the British Delegation in Zagreb informed. What he did after that was up to him. One thing I did do was to get the full portfolio of British Admiralty charts sent out covering the whole of the Dalmatian Coast. I imagine they are still in the Split Ops Room."

"Could be useful. The RSK? You said you would give me a potted history."

"A very potted one too as it is getting late. During the last war Croatia was a puppet state of Nazi Germany so, hardly a coincidence, in 1991 when Croatia obtained independence, it was with German help. The Serbs, in the Croatian border region of Krajina, remembering how the Ustaše had treated them, decided that if Croatia could obtain independence from Yugoslavia then they should do the same from Croatia. So they established a government in Knin and called itself the Republic of Serbian Krajina. An unmarked, mined confrontation line was the result which tends to ebb and flow as each 'side' takes or loses territory; often accompanied by the indiscriminate shelling of school children."

Julian studied his glass and sighed while James, shaking his head, asked, "Interpreters?"

"A good bunch. Mostly girls on the look out for an escape although I think I only knew of one who managed it. An army monitor brought a Croatian girl to stay in his club in London where, hardly surprising, they were spotted together. End of his marriage. End of their relationship while she was left to pay her own way back to Zagreb. Served him right, of course, but I felt

16

more sorry for her as she was promised married bliss in nice, safe Hampshire. Instead she ended up broke and ostracised in the slums of Split."

James simply nodded but Julian hadn't quite finished. Noticing his friend's tiredness he said, "Let me sum up briefly and then I'll let you turn in." James nodded once more.

"The Croatians," Julian explained, "like to think of themselves as being middle European not Balkan. German is their second language although many speak good English while the current Serbian-Croatian hostility is regarded as similar to that between Ulster and Eire…

"The overall tragedy is that rather than having someone of Havel's stature in charge of Czechoslovakia, Yugoslavia has inherited two second-rate leaders: Milošević in Serbia and Tudjman in Croatia."

And with that closing statement they agreed it was time for bed.

Uncertain whether he wanted to drag decomposing corpses from a minefield, arbitrate over the mutilated bodies of innocent children, or even be 'targeted' by a lady interpreter, James had six hours on the train the next day to decide. Yet, on his arrival at home he found that the decision had been made for him in a letter – he deduced that it must have been written before the interview – from the Eastern Adriatic Unit offering a year's contract beginning on 30 November 1993.

That evening James sat watching the sun set beyond Carrick Roads. The light reflecting off the two-mile-wide waterway filled the drawing room with crimson, as it had done so often when he and Caroline had been together. Five years since her death and he still thought of her as if she had gone away for a long weekend but now it had to be goodbye and if nothing else the ECMM was offering that chance… a chance he could take with a clear conscience.

"Bugger it," he said aloud. "This is damned silly."

He knew, he had always known, that Caroline would approve of anything that kept his mind – and even his body – active. She would not approve of the vegetative existence, both physical and emotional, that he had set himself. On the positive side the sailing season would have ended by the time he took up the offer: he would ask for six months and then, if he felt he was doing any good, he would apply to extend for the full year.

"Decision made," he announced to himself, "I'll write the letter in the morning."

As he coasted towards sleep he was surprised to find that he could not stop weeping.

CHAPTER TWO

Sunday 3rd October 1993
Percuil House, Tredenhum Road, St Mawes,
Cornwall, England

Honouring the promise that he had made to himself James Laidlaw wrote to the Foreign and Commonwealth Office accepting their offer, but for six months. His lame excuse for not wishing to serve the full tour was, he explained, 'due to the death of my wife'. As his marital status had never been queried, beyond a tick in a box indicating that he was a widower, a vague response was in order. He was unwilling to commit himself to a period that he might find difficult to complete.

A reply, accepting his proposal from 30 November 1983, gave a choice of dates for a 'medical' in London and, on the assumption that he would be found 'fit for purpose', that physical inspection would precede a briefing in King Charles Street on the same day. He was obliged to sign a copy of the Official Secrets Act and read an enclosed essay titled General Background on the role of the EC Monitor Mission.

The brief medical examination – more a question and answer interview than a prod and a squeeze – was endured, as was the accompanying brief by the FCO.

Before leaving St Mawes a surprise telephone call from another acquaintance he had known in his submariner days had James thumbing through an A to Z of London, searching for Soho's Romilly Street. A lunchtime meeting with Magnus Ian Sixsmith on the day following his medical was suggested and agreed. Magnus, a member of the Secret Intelligence Service since university and now running the Balkans desk from Century House, had given little away.

"James, we use the Lyndsay House at Number 21, for discrete meetings. I know you won't be disappointed by the menu and nor, I hope, will you be disappointed by the ideas I would like to put to you. If you arrive before me just say that you are having lunch with Mr Short."

"Thank you…"

Magnus remembered, "Oh, and by the way I have told them that my guest's name is Wilcox. Better stick to that in case they ask. They never do but…"

James was fifteen minutes early and the door to Number 21 was locked, nor was there any indication, other than the name of the 'house' on a large brass plaque, to suggest that food was served behind the suspended gas lamp, the iron railings and the black door topped by a fanlight. Puzzled, he retraced his steps and ordered half a pint of London Pride in the Golden Lion pub where the long-remembered smell of *Gauloises Caporal* cigarette smoke helped sharpen his appetite. As James entered the bar, the smoker, a small, un-shaven, olive-skinned man sitting beneath the leaded-glass window facing Romilly Street and reading the previous evening's *Le Monde*, looked up. Impassive and bored, he turned back to his newspaper, removed a soggy dog-end from his nicotine-stained lips, flicked a replacement from the blue, paper packet and struck a match.

Knowing that the SIS, and Magnus in particular, did not make such mistakes James returned to No 21 on the dot of 1230 and rang the bell again. Voices from inside preceded a theatrical opening of the heavy door through which he was swiftly ushered without a word being said. Just as speedily the door was closed behind him.

"Good afternoon, sir. Do you have a reservation?"

"My name's Wilcox and I am here to meet Mr Short."

"I'll show you to his table. He will be here at 1240. Precisely. May I offer you a drink while you wait?"

"Thank you, a gin and tonic please and I am sure Mr Short won't mind if it is a large one!"

"He would have insisted, sir."

"Now, if you would like to sit... here..." the waiter drew back a chair half facing a first floor window, "...while I pour your drink. Ice and lemon?"

"No ice. Thank you."

Precisely at 1240 the tall, fair-haired Magnus Sixsmith zigzagged his way between the empty tables with a wide grin across his angular, long-nosed face. James stood. They shook hands warmly.

"Sorry I'm ten minutes late. Making sure neither of us was followed. Not a problem if we were... but you never know." Magnus with his back to the window, but not in front of it, sat facing the dining room that was beginning to fill up: whether with 'escapees' from the Secret Intelligence Service's Century House, a mile or so away towards the river, or with bona-fide diners was not clear to James who presumed that Magnus knew them all but would acknowledge no one. None of the adjacent tables was occupied.

Handing James a menu his host summarized its contents, "They specialise in reasonably exotic European food so let me recommend the pan-fried *foie gras* followed by the duck with fennel and orange marmalade," he stopped, remembering that James, too, enjoyed his food. "Sorry, you choose." James chose the *foie gras* and duck.

Lunch was a smoke screen. The serious business began once the first course had been cleared away during which they had caught up with each other's recent past.

"I hear you are off to Yugoslavia." Alone again Magnus came straight to the point, "That has to be the best way to put Caroline to bed, as it were."

"I have to get away from the house. Her house. It is the only answer." James guessed that Magnus knew more about the ECMM than he did so he didn't elaborate beyond stating simply, "So I am now to be a monitor..."

"I'm glad you are as we need a little help. Not least of all because you were once security cleared to Cosmic Top Secret. You won't have any clearance this time as we need an un-attributable person in theatre. Someone who is part of the scenery. Un-noticed, when necessary. Someone with an easy entrée, when needed."

James listened intently until their duck arrived. Alone once more Magnus continued with his request. Years before, beneath the turbulent surface of the Barents Sea, and close inshore to the north Russian port of Murmansk, HMS *Orion* had eavesdropped on Soviet naval communications. Magnus, a competent Russian speaker, spent weeks listening and recording. James had been the navigator: now it would be his turn to do the snooping.

The Secret Intelligence Service, for reasons that Magnus was not going to divulge, needed to know if United Nation's Arms Embargo Number 713 was being broken and if so by whom. He agreed that this was probably beyond James's remit as a monitor, indeed warships of the NATO Standing Squadron were on patrol for just such duties. "Nevertheless, on the assumption the embargo is being breached..."

"You sound as though you already know that it is being broken," interrupted James.

"We have no confirmation other than that all such embargoes are broken. It's almost mandatory!" Magnus laughed. "Seriously though, it would help us if we had hard evidence and it would help us even more if we knew where the arms are heading once they are ashore. Serbia or, more likely, Croatia. You are not James Bond. All I am asking is for you to keep your eyes and ears open. Other monitors, dockyard workers, crane drivers and so on, might say too much after a raquia or two."

"Raquia?"

"You won't be able to avoid it. Croatia's revolting version of the far more palatable Serbian slivovitz."

James stopped Magnus a second time, "I have no idea where I will be sent. I could find myself spending the next six months twiddling my thumbs on the banks of the Danube."

"The current Head of the British Delegation in Zagreb, Colin Cooper, is with us and while no Head of a National Delegation can, in theory, decide where their countrymen will serve I think you will find that CC may well exercise his famed charm." Putting down his knife and fork Magnus looked directly at James and smiled with the slightest suggestion of a wink.

The duck was superb and on any other occasion James would have devoted more attention to its taste and texture but, unable to take 'minutes of the meeting', he was concentrating hard. He also made a mental note to return under less serious circumstances: assuming The Lyndsay House catered for people 'off the street'.

"We won't pay you of course and if anything happens we will deny all knowledge of you. The fact that you are employed by the FCO for duties with the ECMM will be enough. If in the current unlikely case that you should leave a widow she would be looked after by them."

Magnus was nearly finished. "Over 'pud' I'll explain how you contact me now but it might become more complicated as the whole of 'the firm' is about to move to 85 Albert Embankment at Vauxhall Cross. The other side of the river."

They chose their puddings and once the passion fruit, marinated in Benedictine, had arrived Magnus summed up the meeting.

"The British Consul in Split is Captain Augustin Milna. He is Croatian and was a merchant navy ferry captain so there is not much he doesn't understand about the Dalmatian coast and offshore islands."

"Sounds just the chap I should get to know."

"Even more so when I tell you that he is, as it were, also one of us," and this time Magnus did wink.

"If I end up in Split I'll make contact."

"More than that he'll pass on any message using one of our adapted mobile telephones. His public contact details, which I don't know and would never use anyway as we also have our own secure Telex, are in the Split telephone book. He will be a useful and trusted ally."

"I look forward to meeting him."

"There is one other person I should tell you about for he is a headache despite, in theory, all of us facing in the same direction."

James nodded, still anxious to take notes but knowing that that was impossible.

"The US Defense Attaché in Zagreb operates under the name of Colonel Dwight Ivan Anderson. We're pretty certain that is his real name as there are a number of Andersons in the US Army's officer list and only one with the same initials. But, as an officer with the Defense Intelligence Agency, who can tell. We are convinced that he is going beyond his brief and doing so with the connivance of his superiors in the Pentagon's Department of Defense," Magnus looked closely at James, "up to the very highest levels." He pulled an envelope from his coat's inside pocket, "Here," he said, "have a look at these snaps taken by Milna."

James studied the photographs of two men sitting outside a quayside café. There was nothing remarkable about the shots other than that they appeared to be arguing vehemently.

"What's going on do you suppose?" quizzed Magnus.

"No idea,"

"This could be your starting point as we are pretty certain that the US is intent on breaking, or somehow circumventing, the UN arms embargo as this shows Anderson and the Chief of Staff of the Croatian Army's 4th Guards Brigade, one Colonel Ante Slavić, drinking in a Zagreb café. What they are arguing about, who can tell, but I would lay a bet that it involves Slavić, also a known Serb hater, demanding that America supports Croatia in the destruction of the Republic of Serbian Krajina. Anderson is probably saying that that is out of the question, while secretly doing so."

"If what you say is true…"

"I am only guessing. If I was Anderson I would keep Slavić at a long arm's length until he gets what he wants and the truth can no longer be avoided."

"Why?"

"Slavić is a drunkard. Untrustworthy. He quite openly likes under-age young men, or men of any age come to think of it, while Anderson is, equally pugnaciously, heterosexual."

"I see," James said slowly, wondering if he really did.

"Now," said Magnus pulling a second envelope from a pocket and extracting a single sheet of paper, "here is how we contact each other until you get to Split. Memorise the numbers then destroy them."

James was late home. He slept well and was, unusually, still asleep and not sitting on the end of his bed staring out across Carrick Roads, when his alarm woke him. Three weeks before his flight to Zagreb he bought a number of items of 'white' clothing listed in a Foreign Office letter. Two packets of candles and a small, long-wave wireless all but completed his preparations then, with the arrival of his passport from King Charles Street bearing an imposing FCO rubber stamp announcing that James Laidlaw was a Member of Her Britannic Majesty's Diplomatic Service, he was ready to go.

His gaff-cutter was laid up at Mylor, across the River Fal, while Mrs B's son, Jake, would take his 1956 Bristol convertible for a spin every fortnight. Mrs B herself was provided for and would make sure the central heating worked and the rooms were kept well-aired. James thought of up-dating his will but, with no close relatives, could think of no good reason to replace Mrs B as his main beneficiary.

During the afternoon before his flight James asked a final request of his down to earth, straight talking, Cornish housekeeper. Mrs B was the last link with Percuil House's past, and that of the Lennox family, now James had one entreaty of her that, for five years, he had delayed making.

"Mrs B," he was not confident of her reaction, "I'm not sure if I should say this but I have an immense favour to ask."

"I would do anything for you."

James sighed. This was the point of no return. "When I have gone I would like you to remove all Caroline's clothes from the wardrobes and chests of drawers. Hats and coats from the cloakroom. Her make-up and things from the dressing table. Leave her jewellery, books, pictures and photograph frames where they are." He stopped, "I can't do any of that myself. I just can't!"

Mrs B said nothing.

"Give them to a charity shop of your choice. If I am going to make the break it has to be a clean one."

Had she been able to leap, Mrs B would have done so. Instead she crossed the room as fast as her ageing legs allowed and hugged him: enveloping James in her ample arms, pulling him tightly into her generous bosom. Between shallow sobs she whispered, "If I may say so, not before time."

James was close to tears himself.

"I loved Miss Caroline too you know, and her father. And her mother, who went before them both. But we must look forward. You have been holding us both back for far too long. This old house needs a woman again!" Mrs B paused, "She would have understood some years back. You look after yourself and come back happy once more."

"I will," James promised as he wriggled from Mrs B's embrace for he had one final duty to undertake. Walking around Percuil House's garden he picked a sample of every flower that grew. Mrs B's husband had nurtured each plant and bush until his own death since when it had become James's task and he, too, now knew every flower.

Gathering together as many stems as one hand could carry he tied them with a red ribbon, placed them gently on the Bristol's passenger seat and drove the two miles to St Just-in-Roseland Church. Caroline's grave was next to those of her parents, towards the end of a worn, grass track where, James noticed – as he always noticed – that there was room for just four more tombstones. He knelt at the foot of the most recent one.

Croatia Airways flight OU419 to Zagreb left London Heathrow shortly after lunch on Tuesday 30 November and landed in -4ºC and a heavy snow shower.

Whether James liked it or not, and at that moment he had yet to be convinced he was going to like it, he was now, inescapably, in the Former Republic of Yugoslavia. It wasn't that he 'wanted to help' – he didn't – or that he needed the money – he didn't – he simply had to forget and this was the best chance on offer.

CHAPTER THREE

Tuesday 30th November 1993
Zagreb Airport, Republic of Croatia

As James Laidlaw stood by his luggage, his mind wandering back one thousand miles, someone tapped him on a shoulder.

"Are you with the ECMM?" a heavily-accented voice enquired in English then, without waiting for an answer, added, "If so, come with me please." James joined a gathering herd around a short, tousled-haired, tousled-bearded gentleman holding a clip-board and ordering all to join a minibus bound for the headquarters of the European Community's Monitoring Mission.

Some minutes later, stepping through the vehicle's sliding door, James leaned back to study his new and, he hoped, temporary home for he was facing a prime example of the many 'communist concrete' structures that Russia had built across its 'empire'. Lacking any pretence of charm Hotel Betonska reared upwards, tall, narrow and grey; a long blade of a building standing self-consciously in the middle of a flat and featureless land.

After booking in at the front desk and having taken an exploratory stroll James struggled upstairs with his cases before returning for an introductory brief in a glass-fronted, lobby 'shop' that sported the Union Flag in its window: as instructed by the contents of a brown envelope pushed under his bedroom door. Greeting him in the entrance was the Head of the British Delegation, Colin Cooper. Here he met also the one other British 'new boy': Roger Sampson, a retired Fleet Air Arm pilot who had lost an eye ejecting from his Harrier during the Falklands campaign.

Following Cooper's brief introduction, dinner was a help-yourself affair from huge, semi-spherical urns surrounded by small dishes set upon a large, central table beneath plain wooden walls covered with numerous signs pleading with the 'guests' to 'refrain from removing food'. On lifting the first lid, James discovered that there was no food to remove. Resolving to arrive early on the morrow he hoped to avoid being faced with little more than a bowl of stuffed olives and a plate of soggy pita bread.

Hungry but thankful for the peace of his room James was unsure whether the few ECMM staff he had met in the bar were ex-military people trying to be civilians or civilians trying to do the job in the manner they perceived the military would. Of one thing he was certain: the ECMM's headquarters, with all its influence and power, was in the capital of one of the many adversaries that made up the Yugoslavian conundrum and he was not sure that that was a good thing. He would soon find out for the first day of December 1993 was much as he was expecting.

"Good morning, gentlemen," a tall, ginger-haired, freckle-faced monitor called for attention as he breezed into the room from behind. James and Roger looked back from their arm chairs as the briefing monitor walked to the table at the front. He was still speaking quickly as he sat down, dropping a sheaf of papers untidily onto the desk in front of him. "My name is Andrew Sykes…" and for the next half an hour he gave a potted history of the Balkans beginning, in 1946, with the establishment of the Federal People's Republic of Yugoslavia consisting of Slovenia, Croatia, Bosnia-Herzegovina, Serbia, Montenegro and Macedonia, until its dissolution in 1992.

"At the end of the Second World War the Croatian fascist Ustaše, assisted by Catholic monks, forcibly tried to convert the Serb Orthodox people. In the process they killed at least 400,000 of them. There followed a short period of Četnik revenge but, either way, many of the culprits on both sides escaped justice.

"I am not a Serb apologist," he continued, "and you as monitors, cannot be apologists for any faction. But the desire of the Serbs to live in one state and not to be ruled by other nations, should have been acknowledged. Any settlement, any peace plan, that ignores the understandable wishes of the Serbs only fuels more instability and with that instability come more atrocities. To bring about change in the Serbian leadership, sanctions were imposed by a frustrated United Nations yet, inevitably, the sanctions against Serbia did what sanctions always do: they entrenched those in power, fed nationalism and encouraged self-sufficiency."

Andrew reached for a map, rolled-up and propped against the wall behind him. "I will now show you a map highlighting the dichotomies," he said and, with a flourish, let it unfurl down the front of an easel. "This may look as though it's been drawn by someone with a sense of humour but unfortunately it is not at all funny."

He picked up a pointer, "I want to demonstrate just how mixed up this all is. Starting in the north-west of Bosnia Herzegovina in what is called the Bihac pocket we have Bosnian Muslims fighting Serb Muslims. Moving clockwise towards the east, Croats and Muslims are facing the Serbs while ten or so miles to the south, at Zepce, Serbs and Croats are fighting Muslims. To the north east of the country, around Brcko and

Tuzla, Croats and Muslims are fighting Serbs. Further south, Serbs at Olovo are pitched against Muslims. To the south-west of Sarajevo, at Konjic, Serbs and Croats are against the Muslims. In the far south of the country, at Trebinje, it is a straightforward ding-dong between Serbs and Croats. Moving a few miles to the north, at Mostar, Muslims are siding with Serbs against Croats. North again to Fojnica we have Muslims fighting the Croats. And, of course, across the border into Croatia there is terrible aggression between the Krajina Serbs and the Croats."

Andrew looked at the two sceptical faces, "Is that all quite clear?"

Following further history lessons Andrew studied the still-dazed faces in front of him, "And that gentlemen is that and I for one need a break. But to end this session let me quote from a book called *The Fall of Yugoslavia* by Misha Glenny, the BBC's Central European correspondent." He picked up a battered paperback and read, *Throughout the wars in Slovenia, Croatia and Bosnia-Herzegovina the ECMM monitors were strange figures. They emerged from vehicles, dressed all in white and projecting a clean, even dreamlike quality. It was as though they were emissaries from outer space who had been sent to save the human race from itself.*

At the bar's long, curved counter James ordered a bottle of white Malvazija wine and placed it in front of Andrew on a nearby table. "Thank you for this morning," he said, "but when are we going to be taught how to actually monitor."

"There are no lessons," Andrew replied, "When I asked the same question I was told that all I needed was a pair of binoculars and a walking stick."

Andrew had made his point and there was silence. "Why don't you both have lunch," he eventually recommended. "unless either of you wants to join me in the gym."

"There's a gym?" Roger asked, hesitantly.

"You will find that it will be the only exercise you get," Andrew responded. "For instance I never use the lifts. Anywhere! Walking up and down the stairs is another good time passing measure, or what I call a TPM."

For the penultimate lecture of the day, a French monitor delivered the ECMM's views on United Nations Arms Embargo Number 713 that prohibited the import of arms anywhere into the Former Republic of Yugoslavia. James had been looking forward to this talk; indeed it was the anticipation that had kept him alert throughout the earlier part of the afternoon for he himself had experience in embargo-enforcing patrols. His Royal Navy background had included the Beira patrol, imposing the oil blockade against Rhodesia in the mid-1960s then, having qualified as a submariner, months underwater had been endured shadowing, and sometimes confronting, IRA-bound ships.

By the lecture's end not only had he written no notes but he remained un-enlightened other than that the French, if the briefing officer was typical, seemed not to care whether the embargo was being circumvented or enforced.

In his room, mulling over the day, James lay on his side staring at Caroline's photograph until a fleeting thought startled him back to full consciousness. A growing enthusiasm for this latest 'project' was starting – 'only just starting' he reprimanded himself softly – to eclipse his acceptance, enthusiasm even, for a prolonged mourning. As he stretched back, contemplating his immediate future, he knew that, already, a dividing line had been crossed in his rehabilitation. Tomorrow, and on all the future tomorrows, he resolved to keep Caroline's image in his head and not in a frame by his bed.

* * *

The next day, having endured yet another hour-long history lecture by an outgoing Belgium monitor, a small round, cuddly-looking, retired Royal Navy Commander waddled to the table, theatrically jangling a bunch of keys above his head and introducing himself as Simon Wilkins. "Having been a Supply Officer it was obvious that I would end up as the poor bastard in charge of British logistics. So," he announced, "this is the moment you have been waiting for. The issue of your white uniforms from a shipping container, outside in the snow, that doubles as our storeroom. Follow me!"

That afternoon Colin Cooper pulled James, now dressed all in white, aside by an arm. "I can confirm that you will be going to Knin in the RSK where you will join team November Three. Responsible for monitoring the border region adjacent to Zadar. A much disputed area and one still being fought over despite the current ceasefire. But then everything happens despite ceasefires."

"I had hoped to be involved in coastal duties," James answered in surprise

"Despite my requests," Colin countered, "not too strongly made I have to say, Knin is where they want you. From there it will be up to you to make the first move. Maybe after a month or two."

James nodded unsurely.

Watching his concern, Colin clarified the position, "This will be no bad thing for it will allow you to see both sides of this seemingly intractable dispute."

Despite appreciating the sense of this initial ECMM appointment James argued, "If experience means anything at all then I will be wasting the Mission's time monitoring the hills. I do, though, understand the economics and military relevance of coastal areas and would be better at reporting naval movements than army ones."

"At Knin you will find that Gaspard Chastain, the Head of the Regional Centre, is a wise, intelligent, French career diplomat whose opinions, including his views of the problems on the Dalmatian coast – a region within his area of responsibility – will be invaluable."

James paused, conscious that he was quarrelling with someone who was not only trying to help but who understood the internal politics and nuances of the ECMM. "You are right," he agreed, "Best I cut my teeth somewhere different."

"Good. The weekly shuttle, as we call it, leaves for Zadar at 0830 in the morning. Day after tomorrow."

Throughout dinner that night for members of the British Delegation to the ECMM the conversation ranged widely until, with the cheese plates cleared, Colin tapped a glass, "I asked the chefs to prepare something special this evening and so I hope you will agree, that that veal baked *pod pekom* style was superb." Heads nodded their approval. "Remember it because you will not taste food like that for some time. Now, normally in the UK I would offer you all glass of port but out here I have discovered *Prošek*."

Colin looked over his shoulder. On cue a waiter was approaching with a tray bearing an orange-labelled, screw-capped bottle and five glasses. "This describes itself," he said reading from the label, "as a *specijalno naravno desertno vino*. In other words a desert wine, although many drink it as an aperitif. I enjoy it instead of port and as it claims to be 15 per cent alcohol it does nearly the same, job." Pouring generous measures he smiled, "I wonder what you will think of it."

"It can't be worse than that revolting raquia I was offered last night." James, who liked his evening 'tot', had been introduced to the 'plum-dregs brandy', as he dubbed it, for a night cap, "Never again. It should be banned by one of the UN's embargoes!"

"It fuels every process throughout a monitor's day." Andrew had drunk his fill of the far more acceptable Serbian slivovitz while in Belgrade. "Which is a major disadvantage of monitoring in Croatia rather than Serbia!"

"In that case I am surprised one of the Belgians didn't give us a practical demonstration on how to swallow it without being sick! They've covered just about every other subject."

"*Prošek* is different," Colin claimed. "Now, who shall we toast…?"

As he undressed that evening James realised that, throughout the long day, not one thought of Caroline had entered his head. He slept soundly and if there was any firing outside his window, as there had been during each of the previous nights, he was oblivious to it.

James Laidlaw's last day in Hotel Betonska was one of enforced idleness. With no lectures and nothing to occupy his mind his body needed exercise but as the long afternoon walk dragged out across the flat countryside of uninspiring tracks and lanes his thoughts, inevitably, turned to his late wife. Not only was it the first time he had thought of her for forty-eight hours but it was no longer with the burning intensity that he had known previously. By the time he re-entered the hotel's glass doors the deep guilt that had plagued him over the years was still present, yet noticeably diminished. Feeling strangely at peace with himself, instead of heading for the stairs and the solitude of his fourth floor bedroom James retired to a quiet corner of the hotel's lounge with a mug of tea and a week-old copy of *Le Figaro*.

Leaning forwards to place his empty mug onto the low table, he was aware of someone standing over his chair. He looked sideways up past slim ankles, a knee-length, white denim skirt and white blouse to the fair-haired, blue-eyed face of a lady he gauged to be in her mid-thirties. She was holding out a hand. "Hi," she began, "My name's Camille de Wilde."

James stood. Uncertain of himself, he said simply "James Laidlaw."

"I know," she replied, "May I join you?"

"Please do." He pointed to the arm chair opposite his.

Camille de Wilde sat, crossing her white-stockinged legs as she did so. "I'm with the permanent Belgian Delegation so I am more of a fixture than most of my countrymen who are enjoying the last month of our presidency." James nodded as Camille explained her interruption, "I wanted to have a talk as I hear that you are going to Knin."

"That's right."

"I am responsible for the employment of all interpreters throughout the Mission. Mostly female as you will discover."

"Quite a task."

"I also vet their backgrounds and contracts."

"They must see a tremendous amount of sensitive stuff. I imagine you have to be very trusting much of the time."

"Yes and Knin is a tricky place."

"Does that matter?"

"Not particularly but the girls there do tease the monitors unmercifully."

"How?"

"Well, they are always out for a bit of fun. Not approved of, of course, but inevitable."

"And do they get the fun?"

"Let me just say that eight hours a day cooped up in a Land Rover, and sometimes it is just a single monitor and his interpreter, is…" she stopped. "I believe you have been a widower for five years?"

"I've never mentioned my personal life to anyone out here."

"If it is true then you must be even more careful. They can be rather predatory."

On his guard and edgy James replied curtly. "Are you trying to warn me. If so have you also spoken to Roger Sampson who, I believe, is divorced?"

Camille didn't answer but slowly re-crossed her slim legs, allowing her white skirt to ride higher. Knowing James was watching she let the hem stay where it was: smoothing it down over her thighs to make sure. "You must be lonely. Why else would a youngish widower become a monitor. You don't need the money. You have no family ties. You once enjoyed parties. You must have so much more to give back to Cornwall than to Croatia."

Undecided how to react James settled on attack. Camille knew too much; none of which could have been gleaned from within the ECMM. She was one of very few woman he had spoken to, alone, since Caroline's death. And she was remarkably pretty. "I'll explain…" he began.

"Why not tell me over dinner? I'll book a corner table after the mob have finished." She seemed sure of his answer. He was not.

James had missed Caroline's companionship and he missed her physical presence for they had enjoyed an energetic love life: experimental, imaginative and fulfilling. Now, quite unexpectedly, a craving – no other word would do – after five years of enforced abstinence was sudden… and intriguingly alien.

Yet there had been no suggestion of anything other than dinner at a corner table in a very public room full of colleagues. "Fine," he replied in a voice steadier than his heart was beating,

"Shall I meet you here at seven-thirty?"

Camille smiled and uncrossed her legs even more slowly than she had crossed them. They went their separate ways to change then, later, took their gins and tonic to a far table.

"I asked the cooks to keep some steaks back until we are ready or the newly-arrived Greeks will have taken the lot."

"I don't like to rush."

"Sorry to have bounced you into this but..."

"Not bounced, I could have said I was packing."

"Why didn't you?" Camille asked directly.

James shrugged his shoulders and reached for his glass. "Since you seem to know so much you tell me," he provoked.

"Leaving Cornwall was the first step in your lengthy recovery from grieving."

"...and the second?"

"Possibly having dinner *á deux*?"

"I don't think I should go on."

"Pity!"

They dined and drank well and as the meal progressed James un-wound, knowing that he was in danger of breaking his last taboo: and breaking it without guilt.

Throughout dinner, during which Camille had flirted outrageously, James knew that he was, once more, enjoying the experience of being seduced: yet, as he was to find out, there was still a limit.

In Camille's bedroom – "A cup of coffee, maybe a nightcap. Nothing else!" – each relished the growing excitement of fumbling and mock-hesitancy before falling sideways, laughing together, on to the single bed. With considerably less hesitancy fingers now searched for buttons, for zips, for hems.

"Camille, please don't do that." James was almost as surprised as she was.

"Why not?"

"I like it too much!"

"I want you. You know that don't you?"

"Pretty obvious but I thought it was the Knin interpretresses who were the predatory ones."

"They are, but this is me."

"I'm not ready."

"Doesn't look like that from here!"

"Not ready emotionally."

"Does this help?"

There was a long pause.

"Yes. But it is rather selfish."

"Well…" Another long pause. "You could do the same for me…"

At breakfast James joined Colin, sitting alone. "Tell me about Camille," he began.

"Ah, Camille. I heard you had dinner together yesterday evening."

James nodded.

For a brief moment the Head of the British Delegation dropped his guard, "She's my favourite sparring partner. Wholly platonic of course although I know she is game for more. Quite a reputation but, sadly, she is also a senior member of the Belgian *Staatsveiligheid*. Wouldn't do you know. Someone in my position! Lovely girl. Just the thought is excitement enough for me."

James, his face reddening, stood quickly. "Sorry! Desperate for some coffee," he stuttered, "Back in a second."

A 'one-night stand' – if only a semi-consummated one – was not the way he had expected to meet this particular crisis point. And yet… he was now free of the last vestige of physical guilt, helped by the well-practiced hands and tongue of a member of Belgian's State Security Service. Escape from the final emotional tie would have to wait a little longer.

On his return to the table Colin continued his résumé, "Camille is the only lady ECMM monitor who wears a white dress as uniform. Mind you she would look stunning in your white naval cook's trousers. Or any other trousers come to think of it!"

"I'll bear that in mind."

CHAPTER FOUR

Saturday 4th December 1993
Headquarters, European Community Monitoring
Mission, Hotel Betonska, Remetinečka 106,
Zagreb, Croatia

"Well, goodbye James." Shivering by the mini-bus Colin held out his hand.

"Thanks for all you have done," James turned from forcing his cases into the already-full back. "I'm looking forward to starting work which I won't do if we delay any longer. This snow is beginning to pile up."

"Quite so," agreed Colin turning back towards the Betonska's unhealthy fug and shouting, "Good luck," over his shoulder.

Apart from CC and his own team James had found the hotel home to all the clichéd faults and hang-ups of a multinational headquarters, plus most of the phobias. Now all these reminiscences, and those of Camille's exploring hands, needed to be placed at the back of his mind. He felt no guilt or embarrassment at the latter and certainly no regrets but it had not been part of his unconstructed plan: he was in the Former Republic of Yugoslavia to forget, not to build new memories.

Four uncomfortably-cramped hours later 'the shuttle' reached the coastal town of Prizna and the ferry crossing to Pag island. Here, the driver explained, was as far as he went.

Another bus, waiting on the far side of the narrow waterway, would take the passengers on to Zadar. "We could continue on the mainland all the way but the ECMM has been ordered to use this ferry to avoid the Maslenica crossing forty-five or so miles ahead. That waterway," the driver clarified, "is under surveillance by the Krajina Serbs, the original bridge having been destroyed by them in November 1991. Now a series of pontoons span the gap but that, too, is under near permanent artillery fire."

During the eight minute crossing James and his fellow travellers stretched their legs and lungs in the cool sea air before heaving their luggage into the back of a similar vehicle for the island leg of their long journey. Here they traversed a dry, dusty moonscape with sparse vegetation and few houses then, as they neared Zadar, the realities of war became more apparent through wide-spread destruction and devastation. Although forewarned and braced for the sights James still stared incredulously as they passed ruined house after ruined house and blackened field after blackened field.

"You see," said a companion, "The utmost indignity that can be paid to any family here is to set fire to their home. It is far more than the simple act of destruction. It perpetuates a hatred stretching back over countless generations."

At last the lengthy, overcrowded journey was over as the bus swung around the car park to stop outside Zadar's Hotel Adriatica where James's first impression was one of relief for the hotel's soft Mediterranean-style architecture was far removed from the Betonska's concrete austerity. His second glance took in a boarded up, first floor window by the right-hand corner of the building. Rusting scaffolding suggesting that a modicum of repairs might have been attempted but had, long-since, stopped.

Before he had time to take in more a younger, white-clad monitor was bouncing down the hotel's steps, making straight for him. "James?"

"Yes."

"Stefan Nylander. Acting Head of the Coordinating Centre here at Zadar or the CCZ as we call it. You are most welcome."

"Thank you."

"Good journey? Long and tedious as usual I expect."

"Well it was certainly long but enlivened by a katabatic avalanche. The driver did well to negotiate the rubble after we had pulled a boulder or two to the side."

"Never mind. You made it past that gauntlet. It doesn't happen often but one day someone will get caught. You're safer here than on the road."

Pointing to the crude, semi-repaired, shell damage James laughed, "Doesn't look like it to me!"

"That was over six months ago after the Croats had shelled the RSK: the Serbs always retaliate. And vice versa. I'll show you to your room and suggest a shower before I brief you in the office, after which we'll grab some supper. You're probably starving."

"A Betonska packed lunch doesn't last two hundred miles!"

Entering the brightly-lit, gaily-painted Hotel Adriatica was, initially, a pleasant experience. The main door opened towards a long concierge's desk whose counter stretched to the right, turning into a bar as it did so. But any agreeable first impression now faded, for recent damage and unsophisticated attempts to hide it were everywhere, while the foyer was packed with gaggles of miserable-looking, undernourished people who, James knew from the look of desperation on their faces, could only be refugees. The tattered remnants of what, in many cases, had been fine clothes was a further indication of their reduced status. The children, although clean, had an anxious, near-feral appearance as they and their parents or next of kin wandered listlessly around and through the public rooms.

Stefan left James to take stock of his ground-floor room, a process that was immediately halted as the bare, overhead bulb flickered twice before failing altogether. Seeking natural light James pulled back the heavy curtain covering the grimy window only to face, three feet away and unexpectedly, a rudimentary wall of hollow, red building blocks that ran parallel with the back of the hotel, its upper row of bricks level with the top of the ground floor windows. Although blocking what he assumed to be a sea view at least he now had light but no fresh air for the window latches were rusted shut. He continued his inspection. There was no lavatory paper in the bathroom, no plug in the basin and no bulb in the bedside lamp; not that the latter was likely to be a problem. Luckily foresight had prepared him for these inconveniences and even for the cold shower which, to a submariner, was a luxury and nothing out-of-the-ordinary for a yachtsman.

Cleaned and changed into 'civilian clothes' James found his way to the two, double-roomed suites, either side of the garden end of a corridor, that housed the offices and operations rooms of Zadar's Coordinating Centre. Stefan greeted him, "Sorry if your room was rather airless but we keep the heavy curtains drawn as a precaution against flying glass."

"Presumably that is why the wall is there too?"

"After the last attack we were told by HQ to move out but as all the hotels in the area are as full as this one we simply shifted our offices and bedrooms to the ground floor. You will have noticed the rest of the hotel is full of refugees and displaced people."

"And the difference between the two is…?"

"A refugee has had to cross an international border and gets the full treatment, such as it is, whereas a displaced person has been evacuated from within his own country by the war or by ethnic cleansing. Sadly Croatia does not recognise the Republic of Serbian Krajina as being a foreign country so all those Croats who have been kicked out of Krajina are officially classified as displaced persons and therefore not eligible for help. To make matters easier we refer to them all simply as refugees."

"So presumably all these refugees are Krajina Croats?"

"Yes, therefore they have no refugee status. In Knin you will be dealing with those few Croats who were brave or foolish enough to stay. Their life there is also very difficult. Distrusted of course by the Serbs and, worse still, regarded as traitors by the Croatian government."

"Why did they stay?"

"Bloody mindedness. Too old. Too frail. Now," Stefan changed the subject, "that promised supper where I hope you will meet some of the others. We have a team from the next Greek delegation passing through and one of our lady interpreters is also staying for a day or two as she has friends among those displaced from the RSK."

In the high-ceilinged dining room the ECMM's large, permanently reserved table was set in the middle past which refugees were shuffling to collect loaves of bread and pots of thin soup. Clutching this meagre fare they shambled away to eat in the cramped squalor of their communal rooms or in the gardens and car parks.

"Stefan, I know this is none of my business," James was appalled. "Here we are, all foreigners, about to tuck into fresh meat, salad and potatoes washed down with what you tell me is called Popeye wine..."

"...because of the cartoon on the label..."

"Not bad either but that's not the point..."

"I know what your point is and I agree with you but this is nothing to do with the ECMM. It is the hotel's decision. We continually ask for a separate dining room but our request is always refused."

"I'm sorry to have raised the issue."

"It upsets me, too, because there is nothing I can do about it. I hope the new Head of CCZ can make a change but as he will be a Greek I doubt that he will have much..."

The first shell exploded on the floor above the dining room's inner wall. Before Stefan could finish his sentence an ear-bursting detonation preceded a cascade of plaster and shattered woodwork that scattered plates, cutlery, glasses and bottles. In the brief silence that followed, monitors and refugees shook their heads and, instantly numbed, starred blankly upwards towards the ceiling. The second shell exploded a few seconds later, outside the window in the narrow gap between it and the red brick wall. A blast of searing hot gasses drove slivers of glass, splinters of wood and stone shrapnel past and through the heavy curtains, sweeping everyone and everything to the floor, scattering bodies, tables and chairs like so much jetsam. As the screaming began James found himself on his back alongside a table blown sideways against a wall. He was one of the lucky ones.

In Zagreb, he had been told that both the Serbs and Croats fired their salvoes in multiples of six. With four more to come everyone had to leave the building immediately yet among the ECMM employees and the dozen or so refugees that had been queuing for their soup no one was showing signs of action. Had they ever practiced an evacuation? James did not know. Was there an assembly point or a shelter even? He did not know that either. All he knew was that panic was starting to take hold. Names were being screamed. Relatives, slowly – numbly – staggering to their feet, shaking the debris from their hair and faces as if in a trance, were beginning to check their families: searching for survivors, scrutinising injuries. With the dust slowly settling down the beams of low, evening sunlight now streaming through a vast, ragged gap in the room's outer wall, leadership was vital for an orderly withdrawal of the ground floor. Only those directly involved would know what carnage there might be upstairs.

Ten seconds later the third shell exploded, mercifully outside in the gardens where much of its blast was absorbed by the soft, sandy soil or was deflected by the standing trees and shrubs.

James shouted, "Three more to come. For god's sake get out. Now!" Although in English his message was clear. Pointing at the door he yelled, "Out! Out! Get clear of the building. There are more to come." He turned to face the blood-splattered chaos that was, seconds earlier, a dining room, "Stefan," he yelled. "Is there a shelter?" There was no reply.

Grabbing the father of a bloodied, family group James dragged him towards the exit. "No time to stay to see who is hurt. Do that outside or there will be more casualties. Set an example and the others will follow. Now Go!"

At Reception, members of staff were herding white-faced, grim-jawed families through the hotel's front door from where they were running as fast as they could in every direction. Into the dusk. Away from the car park's security lights.

The sound of an ambulance's siren grew close.

On the hotel's steps James's attempt to take stock was interrupted by the fleeting scream of the fourth incoming shell that preceded another detonation; this time against the right-hand wall of the building, crumpling the metal fire escape. From every un-boarded, upstairs window individuals, their faces contorted with fear and pain, were screaming and gesticulating wildly.

"*Pomoć! Pomoć!*"

Crying to be saved.

James fought against the flow of the elderly on their crude metal walking frames, the middle-aged carrying babies and the young, desperate not to be left behind, clutching at arms, belts, skirts – anything that might guide them to safety. Many had blood running down their faces and bodies from multiple lacerations. Most wore the slashed remains of clothing, exposing bleeding and burnt flesh. All were in shock; wild-eyed expressions of terror, swiftly turning to hate.

Through this pitiful tide James struggled towards the concierge's desk. It was deserted. He swung round and grabbed a member of staff. "Has anyone checked the first floor?" He asked, "Who's in charge of the evacuation? Is there a meeting point? Where are the stairs?"

Someone else grasped his elbow. "They went with the first shell."

"I can smell smoke. Have you telephoned the fire brigade.

"We've telephoned the police."

"Bugger the police. What we need is ladders and hoses."

"I'll ring the fire brigade."

"Have you tried the back stairs."

"That's where the fire is but I know where we keep our ladders."

"Lead on."

In the outside service area, behind the kitchens, two ladders lay on the ground, leaning sideways against a wall. "Grab those," James shouted, pointing, "We haven't much time." Rusting tools filled a plastic crate from where James grabbed a claw hammer and stuffed it into a pocket.

They ran to the hotel's façade with James yelling, "Let's hope these reach the top of the scaffolding. Where the platform is."

In the floodlit car park opposite, four white-clad Greek monitors were smoking nervously. James dashed across. "We need help to reach the planks beneath the boarded-up, first floor window. The wood looks flimsy enough. We should be able to break in."

"No," replied the eldest, "We must keep away. More shells coming."

"Sod that. Those people up there," James pointed, "are trapped and need rescuing. They must escape before those shells arrive."

"I am a general in the Greek army and I order you to stop. This is not an ECMM matter."

"It is precisely an ECMM matter and if it isn't then it is most certainly a humanitarian matter so you can bugger off for a start," James replied angrily, roughly pushing the man aside. "Who's willing to help me?" The remaining three monitors moved forwards together.

"Good men," James said but the officer continued protesting.

"I forbid you to risk your lives…"

James's look of contempt as he growled "Wanker!" into his face, cut the man short.

"Come with me," James demanded of his 'recruits' as he began running towards the building. "The ladders are not long enough to reach the windows so we've got to tell everyone to make their way to the scaffolding at the east end of the hotel. There we might be able to save them."

Arriving at the base of the metal framework he explained further, "From the platform I'll get inside to marshal everyone.

Two of you grab them as they climb out and guide them to the top rungs. One of you stand at the bottom and point them away to safety. Speed is essential as we're expecting two more shells. There is also a fire somewhere at the back of the hotel."

Levering the ladders into place, side by side, James and two Greeks climbed swiftly to the small wooden stage.

Pulling out the hammer and stretching as high as he could James levered at the bottom of the rough boarding and was surprised when it began to come away at the first attempt. Able now to force his fingers inside there was just enough leverage for him to pull the edges back from the window frame. As the rusting nails along the four sides started to give a powerful, noisome smell hit him, followed by a wild clamour of terror that had him scrabbling frantically at the rough wooden edges. Unexpectedly the whole boarding fell outwards in one piece leaving him staring at a dozen terrified faces, young and old, male and female behind whom black smoke was curling in shallow waves along the ceiling. There was no time to lose. There was no time to insist on women and children first. No time to bring out the dead.

"I'll climb inside," he shouted to his compatriots above the cries of the trapped. Hauling himself up he rolled over the windowsill. "Right," he yelled at an elderly woman, "you're first." With no idea what he was saying she knew precisely what he meant. "Out you go." She dropped the three foot onto the platform, itself fourteen feet above the ground. An elderly man followed, then two children were lifted over the edge followed by two more with their parents. The platform was rapidly filling up while those on it were guided to the top of their escape route.

"Come on! Come on!" James encouraged as the emptying bedroom was filled from the corridor beyond. Within moments a disciplined procession had formed as the two monitors outside on the precarious platform kept pace with the human flow. At times everyone concertinaed to a halt as a hesitant evacuee, frightened of heights, disrupted the momentum.

The fifth shell exploded without a warning screech. From somewhere towards the back of the hotel a blast of intense heat swept along the corridor but by then James could see the end of the queue and was certain there would be no more casualties. As the last Croatian slid over the parapet, James called down to a lone monitor he had seen at dinner but not yet met. "I'm nipping back to check the rooms."

"Don't be bloody foolish. The Serbs haven't finished."

"Nor have I!" James snapped. Before disappearing into the hotel's bowels he looked back for an instant. Everyone was well away from the hotel, congregating in bewildered groups at the far side of the large car park. The furthest man, distinguished in the gloom by his white uniform, was the little general.

James raced down the corridor, dodging past improvised beds and piles of dirty clothes. He couldn't make out where the fire was but the smoke, billowing along the ceiling, was creeping lower. He checked room after empty room until turning down the far landing, along the seaward side of the building, he heard a loud whimpering from behind a splintered bedroom door. Slamming it open, he narrowly missed clouting a young woman's face as she lay half off the bed with her head hanging down above a crimson puddle. Blood was slowly spreading down from her temple, through her dark hair, dripping to the floor. All around were the jumbled remains of the room's ceiling.

"*Spremite mog sina*," she was repeating quietly. "*O, molim te Bože spasi mog sina.*"

Fearing that she was close to death, James tenderly but swiftly raised her back onto the bed and dabbed her head with the corner of a sheet. "I don't understand," he said. "Quickly, what is it?"

The woman's eyes opened slightly at the sound of his voice. She murmured, "English?"

"Yes."

Lifting a limp hand towards where the bathroom door had once been she whispered. "My son. Please save my son."

James leapt to where she was pointing. The bathroom's ceiling had taken the major force of the impact for, sprawled across the shattered china base of the shower, was the body of a young boy slowly being crushed by a massive wooden beam. His face was turning blue as his lungs were squeezed empty by the immense weight pinning him down across his chest. He was breathing, but only just. Freezing cold water was jetting from a burst pipe adding to the encroaching hypothermia.

Thinking fast, James knew that his strength alone was not going to be enough. Back in the bedroom he grabbed a rusting metal tie-rod that had fallen from the roof. Slowly levering the beam from the boy's chest he managed to raise it half an inch. Free of the weight for a moment the boy involuntarily gasped but as he did so the spray of water provided enough lubrication for the beam to slide off the rod: this time it fell, with less force than before, across the boy's throat. His eyes were wide, his mouth, but not his lungs, gasped for air, his lips again turning blue.

The fire had reached the far side of the bathroom's wall and was now blistering the paint and cracking the tiles.

"Christ!" James swore to himself, "More care less haste. Try again."

Straining every muscle, becoming hotter with each second, James braced his legs and heaved. One inch. Not high enough. Two inches. Not yet. He needed one hand to pull the boy free and yet he needed both hands to hold the weight.

Speaking to himself for encouragement he muttered over and over again, "You're too young to die. You're too young to die…"

At that moment, and in a shower of sparks, the beam split somewhere above the ceiling. Momentarily, the bottom end swung upwards then fell fall harmlessly to the side of the small, motionless body.

Without caring to see what had saved the boy's life James grabbed an arm and roughly dragged him to his feet as he gasped to fill his lungs with the smoke and dust laden air.

"Is he alive?" the mother whispered.

"He is. Unlike us if we stay here."

"Thank God."

"No time for that. Can you stand?" James asked the woman as he lifted her son upright onto his weakened knees.

"I've got to!"

"Right, grab my arm. We've no time left. I hope you've only been concussed but you still have to help me help you."

"I can make it now that Dino's safe."

"None of us is safe," James rebuked as a wide tongue of flame leapt through the bathroom door. For a brief half second the heat singed its way across the struggling trio as James, in one rapid movement, swung the boy over his shoulders. With his free hand he swept the woman from her bed and half dragged, half carried her into the corridor. As they turned the passageway's right-angled bend towards the front bedrooms the sixth shell detonated behind them. Only partially shielded from the shock wave by the corridor's corner James stumbled, bringing the three of them to a halt.

"I hope that's the last one but we've still got to get out of here." James looked down at Dino's face and, despite the adrenaline pumping through his own veins, announced calmly, "Let's just take stock for a moment."

Dino was breathing normally through badly bruised lips while his eyes no longer stared wildly ahead. "You're a brave little bugger," James praised. "Do you think you can help your mother now? We need to get her to a doctor."

"He doesn't speak much English," the mother replied, "He's only five." James's mind leapt. Only five... his son would have been 'only five'...

Controlling himself he repeated, "You should be proud of Dino, he never complained, never cried but right now we must keep going."

"I'm all right. I can manage by myself."

"You might think so but I want confirmation. You've had a crack on the head and it's still bleeding. And we need to get the lad to a doctor to make sure his throat isn't swelling." As he spoke James glanced down at the woman's face. He hadn't noticed her before, beyond taking in the immediate after-effects of a shell exploding in the roof above her bed. Now, as he looked into her blood and dust-rimmed, brown eyes an overwhelming sympathy swept through him, yet it wasn't a badly hurt Croatian woman he was feeling compassion for... nor a five year old boy he had just rescued. He shook his head of distant memories and yet... and yet... it was inhumane that someone so uninvolved should be swept up in such a bestial act.

"I'm all right," the woman repeated.

"We've caught our breath. Now let's get going. What's your name?"

"Matea."

"And the boy's father. Where's he?"

"Dead."

"Oh God," James almost shouted, "I must go back for him."

"Three years ago."

"Sorry." There was nothing else to say. "Come on. Before the fire catches us."

At the top of the ladder James stopped Matea. "You will have to do the next bit on your own. Think you can manage?"

"You've saved my son's life. I'm not going to let you down."

"That's the spirit. Tell Dino to jump onto my back. Hands round my neck. As tightly as he dares."

Below, a smattering of ECMM monitors and staff had broken away from the far assembly area and were starring upwards.

"Good God. It's Matea," one shouted. To the right, around the corner, three fire engines were already plying their hoses.

James sent Matea down towards willing arms held high, ready to help her drop the last few rungs. Following her onto the grass he prised Dino's little fingers from his throat and lowered him into his mother's arms. She sank slowly to her knees using her son for support. On an impulse James knelt beside them clutching both, feeling the woman sobbing uncontrollably against his chest. Between gulps she looked up into his now-smiling face. Her glistening eyes, full of gratitude, met his. "You saved us," she said simply. "Thank you."

James never knew why he didn't turn away then: while he still could. Nor would he be able to explain why, at that moment, he wanted to kiss her more than he wanted to do anything else. It was not out of love, clearly; nor, evidently, even out of friendship but simply out of compassion. He wanted to show Matea that not everyone was an evil, murdering bastard: he wanted to show her that love still existed somewhere in the Former Republic of Yugoslavia.

Instead he wiped a tear from the corners of his own eyes and murmured, "It could have been anybody," then, remembering the Greek general, added, "Well, nearly anybody!"

"It was you."

"I was the lucky one. And don't forget the other three Greeks. They did well. Now," he said looking past her, "I can see four ambulances. Take your pick."

He stood slowly, offering a hand each to the boy and his widowed mother then, lifting them to their feet, he led them towards a para-medic, the watching monitors making a passage for them.

CHAPTER FIVE

Wednesday 7th December 1993
Headquarters Hellenic Navy, 229 Mesogion Avenue,
15561 Cholargos, Athens, Greece.

The Chief of the Hellenic Navy stood as a tall, dark-haired, deeply-tanned and self-confident naval captain strode into his glass-panelled office, ushered by a Flag Lieutenant.

Before they finished shaking hands the Vice Admiral had already begun, "Demetrios, I am so glad you could find time to call on me. I have been told how busy you are preparing for your next appointment but I just wanted to wish you luck..."

Captain Demetrios Pagonis resented the time he had squandered putting on his best blue uniform when he could have been saying goodbye to... Now he had to kowtow to an officer inferior in intelligence and social standing while going through the motions of being polite. His thoughts were uncharitable and typical.

He didn't need luck.

Pagonis relied on his skills, training and arrogance, conscious that he was a well-known special forces officer who once saved a fellow sailor from assassination during a tricky counter-surveillance operation in the Peloponnese. Couldn't the admiral see he was wearing the medal ribbon of the Hellenic War Cross, Second Class?

Demetrios had told Ariana to meet him for lunch. He wondered how long this farce would take.

"...and remind you that I am expecting great things during your time on the Dalmatian coast. Head of the Coordinating Centre in Zadar isn't it? Don't know the port myself. Closest I got was a visit to Split when I was commanding a frigate. I expect you heard that the Serbs attacked the ECMM hotel with rockets the other day. Killed a good many refugees and a monitor. Never mind. Not for me to tell you your job, at least not as a..."

What was that? Pagonis's thoughts had been far away. I won't be spending much time in Zadar... and certainly not in the hotel...

"...while you must remain unbiased I do not want the Germans, the Yanks, and even the French getting their own way as Croatia builds on its independence..."

What is the fool going on about. I know what I have to do.

"...and there are rumours that when it has re-armed Croatia will move into Serbia. Of course Greece respects the UN embargo and would not wish to see that broken but, well, we all know how duplicitous the Germans can be and the Americans are worse. Just keep an eye open will you. Forewarned and all that... We don't want German influence spreading across Yugoslavia towards Greece's borders..."

Pagonis was hoping Ariana would wait.

"...You are very busy so I'll say goodbye, wish you luck again and ask that you keep in touch. Outside the official channels of course. You know my secretary's number. She will be delighted to pass on any personal messages..."

As Captain Pagonis strode impatiently through the outer office he paused to slip a personal visiting card onto the secretary's desk then, winking at the beneficiary of his leer, picked up his gold-peaked cap and walked out to his convertible Mercedes. It was even warm enough to lower the roof.

He would not be late for lunch and especially not too late for the long goodbye afterwards…

CHAPTER SIX

Saturday 4th December 1993
Headquarters, ECMM's Zadar Coordinating
Centre, Hotel Adriatica, Zadar, Croatia.

While the ambulance with Matea and Dino safely on board pulled away James joined the remaining members of CC Zadar's team gathering in the car park for an impromptu debrief.

As he approached the spontaneous meeting a monitor broke away and introduced himself. "Hi. I'm Didier Levesque, the Ops Officer," he said before explaining all he knew to the assembled members of the ECMM. Stefan had been killed outright by a wood splinter through an eye while three other monitors had been treated for minor cuts and bruises. Miraculously, there had been no fatalities on the first floor, Matea and her son being the most significant of those affected. Five Croat refugees had died in the dining room.

Didier called for questions and first impressions but these were interrupted by the hotel's manager striding across the grass. "Mr Levesque," he reported, "I am very sorry indeed to hear about Mr Nylander. So easy to work for."

"Thank you. Much appreciated but now there must be something we can do to help tidy up and make safe."

"The fire brigade are doing that. Assisted by many of the

refugees who are happy to have a purpose. Something to occupy their minds. We are also taking care of the bereaved and making them comfortable in a staff rest room. The fire is finished but the first floor rooms and dining room are out of bounds."

Didier and his fellow monitors nodded their surprise at the swift efficiency as the manager concluded his report, "We are turning the ground floor lounges and games rooms into dormitories. The kitchens are working but food for everyone will have to be collected and eaten elsewhere."

As the manager returned to the hotel Didier regarded his depleted team, "Now I must go and pay my respects to Stefan should anyone wish to come with me." Looking at James he continued, "Well done, rescuing Matea. She's one of our best interpreters. Because she also has a son we let her use the room as often as she wants."

"My guess is the blow on the head was less severe than it looked."

"Let's hope so as she is an interesting girl. From a Croat family whose parents chose to stay in the RSK at a place called Drniš. One of only two such families still there. When you join Team November Three you are bound to visit it sometime. She's a widow as I expect you have discovered."

"Yes."

"Husband was killed in a hit and run accident by a Serb lorry driver a few years back but she has never been able to hate the Serbs as most Croatians do."

The visit to the mortuary was short, unpleasant and final. Stefan's bloody and smashed face, although roughly cleaned-up, was unrecognisable. "Rest in peace," was all James could mutter as he looked away.

On their return Didier spoke to his team once more,

"Stefan would not have known anything about it. Death would have been instant."

James winced. "Stefan was facing the window. I never saw him again. Alive." He paused at the gruesome memory, "Seemed a lovely person. I wished I had known him longer."

"Too pleasant to be a monitor."

Surprised, James looked across at a thin-bodied, black haired, near-youth whom he had not yet met but who had also been at the dining table. "That's a bit tough," he reasoned. "I know I haven't been here long but geniality has to be a useful attribute I would have thought and certainly better than resentment."

There was no reply.

With little appetite for small talk people began to drift away to their rooms. In the corridor the black-haired monitor caught up with James. "My name's Guillaume Larouche and I have one thing to say to you."

James, anxious to bring the long day to a close, merely smiled in reply for the younger man appeared troubled.

"When I saw how you looked at that wounded Croatian interpreter, the youngish one with the small lad…" James continued to smile for he wasn't sure how many other young lady interpreters there were with a small lad that had been shelled in Hotel Adriatica that evening.

Larouche came to the point. "She's a Croat. I know she works for the ECMM but she is still a Croat that tolerates Serbs."

James, on his guard now was no longer smiling. "What's the problem with that?"

"Don't get involved. People like her are as bad as the Serbs."

An unexpected spark of anger began to burn within James. That, and the hangover from an earlier overdose of adrenaline, was making him edgy. "What are you suggesting?" he countered,

"And what sort of involvement are you worried about. I helped some people escape. That's all. Nothing more. Nothing less. I was probably in their presence for less than ten minutes."

"She now owes you a debt so watch it is what I am saying. "

"Are you also suggesting that, because she is a Croat, I should have left her behind?"

"It wouldn't have mattered much if you had. Serb or Croat. They are all the same."

James was appalled. "Christ," he swore, "she works for the ECMM and you would still wish her harm?"

"There are plenty more girls to take her place."

"That's a terrible thing to say."

"It's true."

"It's still a terrible thing to say. I am off to Knin tomorrow so there's not much chance of any involvement as you so crudely put it." James needed to rebuff the insults. "You must be jealous. No one in their right mind would insinuate such a thing under the circumstances."

"Jealous! That'll be the day."

"So what about all the other Croats we rescued from the first floor?" James's irritation was increasing, "I suppose you would rather we had left them behind as well?"

"Never gave them a second thought." Larouche elaborated, "I don't like Croats. I don't like Serbs and I don't like whoever is supporting them. When you have been out here as long as I have you will feel the same."

"I sincerely hope I won't. Right now I don't give a damn how long you have been out here yours is still an odd attitude to adopt." Keen to defuse the conversation before he lost his temper, James added quietly, "Did you volunteer? Because if you did may I suggest that you chose the wrong employment. At your age there is still time to change careers."

Larouche did not answer directly, "Take it from me, the best way to get through this place is to dislike everybody. Take no sides. The same as everyone else across Yugoslavia where everybody hates everybody else. Start liking just one person on one side more than any other and you're on a slippery slope. You'll start having favourites."

"I'm not sure that an all-embracing dislike is the way ahead," James tried to reason. "Everyone should be taken at face value regardless of nationality."

"You're wrong," Larouche retorted sharply, "Hatred is what makes this place tick and it will be hatred that will be making it tick long after we have left. Believe me."

"You're not English are you?" James's questions was rhetorical: he knew the answer.

"Canadian. And before you ask I don't like the Yanks either."

"Fair enough but I still think yours are rather extreme views."

"Say that to me in another couple of months when you have some experience under your belt."

"I'll hold you to that."

"Good," Larouche replied without grace.

They halted outside James's bedroom door.

"What did you say you did before coming out here?" probed the Canadian.

"I didn't. But since you ask I was a submariner for twenty years and," James added a second fact for good measure, "I specialised in close-quarter Special Forces operations in and around Northern Ireland. So I think I know a great deal more about sectarian relationships than you ever will."

Humiliated, Larouche could not admit that he had been sent to the ECMM by Canada's Department of Foreign Affairs to gain an understanding of how diplomacy works. Having passed out bottom of his graduate 'intake' the critical remarks on his 'end of training' report, just three months back, still hurt. He walked away.

As he tried to enter his bedroom James immediately knew that something was not right for he could only push the door wide enough to allow himself, with some difficulty, to squeeze past. Peering cautiously through the dim emergency security light filtered by the hollow-brick wall James saw that every surface of his room was layered with sand, leaves and shards of glass. Ignoring the mess he crunched his way to draw the curtain shut then, remembering where he had left the match box, lit a candle by his bed. After shaking the duvet clear of detritus he lay back to mull over his first day as a monitor and, as he began to relax, uninvited pictures floated across his mind's eye. The evening had been a nightmare with two contrasting images fighting for supremacy. He recalled Stefan's smiling face before the explosion but this was eclipsed by the sheer horror of his blooded, smashed head just an hour or so later in the mortuary. James knew that it would be the latter image that would remain uppermost in his memory.

He allowed more random scenes to drift by: the apparent near-death appearance of Matea's limp body as he slammed open her bedroom door followed immediately by the relief when she spoke: the thrill of seeing Dino breath deeply in the shattered bathroom: the ache in his own chest muscles that became noticeable only once he had stopped straining at the beam. Yet more phantom images floated behind his closed eyelids: the look on Matea's face as she cradled her son while grabbing at James's leg, as a child might clutch at its favourite toy for security: the fragile vulnerability of the bond between mother and son on the landing as all three struggled to gain strength for the final phase of their escape.

He remembered, too, the overpowering desire to protect Matea and Dino from further trauma… and the fear that he might have been impotent to do so. But it was a feeling of compassion, generated by Dino's tiny hands desperately grasping his neck, that was planting itself deepest into James's mind. That and the sensation of Matea's slim, sobbing body against his as she, too, clutched trustingly at security.

His final realisation, before sleep overtook him, was the similarity in the helplessness he had felt in Treliske Hospital compared with that he had just experienced in one of Hotel Adriatica's shattered bedrooms. He knew that his emotional frailty was not caused by an unknown woman clinging to him on the lawn of a Croatian hotel a few hours ago, but by the love that died in the accident and emergency department of a Cornish hospital five years earlier.

For the second time in recent days he accepted that any longed-for catharsis was going to be slower in coming than he had hoped.

CHAPTER SEVEN

Sunday 5thDecember 1993
Hotel Adriatica, Majstora Radovana 7,
Zadar, Croatia

With his kit loaded in a white ECMM Land Rover James sought Didier in the Operations Room. "I was disturbed by what Larouche said to me last night," he started.

"You have pre-empted me, James. Larouche..." Didier paused, "...is a prime example of why this is no place for the inexperienced."

James nodded his agreement.

"There's one more thing you should know. Having drunk too much raquia on a patrol Larouche once put his hand way up Matea's skirt. She slapped him hard, very hard, and made a formal complaint on their return. That messed up our scheduling as we could never have the two together again. Bloody nuisance but there we are."

Unsurprised by this news James renewed his condolences, picked up his briefcase, said goodbye, and walked towards the hotel's entrance.

The vehicle, laden with 'mail' bags for those few Croats who had elected to stay in the RSK, passed between abandoned Serb houses and the scorched fields that had once helped feed

Dalmatia. Turning inland, a mile from the seaside town of Biograd, they entered an even worse war-torn countryside that reminded James of countless film clips of the 'low countries' laid waste by the Nazi's westward advance between 1939 and 1940. The frequency of deserted houses increased and the road became more rutted where shell fire had damaged it. Burnt out and now rusting fighting vehicles from both 'sides' stood where they had been halted.

Rounding a bend at the top of a gentle slope they decelerated to little more than a crawl in bottom gear. The Belgian driver spoke equally slowly, "The confrontation line is around the corner. Don't do or say anything. I'll handle it. If the trigger happy bastards don't like us, or we do anything sudden, or approach other than at a snail's pace they are perfectly capable of loosing off a full magazine from their AK 47s. I don't think they mean to hit us but as they fire from the hip they could well do so."

"Thanks for the warning."

"They won't be sober either and will make a great issue about our papers, vehicle registration and timings not being correct." The driver squinted at his watch. "I said nine-thirty and it is now nine-twenty-eight. Their cheap watches will not agree so I expect we'll be here a couple of hours while they argue with their HQ."

Two Croatian border guards, gesticulating wildly with their weapons, brought the Land Rover to a halt, Kalashnikovs pointing directly at the windscreen. A third soldier thrust his head through the window, his breath filling the cab with stale raquia fumes and second-hand garlic.

In barely intelligible English he demanded to see identification cards, the vehicle's log book, the driver's international driving licence and the written authorization for crossing the confrontation line at 0930.

Unkempt, dirty, unshaven and unsmiling the soldiers carried out their self-imposed task of delay with a bored enthusiasm. Surrounded by dried mud, dusty scrub and numerous notices warning of the presence of mines, theirs was a wretched existence.

The guards checked, double checked, then triple checked, seemingly unable to match the car's registration number with the number they had been given. They had spent most of the night smoking cannabis and dinking cans of beer with nothing to which they could look forward in the morning other than one ECMM Land Rover. Now was their chance to relieve their tedium at the expense of others, and they had all day to do it in.

During the two hours of enforced idleness James sauntered around the bunker's immediate surroundings until the overpowering stench of human excreta, wafting from every shell hole, forced him to return to the air-conditioned vehicle.

Eventually the three grudgingly waved the Land Rover into no-man's-land, sending it on its way with a salute of AK-47 shots that cracked down either side.

Forty miles later and from the edge of an impressive gash in the earth's surface it wasn't easy to see Knin clearly from the plateau's lip. That morning, as on most mornings, it lay beneath a thin, flat layer of grey smog. At the junction of three valleys, 500 feet below, the town projected an air of desolation with few vehicles on the roads; the large railway marshalling yards empty and the surrounding fields bare of crops and cattle. Not only did the town appear to be desolate and dirty from above but at ground level it was worse. The predominant colours of the buildings, those that were left intact, were shades of grey; the dusty trees and bushes were no different in hue from the hoardings, the street signs and even the people trudging their weary journeys from empty shop to empty shop.

The unfinished cement staircase to Regional Centre Knin's first floor headquarters led directly from an outside doorway in a partially completed detached house on the town's north-eastern outskirts. Waiting at the top was a tall, elegant gentleman wearing white trousers beneath a fitted, short, white jacket that had not been issued from the back of a Quay D'Orsay shipping container in the snow. More probably, James thought back to his brief excursions into the French capital, his 'suit' had been made to measure by Charvet of Place Vendôme, Paris. A white cravat was loosely knotted around his neck. Gaspard Chastain, the Head of the Knin Regional Centre, held out his hand as James stepped into the Operations Room.

"James, you are most welcome," Gaspard began, "especially as we are also very short of transport! And I was appalled to hear of last night's shelling. I've made strong protests to the RSK government, such as it is here in Knin, but I know my words will have been ignored.

"And so it goes on." James replied.

"And so it goes on," echoed Gaspard. "But there is one other thing I must mention first only so that we can dismiss it instantly."

"Yes?"

"I've had a complaint from the incoming Chief of Staff. A Greek major-general."

"Ah," said James, mentally preparing his defence.

"Apparently you swore at him in front his men."

"I did. I called him a wanker."

"A what?"

"En Français, un branleur."

Gaspard raised his eyebrows, "Was that necessary?"

"He was preventing us from saving lives."

"As a diplomat I have to say that that was not very tactful."

"And as a human being?" asked James.

"Ah, now that is an entirely different matter."

"Good." James was already warming to Gaspard Chastain.

Settled into comfortable arm chairs Gaspard confirmed James's appointment. "I am attaching you to Team November Three for a month so that you can understand the work. After that," Gaspard, was vague and raised both hands, "Who knows."

James commented as directly as he could at this first meeting, "As a naval officer I would prefer to be on the coast. Once I have got the hang of things."

"Wouldn't we all," Gaspard teased.

"You don't like it here?" James hazarded.

"Whether I like it or not is immaterial. I am a diplomat. I go where I am sent."

"Whereas I am a mariner and hope some day to go where I can do some good."

Gaspard ignored him. "I have a task for you here before we can think of your next appointment. For the moment you will be working with a French Commando Marine lieutenant called Jack – he prefers the English pronunciation – and Florian, an elderly Belgian air force logistics officer."

James nodded.

"I see you speak French." Gaspard declared.

"Bit rusty," replied James. "I was at Grenoble university before joining the navy."

"Good." Gaspard exclaimed. "My advice is not to let on that you speak it. Stick to English. Theirs is poor so they speak French on patrol and that way you may learn much more!"

Following lunch – of sorts – in the local United Nations canteen and full of bulk if not sustenance Gaspard drove James to a small 'motel' among Knin's eastern outskirts. Downstairs, the restaurant was based around a bar in the manner of a French village café. Upstairs the first and second floor rooms were each equipped with a double bed, a chair, a table, a wardrobe, an en-suite shower and little else: no pictures, no carpets… and no bathroom plugs.

"Do not use the lift. Ever! There are always power cuts and you could be stuck for hours."

After a welcome, but freezing, shower, James met the other Knin-based monitors for dinner in the one seedy, smoke-filled public room. The ECMM had a permanently reserved table in a far corner from the Serb habitués who spent their days drinking beneath a loud television, fixed high on a wall and only tuned to football. The monitor's table was laid with a central pile of paper napkins surrounded by an untidy jumble of knifes and forks. Plastic Coca-Cola and Pepsi Cola bottles were filled with red and white wine respectively. Nodding to the other diners as he did so, James pulled back a chair and sat down.

"James?" A tousle-headed, square-jawed man thrust out an arm. James stood again to look up directly into dark blue eyes set in the lined, well-lived-in face of a tall Frenchman. "Am Jack. Combat diver. What you English call *homme de grenouille*! I marine. I kill!"

Taken aback by this sudden declaration, in pigeon English, James enquired, "You don't enjoy monitoring?"

"*Jamais,*" Jack retorted.

"I am Florian," another voice declared. Standing behind Jack, a balding, white-faced, unfit man, the antipathy of his companion and less welcoming, crept forwards. "Silly," he began in halting English, "why you are with us. Two monitors is enough."

"I'm sure you're right," James readily agreed. "So I hope it will only be for a month."

"Hope so too," Florian replied. "We have our routines. We don't alter. Monday we go to Benkovac. Always Benkovac on Mondays. Tuesday to Karin Plaza…"

"The place that is shelled regularly?"

"Yes. On Wednesday to Drniš."

James remembered the name. "Tell me about Drniš," he asked.

"Once a nice place." Florian answered, "Peaceful. Serbs and Croats lived next door to each other but now…" he made a cutting motion across his neck then paused, allowing James to finish his sentence for him,

"…just two Croat families remain."

"I'm Hans," an elderly German monitor introduced himself, "If you look over there you'll see what tonight's supper is supposed to be." He pointed to a large blackboard leaning against a wall and read the English aloud as though it was not James's mother tongue, "*Wiener schnitzel*, potatoes and bread."

In the short silence that followed, Hans looked at James across the table and asked helpfully, "How much do you know about this place?"

"Only what I've picked up since arriving in Zagreb."

"The actions of this so-called Republic of Serbian Krajina are easy to understand because, now that Croatia has won its independence and is no longer kept in check by the Yugoslavia government, Ustaše gangs may well re-exercise their extreme behaviour."

Surprised by this immediate and brief history lesson – especially from a German who was old enough to have fought in the war – and unable to see the connection, James asked, "Surely not if Croatia wants to join the European Union?"

"You would think so but swastikas and U for Ustaše are daubed on Croatian government buildings and never removed." Hans continued, "Then there is the more formal red and white chequerboard on the Croatian national flag: a Ustaše symbol hated by the Serbs. A number of streets have been re-named after notorious Nazi leaders and if that isn't bad enough Croatia is about to re-introduce the Ustaše currency, the kuna. Replaced by the Yugoslav dinar in 1945 but now set to return."

James understood the German's point, "I rather agree. Not difficult to see why the Serbs want independence from an independent Croatia. Rather unnecessarily provocative. One might even accuse Croatia of exercising a form of constructive dismissal."

"Nicely put James," Hans agreed. "I like that. In the good old days of communism everyone got on with everyone else. In their manner. The more sensible regarding themselves as Yugoslavs, not as Croats, Bosnians or Serbs, Muslims or Christians. The question is, can Croatia do anything about the Republic of Serbian Krajina; this spectre to which it has given birth? The status-quo can not remain for ever. One side will have to give in and, right now, the weaker country is Croatia although I don't think that will last for long. It's what we call the 'view of no horizon.'"

Opinions on the current situation were banded to and fro until deep bowls of lukewarm food were placed without ceremony in front of each monitor.

After two mouthfuls James put down his knife and fork, his mouth puckering, "Tell me," he said to no one in particular, "Do we often have this *Wiener schnitzel*? I feel as though I am chewing my own teeth!"

The next morning, a Sunday, the monitors reported to the headquarters for briefings before breaking for lunch and a 'free afternoon'. As he gathered his meeting's papers Gaspard beckoned cross the Operations Room. "James, may I have a word please." In the inner office he closed the door behind them.

"Yesterday I mentioned that I might have a little task for you."

"Yes."

"Two or three events have forced me to bring my plans forward. The new head of the Zadar Coordinating Centre is coming here on Tuesday before taking up his appointment. Captain Demetrios Pagonis of the Hellenic Navy has arranged his own welcoming dinner in Knin castle that night through some Serb contacts he must have."

"I am not in Zadar's patch."

"That's the second point. The Head of Team Split, which is in Zadar's patch as you call it, is a commander in the Royal Danish Navy and, like you, a submariner."

"If we ever meet we may have much in common."

"I hope not as the Croatian army have arrested him for, and I use their words, 'gathering intelligence.'"

James, surprised, could only ask, "Why on earth does a Danish naval officer need to be doing that sort of thing in Split?"

"No idea but in yesterday's mail I received a letter from a Colonel Ante Slavić, Chief of Staff to the Croat army's 4th Guards Brigade telling me that Bjørn Svendsen, the Dane, was released on the understanding that he stops all monitoring duties and leaves the country within the week. I have telephoned that assurance. Now I need a replacement and the next senior monitor, if there is such a thing, is Florian but as he is verging on senility I cannot trust him to be in charge."

"There must be others?"

"Hans is one of the very best and there are other excellent ones too but, as in many walks of life, the bad get noticed more than the good who just get on with their jobs."

"It was the same in my service." James, unsure where this was leading asked, "So why not Hans?"

"He is too invaluable running the humanitarian side of our work."

"So, where do I fit in?"

"You will be taking over Team Split."

"I'm not sure that I am ready for that," James laughed.

"Bjørn will brief you before he goes."

"This is all a little sudden."

"You are one of the very few monitors with operational experience and I also know," there was a hint of wink, "that CC would like you to be on the coast."

"I see," responded James without expression, "Would there be time to fit in a visit to Karin Plaza before I go?"

"Why?"

"I believe it is Serbia's only outlet to the sea."

"Of course, for what goes out can come in," Gaspard replied before elaborating. "Karin Plaza is obviously of interest to Croatia for it is regularly shelled by their artillery and as there are no military targets one has to ask why. My view is that the beach might be useful for an amphibious assault. Behind the confrontation line."

"Surely, though, it is not sensible to advertise an interest in advance," James commented before considering his reply further, "Anyway, does Croatia have enough landing craft for such an operation?" He paused, "I can tell you how many mini submarines they have, capable of delivering commandos for sabotage operations, but I'm a bit rusty on surface vessels."

"Might be good to check once in Split," Gaspard suggested before returning to the main subject, "Now, Team Split. The situation is not helped by the two lady interpreters living with the two monitors – Bjørn and his second in command, Wilhelm de Meyer. Another Belgian and I'll come to him in a minute. "

"I had been warned about the interpreters."

"Wherever it occurs it is a thorough nuisance."

"And Wilhelm?" James prompted.

"Ah yes, Wilhelm the Belgian. Although he is married he is living with the younger of the two girls. Unexpectedly his wife flew into Split the other day and caught them together in his bedroom. Determined not to lose Wilhelm, Mrs de Mayer... I can't remember her first name... moved in to the hotel to keep an eye on things."

"Did that work?"

"No. So there is now a form of *ménage á trois* in Team Split. *Ménage á cinq* if you take Bjørn and his mistress into the equation." Gaspard laughed loudly, "Even a *ménage á six* if Bjørn's wife decides to join-in from Denmark for his last days!"

Gaspard stopped laughing. "You don't have a wife." It was a statement not a question.

"No," James replied. "No. Not any longer. She died in childbirth." It was the easier answer.

"I'm sorry," Gaspard said. Then, after a few seconds, continued, "In the meantime I need you to undertake the little task I mentioned at the very beginning. Have you ever heard of a Captain Ratko Knežević."

"Who?"

"We don't know much about him which is why I am agreeing that you should take up his invitation."

"Invitation?"

"He seems to know that you are in Knin."

"How come?"

"No idea."

"Tell me about him."

"He is a Serb army officer who speaks perfect English. He

runs a camp in the hills called Gornji Bruška. Beyond Benkovac overlooking Zadar. Training men for a special unit they call the Red Berets although more commonly known as the *Knindže*. A word apparently derived from Knin, the town, and ninja the Japanese warriors of that name. No one has ever been allowed near except the local Canadian platoon commander.

"Knežević has asked you to call on him on Tuesday in civilian clothes and in a Canadian jeep. He doesn't want a diplomat, but someone he can talk military matters with and, as CC has spoken at length about you, I am putting great store in your ability to gain useful intelligence."

James, unsure how much CC had divulged, kept silent.

"Once you have met Knežević then you'll be off to Hotel Split. A five star hotel..." James began smiling until Gaspard corrected himself with a laugh, "...a five-star hotel without the stars!"

Needing time for his brain to decipher all that Gaspard had mentioned James walked back to the motel for cabbage soup and a plastic Pepsi bottle of white wine. As he entered the dining room Hans waved to him. "I am going for a drive this afternoon. Would you care to see some of the countryside?"

"Love to."

"I've borrowed the rickety old Peugeot P4 that is only used for local work."

The elderly German drove to the east of the town, then up the long escarpment until, after half an hour, he pulled to a stop in a high valley etched into the plateau. Switching off the engine he sat, unaccustomedly solemn. "I thought you should see this sad place," he said at last, looking straight ahead. "It's called the Valley of Silence. If you get out you will not hear one sound. No birds singing. No animals calling. No humans laughing. Nothing except sometimes the wind."

"There has to be a reason," James ventured.

"It is where the Ustaše murdered thousands of Serbs in the war. Nothing will come back as long as the bodies remain in their unmarked mass graves." Hans waved an arm across the barren, rock-strewn landscape.

"Thank you Hans," James said quietly, "Do you have anything nice to show me?"

"Certainly. We are going home via Knin Castle so you can see where we are dining, if that is the correct word, on Tuesday night."

At the Regional Centre's base, during the Monday morning briefing, Team November Three was ordered to distribute mail to the two Croat families still living in Drniš. As the Operations Officer, standing in front of a large wall map, put down his pointer Jack stood abruptly to his feet.

"Not right," he protested loudly. "On Monday we go to Benkovac."

"Not this Monday," retorted the Operations Officer.

"Pourquoi?" Jack was agitated. *"Nous allons à jamais Drniš sur un lundi."*

"Jack, the language of the Mission is English."

"Merde á vous," was the intemperate reply.

Exasperated, Gaspard took charge. "Jack," he said solemnly, "I have spoken to the mayor and he can only see you this week on Monday. Also I want James to visit a village with Croatians still living in it."

"Can't that wait?" Jack argued back.

"No!" Gaspard was firm and gave no reason. With a Gallic shrug and harsh whispering to Florian, sitting beside him, Jack slowly sat down.

Gaspard had one other instruction that he knew would not meet with Jack's approval either.

"When you have visited Drniš you then drive to Karin Plaza. At the head of the Karinsko More waterway."

"*Pourquoi?*" Jack repeated petulantly.

"Two reasons." Gaspard answered again in English. "I want James to see what the Serbs call the Serbian Sea and because I need you to call on the headmistress of the local school. It was shelled recently and I must know how they are dealing with the aftermath. And offer help."

Waiting by the Land Rover a lady interpreter, clutching a bulging canvas bag, introduced herself. Miljana, a slim, short-haired girl of, James guessed, about thirty-five years climbed onto the back seat, tossing the mail ahead of her. "These are for the two Croat families in Drniš." She picked up a letter that had spilled across the seat. "Oh look," she exclaimed, "There's one for me too. From my friend in Zadar."

Driving towards Drniš Jack swung the Land Rover off the road to stop, unexpectedly, at a small Serb house close to an unguarded section of the confrontation line. Here, in return for a few American dollars, he filled his and Florian's bellies with fried eggs, fresh bread, jam, cheese, tomatoes, mushrooms and apples.

James asked Miljana softly, "How do they get this food?"

"We are not supposed to like the Croats but we lived with them for years before they were forced beyond the present border. Some friendships are hard to kill and there are a few places where the confrontation line can be crossed by evading the Croatian army check points. It is dangerous but it works."

Returning to the Land Rover Miljana elaborated, "Although we have our historic reasons for hatred I think we have more desire for friendship with the Croatians than they do with us. Yet it was we that suffered so much in the Second World War at the hands of the Ustaše. Until, of course, under President Tito, we all lived side by side."

"The Četniks weren't nice to the Ustaše either."

"We think we had the greater cause when you consider what the Nazis did."

Not wishing to be drawn into comparisons James moved on, "Tell me about Drniš?"

"It is in beautiful, hilly country and was a mixed village, as most were, until September 1991 when it was attacked by the Yugoslav National Army and the RSK's Militia. The tragedy was that the Croats throughout the Drniš municipality outnumbered the Serbs by four to one. So, when they were forced out, there was no one left to farm the land and supply the usual services. Now it is a place full of ghosts with just a handful of people living a bad life; existing on parcels and hand-outs from the United Nations."

James looked down at the packages between him and Miljana, "And teddy bears from Zadar."

"That one will be from a Croatian lady called Matea. My childhood best friend who lived here but who was caught on the wrong side of the confrontation line and has never been able to return to her parents. Now we both pray that one day we can be together again. Her young son likes to send little reminders of himself to his grandmother."

"Matea?" James asked.

"Yes. Her parents are two of those we shall visit. Why do you ask?"

"No reason," James lied. "I like the name."

Florian turned from the front passenger seat to face Miljana, "Can you direct us to the addresses on the parcels? We always get lost."

"Sure," she replied, "From the village square head south-west along the Ulica Stjepana Radica for less than half a kilometre. Then take the minor road to the left. After one and half kilometres take the right fork then, after another kilometre, we will be there. If you recall, it is very isolated."

Along the dusty, stony track Jack guided the vehicle between the dips and bumps until a small, red-roofed bungalow came into view.

Undernourished, Mr Tomić was wafer-slim with excess skin hanging in light folds around his neck and chin. His wife was smaller and, had that been possible, even more emaciated. Both were prematurely hunched with age. Close to infirmity, they sat facing each other by their front door with neither rising as the Land Rover stopped in a dust cloud. Miljana, clutching the bag of mail, walked towards them then, leaning down, kissed each on their foreheads. Jack and Florian sat motionless in their seats.

"Are you two getting out," James asked.

"No. Don't like seeing Serb kiss Croat."

"For God's sake," James exclaimed, "They are human beings. They are elderly. They need all the love they can get. Anyway, the two families knew each other well."

"It's hypocritical."

"And it's their problem not ours. If they want to show affection for each other that too is their problem. Without reconciliation there is no hope."

"I don't want reconciliation," the Frenchman growled, "I want the Croats to take back what they lost."

James slammed his door shut. Allowing a smile to return to his face, he walked towards the elderly Croatians.

On his arrival Miljana excused herself. Five minutes later she reappeared carrying a battered tray laden with fresh bread and mugs of black coffee. Translating she explained, "They make their own bread as the Canadian platoon slips them a sack of flower whenever they are in the area. They grow a few root vegetables which they preserve and eke out through the winter. Three goats supply milk and cheese and they have chickens. Food parcels from Mrs Tomić's friends and her daughter in Zadar help as well. Each time we visit I bring small items for them such as a bag of coffee and maybe an apple or two if I can find any in Knin or when I have managed to pinch some from the UN canteen."

While she was speaking Miljana laid out the packages and letters, starting with the teddy bear. It bore a label tied around its neck written, James presumed, by Matea on behalf of her son. Mrs Tomić asked Miljana to read it aloud which she did and then translated for James. "Dear Grandma and Grandpa. Here is a bear to remind you of Dino. He is nearly as big as me. I am well and staying with Mama in the Hotel Adriatica for a week. She is well too. I love you, Dino."

Clutching the bear to her bosom, tears welling in her eyes, Alicia Tomić muttered, "That's lovely. How kind of dear Dino. He was only two when I last saw him."

Promising to collect any outgoing mail sometime during the next week Miljana and James returned to the Land Rover. "Dino?" James eventually asked, knowing the answer, "Mrs Tomić said her grandson was called Dino."

"That's right," Miljana answered, "Dino's mother is a Croatian interpreter, a widow called Matea Marković whom I mentioned earlier. Why do you ask?"

James, praying that his beating heart could not be heard, answered, "Just curious. Nothing more. As I said, I like the name."

Winding down through the thickly-wooded escarpment that leads to Karin Plaza from the south Jack stopped the Land Rover on a hairpin bend. Pointing north across a blue expanse of calm water he said haltingly, "Why so important for you come Karin Plaza. Fifty nautical miles to the sea through two deep and narrow gorges. Easily blocked, even by amateur civilians with just small arms. Escaping Serbs stand no chance and, anyway, there is no jetty."

James said nothing. He stared seawards thinking not of escaping Serbs but of invading Croats. In the dark. By boat. Under cover of fire. Infantry supported by main battle tanks. He needed to inspect the beach and immediate hinterland closely to assess why it was being shelled so regularly by Croatia.

They continued their descent through the dry scrub that now replaced the trees higher up the hill until, half a mile from Karin Plaza's semi-circular beach, they negotiated a single track bridge, stopping briefly to allow a slow, mule-drawn cart to pass the Land Rover in the opposite direction.

From here Miljana gave directions to the village school, a once red-roofed building but now a pile of light coloured stones from which jutted, obscenely a tall, undamaged chimney. A middle-aged woman, her bandaged left arm in a sling, waved the Land Rover to a halt then walked to the rear passenger door.

Miljana unwound her window. "Hello," she said in Serbian, "We are looking for the headmistress."

"That is me," replied the teacher, smiling grimly through red-rimmed eyes. "Monsieur Chastain telephoned the police station to say that you were coming. Not that there is much you can do."

Miljana relayed the conversation to James. "Actually," he hoped to reassure her, "there is probably much we can do."

"If you think so," replied the headmistress in good English, "park here and I'll take you to my house where the children are."

"You go, James," said Jack. "I'm not interested." Florian

nodded his agreement.

"Well I am," James answered sharply, pulling at the door handle. "Come on Miljana. We have work to do."

The headmistress's house, in a parallel street to the school's, had also been damaged in the recent artillery attack. A large hole in the roof was roughly sealed by a tarpaulin beneath which, and avoiding a steady trickle of water oozing from a split pipe, sat groups of young children aged between five and ten. All were thin-faced. All were haggard. All were frightened.

James asked Miljana to tell them he had come to help search for a newer, safer school. A school that was not going to be bombed. A school that was not going to see anymore of their friends killed and maimed. A school where they could learn in peace.

The children clapped politely. Tentative smiles began to appear.

James took the headmistress aside, "We need to find a place out of the village but close enough for them to walk to. And we shall need a larger building where we can house them properly. Where they can sleep in safety. Do you know anywhere?"

"I'm not sure," the reply was hesitant.

"Well," James was firm, "in that case we had better start looking. Today."

The teacher asked directly, "Do you know Ratko Knežević?"

"I'm due to meet him tomorrow."

"He once promised that we could move to one of the buildings in his camp. He'll collect the children and return them each day," the headmistress paused. "It is even more urgent now but we have heard no more."

"When I see him, I'll hold him to that promise."

The head teacher blushed, "Would you," she said, "Would you. Please. Promises don't count for much these days. They are too easily made and even more easily broken."

"I promise," repeated James before correcting himself. "That is, I promise to ask him to honour that offer." The head teacher took James' hand and kissed it, leaving it wet with tears.

After a long, reflective pause James said earnestly, "Before we discuss anything else I must use your *toilet* please."

"We have no running water so if its only to urinate then you must walk down to the sea and take your shoes and socks off." For the second time the headmistress smiled.

Making his way to the shore James's mind ran through the beach reconnaissance check-list for amateurs contained in a tiny Admiralty publication called *Beachcomber* that had been issued to young officers under training. At the water's edge he removed his shoes and socks before rolling his trousers above his knees. He would not be able to wade deep enough but it would have to do.

Un-buttoning his fly as he wriggled his toes downwards James pushed his feet through the first four inches of soft sand until he could feel the hard, almost solid, sub-surface. Light, portable beach track-way might be needed for wheeled vehicles but not for fighting vehicles. Furthermore, James calculated, the shallow gradient would give foot soldiers a wet landing of only a foot in depth for just five yards. The beach faced north-west with an estimated fetch across the open water to the nearest land of two nautical miles. When 'the Bora' blew a short and nasty sea would build up but, he estimated looking around him, nothing dangerous. The beach exit behind was fine for infantry, indeed the bushes and shrubs would offer a modicum of cover while not hindering a main battle tank before it reached the lateral road at the back. High ground either side would dominate any landing, but from the comparatively safe distance of about a nautical mile.

Judging by the motorboats at anchor the holding ground was good for moorings.

The imponderables were the two choke points he had seen on the map and that Jack had so contemptuously highlighted. Now, one of these deep gorges was held by the Serbs, although he wasn't too sure if that was the current week's situation or the previous week's. The seaward one was definitely held by the Croats but who ever used this conduit, to or from the ocean, would need to establish full control over the whole waterway.

Smiling to himself – thinking that any observer would have just witnessed the longest pee in Serb medical history – James buttoned up his fly and turned for the shore just as a familiar, terrifying noise, tore the air apart above his head. Instinctively he ducked, falling to his knees, and was already waist deep when the explosion knocked him face downwards. He lay, holding his breath, waiting for the fall of debris; praying that a few inches of salt water would offer some protection.

One down, five to go he counted, stumbling out of the shallows.

Even as the second shell landed in the shallow water behind him James's thoughts were already concentrating on the headmistress's house, one hundred yards away, until the searing hot punch in his back lurched him flat across the coarse sand that now stung his exposed skin. Trying to catch his breath he staggered to his feet again, seeking his shoes and socks only to slump back, still winded, desperately trying to suck air into his lungs. The taste of burnt cordite made him retch as he lay, counting the explosions and nursing the lacerations to the backs of his legs.

In the eerie silence that followed the final explosion – James hoped that the Croats were, too, acting according to habit – a low wailing reached the beach, mingling with other sounds: a car's horn blaring unstoppably; men running down the street shouting unintelligibly; a dog whimpering as it tried to lick life back into its owner's now-still, bloody body.

Grabbing his shoes – forget the sodding socks – James ran back from whence he had, a few minutes ago, strolled, anxious to relieve himself.

His legs were bloodied from the second explosion but it was not that inconsequential pain that brought his progress to a halt. James's absence might have saved his own life but it had not saved that of five, possibly more, of the school children. Nor had their headmistress escaped. Dazed, in shock and with what had been her bandaged arm, now hanging limply and pouring blood, she was only half aware of what she was doing. Climbing and crawling across and through the smouldering debris she was pulling at arms, tugging helplessly at legs, weeping inconsolably as the scale of her losses began to sink in.

Miljana was not dead. Much of her lower left leg was missing and part of her scalp hung bloodily down one side of her face, draped across her shoulders as a loosely tied scarf might hang, her brown hair matted with blood. Seeing James she tried to lift an arm. Jumping across the debris he knew that unless he acted immediately there would be little he could do to help. Kneeling by her shoulders he lifted her face onto his lap: only then did he see blood haemorrhaging from her left thigh, above the bloody mass that had once been her calf. She needed a tourniquet and she needed a saline drip... and she needed both – now! The first he could manage. Ripping off his long-sleeved jersey he quickly wrapped it round her upper thigh, his fingers slipping in the blood as they tried to grip the wool. He twisted it tight. Tighter still. The bleeding slowed. The drip would have to wait...

James leaned back against a stone block, pulling Miljana's

head onto his stomach. She opened her eyes, breathing in shallow gasps. "It doesn't hurt any more," she whispered.

"We'll get a drip into your arm as soon as help arrives," he answered wishing he could do more as he felt her tense body slowly beginning to relax.

Suddenly she stiffened, "The letter, James," her voice was little more than a guttural murmur, "The letter from Matea."

James looked about him, Miljana's bag was by her shoeless left foot. "Yes," he said, "I can reach it."

"Read it to me James. Read it please."

"It will be in Croat."

Miljana insisted, croaking more softly now, "Please."

Cradling her head in his elbow he tore the envelope open and read, stopping often for Miljana to translate softly, her voice weakening with each sentence.

Dearest Millie,

I do hope you are very well and that my darling parents are too. Be sure to give them many hugs and kisses from me. Dino is thriving and chose the teddy bear for Mama with particular care as he thought it looked like him!

Isn't it funny that we are both interpreters but for different sides although I do not see it like that as you know. There should be no sides ... decent people have no 'sides'. Only the army and the politicians have 'sides'.

Dearest, I continue to pray that we shall meet again in the sunshine and smell the wild bougainvillea as we walk together by the sea in peace...

You may have heard that we were rescued from the Zadar hotel by an Englishman when it was shelled the other day. So there is some goodness around.

Write by return sweetest. I love your letters and news.

Your oldest friend, Mattie.

As Miljana translated the last paragraphs James leaned closer to catch her faltering words, involuntarily wiping a tear from his eyes, smudging the blue ink. Looking down at Miljana's face he could only read her lips rather than hear her failing voice, "Give it back to Matea with all my love. Tell her," even whispering was nigh impossible, "Tell her it gave me great comfort and peace. Tell her..."

"Yes?" James asked quietly, but there was no answer. He looked down at Miljana's sightless eyes as he felt her body die in his arms.

The dead were dead. The living needed attention.

While the injured children, plus those wounded grown-ups in the street that bordered the beach, were being swiftly triaged and given rudimentary first aide by neighbours, those that were unharmed were shepherded away. The next of kin were being cared for, comforted and smothered by sympathetic arms.

With nothing more for him to do James sat down on a damaged chair. Resting his head in his hands, tears flooded over his fingers. His thoughts were only of the innocent children he never knew: torn to ribbons, reduced to just so many parts.

He could take most things but not this.

As he had lain on the beach, counting the explosions, the exhilarating, pulse-racing smell of the winter-flowering, wild jasmine, that – along with the cordite – had been blasted towards him from the bushes along the back of the beach by a bursting shell, was the most striking sensation: the long remembered scent that Caroline used to wear. How peaceful, he thought. How sublime... how paradoxical. And with that jasmine came memories of his dead wife and of their unborn son as he stared at the obscene line of half-covered bodies, including that of Matea's best friend. It was more than his still-fragile emotions could endure.

Someone would have to tell Matea. Pray God it wasn't him. Then he looked down at the letter, crumpled now, bloodstained and smeared with tears. It was going to have to be him.

CHAPTER EIGHT

Monday 6th December 1993
Headquarters, ECMM's Regional Centre, Ulica Kneza
Trpimira, Knin, Republic of Serbian Krajina.

"I needn't ask how your first patrol was."

"Not quite as I expected," James replied rather more calmly than he felt. While Jack and Florian compiled Team November Three's Daily Report, James, still smeared with dry blood and sand, had been summoned to Gaspard's 'inner office'.

He came straight to the point, "Miljana's body, along with the others, has been recovered in UN ambulances and taken to Knin hospital's mortuary." James took a deep breath, "I'm sorry Gaspard. All we did was make two Croat families happy for half an hour or so..." Unsure what else to add he settled for, "...we saw a great deal of the countryside on our way to Karin Plaza. After that I rather lost interest and concentrated on trying to get dry and keep warm."

"Understandable."

"I made a promise to the headmistress that when I see Ratko Knežević I would remind him of his pledge to provide a secure place for the school."

"He can still honour that promise."

"Especially as he will only have about eight youngsters to look after. I'm afraid we left before knowing the full casualty list."

The next morning, shortly after a rising, watery sun had crested the eastern hills James met Gaspard again in the HQ building.

"Do you have a camera?" he was asked as they walked towards the Land Rover.

"Yes,"

"Normally it is not wise to carry one as the Serbs are apt to smash them on the road side but I know that Knežević will be happy for you to photograph him."

"Being photographed by me may not be the answer!"

"He is accused of war crimes by the Croatians so I think he will want to be seen in a better light."

"Has he committed any?"

Gaspard did not answer directly, "To mask their own considerable criminalities, the Croats will accuse every Serb of such crimes. For his sake, I hope he is tried – if it ever comes to that – by an international court and not in Zagreb."

Gaspard stopped the vehicle outside a barbed wire gate and beneath a large sign indicating that the inhabitants of the camp were from the Anti-Tank Platoon of Princess Patricia's Light Infantry. Inside he parked where directed by a young corporal who then instructed, "Stay in your vehicle. I'll tell the lieutenant that you are here." After five minutes the soldier reappeared and spoke curtly to James. "The jeep will be ready soon, mate. Wait by the guard room," he said pointing.

Looking about him James replied, "Thank you."

"Well I guess that is me dismissed," muttered Gaspard with a thin smile, "I'll be back in two hours."

James waited by the guard room from where he could hear the almost continual crump of high explosive echoing up the hillside from the north-west. Within the open-sided tent, covered by a camouflage net, three soldiers sat drinking coffee and speaking French. No one took any notice of his presence until a Mercedes 'G' Wagon stopped alongside. The driver wound down his window and barked, "Jump in!" James did as ordered.

Clear of the Canadian camp the driver was uncompromising in his displeasure at driving a civilian, "We don't usually waste our time with the likes of you. It'll take half an hour to get to the Gornji Bruška training camp. Once I've dumped you I'll leave. I don't like to hang around that place."

"Why?"

"Full of Serbs. Up to no good. Most nights we watch them patrolling through no man's land into Croatia. Serve the buggers right if they get a bloody nose."

"Do they?"

"No idea but I hope so."

"You don't like the Serbs."

"No."

"So you prefer the Croats with their Nazi symbols and self-righteous attitude?"

"Not particularly. My view is that this is a military situation and one that would be easier to contain, or even solve, without damned politicians muddying the waters."

Feeling that it would be a further waste of the driver's time trying to engage him in a sensible conversation, James could only mutter, "Thankfully, that's your personal opinion."

But the driver hadn't finished, "Why are you visiting Knežević anyway. He doesn't give interviews except to senior Serb officers. I'm surprised he's bothering with a non-combatant."

For the second time since leaving Zagreb James found himself on the defensive with a Canadian and, for the second time, decided to attack. "Since you ask, I'm not a civilian."

"You bloody well look like one."

"That may be so but it is often a good idea not to make it seem so blindingly obvious."

"Okay bud, tell me what your background is."

"In short," James said, without needing to stretch the truth, "I am a British Royal Navy submariner and a specialist in maritime special forces and counter-insurgency operations." No point in explaining that he was retired.

"I would never have known. I guess you have a story or two to tell." The driver's tone was moderating.

"Another time I think."

"What rank are you?"

"Commander."

"Oh. Sorry, sir." The unexpected politeness brought a smile to James's eyes.

"Why are you so far inland?"

"I'm collecting background material before I move to the coast."

The road was rough and became bumpier once the Mercedes began winding its way between the rocky outcrops and narrow defiles of the hills that overlook the Adriatic, flickering on the far horizon in the cool December sunlight.

At last the track curved sharply to the left then, unexpectedly, the smartly painted gates of Ratko Knežević's Gornji Bruška training camp halted further progress. Ahead, white-painted huts faced the coastal plain beyond.

A red-bereted soldier marched towards the Mercedes's passenger door. "I've telephoned the captain," he announced to James in near perfect English.

As the Serb soldier stood back a tall, pinched-faced, grey-cheeked officer in well-pressed combat uniform was striding towards the gate. Saluting James he reached for the door handle.

"Blimey," muttered the driver, "Never seen the captain salute anyone else before other than another bloody Serb."

"There you are," James grinned over his shoulder, "never believe everything your eyes tell you." Riding his new found status with the Canadian driver he then ordered, "Please be back in two hours. I have other visits to make."

"Yes, Sir," the driver replied, sharply emphasising 'sir' and hardly containing his surprise. "Sure thing commander."

James stepped into the cool air.

"Commander Laidlaw," Knežević began, "I am so glad you could take the time to come and see me."

"The pleasure is mine," James answered cautiously.

"We'll go to my office where I can explain what I do and why I have asked you to come here."

As they walked down the dusty track James knew that he was in the cleanest establishment he had yet to visit since his arrival in the Former Republic of Yugoslavia. In the near distance he could hear rifle and pistol fire as though from a firing range. Those Serb soldiers that passed were dressed smartly, each one saluting their 'boss'. There was nothing slovenly about their appearance nor was there anything sloppy about a platoon of troops marching towards him, wearing a uniform that, somewhere in his mind's recesses, he knew was familiar. He shook his head as though to jog his memory but with no result.

Reaching a newly-painted, wooden hut Knežević swung open the door. Inside the air-conditioned building framed photographs of military personnel were hung on the corridor's walls as a school might display it's football teams from down the years.

The captain's office, thickly carpeted beneath a window the

length of the wall, faced south-west towards Biograd, visible in the far distance.

Knežević pressed a bell and within moments a soldier entered bearing a tray with coffee, milk, sugar, biscuits, cups and – James smiled – even saucers.

Settled into armchairs the captain explained, "You would have heard considerable artillery firing along the edge of the confrontation line." James nodded as Knežević continued with a grin, "I didn't arrange your visit to coincide with that but right now there is a three pronged attack taking place from Croatia, northwards towards the Maslenica bridge crossing which they seem determined to control."

"Understandable I suppose since it is the direct road link between the coast and Zagreb."

"Of course," replied Knežević, "I am alive to Croatia's problems but if they were to be less keen on resurrecting old symbols I might even see their point of view. Now I hope for a balance that allows Serbs to continue living where they have lived for hundreds of years. And if I had a wish it would be to return to the Yugoslavian status quo but as I don't have that luxury my aim is to make sure that the Serb soldiers that are sent to me are trained to the best possible standard. Sadly, I receive so few that those that I send back, having earned their red beret, are too few to make a difference to the army as a whole."

"Maybe your standards are too high for the calibre of men you receive."

"A valid point. When the Yugoslav National Army left Croatia we were a good army and now we are an even better army because we left the worst behind on the coast. The Croats are poor soldiers led by poor officers."

James, with no idea why he had been summoned to

Knežević's lair, lent forwards but the captain was not yet ready to talk in details. "These exchanges of artillery fire are tedious and although I have no authority over the Serbian army I do not approve of the targeting of innocent people."

"Nor do I," James interrupted, anxious to move the conversation away from the general towards the specific. He needed to know why he had been summoned, "A few nights back I was staying in the hotel Adriatica when you fired six shells into it."

"It was not me and it should not have happened."

"Did it not also happen to a school on one of the outlying Islands not so long ago?"

"You are correct but I can only advise."

Becoming irritated, James felt it was time he addressed his most important concern even if Knežević continued to hold back, "The artillery bombardment of Karin Plaza last night. Was that part of this Croatian push that you have just mentioned?"

"How did you know about Karin Plaza?"

James, unsure if he was being purposively side-tracked, replied with a straight answer. "I was there to see what help we could offer the junior school to save further bloodshed."

"They lost five I think."

"And one of our lady interpreters."

"A bad business."

James turned on the offensive, "Is that all you can say!"

"It happens."

"They are your fellow countryman. You don't approve of Serbia shelling Croatian schools and yet all you can say when Croatia shells a Serb school is that it is a 'bad business.'"

Knežević narrowed his already thin eyes and looked coldly at James. "It happens all the time and, yes, it is a bad business as I disapprove of indiscriminate shelling by either side. It may be a little late now but I had already ordered my men to prepare one of our huts as a school room."

"And transport?" James felt he was back on more secure ground, "Can you supply that too?"

"I have asked the school teacher and some of her parents to come here tomorrow." James nodded as Knežević continued, "And before you ask, I am sending a car for them. Then they can see what is on offer."

"That is very good of you. Thank you."

"One thing you may have missed. Here we are also within range of Croatian artillery and although, surprisingly, we have never been targeted, the children's presence may change that."

"Not even the Croats could be so cruel."

"Their record is not good as you have experienced for yourself."

"So what is it that you do here?" James persisted. "You say you don't approve of shelling indiscriminately and that you are training men to a higher standard than the normal. Either you are at war with Croatia or you are not?"

"We are not at war, at least not an all-out war, and your own training will tell you that when the fighting starts it is a sign of failure so I see my job as one of trying to prevent full scale conflict. *Si vis pacem, para bellum*! As the Roman Vegetius said, Let him who desires peace, prepare for war."

"Thank you, I am familiar with the Latin."

"The Croatian army intends to wage war with the aim not simply of defeating the Krajina Serbs but exterminating them."

"How do you know that?"

"One of my late bosses is a Colonel Ante Slavić…"

"…I have heard of him…" James interrupted.

"…now the Croatian army's Chief of Staff in the Split area. He knows my views on his personal poor military capability and tries to get his own back by never failing to let me know, by one method or another, how well equipped and trained the Croatian army is becoming."

"Is that true?"

"I hoped you would tell me!"

"You know that is impossible. As a monitor I am unbiased and neutral."

"And in your other role? Are you neutral in that too?"

"What other role?"

"Come now. I know you worked with British Intelligence in your diesel-electric submarines off northern Ireland and north Russia!"

"If you asked me here to discuss my naval career then I regret that I must leave."

"Please, Commander, not so hasty. You should remember that the interpreters, on both sides, have their own agenda and that includes those that work in your HQ in Zagreb."

"News to me," James replied plainly.

"Some feel as I do. Tito taught us that we are all Yugoslavs so allow me to give you a warning. Slavić is a dangerous man. Fat and lazy but still dangerous. He is in league with the Americans and Germans in Zagreb so that he can facilitate their embargo-busting plans for his own advantage... and by the way, as it happens, I am married to a German lady but I can't stand them as a race."

With an uneasy start James realised that he recognised the uniforms worn by the platoon that had passed them earlier, "And for your part, what about those Italian soldiers we passed?"

"I am glad you saw them."

"On purpose I presume? Not very subtle."

"I don't deal in subtleties. I'm a soldier."

"So, why are they here? Judging by their uniforms they are

from the San Marco Battalion."

"How observant. These men are good amphibious soldiers and as Italy is keen to take back that part of the Northern Adriatic it lost to Germany at the end of the war I have been asked to train selected groups to do just that. They come in via Belgrade."

"Now that really does surprise me."

"You see, all thoughts of European military integration are meaningless. Here you have Croatia rearming with German and American help. The French too are supportive, while the Greeks, Russians and Italians back Serbia to the point that we are even training some of their men."

"And you have proof of this re-armament?"

"Not in so many words perhaps but I believe that it should be your Mission's duty to expose such a serious international crime. However, I am being truthful when I tell you that if Slavić knew that anyone was undermining his work with the Americans and the Germans he would not hesitate to ..." Knežević drew a finger across his throat.

"Which, as a monitor, is a good reason to stick to the rules," James suggested.

"Nobody else does."

The captain put down his coffee cup and stood. "Let me show you the camp, your driver should be back by the time we return." Hanging on a hook behind his desk was a webbing belt with four grenades clipped to it. Knežević lifted it down, buckled it around his waist, smoothed his red beret onto his head and ushered James from the room.

Outside they stopped for the captain to point towards the Adriatic in the far distance. "There you are, we are back from the confrontation line by about ten kilometres. You can see Biograd on the coast about twenty four kilometres away. We are well within range of their heavy artillery and yet they fire at Karin Plaza where there are no military targets."

"And Serbia retaliates?"

"Not every time."

"Often enough to cause casualties to civilians."

"I have no artillery. I try to stop the Serb army but I have little influence over day to day operations. My way of retaliating is to train Serb soldiers to be better than their Croat counterparts, which is not difficult."

James remained puzzled, certain that Knežević was holding something back. He tried again. "The Croats must think that Karin Plaza has something to hide. Something that needs destroying and I wonder what that is." Knowing that he was moving beyond his duty as a monitor James reasoned that, in civilian clothes and talking military tactics and not political strategy, he could play a different card, "Salt water maybe," he suggested, knowing the answer. He also believed that Magnus Sixsmith would not be pleased if he missed this opportunity.

Knežević replied slowly and carefully, "With your background I knew it would not take long. Sea water is the clue: that and a beach with suitable gradients, but approaches that are dominated by Serbia..."

James took up the unspoken challenge, "...yet a population so cowed by bombardment that they might flee." He was beginning to understand the reasons behind the artillery salvos and, incensed by his experience the day before decided, by offering a warning, to remove one small piece of his armour. "I know I needn't tell you this but they are goading you," he said firmly. "They are forcing you to take action. To reposition your defences. To open gaps up elsewhere."

"Tell me more."

"They may be calling your bluff by pretending that they will launch an amphibious assault cross the Karin Plaza beach…"

"They don't have the landing craft," Knežević interrupted.

"I am sure you will have worked it out for yourself but the Croatian occupation of Karin Plaza would be like an intravenous injection into the heart of the RSK. And if they arrived by sea and found it not only uninhabited but undefended so much the better. It would save their heavy armour quite an overland journey."

"So we strengthen our defences at Karin Plaza instead of elsewhere despite the amphibious threat being negligible?"

"I couldn't possibly tell you what to do other than to suggest that that is what they may be hoping by their aggressive action. In which case you will have to ethnically cleanse the place yourself…as it were!"

"We would be doing the Croats' dirty work for them."

"Quite so. It is, as they say, your call."

As the guided tour continued James's admiration for Knežević as a soldier increased. He would have much to tell Magnus back in London. He might have some news for Gaspard too.

The excursion around the camp ended at the main gate where, as Knežević had predicted, the Mercedes was waiting. The captain turned to his departing guest, "I suggest that this visit never took place," he said.

"I was going to propose the same," replied James, "although too many people know already."

"Only the Canadian lieutenant, his driver and your boss."

"As well as Karin Plaza's headmistress."

"True, but I think we know who we mean."

"You may do but I don't!" James replied simply.

Back at the ECMM's Knin headquarters James followed Gaspard to his office where the Frenchman came straight to the point, "What did Knežević want to see you for? Alone?"

"He runs what we in the British navy call a tight ship. Training Serbs to a level beyond the norm for this part of the world. He is also training Italians in case the chance ever comes to take over those parts of the Istrian peninsula lost to Yugoslavia – now Croatia – at the Paris Peace Treaty in 1947."

"I knew something was going on along those lines."

"There is more. The other day you mentioned a Colonel Slavić. He and Knežević know each other well. Or, rather, they did before Croatia's independence. The captain is convinced that Slavić is supporting, even facilitating, American and German efforts to break the embargo of arms shipments to Croatia."

"That would tie in with the rumours that I have heard here in the RSK and from my own Quai d'Orsay people. Now that you have given me a form of confirmation, there is another reason why I am keen to get you to the coast."

"Meaning?"

"You will have to do it in your own way but it will be more than useful if you can provide firm facts and figures on any embargo infringements."

"Is that not the duty of the various navies patrolling the Adriatic?"

"There are some nation's navies that are not so keen on enforcing the embargo. Thus it falls to us to double check. And yet," Gaspard elaborated, "as you have just said, it is still not the ECMM's task to monitor the embargo."

James nodded.

"But as individuals reporting through our own national chains of command…" the Frenchman hesitated for a moment, "…well, that is an entirely different matter."

"And France's position in this is, I believe, not entirely altruistic?" James was fishing.

"I am a diplomat. It is my business to assess the truth, analyse it and report back to my own headquarters as well as through Zagreb and Brussels. What happens to those assessments is not my concern." Gaspard paused before adding hesitantly, "Rather as I imagine CC does with your MI6."

James did not feel the need to declare his own interest in gaining intelligence on embargo busting other than as it affected his job as a monitor. Too many people were putting two and two together...and coming up with the correct answer.

"So," Gaspard spoke softly now although there was no one else in the room, "Because of what you have just told me, coupled with the sacking of Bjørn and the presence in Split of Mrs de Mayer, I have decided that you should move to Split sooner rather than later. Tomorrow you will leave in my Land Rover."

"I understand."

"Wilhelm will probably leave the mission soon if his wife has anything to do with it. Assuming that will happen I have warned Patrick O'Hara to stand by to join you."

"I understand," repeated James, delighted at this change in his programme so soon. The growing prospect of getting his teeth into a real project more in keeping with his experience was exciting. "So Demetrios Pagonis, will in the end be my immediate boss."

"Correct, but he still has to answer to me and carry out his duties in accordance with my directions."

"Do you know him?"

"Although he's been in Knin for a day or two, he has yet to call on me. I think he has spent most of his time arranging tonight's dinner in the Castle. He obviously has a number of Serb friends."

James stood to leave but Gaspard held up a hand. "There is a final reason why I need to get you in place sooner rather than later. I have heard that I will be leaving the mission shortly after Christmas."

James looked up, surprised and saddened by this news for he had warmed to Gaspard. "Do you know who your relief is?" he asked.

"He will not be a diplomat but a member of the DGSE. The *Direction générale de la sécurité extérieur.* The equivalent of your Secret Intelligence Service."

"Why the change?"

"Probably as a result of problems with the embargo. My government has long suspected complications and wants... how shall I put this... to exercise a less diplomatic approach."

James, sensing something he could not put his finger on, asked a more direct question, "Do I take it that your successor will not be impartial?"

"I couldn't possibly answer that. I know of his reputation but that, too, I shall leave for you to assess. All I can say is that you will probably discover that his approach is different from mine..." Gaspard paused, a smile on his lips as he remembered a saying he had been taught by Hathaway, "and I think you will find that he is the sort of prudish man who would spell your word fuck with a ph."

They both laughed loudly.

"And where are you going?"

"French ambassador to the United Arab Emirates."

"Bravo, Gaspard. You deserve something like that after here. Does the new Head of the Regional Centre have a name?"

"Jean-Claude Sublette. I believe he has been sacked from his current post and will be sent here to see if he can improve."

"Is this the right place for a failure?"

"Is any place the right place for a failure!"

There was a short silence during which Gaspard stood to

unlock a corner cupboard from inside of which he took two cut glass tumblers and a bottle of 45 per cent proof *Pastis*. "Grenoble University I think you said?" he asked over his shoulder.

"I did."

"Then you will be familiar with this aperitif?"

"Love it!" replied James.

"I don't have many chances to drink it here but I keep a bottle or two for occasions such as these."

"Is right now so special?"

"To me. Yes. While I am obviously happy with my next appointment I feel as though I am leaving with my task only just beginning. The exposure of Croatian re-armament."

"I thought we agreed that that is outside the ECMM's remit!" James teased.

"It is but the honest discovery of what might or might not be happening is certainly a matter for the European Community as a whole. We can of course take no direct action other than alert Zagreb who, I trust, will alert Brussels. What happens after that is not our concern. What, though, is our concern, and I think I am speaking for both of us, is that our countries know what is happening. For my part I will keep the Quai d'Orsay informed and, I'm sure for your part you will keep CC informed."

James nodded noncommittally and took a sip of the pungent anisette.

Gaspard had not finished, "I have a bad feeling about Demetrios and I have a bad feeling about JCS as he is known. Although France supports Croatian independence it does not, officially, support that independence at the expense of the Krajina Serbs. Nevertheless, I fear that, with the Greeks taking over the presidency and my job being taken over by a DGSE man, diplomacy will be set aside by individuals if not by the countries they represent.

"And the reason why I am telling you this is that I believe you are a straightforward man keen to see fair play. Breaking the UN embargo, if that is happening and we can assume nothing without hard evidence, is not fair play and I see trouble. Now, just when I find I have a British monitor, for the first time since Hathaway, whom I can trust to report correctly and fairly, it is me that is departing."

There was a silence while both finished their *pastis*.

As James stood for the second time to leave Gaspard once again motioned him to sit. "Before you go I think you should know that I believe the Greeks, and in particular Pagonis, will make it very difficult for the Germans by the time they take over next summer."

"By which you mean…"

Gaspard interrupted him, "They will make promises for the future that the Germans will not be able to honour."

"That's quite a prediction."

James smiled at Gaspard's reply, "It is what I'm paid to do. The trouble with Greece is it has yet to decide whether it is a Balkan state or a European one although from what little I have gathered Pagonis goes for the Balkan option and will do all he can to embarrass Croatia."

"Thank you for that," James said putting his empty glass on the coffee table between them. "I'd better get back to the motel and change for his dinner."

"Wrap up. There's no heating in the castle."

Gaspard was right, the castle was cold and, if James had not had the foresight to take two Coca Cola bottles of red wine from the motel, it was also 'dry'. The food, a self-served, mixed grill, was unexpected in the rare variety of cooked meats and although the up-to-now mysterious Captain Pagonis made a brief speech, apparently introducing himself as the saviour of the Krajina Serbs, few could see him in the light from the cheap, spluttering candles that failed to illuminate the huge, draughty, thirteenth-century hall. James was relieved when a clearly put-out Gaspard offered him an early lift back to the ECMM headquarters and a welcome cognac.

In the morning James paid his meagre motel bill – more than covered by his allowances – and met the Land Rover's driver.

Passage to and across no-man's-land was completed without hindrance and so twenty minutes after passing into Croatia the Land Rover was pulling up outside Hotel Split – the five-star hotel without the five stars – on the coast, in the south-eastern suburbs of the town.

Inside the glass, revolving door a large entrance hall reached to the far side of the building where a reception desk stretched, seemingly for yards, beneath an equally long, west-facing window. To the right of the front door a horse-shoe shaped bar, whose seating area lay behind a cordoned off area containing tables and chairs, catered for the thirsty. It was a popular venue.

Having checked-in with reception and been allocated his room James, escorted by a member of the ECMM's Forward Logistics Group, made his way, via a lift, to the fifth floor. "The ECMM has taken over the whole of this floor for offices, stores and bedrooms," the Belgian logistician explained, "and as we are co-located it makes sense for Team Split's offices and accommodation to be administered by us in an addition to our everyday duty of supporting all monitoring teams in Dalmatia, the RSK and neighbouring Bosnia Herzogovina."

The lift doors creaked open to reveal a chair at which sat an unshaven, armed, Croatian policeman, slumped with both elbows on a table in front of him, staring straight ahead down the long corridor. He did not look up as James wheeled his suitcases onto the landing.

Room 519 opened, via a short lobby with a bathroom on the left, into a rectangular room dominated, at the far end, by a large French window. James slid open the glass door and stepped onto a small balcony that faced west and a panoramic view of the entrance to Split harbour. To the left, eight miles away across a broad expanse of dark blue water, was the island of Brač. He stood for a few minutes, rejoicing in the sight of the sea and breathing deeply.

Content that he was back where he belonged, then suspecting, correctly, that they would not come looking for him James found his way to the Terrace Bar at the southern end of the first floor hoping to find Bjørn and Wilhelm. A covered area led through glass doors to a sun-deck that, looking out over the Adriatic, resembled the bridge of a ship. To his right, two white-clad monitors and their lady interpreters were sitting at a corner table, empty beer bottles scattered before them. James introduced himself. Neither offered to shake his outstretched hand.

"Well," he said in the silence that followed, "I'd better get a beer."

When he returned Bjørn spoke for the first time, "I won't hide my feelings. Your presence here is not welcome."

Taken aback James could only utter, "I'm very sorry to hear that."

"I have no proof," offered Bjørn, "but I believe you are behind my dismissal."

James, learning quickly the idiosyncrasies of the monitoring mission, was on his guard, "How come? It was not my idea to take over Team Split. I have only been in the country a handful of days."

"That may be so but I've heard of you through my own

submarine service and I don't think you are as straight as you would like us to believe."

"I left the Royal Navy some years ago."

"What have you done since?"

James ignored the question and turned to Wilhelm. Intending to provoke he asked, "And how do you find my presence here?"

"Unnecessary," was the Belgium lieutenant's short reply before looking at his watch. "There will now be three monitors where there is hardly work for one."

"I thought that Bjørn was leaving us."

Bjørn snapped back, "Not if I can help it."

It was time to come to the point. "Have the Croats not asked you to leave?" James asked.

"Only Colonel Slavić, but I think I can expose him."

"Colonel Slavić?" James asked innocently.

"Chief of Staff of the local army brigade."

"And how can you expose him?"

"He's in cahoots with the Yanks."

"For what purpose?"

"He didn't like what I was finding and has dressed it up as spying in order to get rid of me."

"And were you spying?" James asked, unsure that spying was the correct word.

"I am here to monitor."

"Monitoring must involve some intelligence gathering, surely?"

"I've no idea what is going on but when I asked Slavić about his friendship with Colonel Anderson, the US Defense Attaché, things quickly became nasty. So, I started putting two and two together and did not like the answers I was coming up with."

"Which were?"

Bjørn was suddenly defensive, "Let me just say that I was getting suspicious that they were seeing a good deal of each other here in Split and on the islands so I thought I should just see why…"

"And did you?" James persisted.

Bjørn thought for some time before answering, "Slavić thought I was tailing him and didn't like it."

James, unconvinced that Bjørn was telling even a small part of the truth, pressed further, "Where were you this morning?"

"In the harbourmaster's office checking up on ferry movements."

"And I take it Wilhelm was with you?"

In the silence that followed James looked in turn at Wilhelm and his interpreter, both blushing visibly.

"No. I tend to do that sort of monitoring by myself."

"You don't trust Wilhelm to keep his mouth shut?"

There was a long silence.

At last Bjørn spoke, "I'm not going to sit here and listen to this from someone I do not know. We are going to lunch and then we will be back on patrol."

"To where may I ask?"

"Brodosplit shipyard," was Bjørn's immediate answer.

"I thought you were no longer a monitor."

"Says who?"

"Gaspard Chastain for one," responded James. "So would it not be a good idea if I came too? To get acquainted."

"No room in the Land Rover. Both the interpreters are with us."

James looked surprised. "You need two interpreters to visit Brodosplit?"

"Certainly, we plan to split and cover different sections of the shipyard."

"Friendly bunch!" James muttered to himself as they left.

Team Split returned for tea on the hotel's terrace with laughter booming down the corridor as an advance warning. The monitors, each with their interpreter clinging to an arm, sank into the two sofas opposite James. A wave of garlic, wine fumes and cheap scent drifted across the low table between them: odours that were unlikely to have been acquired among the slipways, welding shops and boardrooms of the Brodosplit Shipyard.

The interpreter next to Bjørn giggled and squeezed his hand. James looked at her blonde hair, he looked at her long legs that stretched from beneath a short, heavy-cotton blue skirt and he looked at her heavily made up blue eyes and flushed cheeks. Wilhelm, looking nervous if not shifty, said nothing as his own mistress slowly stroked an arm...

The Terrace Bar door crashed open. Five heads swivelled. A woman, barely in control of her anger, stamped across the decking, heading directly for the Belgium. Guessing that this had to be Mrs de Mayer, James turned his attention to Wilhelm's face in time to see it being slapped: violently with nothing feminine about the force used.

"You bastard," Wilhelm's wife screamed as her husband began to massage his left cheek, already turning crimson. "I watched you four having lunch..."

"You can't have done we were at the Split shipyard..."

"Don't lie to me," Mrs de Mayer shrieked before hitting her husband with even more force. Satisfied, for the moment, she turned to the second object of her anger over whom she was now towering. "You are a whore and I will be telephoning Mademoiselle de Wilde to have you kicked out."

Mrs de Mayer turned back to her husband to pull him sharply to his feet, "You are coming straight home with me.

Immediately!" she yelled. With the cowering Wilhelm firmly under tow she stormed towards the door that had only just clicked shut while her husband's lady friend fled in the opposite direction, her sobs echoing as she descended the stair well towards the ground floor

James turned to Bjørn, "This is serious."

"If I was you I would keep out of it. None of your business."

"It is my business as I have been sent here to re-start monitoring."

"What precisely do you mean by that?"

"I have no idea where you were today but obviously it wasn't the shipyard."

"Now look here, James. I don't want to fight with you, after all in a different world we were contemporaries, but…"

James stopped him. Raising both hands he said, "I have no intention of fighting you either but I don't think the European Community Monitoring Mission is being well served. There are far more important things for us to be getting on with. Together." He emphasized the last word.

"Such as?"

"The breaking of the embargo for a start."

"Load of nonsense. Visit Ploče and you will find no evidence. Apart from that, you've probably seen for yourself the appalling state of the soldiers. Well, let me tell you, the officers are certainly no better and I guess that's the way it will stay. Frankly it is not worth the country importing arms as there is no one capable of using them and no money to buy them if there were."

The woman at his side nodded her head vigorously.

Bjørn hadn't finished, "Croatia is not likely to risk future membership of the European Union, and even of NATO, by breaking a United Nations embargo. And for what purpose?"

He answered his own question, "An attack on the Republic of Serbian Krajina, even if it were feasible, would certainly gain the country few European friends." Bjørn thought for a moment then added, "Except perhaps in Germany."

James, seeking a more positive way ahead and anxious to learn more, made a conciliatory suggestion. "Why don't we meet this evening over dinner and you can brief me on the situation. Maybe discuss the future as you see it, with your experience."

"Sorry, not tonight."

"Tomorrow morning then?"

"Busy."

James watched Bjørn as he stood, tugging his interpreter to her feet and towards the main door but their way was blocked by the abrupt appearance of a large, long-haired, loosely-jowelled colonel in the Croatian army. Ante Slavić was not alone. Either side of him were two military policemen with their pistols trained on the Danish submariner's stomach.

"Not so fast, my friend," the colonel ordered quietly.

"What the hell's this about, Ante?" Bjørn demanded in return.

The colonel looked around at the otherwise empty terrace. "You are under arrest," he announced, adding for good measure, "For the second time."

"I continue to plead diplomatic immunity."

"Not this time. That may have worked a few days ago but now that you are no longer a member of the European Community Monitoring Mission I shall treat you as a common criminal."

"Let me call my boss in Knin."

"I beat you to it. He confirmed that you have been dismissed and that you are on your way home as soon as the flights can be fixed."

"I don't believe you."

Ante Slavić pointed to the telephone at the end of the bar. "You know his number. Telephone him yourself."

Bjørn gaped open mouthed at the two HS 95 pistols. This was grave and the colonel was in no hurry. After an agonising fifteen seconds the Dane broke the silence, "What am I accused of now?"

The colonel was ready with his answer, "This morning you were seen, in your white uniform, entering the harbourmaster's office. My officers reveal that during that time you were illegally conducting your monitoring despite Monsieur Chastain having specifically ordered you to cease."

Bjørn opened his mouth to speak but another glance at the two pistols silenced him. The colonel continued, "That was part of the deal I had with Monsieur Chastain to prevent you being charged and facing a Croatian court rather than being sent home."

"I... I..." Bjørn stumbled.

"Well," interrupted the colonel, choosing his words with care, "I could re-charge you with the original crime of intelligence gathering, specifically against ECMM regulations, and let events take their course but I can't be bothered. As soon as you're out of my country the better it will be for all of us."

"Meaning?" Bjørn asked.

"Meaning," parodied the colonel, "that you will come with me to the police station where you will wait for the next flight to Zagreb onto which you will be escorted. Once in Zagreb you will be detained in the airport's cells until the first suitable flight leaves for Denmark."

Bjørn could only take in so much. Feebly he muttered, "My kit... what about my kit?"

Ante Slavić leaned back on his heels and let out a mammoth snort. "Ha! Your kit. Yes your kit. And all your notes?"

"Who will pack my kit?" repeated the Dane.

Looking beyond Bjørn Slavić pointed towards the lady interpreter, now standing behind a wicker chair trying to make herself less prominent. "You!" the colonel half shouted at the woman, "you know his room well enough. You pack his kit. A car will collect it from the foyer in precisely one hour's time."

The colonel nodded at the two military police escorts in turn. "Right," he ordered, "Take him downstairs." Without a backward glance Bjørn Svendsen was gone, dropping a bunch of keys on the carpet as he left.

The colonel stepped towards James. "By your uniform you would appear to be a monitor as well."

"Arrived today. James Laidlaw's my name."

"Good. Let's hope for a little more honesty," exclaimed Slavić. Reaching the door he bent to pick up the key ring. "I expect you'll be needing one of these," he said tossing them towards Bjørn's mistress. Turning once more to James he snapped, "I'll be in touch."

"Goodness," exclaimed James to himself as the door shut behind the colonel's ample figure. "That was quick. I wonder if it is always like this on the coast?"

James strode to the surviving interpreter's side. Not unkindly he said, "I think you had better remove Bjørn's bedroom key. I'll need the others."

Studying the keys for a few seconds she un-clipped one.

One of those remaining fitted the lock on Room 511, two doors down from James's room, the other two appeared to belong to a Land Rover. Opening the office door to Team Split's Headquarters James entered a mirror image of his own bedroom with the double and single beds replaced by a large table and six chairs while the wardrobe contained an untidy jumble of books, maps, white flak jackets and helmets. On the long wall above the table a large map covering the coast from Istria in the north to Dubrovnik in the South and from the Adriatic in the west to the border with Bosnia-Herzegovina in the east, had been roughly nailed. A number of coloured pins jutted from its surface.

James, astounded by the swift turn of events, sat by the telephone, deciding his next move. Bjørn had left the mission, of that there was now no doubt, but the status of Wilhelm remained uncertain. He leafed through an ECMM directory and picked up the telephone.

"Chastain," Gaspard answered almost immediately.

"James here."

"I wondered how long it would take you to ring. I have just been speaking to Colonel Slavić."

"That didn't take him long either. I don't suppose he was very happy."

"I don't agree," Gaspard argued politely, "I think he was glad for an excuse to push Bjørn on his way rather than wait another four days. Not least of all he probably didn't trust him not to abscond from the shuttle bus and make his way back to his girlfriend."

Gaspard then sighed before adding, "Events seem to have moved faster than I had anticipated."

"Well there is more which you probably don't know about."

"Yes?"

"Wilhelm's wife caught the four of them having lunch in Split this afternoon. Back in the hotel she fronted up to her husband to tell him that she was taking him home."

"To Belgium or back to his room?"

"Belgium. Then the lady interpreter ran away in tears while

the other one is currently packing Bjørn's kit to be collected by a police car."

Gaspard thought for a moment, making up his mind, "I'll be with you tomorrow lunchtime and will see if Camille can fly down by then. Unwittingly we seem to have the ideal opportunity to sort everything out in one go. Make a clean break of the past with two new monitors."

"Brilliant, Gaspard," James thought for a moment before commenting further, "But, to be serious, I am far too new here to set up a reconstituted Team Split on my own, without a handover and within a week of arrival."

"I will be bringing Paddy O'Hara with me. You've met him. A lieutenant-colonel in the Irish army."

"You mentioned him earlier. Should he not be the Team Leader?"

"I rather hope you will both be leaders of two new teams. As I hinted when last we met."

"I remember."

"You may care to divide the offshore islands between you. Especially as Paddy is also a yachtsman."

"Sounds even better."

"I have some other telephoning to do," Gaspard explained, "so I will end by saying that I intend calling on Colonel Slavić while I am on the coast to tell him of our future plans. I hope you will join me at the meeting."

"Certainly," James smiled, "He seems a very positive sort of chap."

"You must have caught him on a good day," Gaspard laughed, "I wonder if you will think the same after your next encounter."

"I look forward to it."

"*Bien*," Gaspard finished, "*A bientôt et bonne chance.*"

"*Merci.*"

James replaced the telephone as the door swung open. Nursing a crimson slap mark on his left cheek Wilhelm entered the room, drew up a chair opposite James and sat down. Mrs de Mayer hovered in the doorway behind him.

"I need to talk to someone," Wilhelm began.

"That someone is not me." James was not in a mood to help. The man was rude, he was cheating on his wife, he was making false promises to a lady interpreter... and he was deceiving the ECMM. "I don't know you and..."

"You unpleasant bastard..."

Wilhelm was halted by a voice behind him hissing loudly, "Who's the bastard?"

James looked up. "Mrs de Mayer," he began quietly, "none of this is anything to do with me but I think it would make sense for Wilhelm to speak to Gaspard in person when he is here tomorrow afternoon."

Mrs de Mayer shook her head and, turning to her husband growled, "Come, Wilhelm. I'm not letting you out of my sight."

James stopped her and, with a smile, asked, "Fine but may I borrow him tomorrow morning – just for an hour – so that we can go through the team's terms of reference?"

"No." Mrs de Mayer responded unequivocally as she dragged the hapless Wilhelm into the corridor leaving James to search the files for clues as to what the two Team Split monitors had been up to during the previous months rather than what they said they had been doing in their daily reports.

The long day had yet to run its course. After dinner James, surprisingly tired and for once with a full stomach, was looking forward to turning in but as he reached the door to the stairs – he might as well start this Time Passing Measure on his first day – he hesitated with his back facing the lobby bar and main entrance. Behind him, a violent conversation was being conducted in loud shouts accompanied by the passionate banging of a table. He turned towards the American voices, their distinctive southern drawl alien to Croatia. As he did so, a single, sharp crack reverberated around the near-empty foyer.

Horrified, he watched a man in Croatian army fatigues slowly collapse onto the carpet with blood already oozing from the side of his head. Beside him another soldier, stunned and ashen faced, gazed dumbfounded at his falling companion. A 9 mm Browning pistol dropped between them as the victim, blood now gushing from the exit wound, began twitching in his death throes, arms and legs smearing blood across the green, patterned carpet. A widening pool of red quickly surrounded the fallen pistol turning it into a minute island of black.

James's first instinct was to help. His second impulse was to turn his back on a problem that had nothing to do with monitoring and, almost certainly, everything to do with an overdose of raquia, anger and bravado.

He choose the second option.

CHAPTER NINE

Thursday 9th December 1993
Room 519, Hotel Split, Put Trstenika 19,
Split, Croatia.

With a marginally clearer idea of what lay ahead, plus the thought of a constructive meeting with Gaspard, James slept as well as he had since leaving England. As Slavić was becoming an enigma – his name was cropping up more often – it would, too, be good to meet him properly and, as it were, on neutral ground.

He also needed to discuss Ratko Knežević's views with Magnus Sixsmith.

In the meantime James made his way down the stairs to breakfast. Reaching the ground floor he glanced towards the lobby bar where a large ragged section of the carpet had been roughly hacked away. Two Croat policemen were arguing with the barman who, gesticulating wildly, was imitating the holding of a pistol to his own head. James watched for a moment too long. Noticing his interest a policeman excused himself and walked across.

"I see you are with the ECMM?" he began in English.

James was vague. "Yes?"

"Did you witness this game of Russian roulette?"

"There was no game of Russian Roulette?"

"So you did not see the killing?"

"I did not see any Russian Roulette."

"A man died here last night while playing Russian Roulette."

"Either he committed suicide or he was murdered."

"You seem very sure. Where were you."

James pointed the five yards towards the stairs.

"Then how can you be so sure."

"I saw a soldier in combat dress falling. Before that there had been an argument with another soldier. They were shouting at each other in American."

"Did you see the shot being fired?"

"No."

"So how can you say that it wasn't Russian Roulette?"

"You don't play Russian Roulette with a 9 mm pistol. Or any weapon with a fixed magazine."

"We were told it was a revolver."

"You haven't recovered it?"

"No. Nor the man who survived."

"Then if I were you I would start looking for an American mercenary and a 9 mm pistol. The first shouldn't be too difficult."

"There are hundreds of them. Describe this one."

"Well," James said, anxious to continue on to the dining room, "I am glad to say that that is your problem but for the record and from the brief glance that I had the man you should be looking for had a tattoo on his right neck, below the ear. Just too far away to say what it was, but possibly a bird of some sort. A bald eagle perhaps?"

"We may need to speak to you again."

"Quite so. James Laidlaw of the ECMM. Operations Room on the fifth floor."

"Thank you."

As he helped himself to olives and pita bread James felt a hand creep around his waist.

"Hi," a female voice purred in his ear.

He spun round. "Camille!" he exclaimed. "You're early."

"I caught the first flight."

At their table James smiled, "You had better brief me before Gaspard arrives."

"I will, but not here," she replied, glancing at the nearby table of Greek logisticians, "What about your room?"

James's smile broadened.

"Why do you grin like that? It was a lovely evening but today I am on business. And, you will be sad to know, I am catching the evening flight back to Zagreb."

James continued to smile.

"I must thank you for saving the life of one of my very best interpreters."

"Matea?"

"Yes. Maybe she can thank you in person if she hasn't already done so."

"I don't need thanks. It had to be done."

"Let's discuss it over a cup of tea."

In his room James filled his travelling kettle. "Earl Grey?" he asked.

Camille nodded enthusiastically, "A rare treat," she said, then, "I believe you saw what happened to my interpreters yesterday?"

"Clearly they are both living with the monitors but is there a regulation that forbids it."

"No, but if it interferes with good, accurate monitoring it has to be frowned on."

"From what little I have seen that would be the case."

"If both Bjørn and Wilhelm leave then that, in effect, sorts the problem out."

"You won't sack the girls?"

"Good interpreters are hard to come by, particularly reliable ones. I also believe that Gaspard has plans for the future of Team Split but we had better wait until he arrives…"

"Surely it is not always the girl's fault. The monitors are just as…" James paused, seeking the right word, "…lonely."

"The girls are doing it in the hope that they might be able to forge a life elsewhere but the men are doing it because, as you say, they are lonely, off duty and certainly bored."

"Boring is not how I would describe my first few days with the ECMM!"

"I don't know if you are lucky or unlucky."

James wasn't sure either. "You mentioned Matea?" he said.

"As she has a house in Split I have made plans to move her here."

"Fine."

"Her parents remained in the Republic of Serbian Krajina after the rest of the family were 'cleansed'. So she has no reason to like the Serbs especially as she's a widow after a Serb ran over her husband."

"Yes, I knew that and I also met her parents in Drniš."

"She is one of those lovely people who tries to see some good in everyone."

"A noble attitude."

"It is indeed but sadly she has made a number of Croatian enemies because of this same 'noble attitude', as you call it."

"Is that why she is keen to leave Zadar?"

"Not really. She is equally well known here."

"Thanks. I'll bear that all in mind."

"Now I need to interview the two interpreters downstairs."

"Why don't we meet in the Ops Room before lunch.

Gaspard should be here by then."

Two hours later a polite knocking on the Operations Room door preceded the arrival of Gaspard. After kissing Camille and shaking James's hand he said, "I've booked a table in the public dining room. Patrick will join us there once he has checked in. Then we can thrash out the immediate future."

In the foyer, Gaspard led James and Camille to the bar where a curly-haired, white clad monitor stood, glass in hand staring down at a large, rough hole in the carpet.

"Ah," Gaspard said, "I knew you would be here."

Patrick O'Hara but down his beer as his deeply-lined face spread into a wide grin, light-blue eyes smiling. "Didn't know where else to go. Never been here before."

"Great to meet you again, James," Patrick said. "I think we may get to know each other rather well judging by what Gaspard has hinted."

As James nodded his agreement the Irishman butted in, looking down at his feet, "Odd shaped hole in an otherwise good carpet. Strange that!"

"I'll explain later," James answered.

"You had something to do with it!"

James shook his head.

Pointing to Patrick's beer glass Gaspard ordered, "Finish that, Paddy. We'll have some good wine with lunch."

The downstairs dining room, looking out over the Adriatic through one vast window that ran the full length of the sea-facing wall, displayed fading delusions of opulence. Indeed, the hotel had known better days, as traces of the original décor and an earlier ambiance still lingered.

Gaspard had chosen a table next to the window. The maître d'hôtel knew the ECMM were good payers, they also chose the more expensive dishes and better wines, sometimes even the few French wines that remained. Gaspard's request was easy to honour and good for the hotel's finances.

With all seated, and having made their decisions from the limited menu, Gaspard looked at each monitor in turn. "Allow me to start," he began, "This is not how I wanted things to turn out for it had been my intention to expand Team Split into two. However," Gaspard paused momentarily, "seemingly unconnected events have, for the moment, put paid to that idea."

He paused to take a sip of French wine, his eyes widening with pleasure. "The first was the sacking of Bjørn and the second was," he thought for the correct expression, "the equally unexpected arrival of Mrs de Mayer."

Gaspard, enjoying his first taste of civilisation for weeks, paused again, "These events are linked through the two interpreters and while living with a monitor is not against the ECMM's terms of employment, when such relationships lead to falsification of daily reports then a line has been crossed."

Gaspard continued, "There has been chaos in Team Split for some weeks now culminating, all of a sudden, with me having to replace two monitors and as this coincides with the proposal to expand the monitoring area as far south as Dubrovnik it is convenient to make a clean sweep. But before I continue, I will ask Camille to say something about the two lady interpreters."

Camille obliged, "I have decided to keep both employed for a number of reasons. Their English is impeccable, as interpreters they are reliable, they are both local girls who know the area and the local personalities."

Camille looked round the table, smiling.

"However they have been sent on leave to," she caught the eyes of James and Patrick, "recover. So," she explained, "I have moved Matea, whom James has already met, to join Team Split on a temporary basis."

Camille looked at Gaspard and nodded.

"Thank you," he said, "I'm appointing James as team leader with you, Paddy as his number two. Eventually Patrick will be responsible for the area to the north as far as Sibenik and James to the south as far as Dubrovnik. New monitors will be appointed as soon as they become available."

So far so good for his aspirations, James thought. In fact, better and better.

"This afternoon we have a meeting with Colonel Slavić and as he is our point of contact with the army it is important we keep him on our side. The ECMM has, or should have, very few secrets from our hosts."

Gaspard looked around the table, "Now let us enjoy the rare chance of a tolerably-good meal."

After lunch, Gaspard dropped Camille at Split airport where her parting words to James ushered an unexpectedly-welcome sensation through his body, "I'll send you Matea as soon as she is ready," and with a theatrical wink she walked towards the departures hall.

The Croatian Army's 4th Guards Brigade was close by as Gaspard explained, "They have their headquarters at the Hotel Resnik. Bang on the coast. We don't have an interpreter for this visit," he explained, negotiating the airport's many exit roundabouts, "as Slavić's English is good enough."

Hotel Resnik, a collection of linked bungalows facing south and lining the beach, had once been a popular tourist hotel but now the owners were happy to welcome the army and particularly Ante Slavić's hard drinking officers, both commissioned and non-commissioned, that made up the brigade's headquarters.

Leading his small team into the foyer Gaspard was met

by the Croatian colonel, standing by the concierge's desk, a large glass of white wine in one hand, a cigarette in the other and booming, "Gentlemen, welcome to my headquarters." No one had time to respond as he added, "Come, I have prepared drinks overlooking the sea," and led the way through the hotel to where a table and chairs were waiting. "There," he said, "what a view."

Before they sat Gaspard introduced James and Patrick, "Team Split's new monitors."

"I have met James but did you not also have one called Wilhelm I think," observed Slavić.

"He has retired from the Mission," Gaspard replied simply, "and you know what happened to Bjørn!"

"He was not behaving properly." Slavić answered bullishly before moving on, "and you, Commander Laidlaw, you too were a submariner."

James raised his eyebrows at the use, for the second time in recent days, of his old rank but before he could say anything Slavić answered the un-asked question. "I know much about you for I have access to your Royal Navy's Officers List. I do my homework so I do hope you're not tarred with the same brush. I think that is the expression."

"I'm not... and it is," replied James with a cautious smile.

Slavić looked back at Gaspard, "So, you have a new team. Do you have new instructions?"

"No," the French diplomat replied, "The team's orders are as they always have been for those on the coast. They remain in line with the Memorandum of Understanding signed between the European Union and the states of the Former Yugoslavia in July 1991."

"Please remind me," prompted the Croatian colonel.

"With pleasure," answered Gaspard before counting them

off on his fingers, "The Split team will monitor and report on the state of the economy and infrastructure. I am particularly keen that they obtain a list of businesses, so that we can determine their past, current and future situations with a view to offering financial support once life returns to normal. Secondly the Team will report all ceasefire violations and assist with the separation of opposing forces by mediation. To do this they will work with the United Nation's Military Observers and report on troop movements and strengths. Finally they will develop priorities for the economic reconstruction specifically using information gained from their monitoring of the local industries."

Gaspard, drew a breath and raised his glass in the direction of Ante Slavić. Smiling, he said, "I hope that satisfies you."

"No question of military intelligence."

"None whatsoever. And to do all this I will be forming a second team. Between them they will monitor from Sibenik in the north down to the port of Ploče in the south. Then, eventually, as far as Dubrovnik. Including the off lying islands."

Slavić looked up sharply, "Which islands?" he demanded.

"All of them. The economic future of Dalmatia depends to a considerable extent on the regeneration of tourism on the islands. There is also the sardine fishing industry on Brač and Vis and of course the export of the famous white stone which was used to build the White House in Washington. Not to mention the lavender fields of Hvar and the exporting of olive oil."

"I do not think visits to the islands will be necessary." Slavić began insisting

"Why?" Gaspard was equally adamant.

"They are self-sufficient, they are self-contained and the war has not really affected them."

"There are no tourists and little fishing."

"They will return."

"Not unless money is spent on the hotels which are unoccupied and often closed. Neither situation doing their maintenance any good. Money will be needed and it is the monitoring mission's duty to help assess and decide priorities."

Slavic's eyes, partially concealed by his drooping eyelids, sparkled as he said with a near-menacing tone, changing the subject very slightly, "Nor do I want you visiting the port of Ploče ."

Gaspard was caught off guard, "What do you mean by that exactly?"

"The army looks after the port, not the European Union."

The atmosphere was turning. James, with no knowledge of the area, nor of the niceties of who monitored what – even had there been a dividing line of responsibilities – switched his attention from Ante Slavić and Gaspard as each spoke. Gaspard remained cool and factual, Slavić was becoming animated, cheeks flushing, eyes darting.

"There are no limits to our monitoring if we believe that it is in the longer term interests of your country," Gaspard persisted, "and Ploče, like Pula in the north where we have been monitoring since the beginning of the Mission, is a civilian port. It is not a naval base."

"Of course I can't stop you," Slavić was suddenly conciliatory, adding quietly, "But what do you hope to achieve?"

Gaspard declined to answer directly, "Ploče is a commercial enterprise much in the same way as Brodosplit shipyard is a commercial enterprise. Indeed, many of the raw materials required by the shipyard are currently imported through Ploče. My monitoring team will try to ensure that that continues. James, as you know, has a career in nautical affairs and so I'm sure he is the ideal man to lead the monitoring."

With the beginnings of a grin replacing his previous malevolence Slavić poured himself a glass of wine and looked at both Patrick and James in turn, "I hear that you are a yachtsman, James. A yacht owner?"

"How the hell does everybody know so much about me?" he replied.

"The former Republic of Yugoslavia is full of intelligence gatherers, some of whom quite wrongly swap information like others might swap stamps."

"Well yes I do own a yacht," James looked at Patrick, "and you Paddy?"

"I don't have one at the moment."

"Fine," said Slavić "I keep mine in the Split Marina. Maybe that way I could show you the islands over a couple of weekends. Right now let us drink to the success of the new Team Split."

An hour later, as they were leaving his headquarters, Slavić took James's arm and led him behind the Land Rover. Out of sight. The grip on his wrist was rough and the Croatian's once-expressionless eyes, had re-found their earlier malign glint. James pulled his arm away. "I meant what I said, James, I would like to take you to the islands. But by ourselves." He fished in a breast pocket. "Here's my card and please call me Ante."

James, unsure that he was ready for a first-name friendship, turned abruptly for the passenger door, mumbling, "Thank you," over his shoulder as he opened it.

The drive back to Hotel Split was largely in silence, broken just once by Gaspard. "James," he said, "I would like you to keep an eye on both Ploče and the islands. Officially."

"Slavić is not keen on us visiting either."

"The harbour is a commercial enterprise that we have every reason to monitor and he knows that. He's just blustering as a matter of principle. As for the islands," Gaspard continued, "why not take up Slavić's offer to sail across with him. You might learn more than if you went on an ECMM patrol."

"Good idea."

"Best of luck," Gaspard finished as he began to drive away from Hotel Split's car park, "But be careful. I don't want any more of my team arrested."

As they re-entered the hotel a small, nervous-looking man, shiftily searching around him as he approached, handed James a scruffy, brown envelope. "The commander was very good to us, he wrote this in the airport lounge before boarding the aircraft for Zagreb," the man whispered.

James looked at the unfamiliar handwriting addressed to James Laidlaw, ECMM, Hotel Split, but before he could comment the man had run from the building.

In the privacy of room 519, James slit open the envelope. He read quickly:

James,

I have little time as we are about to be called forward to the aeroplane. I apologise for being rude especially as I accept that all this has nothing to do with you.

Nobody is what they seem. My advice is to treat every Croat and American very carefully.

Some will try to befriend you, as they tried to befriend me to get me to support their fanatical idea that every Serb should be removed from Krajina. That is not of course anything to do with the Mission (although the Croats seems to think it should be).

I think my arrest may have more to do with the Croats having a guilty conscience over what they think I may have discovered than anything else. I am certain the local authorities have something to hide. I was on to something but couldn't quite put my finger on it.

Good luck.
Bjørn

James was surprised that he was not surprised by the contents of Bjørn's letter and not astonished either that he could place names where Bjørn had purposefully avoided them. Even so, he had taken a risk that the envelope would be opened by a third party but there was no sign of that.

Picking up the hint that whatever Anderson and Slavić were up to should not concern the Mission he decided that the contents were best kept to himself. If asked, James resolved to explain that the letter was merely a simple personal apology for the way he had been treated by the outgoing leader of Team Split. In the meantime he locked the envelope in a suitcase.

The next morning Split's new monitors gutted their cluttered Operations Room. Anything that appeared to be relevant was saved, to be studied in depth later, the rest was bagged up for the Forward Logistics Group to burn.

On the terrace that evening James and Patrick watched the sun sink beyond the distant islands. "Do you know what, Paddy, I think we should pay an early visit to Brač and Vis. Find out what it is that Slavić does not want us to know about."

"Agreed, and you can add Ploče to that list."

"We should find out when Bjørn last visited these places and what he wrote in his Daily Reports."

"By the way," Patrick changed the subject, "Do you know the new interpreter? I couldn't help noticing Camille wink at you when she mentioned Matea's name."

"I dragged her and her son outside when Hotel Adriatica was shelled the other day."

"Didn't realise that was you."

"Right place. Right time. Nothing more."

The next day James and Patrick finished their search of the previous Team Split's files but with little to show for their efforts. Bjørn and Wilhelm had conducted few patrols outside the city, although ferry receipts suggested that the Danish commander had visited, Brač, Hvar and Vis on a number of occasions and apparently alone each time.

"Interestingly," observed James halfway through the morning, "There are no reports on Ploĉe."

"Maybe that should be our first patrol," Patrick replied.

"Let's look at the diary."

The telephone on the table by the window rang sharply. James picked it up, "Team Split."

"Ah, James," the heavily accented voice was unmistakable, "it's Ante here."

James was cautious, "Good morning, colonel."

"I had been wondering if you would care to join me for a day's sail this Saturday? Just the two of us but I now see I have to be in Zagreb."

Without hesitation James replied, "Just as well, Colonel, as it's a bit too soon. Over the weekend Patrick and I are going to drive around the local area. Getting a feel for the place."

"Quite understand," but Slavić was insistent, "What about the 18th?"

James muttered his thanks, said he would give the offer some thought and replaced the telephone.

"What was that about?" asked Patrick.

"Slavić suggesting I might like to go for a sail. Just the two of us."

Patrick teased, "I think he fancies you!"

"I'm not sure that that is a joke!"

For the second time the telephone rang and for the second time James answered it, "Team Split."

"Mr Laidlaw?" There was something familiar about the caller's voice.

"Speaking."

"Do you remember me? Matea Marković. You helped…"

"Of course I remember you, Matea," James was just a little too quick. He slowed down, "How is Dino?"

"He's fine and so am I."

"I gather we are due to see you in Split?"

"You have obviously been speaking to Camille."

James laughed, "I had no choice." Then, on an unexpected impulse, he asked, "Do you sail?"

"What a funny question?"

"Not really but I have a feeling that we may be doing some monitoring by boat."

"As it happens my parents owned a yacht that we kept up the river from Šibenik. Then the war came and she was sunk by Serb artillery."

"Sorry to hear that."

"It's simply the way it is," Matea replied without self-pity.

"I know you didn't telephone to talk about sailing," probed James.

"I was wondering when you would like me to start work. I moved into the family house last night. The other side of town."

"When would suit you?"

"Tomorrow?"

James thought for a moment and put his hand over the telephone's mouthpiece. Looking across at Patrick he mouthed, "It's Matea. Ready to start work tomorrow. What do you think?"

"The sooner the better."

"Matea," James spoke again into the handset, "Wonderful. Come to Team Split's Operations Room at nine o'clock then you can help us plan our schedule for the coming weeks."

"I'll be there."

James sat down at the table, pulling a desk diary towards him. "Let's start with the Brodosplit shipyard."

"That might then give us a real reason to visit Ploče."

"I wonder what actually comes through the port?"

"I was wondering that too."

"Let's do some guessing over lunch."

James looked squarely at Patrick across a communal bowl of olives. "I visited Ratko Knežević a couple of days ago. At his invitation."

"I had heard."

"He told me that he believed Slavić is trying to persuade the Germans and Americans to break the embargo. Then, it would appear, we have Bjørn watching both Slavić and Anderson visiting the islands while Slavić not only puts us off visiting them but he all but forbids us to monitor Ploče."

"I think," Patrick said slowly, "this may begin to add up as Slavić always seems to be in the middle."

"He is violently anti-Serb."

"Along with ninety five percent of Croatians."

"We also know that the Croat army, in its current state, would be no match for that of the Republic of Serbian Krajina particularly if, as we must assume, it would be supported by the JNA."

"But we also know, from what you witnessed in the hotel's foyer, that there is a growing number of American mercenaries training here. So we should monitor the Croatian army to see whether or not it is being rearmed and trained by foreign powers. Second we should watch Ploče very carefully. The airfields are already under surveillance but anything that comes through them has to be lightweight compared with what a major port can handle."

"The islands," Patrick continued the summary, "remain an enigma that we can not ignore. Possibly as rear logistics bases for building up stores, unseen until they are needed?"

"Maybe I should take up Slavić's invitation sooner rather than later. It may just give us the clue we are looking for and on which we can then act."

"Tomorrow Matea can help us establish a proper patrolling schedule."

"May I suggest we don't mention the islands to her quite yet. She may be one of the better interpreters but she is still an unknown factor."

"Agreed."

CHAPTER TEN

Colonel Dwight I. Anderson of the United States Army looked towards his office's frosted glass door as it swung open.

"Good morning, colonel," trilled his 'all-American, mid-western-gal' secretary. "I have Colonel Ante Slavić here to see you. As arranged."

"Sure, Michelle. Show him right in."

"Hi, Ante," Dwight Anderson, grey crew-cut hair, grey-skinned, lean and business-like, strode across his office, right arm outstretched. Despite the floppy-maned, floppy-jowelled Ante Slavić exhibiting, in Anderson's West Point view, the antithesis of military appearances, they were established colleagues, if not friends. Their wives, however, had not met. If he thought about it at all Anderson had never heard Slavić mention a partner and so had not enquired. Each was, though, wary of the other despite having a common interest: the subjugation of the Serbs.

"How're you're doin'?" asked Anderson.

"*Dobra, hvala,*" replied Slavić. He knew that Anderson was keen to exercise his limited Croatian, nevertheless, beyond the everyday greetings of 'good' and 'thank you', it was easier to speak English. "You hinted that you had some ideas that might interest both of us?"

As the Chief of Staff to the Croatian Army's 4th Guards Brigade, a life-long habitué of Split with a hatred of Serbs and everything Serbian, Slavić had been the ideal contact for Anderson to involve in his nefarious tasks.

"As you know, Ante, we are keen to install a covert military facility somewhere within Dalmatia. Preferably as close to the coast as possible. A small administration team to begin with. Just a few guys but they will need room for a helicopter pad which we will build."

Slavić smiled smugly for he believed that the Americans were now 'coming on-side' but he said nothing as the attaché continued, "You know me well enough to appreciate that I speak with the authority of the White House and that, coupled with the President's determination to help establish Croatia's stability as an independent sovereign state, is a darn good endorsement of our intentions."

"Does that include breaking the United Nations embargo on arms imports?" asked Ante Slavić optimistically.

Anderson did not answer the question directly, "We don't pay much attention to UN embargoes unless they directly, and adversely, affect American interests."

Slavić recalled that, in anticipation of those 'American interests' his country had already given the United States a Russian 500 kilogram mine, a sample of their most modern torpedoes plus the encryption codes used by their army and navy. He could hardly now refuse an additional request, this time for a patch of 'uncontroversial' real estate if that would help to mop-up the Serbian forces in Bosnia-Herzegovina. Aloud he said, "Why do you want this place?"

"We need a deniable foothold from where we can help monitor inshore shipping with a light helicopter supplied by the Sixth Fleet," lied the United States' Defense Attaché. "I've been looking at the maps and reading a bit of World War Two history. The disused airstrip on Vis would suit us very well. What do you think?"

What the Defense Attaché should have said was the clearing of the Serbs from Bosnia Herzegovina would be a vote winner in support of his President's bid for a second term of office. He could also have emphasised, which would have been much to the Croat's delight – but not quite yet – that the American people, fed up watching pictures of Serb atrocities, were demanding that the White House brought the killings to an end.

Aloud he said, "Ante, if you want our help you're gonna have to continue paying for it! So keep those Serb atrocity stories coming in." Dwight Anderson's mouth was working in opposition to his mind. "No need to mention the similar Croatian obscenities…"

"There aren't any…" Slavić interrupted.

"…Goddamit man, of course there are and we are doing our best to keep those away from ABC News."

"There aren't any," repeated Slavić. "So," he was determined to move the conversation forward, "with your help we can liberate Knin and the Krajina region first then force Milošović to sign a Peace Accord. You know that Germany approves our plans. Will America?"

"Not yet Ante," Anderson answered deceitfully, "but I agree it is a good long-term strategy. However, your country is far from ready. Give it another year. In the meantime we need this small piece of land I mentioned."

Anderson knew there was a danger of allowing Ante Slavić

to get too close. At the moment all the Croat needed to know was that the US was prepared to consider breaking the embargo in Croatia's favour. What else America planned the Croat did not need to know.

"I've got just the place. On the island of Brač. It's an ex-Yugoslav National Army base and even has a paved airstrip surrounded by a substantial fence. Not been used since the soldiers left in '91. Kilometres from anywhere. Hidden from view in a shallow dip in the land it is so secret that it's never been put on the map. Almost impenetrable undergrowth has grown up all along the perimeter fence which, itself, is on the far side of high ground for almost 360 degrees. We made sure of that. We also made sure that the locals thought we were excavating a new quarry."

"I'd better take a look." Dwight needed to carry out any reconnaissance on his own but Slavić had other ideas.

"When I get back to Split on Monday I'll check-out my yacht. It's winter so she will be grateful for an outing. My boys keep her ready."

Dwight Anderson did not know this side to Ante Slavic's life and hoped he never would for the American colonel was not a sailor. Thinking optimistically, he could see nothing wrong with the car ferry and if he could get a grid reference out of him he would slip across while Slavić was still in Zagreb.

"Let me pull out a map," he said helpfully, crossing the room to a wide, low chest of drawers. "Here you are. Scale of one to one hundred thousand."

Slavić studied the sheet for a minute or so, bending down with his face close to the paper. Short-sighted, he was too vain to wear glasses for it was not good for the image among his young soldiers. Eventually a stubby finger jabbed at a place that suggested only rocky outcrops, unkempt wild olive groves and dry, uncultivated, Mediterranean scrubland.

Anderson considered it perfect but said aloud, "Why did you not show me this place during our visits?"

"You never mentioned taking over real estate, just accommodation and a helipad... This place on Brač, do you think it will do?"

"Not sure, Ante. Do you have anywhere else?" Anderson was keen for Slavić to remain in Zagreb for a few more days.

Disappointed Slavić replied, "Oh! I'll ask around. As you said there was something similar on Vis Island but it's overgrown and would require considerable engineering work. I'll stay in Zagreb over the weekend to find out. I'll be in touch."

"Thanks but don't make it too obvious," Slavić was not a reliable ally, but he was a vital one if America was going to help break the Serbs of Krajina. One day – not yet – Anderson would take him further into his confidence. Thinking quickly, he said, "I'm taking the wife away for a few days tonight so if you come up with anything while you are here let me know on Monday."

"There is one other thing I should mention," Slavić began, "I have arrested the Danish monitor from the ECMM's Team Split."

"Why?"

"He was becoming too inquisitive. Not too much but I felt it best to have him dismissed. Had the ECMM asked for proof I would have invented something."

"Well, I guess that is up to you."

"I don't think he knew anything definite but he did spend much time pacing out the waterfront in Split and asking awkward questions in the harbourmaster's office."

Anderson was not happy with this news. "I hope you haven't alerted the ECMM. Roused their suspicions."

"No problem, Dwight. The ECMM agree that intelligence-gathering is not in their remit. But the new monitor…"

Colonel Anderson butted in, "Commander Laidlaw?"

"How did you know?"

"It's my duty to know."

"He has only just arrived…"

"I know! And I know his background."

"…and has said that he intends monitoring the islands and, worse, the port of Ploče."

The United States Defense Attaché looked up, no longer bored with Ante Slavić's ramblings.

"Then I think we had better stop him."

"How?"

"That's up to you."

"I can't arrest every ECMM monitor."

"You can't stop them having accidents," Anderson said very slowly then watched a malevolent smile creep across the Croat's face for Slavić had another idea. He would work first on the Englishman, maybe even turn him into an ally, draw him into his net then…

But Dwight Anderson hadn't quite finished, "And don't forget that the head of the ECMM's Coordinating Centre in Zadar is about to be a Greek."

"That's not good news either."

"Quite so. We may be in for an interesting few months. Are you up to it?"

"Of course."

"Well I hope so Ante, your country has much riding on this scheme."

"I'll see if there are any other areas that might suit you."

As the Croat turned to go Anderson stopped him. Sliding open a drawer in his desk he said, "Wait, Ante. I nearly forgot.

Here are the two bottles of Old Spice after-shave you asked for."

"Thanks," Slavić smiled, "My boys will be delighted. You can't buy it here anymore."

"Luckily our small Embassy shop sells it." Anderson looked up as he held out the two cream-coloured, mock-stone bottles then, puzzled, said. "I didn't even know you were married let alone had any children. At least not of shaving age."

Ante Slavić reddened, mumbled his thanks again and turned for the frosted glass door.

Five minutes after the Croatian had left his office, the United States Defense Attaché pressed a buzzer.

"Hi, Michelle."

"Yes, colonel," she answered.

"Fix my car will ya. One of the 'unofficial' Opels, with the Zadar license plate. And a hotel in Split for tonight. Not the ECMM one. Warn them I'll be late. I'll drive myself."

"Sure thing, colonel."

"Once I've left, better tell Mrs Anderson that I've been called away."

"Sure thing, colonel."

"And get the Defense Intelligence Agency in Washington on the secure 'phone. Brigadier-General Westernburger of the Joint Special Operations Command. If he's not in the Pentagon you might find him at Fort Bragg. Your problem! Then I don't want to be disturbed for half an hour."

"Sure thing, colonel."

Dwight Anderson unlocked a large, walk-in safe that formed part of the inner wall of his office. Inside, he pulled down a canvas hold-all, unzipped it and laid out the contents on a shelf. The jacket, trousers and baseball hat matched the camouflage of their container. So they should, he thought, Croatian Army issue, 'Mediterranean-style', disruptive pattern fatigues with no names. No markings. No rank. No identification. Although clean they had been well-worn be a previous owner.

Looking at a felt-lined tray of various issue hand guns he thought for a moment before choosing a 9 mm, HS 95 pistol. His selection was not a random one for this was his own personal property: unmarked, untraceable and so had never appeared in the US Special Activities Division records: best of all it was standard issue to all Croatian Special Forces. He cupped it in his hand, tossing it up and down a few times, remembering the weight and balance, the pull of the trigger. Sliding the working parts to and fro he checked it's serviceability. You never knew when two extra rounds might make all the difference. As his DIA-issued, 9 mm Browning held just 13 rounds he clipped the HS 95's 15-round magazine into the pistol grip and smiled.

A soft chamois-leather shoulder holster and a pair of night vision binoculars followed the pistol into the bag. It was a day or so before the new moon, there might be just enough star light even for these first-generation goggles.

The dark red telephone on his desk rang once, quietly. The Attaché crossed the room in three swift strides to snap, "Sam! Its Dwight. Sorry about the time difference."

Colonel Anderson waited for the brigadier general's good-natured obscenities to die down before paying more attention, "Listen up, Dwight," Sam Westernburger began to explain. "I hope you're ringing to tell me you have found a suitable facility because the logistics and twelve men sailed from Norfolk, Virginia in USS *Drake* three weeks ago. They are bringing with them two flat packed huts and aluminium planking for the helicopter pad. More will come when they are established but it's going to take time. Right now they are due to join the Sixth Fleet on 22 December. It would be good if they could get established ashore on that day."

"Sam, we're in luck."

"You've found a secluded area?"

"Better than that, I've got you a real airstrip. Not one that we will have to build. Brač Island. A deserted military facility not marked on any map. I'm off there right now. Alone. My staff think I'm going to Zadar. If I'm not back in 48 hours Brač is where you'll find me!"

"If it can take a C-130 that will please the team as ferrying everything ashore by heli will take more months than we have. Especially as the aluminium planking for a 3,000 foot runway will have to be triple-handled from Norfolk to Naples and then from there to the Fleet and from the Fleet to ashore in any number of lifts…"

"I'll let you know."

"…whereas the C-130 can load in the States and, via refuelling stops only, land direct into this island of yours."

"I'll let you know, Sam." Anderson was impatient. He listened for a few more seconds then barked once more, "Sure. Sam. Take down the lat and long." He paused. "Ready?" Anderson dictated, "Approximately 43° 17 N and 16° 40' E. No idea how long or in what direction the runway lies but it looks as though it might be about 1700 feet above sea level. Get the satellite-intelligence guys to check."

The Defense Attaché listened again before finishing the call, "OK. Roger to all that, Sam. Good night or whatever goddam time it is with you!"

CHAPTER ELEVEN

Monday 13th December 1993
Team Split Office, Hotel Split,
Put Trstenika 19, Split, Croatia.

The knock on Team Split's office door was quiet but firm.

"Come in!" shouted Patrick and James enthusiastically. The door opened to frame the silhouette of a trim, neatly dressed Croatian lady.

"Matea," James said rising from his chair, both arms outstretched. "How lovely to see you again." He turned towards Patrick, "and this is my fellow monitor. As he is from Ireland we call him Paddy."

"Welcome to Team Split," Patrick said, "James has told me much about you."

"I haven't had a moment," responded James truthfully then looked at Matea for the first time since Hotel Adriatica where her hair had been bloodied and tangled, her face covered in soot and her clothes dishevelled and torn. Now, he was seeing a well-dressed, slim, youngish woman, possibly in her mid-thirties. Her well-brushed dark hair, and plenty of it, reached below her shoulders in a manner that James could only think of as luxuriant. But it was her dark brown eyes that gripped his attention: the no-nonsense eyes of a mature woman who had seen much. Delicate crinkles splaying away from their corners added width and sensuality to her smile. They also hinted at a determination that might otherwise have been belied by her slight figure. She was coolly dressed in a long, fawn-coloured cotton skirt topped by a flowered blouse. Over her arm she carried a light pullover and, despite the warm sun, a mackintosh.

"How is Dino?"

"Fully recovered thanks to you."

Settling with coffee James explained the situation, ending with a brief summary, "So, that's it. Both of the old monitors gone, both interpretresses on indefinite leave. Team Split recovering."

"Interpretresses?"

"Yes. I like the word. Reminds us that you are feminine and that we must behave ourselves."

"In which case you are the first monitor I have met that worries about how they behave in front of the…" Matea paused to get her tongue round the word, "…interpretresses!"

James, smiling at Patrick said, "I think we had better push on." The Irishman nodded and pulled a third chair up to the table. By lunch a patrolling schedule had been agreed starting with the Brodosplit shipyard followed, a day or two later, by an exploratory visit to Ploče's port manager: all approved by Gaspard over the telephone.

"Slavić is not keen on us visiting Ploče," James said, "but as he is not in our command chain we needn't involve him with our programme."

Matea looked up, startled.

"Do you know the colonel?" James asked.

"Vaguely," Matea was blunt.

"You don't like him?" suggested James.

"He's an army colonel. Can we leave it at that for now." She thought, then, for a long moment before asking, "What other places do you mean?"

"The offshore islands. He seems happy for us to visit them but only in his yacht."

"Be very careful about accepting such invitations for he is not the social, friend-to-all that he may pretend."

James muttered, "Of course."

Matea stood and, smiling at each monitor in turn, wished them a good evening. "I'll be in at nine tomorrow..." then she checked before turning to go, " Brodosplit you said...?"

"That's right and I've asked Josip Naglić, our Croatian Liaison Officer, to come to the office tomorrow at eight in the morning to help fix our programme with the relevant authorities."

"I know him of course and as he speaks perfect English I'll leave you to it," she smiled, "Now I must go and collect Dino from..."

James stopped her. "Matea," he said gravely, "Before you leave there is something I have to give you. It's in my room if you would care to come with me."

James opened the door, ushering a puzzled-looking Matea ahead of him and, as they entered Room 519, he waved a hand towards the one arm chair. "Do sit down," he said reaching inside a drawer for the letter that Miljana had given him... then he turned away, embarrassed that there was moisture in his eyes. Hoping she wouldn't notice, he blinked heavily before facing her. This was the moment he had been dreading...

"Matea, I am afraid I have some very bad news and there is no way I can give it to you other than in straightforward terms."

Matea was staring aghast at the blood-smudged envelope in James's hand, "That's the letter I sent Miljana..." she stopped already fearing the answer before she asked the question. "What are you doing with it?"

James began hesitantly, "I'm sorry…" he looked down blinking more quickly, "I'm so sorry… but Miljana was killed last week in Karin Plaza. By Croatian artillery." Having started he was stronger now and able to continue more surely, "I was with her. She asked me to open your letter and read it to her, which I did while she translated. She knew she was dying and in her tragically-last words she said, 'Give it back to Matea with all my love and tell her it gave me comfort and peace. Tell her…' but… I am afraid we then lost her."

Matea, stunned but composed, stretched out a hand for James to place the letter gently in it. "I am sorry for you, James," she said. "Sorry that you saw my friend die."

She paused, not yet able to come to terms with this news. That would happen later, in private. For the moment all she could bring herself to say, without bursting into tears, was, "I am glad you were with her when she went. Now you will always be my final link to my dear best friend… to those more peaceful days." Matea paused again then, saying nothing, fled from the room. James listened to her running footsteps fading down the corridor towards the lift.

He sat for five minutes, before striding swiftly back to the Operations Room.

"Seems a nice, no-nonsense lass," Patrick commented. "Although rather upset as she ran past the door. Nothing wrong I hope, before we even start work?"

James explained, ending, "Her husband was killed by a Serb and now her childhood girlfriend, a Serb, was killed by the Croats. Quite what she will believe anymore is difficult to guess especially as some of her countrymen find her lack of hatred inexcusable."

"The colonel included."

"The colonel included," James echoed, "I wonder if she will ever learn to hate."

"Anything is possible out here," replied Patrick.

After lunch James returned to tidy up one or two details while Patrick studied maps and charts in the warm December sun.

The telephone rang, James picked it up. "Laidlaw."

"Ante Slavić here."

"Good afternoon colonel. You've just caught me."

Slavić's forced, gasping snort of a laugh down the line made James jump. Holding the hand-piece well away from his right ear he was still able to listen, "Do you remember I mentioned a sail?"

"Yes,"

"Now that I am back from Zagreb I thought you might like to visit Brač this Saturday. Then I can demonstrate how self sufficient the islands are and how they need no patronising by your monitoring mission."

James did not answer directly, "I thought that Croatia was keen to join the EU?"

"For that reason I would like to show you how the islands are able to look after themselves."

"I accept, but with one condition."

"I don't make conditions."

James ignored him. "I will bring an interpreter."

"This is a private visit. And," he added, emphasising his irritation, "I speak good English."

"I know but I would feel happier with an interpreter."

There was a long pause during which James could hear Slavić breathing heavily. The thought of the sail was exciting; the thought of visiting the nearest island was professionally satisfying and the thought of doing so in the company of Colonel Ante Slavić was an intrigue worth looking forward to.

Eventually Slavić broke the silence, "Fine," he said slowly, "it's about a two hour passage, given a fair wind, from the ACY Marina in Split to Supetar."

"ACY?" asked James.

"Adriatic Club Yugoslavia. Five kilometres from your hotel. The other side of the harbour from the ferry port. Bring a picnic lunch and I'll supply the wine."

"Thank you. Time?"

"If we can be ready to sail at 10 o'clock on Saturday we should be moored in Brač by noon."

"We will be there at nine forty-five."

"I will aim to be back in Split by 6 o'clock. Again, weather permitting."

James, knowing the vagaries of sailing, muttered, "Quite understood. Looking forward to it."

"So am I," replied Slavić putting the receiver down, glad that James could not see the satisfied smirk that spread across his face. He rubbed his hands and reached for a glass.

At 8 o'clock the following morning James greeted the Croatian Liaison Officer at Team Split's door. "I'm sorry we have not met before," Josip Naglić said in near perfect English, "but things were getting a little messy in Team Split and I thought it best to keep away."

"Very wise," replied James, "unfortunately I couldn't!"

"I hear that the two lady interpreters are on leave sorting themselves out."

"You hear correctly," James agreed, "So we come with a new interpretress."

"Is she by any chance Matea?"

"Yes,"

"I'm so glad. She's had quite a rough life. I expect you heard that she was nearly killed in Zadar a few days ago."

"Yes," James said without elaborating further, "I was there."

Determined to help the new team Naglić agreed the visit to Brodosplit that afternoon. He picked up the telephone and within ten minutes it was arranged.

"That was quick," James declared, "is it always so simple?"

"Very seldom and I will tell you why. Most organisations in the area, including Brodosplit, are fed up with the same monitors asking the same questions and always with the same nil results."

"The results will come when the problems between Croatia and the Republic of Serbian Krajina have been resolved."

"Many know that but they choose to ignore it. They are impatient. As you will appreciate most of the intellectuals and people with money and influence escaped abroad. That has left mainly low grade people without much imagination to run the businesses and the government, both local and central. Even the military was not immune as the good leaders were mostly Serbs who departed with the Yugoslav National Army. And," he ended with a laugh, "the Croatian police force has never attracted the intelligentsia anyway."

"We must work with what we have."

"There are of course a number of exceptions although most of these will be found on the islands and in the very few international businesses that remain."

"Does that include the port of Ploče."

"You will be able to make up your own mind. Currently it is run by a Scot but even he, sadly, has his limitations."

"Such as?"

"He's rather keen on delegating."

"Good idea."

"While I could agree with you it is during the times that he is away that I believe strange things happen."

"Such as?"

"More offloading takes place at night then used to be the case."

"Meaning?"

"I have no idea. Perhaps this is something you should monitor."

"I hope to but Colonel Slavić is not keen on us doing so. He told us that the Croatian army is responsible for the port. Not the European Union."

"Oh yes, Colonel Slavić. Luckily he's not your liaison officer and he's wrong anyway. The army has a presence in the area but only as a back up for the police if needed."

"You will see on our proposed itinerary that we had hoped to drive to the port the day after tomorrow. Thursday."

"No reason why not. I will telephone Dougal McGregor and fix that too."

In the early afternoon Brodosplit's Chief Executive Officer greeted James, Patrick and Matea at the entrance to his boardroom. Once seated around the table with cups of bitter, black coffee and the obligatory glasses of raquia James felt that he should start with an apology.

"I'm very sorry for the late setting up of this visit," he began, "especially as you were visited by our predecessors only last Wednesday."

Matea effortlessly translated James's words while he studied the Chief Executive Officer's face.

Looking at James the CEO held up both hands in mock despair, "We have not had a visit from the ECMM for many months. And although we don't welcome them we know they are necessary so we were a little surprised that you were no longer taking any interest in us. Especially as we will be one of the major factors in the regeneration of Dalmatia's economy."

Conscious that he was in danger of making Team Split look foolish James repeated his apologies. "I was under the impression that monitors had visited you recently."

"No," the CEO replied then, anxious to move on, continued, "Let me explain what we do and then I will hand you over to my Operations Manager for a tour of the shipyard. He will be happy to answer any further questions."

"How kind."

"We used to build warships. Mostly of the corvette size and we have an acknowledged expertise in small submarines. Especially the Mala class of swimmer delivery vehicles."

Determined to show a rapport rather than a purely monitoring persona James butted in, "Very good they are too. I have worked with them and found them impressive."

"You know about submarines?"

"I was a submariner for most of my naval career."

The CEO straightened his back very slightly. "Then we may be able to discuss all sorts of things. One day."

"And I look forward to that day. "

"We don't build any military or civilian vessels now. But we try to maintain our expertise for the day when we can."

"I believe you once built an 800 ton landing craft."

"First of the Silba class. We launched it earlier this year but since then nothing, although we would like to finish two more."

The CEO passed round a list of civilian ships, mostly passenger ferries, they were currently refitting. "These jobs help us to retain our skills but obtaining raw materials is not easy."

"And where do those materials come from," asked Patrick. Matea translated.

"Before the war we imported steel plate through Split

so it was delivered direct to our doorstep but Split docks are now taken over mostly by ferries transferring refugees along the coast and the few general-cargo container ships that are prepared to run the gauntlet."

"Gauntlet?"

"The embargo! NATO navies, yours included," the CEO looked carefully at James, "put many civilian shipping companies off from accepting cargoes for Croatian ports even if they are not carrying weapons. They get delayed and they get hassled."

"That's not right." James watched Matea as she translated.

"It happens. The British and Dutch navies are the most diligent. American and German warships are not so fussy. Sometimes their inspections are over very quickly."

Matea paused in her translation to glance at James but the CEO had not finished his résumé.

"Maybe if any good comes out of your monitoring you can get the message to whoever needs to hear it that enforcing the embargo may be working too well. And I for one, even if the United Nations doesn't " he laughed briefly, "would be prepared to accept the import of a few weapons if it means that we can get the thousands of tons of the steel we need to keep my business going. Right now it comes in insignificant packets overland from Ploĉe."

"You make the point well," James said, "I will certainly emphasise that."

The CEO looked at his watch, pressed a buzzer on the table and spoke to Matea. "The Chief Executive," she translated, "will hand you over to his Operations Manager. He says that you will not see any ships under refit as that happens in the main sheds until after re-launching. Then they are fitted out in the open but currently he has no vessels at that stage."

A short, jovial tubby man in a light grey suit that he had bought long before he put on weight, entered the room. Once introduced to the monitors he moved to the door, stopped and looked back. "Come," he eventually said in halting English, "I show you."

Outside, he stopped. "We do not allow visitors to enter the sheds," he explained implausibly, "in case you breath dangerous dust. But," he continued with a smile, "as we walk past the buildings you will be able to look beyond me. I have ordered that the doors be left open this afternoon to let in some of this warm, fresh air."

As good as his word the Operations Manager, with a theatrical choreography each time they changed direction, allowed James and Patrick to look past him and into every shed without making it obvious to a casual observer.

Eventually, back in Team Split's office Patrick asked, "You're the naval officer. What did you see?"

"It wasn't very subtle of the Operations Manager but I guess it would have looked innocent enough."

"Yes, but what did you see?" insisted Patrick.

"The first question is why did he want us to see a Silba class tank landing craft," answered James. "As you saw, it is actually nearing completion, despite the CEO's assurance that they are not building anything. My first guess is that soon she will be Croatia's second LCT in commission and my second guess is that they wanted us to know that."

"Not much use to attack the RSK. It's landlocked."

"Not sure that you are right, Paddy. Let me show you on the chart."

James opened the large wardrobe, now fitted with shelves to house the books, papers, maps and charts in an orderly manner. He drew out British Admiralty chart 515, unfolded it across the table and placed a finger on Karin Plaza at the head of Karinsko More. "That is Serbia's outlet to the Med. It is also the entrance to Serbia if a military force wanted to move in with heavy armour."

"These Silba LCTs?" asked Patrick, "What can they carry?"

Thinking back to his amphibious warfare courses James recalled, "Each one can lift three tanks or 200 troops. Quite a cargo."

"So," Patrick began to tally up what they knew, "Prognosis number one is that the Croats, no matter how much they may want to, are not in a position to attack, let alone overwhelm, the RSK. Even with two of these LCTs there are very few serviceable main battle tanks and even less fighter aircraft."

"That's how I see it."

"Prognosis number two. For Croatia to achieve its aim it needs to break the embargo."

"And to break the embargo it will need, if it is not getting it already, foreign help."

Patrick concurred, "Do you believe that statement about Croatia-bound cargoes not being accepted by the shipping companies?"

"I got the impression that the CEO was implying that if a ship owner knows that American or German ships are on patrol then he will risk loading a cargo for a Croatian port. But not if the British or Dutch navies are on duty."

Patrick agreed, "And it ties in with all we have heard via, for instance, Ratko Knežević and Colonel Slavić."

"There is only one way to find out, Paddy. Ploče this coming Thursday. Now I have to make a telephone call from the Land Rover."

"Don't you trust the hotel's telephone exchange?"

James smiled, "Certainly not!"

In the car park James climbed into Team Split's white-painted vehicle. He dialled a number.

"Short here."

"Wilcox," answered James. "In my car."

"Any news?" Magnus wasn't wasting time with small talk.

"Snippets so far. Can you get all you have on a Serb army captain called Ratko Knežević. I am keen to know how genuine he is."

"Next?"

"I need to know when the US and German navy ships are on the embargo patrols."

"Reason?"

"Pretty certain Croatia is being rearmed through the port of Ploče."

"Proof?"

"None yet but anything more you have on Ante Slavić and his relationship with the US Defense Attaché in Zagreb will certainly help. Remember you showed me pictures of the two of them together. Arguing."

"Reason?" Magnus repeated.

"Pretty certain they are even further in cahoots than we thought."

"How so?"

"Rumours so far but…"

Magnus cut him short, "I assume that Slavić is offering the American facilities or even being forced to offer facilities. As you know we don't trust the Yanks and are keen to have first hand intelligence on any embargo breaking operations."

"I'll do my best. Lastly, anything you have on a Lieutenant Colonel in the Irish army would be helpful. Name of Patrick O'Hara."

"Why?"

"Its all changed here. I am now teamed up with O'Hara as the only two monitors in Split. The others have been sacked."

"I heard gossip. Tell me why via the Consulate. Next?"

"I was in Karin Plaza last week when it was shelled by Croatia. Thanks to needing to have a pee I escaped injury but my Serbian interpretress was killed along with five children and a number of older civilians."

"Heard that too. The normal complaints have been made to the UN but as usual nothing will come of it. Is that all?"

"I am off to Ploče on Thursday and then sailing to Brač with Slavić in his yacht at the weekend. Purely social you understand! If you have anything for me before that call Room 519 and I can ring back from the Rover."

Magnus replied sharply, "James," he said, "I told you Captain Milna, our Consul, has been issued with one of our secure, mobile sets and I have instructed him to let you use that."

"Sorry. Quite forgot. Much going on."

"Fine but no more public telephone calls unless in an emergency."

"Roger!" replied James,

"Not a big problem but we might as well make it as difficult for 'them' as possible."

"Quite so," James said, then, "Good bye."

"Bye."

James unplugged the telephone and returned to the Operations Room.

"We're on for Thursday," Patrick reported. "Josip gave me Dougal McGregor's number so I rang him direct to confirm. He's expecting us at noon. As it's about 65 miles down the coast he'll give us lunch."

Early the next day the telephone rang in the Operations

Room. James picked it up.

"Commander," the voice almost shouted, "Its Ante here."

"Good morning colonel." James replied quietly in contrast.

"I hear you are planning to visit Ploče tomorrow."

"Correct."

"Did I not advise against that?"

"You said that you did not want monitors there as the port is a Croatian army responsibility."

"I did."

"Your army does not take any part in checking what goes on."

"What happens at Ploče is not your business so I can assure you that all is conducted in accordance with international law."

"With respect, what goes on at Ploče is very much our business and if you do not think so then I must refer you to the Brioni Declaration in, let me think," James paused only to drive the point home, "June 1991 wasn't it?"

There was silence.

"Then a month later, also at Brioni, a Memorandum of Understanding was signed establishing the monitoring mission and laying down its remit and one of those is the requirement to monitor the economic viability of your country. Ploče and its imports and exports – or the lack of them – has to be a major key to any future growth."

As the silence from Slavić continued James asked, "Are you still there?"

"Don't forget our sailing date on Saturday," was Slavić's reply before he slammed the receiver down.

"I won't," James replied to the dead handset.

Matea arrived in the Operations Room at eight thirty the next day. "So," she began, "we are off to Ploče?"

"That's right," replied Patrick.

"It's a lovely drive."

The views were indeed magnificent especially as Matea brought them to life with a running commentary on the villages and islands they passed. Speaking from the front passenger seat she changed the subject and, turning to James, said over her shoulder, "You know, James, Colonel Slavić is not going to like this."

"It is within our constitution."

"He regards Ploče as his own..." she paused looking for the right word, "...in English you would call it his own bailiwick."

"Nicely put and you are right which is why I am suspicious of his motives."

Matea, defended her fellow countryman, "He is probably suspicious of yours too."

"Meaning?"

"Ploče is a major key to our economic future. He doesn't want the EU messing that up."

"By finding things we shouldn't find?"

"I hope my country is not doing anything you shouldn't know about," countered Matea.

"Do you not want to see Croatia whole again?"

"My husband was killed by a Serb," Matea replied, her voice unexpectedly close to cracking, "Dino was nearly killed by the Serbs and the Serbs have done other terrible things when the RSK was first established. On the other hand my best friend has just been killed by a Croat and now, not content with destroying Serb schools and killing the pupils, Croatia is reintroducing old Nazi emblems and currency so I... I... I don't know what I want."

"I'm sorry," James said placing a comforting hand on Matea's shoulder from behind. "It's not our country. We can have no idea how difficult it is to know what to wish for."

Five miles before they reached Ploče the road turned inland with dirt tracks leading off to the right that then snaked their way to the peak of the small peninsula covered with low scrub pierced through by juniper trees and dominating the port and its approaches.

Descending once more to sea level, at the head of the natural harbour, they skirted the beginnings of a new construction before facing the commercial port's entrance gates, manned by two bored Croatian policemen. Following a brief conversation with Matea the flimsy barrier was raised slowly.

Dougal McGregor was standing outside the office building door warming himself in the pale sunshine.

"Welcome to Ploče," he began, "Come upstairs and tell me how I can help you."

James introduced Patrick and Matea, "I hope we won't need Matea's services," he laughed, "but she is most welcome to join us."

Settled in to McGregor's comfortable office overlooking the bay the Port Manager eyed James, Patrick and Matea in turn. "I'm not sure that we have ever had a visit from the European Community Monitoring Mission and if we have it was certainly not in my time."

"How long have you been here?" James asked.

"Two years with two to go."

"I see construction is underway on what looks like some new deep-water jetty."

"With so little traffic and no money we have terminated the work."

"What sort of cargo do you now expect?"

"A limited amount of domestic goods. Shipments that can easily be transported by lorry. As you will know, the railway system collapsed many months ago."

"And do you personally meet every ship that arrives?" James was inquisitive.

"I have staff that must be kept busy."

"So you don't check the cargo manifests."

"Not usually."

"And the Croatian army? Does it show much interest in your activity here?"

"Never see them."

The conversation continued without, as far as James was concerned, dealing with specifics. He and Patrick had, earlier, agreed the low-key manner in which they intended this first meeting to proceed.

Having exhausted the small talk James stood, "Would you mind if we looked around," he asked, "I, for one, need to stretch my legs after that drive."

"Certainly," replied McGregor, "then we'll have some lunch."

Leaving the Port Manager with the previous week's English-language newspapers the trio walked out into the fresh air.

"Dougal didn't seem too fussed what we saw or where we went."

"I also got the impression he didn't really know what was going on."

Walking towards the deep water berth the absence of workers was noticeable apart from those manning a single crane unloading steel plates, one at a time, onto a lone flatbed lorry from a cargo ship, wearing a Monrovian flag of convenience.

"It will take years for Brodosplit to build a ship at that rate," observed Patrick wryly. "And if they break the embargo at the same speed ..."

"...Croatia will never re-arm."

James pointed to his left. "The security on the way in was minimal which would be surprising for a country that has something to hide. Nevertheless, over there, close to the jetty, I wonder what those large iron gates are protecting."

Patrick agreed, "Every commercial port has its secured compounds. However it might be useful to have a look at this one."

"I suggest we just walk past on our way to the ship without appearing too interested." The three, in line abreast, headed for the ship while James, taking a hint from Brodosplit's Production Manager walked on the outside of the trio, looking past his colleagues.

Abreast the Monrovian ship and between it and the compound he slowed down, eyes now concentrating on the dust at his feet, "Don't stop walking but tell me what you see."

"Tank tracks?" hazarded Patrick.

"M-84 main battle tank I guess. A variation of the Soviet T-72. Many went to the RSK when the Yugoslav National Army moved out so we must presume that someone is importing their replacements and that someone could be the Ukrainians or Germans as they make the engines."

The three followed the tracks towards the ship where they ended abruptly alongside the flat-bed lorry. With no other activity to attract their attention the trio returned to the main office.

Over lunch, which James was surprised to find consisted of fresh salads and cold meats all – he presumed – bartered from a visiting merchant ship, Dougal MacGregor spoke about his work, "I don't expect you saw much. Apart from the domestic goods I mentioned you will see that we are importing steel, but in tiny amounts for Brodosplit. They can build nothing substantial with the amount we send them."

Once they had said their goodbyes James took over the driving for the return journey to Split while Matea, pondering the first signs she had seen that her country might be re-arming, needed reassurance although she was not sure in which direction.

"James," she began, "We are militarily weak. Serbia is far stronger but with foreign help we could match them."

"Equality of power would certainly be a welcome stabilising factor."

"But if the balance is tipped too far in our favour then I can see the Croatian army taking revenge against Serbian civilians and that would mean more bloodshed."

"And you wouldn't want that?" James knew he should tread carefully for she had many personal reasons to hate the Serbs: all that they stood for, all that they had done and for all that they were capable of doing.

"No!" her reply was emphatic. "I do not like what evil things the Serbs have done but I also know that they have been provoked and I do not think that two wrongs will make everything right again. We Croatians should accept the status quo and allow the Krajina people to live in peace." She thought for a moment, "And the Serbs should do the same. Both sides should be satisfied with the land they have. Intimidating the Krajina Serbs by resurrecting wartime symbols and names will not help."

"So you would not support any outside assistance in re-armament?"

"No." Matea replied firmly before offering an observation that surprised James, "And, furthermore, I don't think we should try to discover any."

"But if the UN knows it is happening then they can act to stop it. But they won't know it is happening unless we know that it is."

Matea thought for a moment. "Oh dear, I know I should not have opened my mouth! As a Croat, of course I want my country to be as strong as those who threaten us but I don't want it so strong that it does the threatening."

"That makes sense but sadly is rather simplistic."

"I know. Which is why it is just a personal wish."

"All I can promise is that my reports on whatever I find will be balanced and truthful."

"I still don't want you to find anything."

"In that case a form of military stalemate will remain in place until the politicians sort it out and in this part of the world I do not see that happening."

"So you think war between us and Serbia is inevitable?"

"If Croatia re-arms. Yes."

"And if you do find something then the UN will stop Croatia rearming so there can be no more war."

"Unfortunately with the Americans and Germans involved in embargo-busting the UN will be powerless."

"So there is not much point in producing any evidence."

"If you put it that way, no."

"So why report anything?"

James was not sure of the logic behind Matea's comment, "You know that that is not easy for me to do."

"Then all I can ask is that you are balanced. Without favouring either country."

"Not difficult. After all both sides have nearly killed me with their artillery shells and that's a pretty balanced experience!"

Matea stifled the unexpected beginnings of a giggle…

Cresting the hill to the north of the harbour James slowed the Land Rover, leaned forward and stared ahead in the lowering light. Four Croatian army soldiers were standing in the road their rifles pointing directly at them. With the Land Rover stationary four more men appeared from a second vehicle parked opposite. AK 47s were not only pointing at each of their heads but now at all four tyres.

James wound down his window while turning to Matea over his shoulder, "Ask them what the hell they want?"

Before she had time to respond a soldier snatched open the rear door, reached inside and dragged her out by a shoulder.

"Now look here…" James roared swinging open his own door. It was slammed back hard against his arm and an assault rifle levelled once more at his head.

Standing outside, Matea was involved in a heated, but largely one-way, argument. The more she smiled, remaining composed and speaking softly, the more agitated and verbose her would-be assailants became.

Inside, James and Patrick waited with increasing and impotent concern as they heard the name 'Slavić' mentioned several times along with 'Serb' and 'Ploče'.

After three minutes, their rage exhausted, the soldiers shoved Matea roughly back in to the Land Rover. The men on the road in front stood aside and, lifting their weapons in the air, waved them off. As James moved away, slowly to avoid further aggravation, a burst of automatic fire passed down either side; the sharp cracks making them flinch and duck instinctively. Around the first corner, he accelerated and, calmer now, asked Matea. "Are you all right?"

"I'm fine."

"I couldn't help overhearing one or two names."

"They wanted to know where we had been but they obviously knew as the track that led up the hill ends at the peak. They were watching us from there. Acting under Colonel Slavić's orders."

"They seemed to get rather personal towards the end."

"Nothing unusual. They told me that I should not be involved in the monitoring of Ploče if I knew what was good for me. When I said that this is my job and that I have been doing it for many years they called me a Serb lover and a traitor to Croatia."

"Did they mention the embargo?"

"Nobody ever mentions the embargo. Ploče is an army matter, they said, and if I was involved in any more monitoring of the port they will harm Dino."

"Bastards!" Patrick swore then apologised, "Sorry Matea but that is bad news despite the fact that you seem remarkably calm."

"I've heard it before. The threats, all fuelled by too much raquia, are nothing new to any of us interpretresses. On the other side of the confrontation line the girls are accused of being Croat lovers," Matea giggled softly, "and traitors to Serbia!"

"We are due to sail with the colonel on Saturday. It will be interesting to see if he makes any mention of today."

"I suggest that we do not discuss embargos. To anyone. Ever!" Matea added.

CHAPTER TWELVE

Saturday 18th December 1993
Adriatic Yacht Club Marina, Marina Kaštela,
Split Harbour, Split, Croatia.

At a quarter to ten, precisely, Matea and James stopped on the marina pontoon to face the stern of Ante Slavić's yacht whose name, *Helena*, was painted across her counter in gold-leaf. The sun was shining and the wind had died during the night leaving a flat, oily-calm sea, unruffled by even the slightest of zephyrs.

"Don't forget, Matea," James said quietly, "No mention of monitoring even if the colonel raises the subject himself."

"Nor embargoes! Nice to get away from it all."

"I hope you have enough fuel." James shouted down as Ante Slavić lifted a cardboard case of wine from the cockpit down through the main companion hatch.

"I hope we have enough wine," was the cheerful reply.

Slavić reappeared and, stepping up on to the stern deck, offered Matea a hand a short plank that bridged the narrow watergap from the jetty. James joined her in the cockpit to admire a beautiful, wooden ketch designed and built shortly after the end of the Second World War in a northern European country and of about thirty eight feet in overall length. The varnished hull was immaculate, the brass-work polished and the paintwork in good order despite it being the middle of winter, nor were there any stains on the well-scrubbed, teak decks. Everywhere gear and rigging were in shipshape order and James nodded approvingly. What ever else he might have thought about Slavić he had not expected him to be the owner of a well-kept yacht with an obvious pedigree. He wondered how, in his physical state, that verged on the obese, the colonel could look after, let alone sail, such a vessel.

The question was answered with the appearance from the cabin of a smiling, dark-haired youth of about fifteen.

"This is Viktor," Slavić said, holding the boy's shoulders from behind, pushing him towards Matea and James. "He is my permanent crew. From a fishing family. Knows the sea but doesn't speak much English."

Matea and James each shook Viktor's hand.

A second youth, of about the same age, stepped up out of the cabin.

"Ah," uttered Slavić, "and here is my second permanent crew. This one is Bruno." James looked at Matea and smiled.

"Quite a team you have, colonel," James began, "Any more?"

"That is it. They look after *Helena*. Scrub and clean, service the engine, the sails and rigging so that she is ready throughout the year."

"Very wise," replied James, unexpectedly conscious of an overpowering smell of after-shave. He looked slowly at both youths, hardly old enough to need a razor. He never used the stuff himself but years in the confined and airless atmosphere of diesel-electric submarines had taught him to recognise various aromas. This was unmistakably Old Spice.

Settled in the ketch's cockpit, Slavić issued orders. The engine was warmed up. The stern warps were brought on board from the jetty and the head-rope recovered from the mooring buoy. Slowly Viktor eased *Helena* away from her berth while Bruno, optimistically, loosened the gaskets from the mains'l ready for hoisting.

With *Helena* heading for the open sea, Slavić invited James below where he uncorked a bottle of white wine and filled three glasses almost to the brim. "I don't get to sea as often as I would like," he explained, "so for much of the time the boys use her as payment for keeping her shipshape."

"Seems a good arrangement."

"It is, and today I want to show you how peaceful Brač is and how the islanders need no outside interference."

"Fine by me."

"But I am still not sure why you have brought the interpreter on a private visit."

"As a monitor no visit to an island can be classified as private."

In answer Slavić handed James two glasses and motioned towards the companion hatch. "While the sun is shining we must drink on deck."

With the boys taking turns at the wheel and with *Helena*'s diesel engine pushing her towards Brač at five knots they covered the nine flat-calm nautical miles to the port of Supetar, on the island's north-western coast, in under two hours. Time during which Slavić gulped at his wine while James and Matea sipped theirs. One of Bruno's more obvious tasks was to ensure that his skipper was never thirsty.

Once the two boys had expertly moored *Helena* stern-to on the town's deserted quay, Slavić announced that he was taking his guests for a pre-lunch aperitif. On their return he expected to find the picnic lunches that Matea had packed for herself and James laid out in the cockpit and his own warming in the oven. Ashore, the colonel led his guests to a café at which it was clear he was well known for an open bottle of white wine and three glasses were waiting on the table.

Apart from *Helena*'s crew the café was empty, as were the others they had passed on their way around the town's horseshoe-shaped quay: the harbour itself was filled with unemployed fishing vessels tugging gently but vainly at their moorings.

"Brač has a good ferry service, colonel, but that one that has just arrived had only three cars on it. Do cargo ships dock here as well?"

"No, the white stone is exported on lorries. As is the wine of course, which is much better than that produced on the mainland. The Croatian people will always need wine so that industry is safe." He thought for a moment, "they also need the best olive oil so that, too, is safe."

"Not much fishing today," James observed.

"It's Saturday."

"Of course," James replied. "Is there an airport?"

"No," Slavić answered quickly before adding slowly, "Maybe one day."

"So this port is the only key to the island's future."

"Along with Sumartin at the other end of the island but that is for even smaller ferries."

James nodded. He had come as close to 'monitoring' as he dared. Now, backing off, he relaxed, looking at his wine glass while slowly becoming aware of the drone of a propeller-driven aircraft just audible above the gentle lapping of the sea against the harbour's low stone wall. James sat up ready to turn round but Slavić, with surprising speed for his bulk, leapt from his chair, pointing across the harbour, "Good heavens!" he exclaimed "Did you see that."

James turned towards where the colonel was pointing and

as his eyes swivelled around the harbour he caught a fleeting glimpse of himself in the reflection from a glass-fronted billboard. "What did you see?" he asked after a brief pause.

"A huge fish. Leaping clear of the sea."

"Sorry I missed it."

While the level of white wine in the bottle slowly sank, most via the colonel's throat, they talked of many things: the weather, the white stone exported around the globe and the sardines. "Yes, the sardines," Slavić mused, "During the last world war the islanders lived almost entirely on sardines and they can do so again if needs be." Then he changed the subject. "Now," he announced, "lunch on board while there is still the sun."

During the return journey to Split Slavić, lounging back in the cockpit, summed up the day, "Commander, you saw with your own eyes that Brač needs no help from the European Union."

James was studied in his reply, "I am not sure that I can agree with you," he said slowly.

"How come?"

"I saw a good deal of under-used fishing vessels, no private yachts, just three tourist cars, no lorries and many closed cafés."

"The people will come the moment the present crisis is solved. Therefore I do not think you need bother the ECMM with your monitoring."

Anxious not to abuse the colonel's hospitality James played safe with a simple, "Thank you."

Half an hour before their arrival Slavić beckoned James below. "Look," he said, pointing to the chart table. "I have no modern instruments, just paper charts, compasses, a lead-line, a towed log and a sextant." James raised an eyebrow surprised, yet again, that Slavic could be so traditional.

"I admire that," James's respect was genuine, "I too, use a

sextant." Reaching into a pocket he placed three photographs on the chart table. "Here," he said, "this is my fifteen-ton, gaff cutter *Sea Vixen*. Of course, not as beautiful as *Helena*," James flattered, "but every bit as seaworthy. I keep her on moorings at a small village called St Mawes. Near Falmouth in the far south-west of England."

Slavić picked up the pictures in turn, studying each one carefully. Eventually he commented, "Very distinctive. Heavy displacement. What does she draw?"

"Nine feet," James replied.

"That's deep!" Slavić exclaimed, "You can't get into the shallow anchorages. *Helena* only draws six feet."

With the ketch secured in her berth James and Matea gathered up their few possessions and said goodbye while Bruno and Viktor replaced the covers on the unused sails.

"What did you make of all that?" James began as he manoeuvred the Land Rover away from the marina.

Matea wasn't sure, "Slavić seemed unusually nice."

"There was a reason for all this that I have yet to understand. Already one or two things do not add up."

"Tell me."

James needed to marshal his thoughts. "I will need to think for he is determined to make me believe that Brač is thriving when obviously it isn't. So what is he hiding?"

"No idea?"

"When he said he saw a huge fish jump he hadn't seen anything."

"So?"

"You may not have heard it but an aircraft was flying over the hills to the south."

"I took no notice. It was one of the little 'planes that people hire at Split to take them for a joy ride across the islands."

"How many people do that these days?"

"Not many."

"You have to believe me when I tell you that it was a large, four-engined aircraft that I heard."

"Doesn't prove much."

"Ah but I also caught a fleeting glimpse of it reflected in the glass-fronted billboard by the café. I didn't have to look round. I would know it anywhere."

"What was it?"

"A military Hercules C-130 heavy lift aeroplane and," he said with emphasis, "it was very low and flying in a south-westerly direction."

"Slavić said there was no airport and I am sure he is right. There was a grass one on Vis island, left over from the last World War, but I've never heard of one here."

"There has to be," James was adamant.

Matea was equally unwavering, "There is no airfield, Ante Slavić said so himself."

"And you believe him?"

"Despite everything he is a colonel in my country's army."

James was contrite, "Of course, I'm sorry."

"Who owns these Hercules?" asked Matea, her worries returning.

"Dozens of air forces around the world but Croatia is not one of them and, you will be pleased to know, nor is Serbia."

"Could it have been American?"

"More likely one of the other countries in the northern Mediterranean area," James was anxious not to alarm Matea.

"Who are they?"

James thought for a while, adding them on his fingers, before replying, "Italy, France and Greece."

Matea was silent for a moment, then asked, "Anything

else?"

"Yes, there is another little puzzle. *Helena* is kept ready for sea throughout the year. By the look of all of the other yachts and motorboats she is probably the only vessel in the whole marina that is kept in that state. Every other one is run-down, neglected even to the point of being unseaworthy. So," he asked, "any ideas why that should be?" James asked before attempting to put words in her mouth, "Apart from an instant escape route?"

"None," Matea replied, not taking the bait.

"Finally, any clue why Slavić keeps charts from here all the way to the Bay of Biscay?"

"None," repeated Matea.

"Nor have I other than that he wanted me to know."

They drove on for a few minutes until James broke the silence, "Do you realise, Matea, that not once did Slavić mention Ploĉe, nor the embargo nor even the war. Subjects suspiciously conspicuous by their absence."

"I was thinking that too."

"He has been quite jolly all day. Shiftily so!"

"Maybe that was the wine…"

"…or the presence of the two lads?"

On their arrival at Hotel Split James walked Matea to her car while announcing, "I'll do some thinking then we can talk about these little puzzles on Monday."

Patrick was sitting in the Terrace Bar and stood as James entered the room. "You look as though you need a drink," he said.

"Gin and tonic, please. I've seen enough white wine to last me a month."

"Bad as that."

"I didn't want to keep up with Slavić's drinking and so made three glasses last the whole day."

"Tough!"

"Let me explain."

Over the next hours the monitors compared notes, ideas and opinions, continuing to do so in the ECMM's empty dining room where the Greeks had left little food; mostly bread and dried ham.

"Slavić's behaviour has to have something to do with the possible presence of an airfield. That Hercules was flying low for a purpose."

"Nationality?"

"Not sure. I told Matea that it might have been Italian, French or Greek but only to try and put her off the idea that it could have been a Yank. Which I suspect it was."

"Proof?"

"Just a hunch based on the fact that Slavić did not want me to see it."

"No proof!"

"No proof!" agreed James

"Right," said Patrick, "Let's go back to the office. The largest scale map we have of Brač is one to one-hundred thou. Might give us a clue."

Patrick selected the map of the Dalmatian coastline that included Split and the adjacent islands, then smoothed it out across the large desk.

"I'm no aviator," James declared, "but from the briefest of glimpses I would say that it was flying towards the south-west, on the down-wind approach leg for a landing into the prevailing wind."

"You said there was no wind."

"There wasn't. I am also assuming that the aircraft was on a standard left hand circuit so the pilot could see the runway out of his side of the cockpit before turning 180 degrees to port and a landing approach towards the north-east..."

"Supposing you are right..." interrupted Patrick.

"I'm a submariner so it is an uneducated assumption!"

"Just suppose you are right," Patrick repeated, "there is nowhere flat that I can see until..." he stabbed a finger on the map, "...you get to the north of the seaside town of Bol. Nothing marked there. No villages. Not even roads but it does appear to be reasonably level ground."

"That would certainly tie in with my projected flight profile."

"Makes sense to me," Patrick said

"There is only one way to find out and that is..."

"... a spot of monitoring of the Zlatni Rat tourist beach."

James looked up, "As we have to start somewhere a day or two there is as good a place as any."

"It's Christmas at the end of next week," Patrick observed, "and the new Head of the Coordinating centre is due to join Zadar sometime before that. Perhaps we should delay till the New Year."

On Monday Matea joined James and Patrick for breakfast where James pulled a piece of paper from a pocket, "On my way I looked into the Ops Room. Someone from the Forward Logistics Group had stuffed this signal under the door."

"It seems," James paused, unfolding and staring at the flimsy sheet, "to be rather sensitive. Let me read it to you." He smoothed out the creases.

This is Captain Demetrios Pagonis your Head of CCZ. I shall be carrying out my initial inspection of Team Split on Wednesday morning at 0900.

I expect to see your patrol reports for the previous three months and your planned schedule for the next month.

There then followed a short list of detailed administrative instructions for his visit ending with,

I shall bring my own interpreter. We will stay to lunch.

Patrick frowned. "Demanding isn't he?"

James, puzzled by Pagonis's assumption that he and Patrick knew Split well, agreed, "I don't think he has listened to one word that Gaspard has told him."

"In which case he is in for a bit of a surprise," suggested Patrick, "Although, to be fair these are all points that I would raise when taking over such an appointment. Even so he needn't be so bullish at this stage."

James, also concerned at the brusque message, mused, "I was expecting something a little more user-friendly such as a social call first to hear our problems and how we intend solving them."

"Let's be positive." Patrick took a slurp of tepid coffee, "With Matea's help, and that of Josip, I can draw up a list of personalities but as far as patrol reports and the future are concerned we shall have to come clean!"

"Its not my job to comment," Matea laughed, "but I am not surprised. The Greeks have a different view of their role. After all they are the only monitors who can call themselves 'local'."

James and Patrick looked at their interpretress, taking a large bite out of an olive sandwich. "Got it in one, Matea," they said in unison as though from a pre-prepared script.

She blushed.

As James, murmuring aloud to himself, began scribbling a draft reply, Matea cautioned, "No one will want to work three days before Christmas. Especially not with the ECMM."

"So I shall tell Pagonis that while we welcome his inspection we have no patrol reports to show him; we can't fix up any visits before the New Year and neither Patrick or I have the slightest idea what is going on along the Confrontation Line."

"Well," Matea replied, "if that is the truth then that is the truth."

James crumpled up his first version and began again. "Not much more we can do at this stage," he said, looking up at Matea, "so I'll see if I can call on the British Consul tomorrow. You know your way round the Croatian telephone directory…"

"I also know my way to the Consulate."

"I'm sure Her Britannic Majesty's Consul speaks English," James teased. He needed to visit Mr Milna, his link to Magnus Sixsmith, alone.

"You'll get lost. And, anyway, his secretary is a friend of mine"

Not wishing to rouse suspicions James relented. "You win," he demurred and the next morning Matea led him to the Riva, Split's wide, tree-lined waterfront. The consulate, at number 10/111 and half way along the Obala Hrvatskog narodnog preporoda, was where the jolly-sounding Augustin Milna suggested they met. Outside the Consulate's front door the retired merchant mariner greeted them among the pedestrians meandering the wide breadth between the waterside and the tables and chairs of the numerous café's scattered beneath the extensive, imposing façade. While Matea remained in an outer room, catching up with her friend's news, James was ushered in to the large, first floor office.

"I am sorry to see you at such short notice and so soon before Christmas," James began as he shook hands with the short, russet-faced, impeccably dressed gentleman. Feeling, instantly, that he was in the company of a friend he continued, "I should have called as soon as I arrived in Split but much has been going on,"

"My dear commander," Augustin replied, "it is a pleasure to meet you at any time. Luckily you caught me before I take my motor boat home this afternoon."

"And where's that?" asked James.

"Milna. On Brač. Where my family comes from, hence my name." The Consul walked to the window and pointed to the right. "There," he said. "Not three hundred of your English yards from here, moored stern to the wall, is my vessel. On a flat calm I can be on my other mooring, ten nautical miles away, in twenty minutes."

"Thirty knots."

"More if I am really in a hurry."

"Ah," muttered James thinking ahead before changing the subject, "You know my colleague Magnus Sixsmith?"

"We are old friends. He told me to expect you sometime but that you would make the first move when ready."

"Well, here I am!" James laughed.

Over the next hour the two discussed life on Brač, the island's economy and its future until James looked at his watch, "Good heavens!" he exclaimed, "It is time I took Matea back. We have to prepare for our new boss's first visit tomorrow."

Augustin looked around him. "Before you go, " he said, needlessly lowering his voice, "I know what Magnus wants you to do..." James nodded. "...I cannot tell you where to start or even if there is anything that Croatia has to hide but there are one or two things I do not understand..." He paused, "...and I speak as an islander who, like the rest of us on Brač, Vis, Hvar, Korcula and the others, do not regard ourselves as true Croatians. We think and behave very differently."

"I'm glad to hear that," James said before stating, at last, the reason for his visit, "Magnus tells me that you will pass messages."

"I will but you must bring them here in person."

James decided that it was better to strike sooner rather than wait.

"Last Saturday, myself and Matea sailed to Supetar with a Colonel Slavić…"

"I know Slavić," Augustin said without emotion. "He has a beautiful yacht but not so beautiful personal habits."

"I won't ask." James commented before continuing, "Then you might be interested to know that he is actively trying to prevent me from monitoring the islands – particularly Brač – as well as the port of Ploče."

"Maybe that doesn't surprise me. He is too much of a loose cannon as you chaps would say. Too extreme. He also drinks greatly."

"You mentioned that there were one or two things that you didn't understand."

"I cannot put my finger on them but very recently there has been unusual aerial activity over the island. Almost always at night. This is strange as we don't have an airfield. Even Vis once had an airfield but us… never."

James nodded.

"Our economy relies on fish, the white stone, wine and olives rather than on tourism because we are not allowed to advertise on the mainland. Also the fishermen are prevented from selling their catch in Split so they only land what the islanders themselves need."

"Why do you suppose that is?"

"If we have to suffer so must you is, I suppose, the attitude on the mainland," Augustin declared before thinking for some while, eventually adding, "but I am not sure that I can explain the other things."

"The aeroplanes?"

"Yes,"

James stood but the Consul held up his hand. "Don't forget that I will pass messages to Magnus when ever you are ready. I will call you if I have anything from him."

"Thank you."

"Any time you need a fast lift to Brač or Vis let me know. No questions will be asked! Here is my business card with my private numbers for both here and on the island."

"That is very kind."

Twenty minutes later James and Matea joined Patrick in their hotel.

"How did you get on?" James asked.

"I didn't," replied Patrick, "Not a soul keen to see us till after the New Year."

"At least that should keep tomorrow's visit short."

"Pagonis will be here at 0900 and I have warned the hotel that there will be two extra for lunch."

CHAPTER THIRTEEN

Monday 20th December 1993
Headquarters, Direction générale de la sécurité
extérieure, 141 Boulevard Mortier,
Paris XX, France.

The Director of the DGSE inhaled a long draught of nicotine through his un-tipped Gauloises Caporal and, even slower, blew the pale-blue smoke across the room towards the door. Not for him the milder Gitanes: they were for ladies, they even had a gypsy woman on the package. Right now he needed the strongest cigarette to mask the notorious body odours of his next visitor.

A knock heralded the arrival of Jean-Claude Sublette and the Director was not looking forward to the arrival of Jean-Claude Sublette. He smelt, he was inefficient, he was rude and he spoke with the rough accent and syntax of the Brest peninsula: a patois that exasperated the Director's refined persona. JCS, as he was known, wasn't even particularly 'French': he didn't smoke, he didn't drink wine, he was *bégueule* and, according to his confidential reports that the Director was replacing in a drawer, he was a misogynist. He may even have been 'more' than that but there was no substantial evidence.

JCS's only saving grace was a love of the sea, which, the

Director sneered to himself, was hardly surprising if you lived at Camaret. Pity he hadn't joined the navy instead of inflicting the intelligence service with his incompetence and poor personal hygiene.

Jean-Claude Sublette was also about to be threatened with dismissal: an event that, should it prove necessary, would give the Director a pleasure otherwise unknown throughout his dealings with this most useless of agents. JCS was not up to the next assignment but as he, the Director, had no time for the European Union either he relished the thought of one flawed man doing his best to destroy a flawed organisation.

"Ah, *bonjour* Jean-Claude." The Director didn't rise to shake hands. Trying to keep the sarcasm as light as possible he enquired, "I trust the journey all the way from Camaret was not too arduous."

"*Merci, monsieur,*" Sublette replied, wondering why he had been dragged to Paris on the Monday before Christmas. He knew he had not made a success of his previous employment in Algeria – the heat, the smells (the irony would have been lost on him!) the very Algerians themselves – but had hoped for the expected fortnight before discussing the next assignment.

The Director did not want to waste time with the interview, "As you have been informed, you will not be returning to your old job. Instead I am sending you to the European Community Monitoring Mission based at Zagreb. Croatia. You will take over from a Monsieur Gaspard Chastain of the Quai d'Orsay as the Head of the Regional Centre in Knin. Capital of the Republic of Serbian Krajina. Look it up!"

The Director's last words were muffled by a handkerchief pressed close to his nose as the stink from Jean-Claude Sublette's unwashed body slowly gained ascendency over the Gauloises. As soon as the Director could terminate this discussion the sooner *La Piscine* – as the DGSE headquarters building was nicknamed – and, indeed, the whole of Paris's *vingtième arrondissment*, could begin to breathe again.

"You know who to discuss matters with in the administrative department. Dates, allowances, travel arrangements and so on. I've warned them," the Director smiled, "you will be calling this morning."

Jean-Claude tried to argue. *"Non!"* The Director held up a hand, "You are lucky you still have a job, but if you make a mistake this time then it will be the last mistake that you will make with us."

Jean-Claude drew a breath of second-hand smoke. He wanted to ask just one question. *"Non!"* repeated the Director, "Listen to me. If you can make your mark with the ECMM while upholding France's position in relation to Greek aspirations in the area – Greece is taking over the Presidency as we speak – then I may look more favorably on any subsequent appointment. You must remain un-biased in public of course but remember that France has an interest in Croatia's future as an independent nation state."

"I understand monsieur."

"What you don't understand is that your immediate inferior, on the coast, is a Greek naval officer. He doesn't like Germans and I don't think he likes the French very much either."

"I am sure I can handle him," Sublette said with little conviction.

"I hope so," answered the Director, equally without conviction. "We are all working there, including Mossad and the KGB, so I need to know how much interest the UK is showing. They have a man called Laidlaw as a new monitor but we also know that he was briefed recently in London by MI6's head of the Mediterranean desk. A Monsieur Sixsmith."

Still not prepared to listen to his junior the Director finished the interview. Speaking around the side of his hand he said, "Be ready to leave as soon as Christmas is over."

Sublette made a last attempt to speak, "*Non!* It's your last chance to do something useful. Now get out of here. Brush up on your English and for God's sake go and take a douche! You know where the washrooms are."

"*Oui, monsieur. Merci.*" Outside the office Sublette stopped momentarily, shaking his head. Inside, the Director opened the three tall windows that faced an inner court-yard then walked around the room blowing smoke into every corner.

Bien, mused Jean-Claude Sublette as he sought out the administrative section, if that is how to behave as a senior officer in the DGSE then he had better get in some practice.

CHAPTER FOURTEEN

Tuesday 21st December 1993
Headquarters, 4th Guards Brigade, Hotel Resnik,
Njiva Sv. Petra 6, Kaštela, Croatia.

Colonel Ante Slavić placed his wineglass on a table before picking up the telephone. Levering himself back in his chair he rested his feet on the desk. Looking past his shoes, through the French windows that led to a small, private terrace he could make out Brač island's highest hills, thirty kilometres beyond the western entrance to Split Harbour and now silhouetted by the setting sun.

He dialled the United States Defense Attaché's office in Zagreb. The telephone rang just once.

"Anderson!" Anderson grunted.

"It's Ante,"

"You'd better be quick. I'm on my way home."

"I thought you might like to know that I went to Brač with Laidlaw last Saturday."

"I didn't realise you were taking the Limey."

"I wanted to show him there was no point in monitoring the island."

"And?"

"He may now have a reason. Not as a monitor but as an intelligence officer."

"He isn't."

"Maybe not but I don't trust the Brits and especially this one as his background is in maritime special forces."

"I know, I know," Anderson had better things to do with his Saturday evening, "So why are you wasting my time. I'm taking the little lady out to dinner."

"You didn't tell me that you were flying C-130s into Brač airfield."

Anderson sat upright, instantly on his guard. Stalling for time. Thinking quickly, "Need to know, buddy. Need to know."

"I thought we were in this together," Slavić said raising his voice, his face reddening.

"Calm down. Here's the deal. You told me about the airfield. Right?"

"Right!"

"So I went and had a look. Right?"

"I didn't know you were going to do that."

"Need to know," Anderson repeated. "I cleared it with what passes for your Defense Ministry. They agreed to a daylight Hercules reccon flight last Saturday and one USMC helicopter proving flight that will take place tonight. I have yet to have the C-130 report as they are probably still flying back to Norfolk, Virginia."

"I thought you just needed a secure area for a small admin team. Just a few guys and a helipad…"

Anderson cut him short, "Buddy this is beyond you now. We are grateful for your initial help in suggesting the place. Maybe we will use it, maybe we won't."

"What for?"

"Need to know."

Jebi ga! Slavić swore violently in Croatian then, calmer for his outburst, said, "I need to know. It's in my operational area."

"Calm down, Ante. All in good time. On Saturday the aircraft flew down the length of the airfield in both directions. It also flew over other flat areas across the island to allay suspicion. Getting to know the topography so that they can brief the small admin team I mentioned earlier. That is all." No need to explain that a number of high level, infra-red photographic missions had already been flown over Brač in the dark.

"Your 'all in good time' may be too late."

"Why?"

"Laidlaw also saw the aircraft."

"Sod you, you dumb bastard." It was Anderson's turn to swear, "Why the hell did you take him there. Last Saturday of all days?"

"I didn't know. It was a weekend for God's sake."

"Sod you!" Anderson repeated violently and slammed the telephone down. Perhaps he had better start keeping Slavić closer to the plan.

"Bugger Laidlaw!" Slavić shouted in English at his own mute handset before he too slammed it down. Beyond his raised feet the darkening silhouette of the distant Brač hills now loomed forebodingly as the sun dissapeared behind them. He leaned forwards for the wine bottle.

CHAPTER FIFTEEN

In the soft glow of the cockpit's panel lights Lieutenant-Colonel Joe Martinez, United States Marine Corps, glanced towards his co-pilot in the left hand seat. "Ready, Hank?" he asked.

"Ready," came Major Bennett's brusque reply.

"Ready in the back?" demanded Martinez over the intercom.

"Ready in the back," answered the Crew Chief, Master Sergeant Chuck Lewinsky, as he checked again down the length of the helicopter's interior, lit by dimmed red lighting. The only clue he had to the contents of the large wooden crates were the words USS Drake. *Logistics Grade Two – Star Three* stencilled in white on each one. Even the twelve personnel, further aft, were unidentifiable in their disruptive-pattern uniforms that carried no badges of rank and no formation insignia. The crates were heavy, very heavy, and with the passengers and their personal kit the aircraft was carrying its maximum permitted internal payload weight of 30,000 pounds. The problem of unloading them at the far end was taxing Lewinsky's imagination...

In the cockpit Martinez ordered, "Switch to NVG," as he leaned forward to dim further the already dull lights that were illuminating the array of dials and instruments. On the right side of his helmet he pressed a rocker switch before folding down his night vision goggles. It would take thirty seconds for his eyes to become used to the mottled-green effect that was to be his view of the world for the next two hours. In the ship's flying control compartment, above the forward end of the flight deck, the lieutenant-commander in control of aircraft operations reduced the deck lights until they were all but out. He called the ship's bridge. "Bridge. Flyco."

"Bridge."

"Charlie Seven Six Delta ready to lift off. Fifteen souls on board."

USS *Drake*, a Raleigh class 'landing platform dock', temporarily assigned to the United States Navy's Sixth Fleet, was slowly turning to bring what light wind there was fine onto the port bow. The ship's speed of sixteen knots would help.

"Roger," replied the Officer of the Watch, "coming on track," he paused, watching the gyro compass repeater, "...now!"

"Six Delta this is Drake," the lieutenant-commander called the helicopter on the ship's secure, flight-deck communications loop, "You are cleared for take-off. Wind across the deck is red fifteen at twenty knots. Ship's position confirmed at forty-three degrees nineteen minutes decimal nine north, fourteen degrees fifty nine minutes decimal seven east. Initial vector nine two degrees true. Distance seven one nautical miles and closing. Cleared to 2,000 feet until outside controlled airspace. Then at your discretion. No further calls. Have a good flight."

"Six Delta," Martinez replied. "Roger. Out."

The helicopter's co-pilot entered the ship's coordinates into his computer, glad to have confirmation that his initial flight plan, course and distance tallied with those now endorsed by the ship. Looking at his dimmed instruments through his goggles he confirmed fuel state, hydraulic pressures and temperatures. All were within their operating 'tolerances'. He called his pilot, "Take-off checks complete."

Joe Martinez's CH-53E Super Stallion did not 'belong' to USS *Drake*. The ship's own Sea Knight, a twin-rotor, Chinook look-alike, had had to be parked on another deck for the two hours that it took *Drake*'s crew, under Chief Lewinsky's supervision, to load Six Delta with the large wooden containers. The embarked personnel were from the recently established United States Air Force Special Operations Command and the US Navy's Joint Program Office for Unmanned Aerial Vehicles: together, known in US parlance, as the JPO-UAV. USS *Drake*, herself, was not part of the US Sixth Fleet either but had loaded her cargo in secrecy at the Norfolk Naval Base, Virginia, before making her sedate way across the Atlantic and through the Mediterranean, collecting her passengers before departing Naples.

Six Delta had been allocated this task for the ship's own Sea Knight did not have the internal capacity to lift such a bulky and heavy cargo. Quite how they were going to unload the crates at their destination Joe Martinez had no idea either and he had almost as little idea of that destination other than its geographical position, the coordinates for which had been firmly punched into the aircraft's computer following the pre-flight briefing on board the Amphibious Command Ship, USS *Mount Whitney*, earlier in the day. Martinez did, though, hope that the United States' Navy's special forces sailors from SEAL Team Six's 'reception party' would be available at their destination to help offload the cargo. If not, then the aircrew and passengers would have to manhandle it as best they could.

His orders had been clear. After sunset he was to land on USS *Drake*, load the assigned stores and personnel then transport them to an unmarked airfield two nautical miles north east of the small town of Bol on the Croatian island of Brač. Once empty he was to return to his own 'carrier', a Sixth Fleet assault ship.

Outside and ahead of the cockpit a lone aircraft-marshaller held out two florescent wands each at shoulder height and parallel with the deck. As the marshaller lifted the lights above his head Martinez applied power while slowly raising the 'collective stick' with his left hand, allowing the seven massive, titanium and glass-fibre, composite rotor blades to bite easily into the cool night air. With his wheels ten feet clear of the deck and able now to judge the wind's effect he slid his aircraft over USS *Drake*'s port side, slowly transitioning to forward flight and a gentle climb. Once clear of the landing ship's superstructure, and rising through 200 feet, he steadied Six Delta onto the course for Brač Island.

From now on they were alone and in radio silence. The next thing Martinez hoped to see, apart from shore lights, would be the shaded glow of dim landing-strip markers laid by the SEAL Team that had, a few days earlier, swum ashore from a submarine in order to guide in this first aircraft. The only other aspect of the operation that he was aware of was that a C-130 had carried out a series of low passes by day and night over the airstrip which was, and this was now the sum total of his knowledge, at the top of a 1,500 foot escarpment that led up from the narrow coastal plain above Bol. The moon was waxing, well past its first quarter, and so, with luck and no cloud, all would be plain sailing. Whoever they were in the rear of his aircraft had to be worth the risk.

"You have control," Martinez ordered his co-pilot once Six Delta was at 2,000 feet above the sea and flying, straight and level, at 150 knots along the planned course of 92 degrees. The estimated flight time, allowing for the slight headwind, was thirty minutes.

"I have control," Bennett answered.

With his folded aeronautical chart laid across his right knee, clear of the helicopter's cyclic stick between his legs, Martinez marked off the distance to run between his forefinger and thumb. Outside the cockpit windows all was not quite black for the moon, high in the sky was throwing a dim, narrow triangle of cold light across the calm sea, to the right of Six Delta's track.

"I'm just picking up shore lights now, skipper. At our eleven o'clock, maybe ten miles. Must be Bol," Bennett reported.

The lieutenant-colonel glanced through the helicopter's port side windows then back at his chart. "Yup. That's it. On track. Keep her steady at 2,000 feet. Plan to pass well to the south of the village before turning inland for the airstrip. No need to alert the locals. I'll take over from there."

"Roger."

Martinez waited five minutes as Bol's few lights passed down the aircraft's port side, five miles distant, then he called his co-pilot, "OK, Hank. I have control."

"Roger, you have control."

Martinez began the gentle turn inland aiming to pass between Bol and their landing site to the north east with a calculated clearance of 300 feet to spare beneath the fuselage as they crossed the top of the escarpment. Visibility was good as he began to make out the escarpment's edge, now off to starboard. Beyond, at right angles to the moon's path, he thought he could just detect the light reflecting off the airfield's paved runway. Any moment now he expected to see a box formation of faint yellow lights…

"Christ!" he shouted.

"For fuck's sake, skip," Bennett yelled as Six Delta began

shaking violently. "What the hell are you playing at?" Red warning lights flashed on the panels in front of the two pilots, blinding them through their goggles. The screech of warning alarms deafened their ears.

The aircraft lurched suddenly downwards tugging violently at the pilots' shoulder straps.

"Pull up! For Christ's sake! Pull up, skip."

"I can't hold her. I can't hold her," Martinez screamed, heaving on the collective stick with every ounce of strength his left arm could summon. The juddering increased violently, the noise of the aircraft breaking up in mid-flight now blanking even the alarms squawking in their earphones.

The heavy containers in the back began to break loose from their lashings.

"We're going down Hank," Martinez shrieked again, his face twisting with terror. "We're going down. Mayday, Mayday. This is Six Delta Mayday, Mayd…"

It was all over for USMC Super Stallion, call-sign Charlie Seven Six Delta. The main rotor gear box, fragmenting into a thousand shards of metal, shook the aircraft far beyond its designed limits as nearly thirty tons of dead weight plummeted, corkscrewing 2,000 feet downwards towards the foot of the escarpment, disintegrating all the time. The main fuselage and fuel tanks smashed through the roof of a stone building killing all inside instantly before incinerating them and the aircraft's passengers in the searing flames and scorching heat of burning aviation fuel. The cockpit and the three, massive General Electric T-64 engines continued their headlong tumble down the last of the mountainside, coming to rest by the one road that leads into, and out from, Bol. The two pilot's bodies were flung clear then torn apart as they spun through the low olive bushes, tall cypress trees and across the sharp rocks.

One hundred and fifty nautical miles away and at 32,000 feet above sea level a radar operator, hunched over his screen in a United States Air Force Boeing E-3 Sentry, airborne warning and control aircraft, called his commander over the intercom. "Sir, USMC Six Delta has just dropped from the plot. Could be he's masked by the hills…"

"No," was the terse reply, "The pilot just sent an incomplete Mayday. Mark the position."

"Shit!" the radar operator swore. Quickly collecting himself, he replied, "Roger Sir. Marked at forty three degrees sixteen minutes decimal one north, sixteen degrees thirty nine minutes decimal nine east."

CHAPTER SIXTEEN

Wednesday 22nd December 1993
Room 519, Hotel Split, Put Trstenika 19,
Split, Croatia.

When he woke James knew that Wednesday 22 December 1993 was not going to be a normal day. During the night there had been the usual sporadic gunshots in the street below his west-facing window but the number of helicopter movements in and out of Split hospital's landing site, two hundred yards away, was of an unusual frequency. As far as he had discovered during the few days since his arrival on the coast, routine events in the hospital had nothing to do with the ECMM, and yet, as he dressed, James felt an unease. In the dining room Patrick was already spooning olives and cold meats into a shallow bowl.

"What was going on last night, Paddy?"

"Dunno, James," Patrick replied without concern. "Why?"

"Lots of helis landing on the hospital pad."

"Never heard them. My room's the other side."

At ten minutes to nine James pushed back his chair. "I'd better go and meet Pagonis."

"I'll be in the office, chatting up Matea."

"Good luck," James smiled with mock jealousy, "Maybe she knows what happened."

In the foyer James paced to and fro. He was not nervous,

indeed far from it, but he still had a bad feeling about the day until a movement through the large, glass doors caught his eye. A black Toyota all-terrain vehicle had drawn up out of which was stepping a tall gentleman in a light grey suit, over his shoulders an overcoat was slung casually while a wide-brimmed, mauve fedora was pulled low over his eyes, concealing his face. An equally tall lady with slim, stockinged legs beneath a short, dark skirt was walking round from the far passenger door. James turned away. Pagonis was still en route.

"Commander Laidlaw," a voice called. James swivelled on his heels. Surely not. Where's the white Land Rover, the white uniform, the...?

"Yes?" he said, tentatively.

"Are you not expecting me?" the voice demanded in English.

"Sorry, no," James was apologetic, "I'm waiting for an ECMM monitor."

"I am Captain Pagonis of the Hellenic Navy," Captain Pagonis declared angrily, "Did you not receive my signals? And do you not remember me from the dinner in Knin castle?"

James, momentarily taken aback, felt that a softer approach would be more disarming. "I'm so sorry, Demetrios, it was pretty dark in the castle. Didn't recognise you or your car..." he paused, cautious not to offend so soon in their relationship, "... and I was expecting a white uniform."

"I am not in the field. I have no need to wear the white clothes."

"Quite so... well..." James was hesitating, now unsure of himself, "Do introduce me to your friend."

"We'll do all that in the office. I hope the coffee is good."

James led the duo towards the stair well.

"Why are you not taking the lift?"

"We don't use the lift because on Wednesdays there is…"

"I am not in Team Split. I will be waiting for you on the fifth floor," and with that declaration Pagonis and his companion strode through the open lift doors, before James could finish his sentence.

"Silly bugger," he muttered, grinning broadly.

By the time James stepped onto the fifth floor landing the weekly nine-o'clock emergency alarm had been sounding for two minutes. The bored Croatian policeman was taking no notice, remaining slumped at his desk with his head in his hands.

Knowing he had a few minutes grace James walked to the Team Split office. "Morning, Matea," he beamed, "You'll never guess?"

"Don't tell me, he's not coming."

"Close. He'll be eight minutes. Stuck in the lift. Tried to warn him but… well there we are!"

"Brilliant," said Paddy.

As the lift doors eventually shuddered open James said without a trace of mockery, "Ah, Demetrios. Welcome to the fifth floor."

"Did you know that was going to happen?"

"Yes. Every Wednesday morning at nine o'clock, give or take a minute or two, they switch off the electricity for ten minutes to test the…"

"Why didn't you tell me?"

"You had already gone," James smiled.

As they had rehearsed the evening before James now stood to one side of the wall map with Patrick opposite clutching a pointer while Matea prepared 'instant' coffee and powdered milk.

With his audience seated James introduced his team before

inviting Pagonis to do the same. "And by the way we do not use our past ranks here as we are all monitors…"

The Greek interjected impatiently, "Let's get on with the brief shall we. I am Captain Pagonis and this is my interpreter," he said resting a hand on the woman's thigh, "Karla."

"Good, now we know each other I'll begin but I should warn you that it will be rather short!" James outlined the geographical extent of Team Split as it stood at the moment. "The two of us are responsible for all monitoring in accordance with ECMM guidelines from Sibenik in the west to the port of Ploče in the south-east, a straight-line distance," he emphasised, "of over 150 kilometres. We are also responsible for the confrontation line in one direction while in the other we cover the offshore islands."

Pagonis held up his hand, "I know all this," he said reaching into an inner pocket to retrieve a large cigar. Karla produced a lighter. Comfortably surrounded by smoke, the Greek waved towards the map. "It is a large area but you have conducted just two patrols since you arrived. I do not consider that productive."

Controlling a rising annoyance James ignored the accusation, "It is indeed a large area and it is also the key to Dalmatia's economic recovery when, or if, peace finally comes. Or when Croatia and Serbia reach some form of rapprochement. In whatever form that may take," he added. As Pagonis stared at the map in silence James continued. "So, Gaspard has ordered Patrick and myself to prepare to divide Team Split into two, sometime in the near future."

Pagonis remained staring ahead, his face expressionless.

"Until then I intend to concentrate on the islands and ports to monitor the incoming, commercial cargoes."

"That is not your job!" Pagonis almost shouted, making Matea jump. "While I am the Head of the Coordinating Centre you will monitor the confrontation line. So far all you have done is visit Brodosplit and Ploče. Such businesses will look after themselves."

"Fine," said James, "Perhaps you will tell us what our job is if it is not to meet the ECMM mandate which, on the coast, is to monitor the fluctuating state of the economy so that when the time…"

"Your job on this side of the border," Pagonis interrupted, "is to ensure that any and all Croatian aggressions against Serbia are monitored and reported. It is not to concern yourselves with commerce."

James shook his head.

"Do not shake your head," Pagonis commanded, "From now on you will obey the priorities that I will be issuing."

James, still and silent, waited for Pagonis to finish.

Patrick, open mouthed, entered the fray. "Demetrios," he began, exercising his softest Irish lilt to the full, "I am not sure that you quite understand the rather delicate position that we find ourselves in."

"I am not interested in your position. I am only interested in you doing what I order."

"Then," James backed up his Irish colleague, "we shall have to discuss this with Gaspard. I suggest we fix a meeting between all of us before he leaves the Mission."

"No!" Pagonis spoke loudly. "I am the HCCZ. We do not need to involve Monsieur Chastain. You, commander," his cigar pointing directly at James's stomach, "are wrong and I will not have you questioning my orders."

James smarted at this allegation. Indeed as he was not happy with Pagonis's physical presence either, it was time to introduce some realism. Looking at Matea and Karla in turn he said, "Ladies, will you kindly leave the room as I do not think that what I am about to say is for a woman's ears."

"Karla. Stay!" Pagonis ordered. Karla stayed.

Matea, looking pale, walked slowly out of the room shutting the door quietly behind her. Then, on an impulse, she re-entered the office and sat down, smiling confidently up at James.

"Now Demetrios," James said slowly and deliberately, "you listen to me."

Pagonis, taken aback, drew on his cigar with hollowing cheeks. He was not used to being confronted by inferiors. He would wait to see what this British monitor had to say then he would swoop.

"I am a retired commander in the Royal Navy and Patrick is a serving lieutenant-colonel in the Irish army. We are both experienced officers but right now, like you, we are monitors with the ECMM. Nothing more, nothing less. We know what we have to do here in Split. We also know and understand the ECMM's priorities for monitoring on the coast. As it happens we have been here for less than a fortnight taking over from two monitors who left leaving no handover notes."

"I know all of this." Pagonis spoke loudly, "Get on with what you have to say then you will listen to me."

"No, Demetrios I will not." James was angry now and not inclined to curb his irritation, "And I will tell you why not. You do not dress as a monitor, you flaunt an un-accredited interpreter, you drive an unregistered car. Until you behave correctly and earn our respect I will bypass you and your orders and deal only with the Head of the Regional Centre…"

Shaking with rage, Pagonis stood.

"Sit down for I haven't finished!" James ordered. Surprisingly Pagonis sat, open mouthed. "We shall continue to monitor not only the ceasefire violations but the commercial needs of the coast and while we do that we shall also keep an eye on cargoes that not only come through the airfields but also through Ploče and, if necessary, those that arrive direct into the islands."

"You will not!"

James, still speaking deliberately and calmly continued, "What you do not know is that I have already visited Brač..."

"I have seen no patrol report."

"It was a private visit. We have, as you know also visited Ploče and I hope you will have read that patrol report."

"Not yet..."

"I am not happy with the cargoes of those ships that have managed to evade the maritime inspections so why do you not approve such monitoring." Knowing well that it would hurt Greek sensibilities James added, "Or do you wish to support the illegal re-arming of Croatia?"

"It will never happen. This country is broke. It cannot pay for new weapons. You will be wasting ECMM time," Pagonis paused. With no one willing to break the silence all waited, "... especially..." the Greek continued, "...as I have promised the Croatian Chief of Staff, a Colonel Slavić, that the ECMM will no longer patrol the islands and ports."

James and Patrick looked at each other in astonishment. "You've done what," they exclaimed together.

"I hope you are not questioning my orders." Pagonis retorted sharply.

"As a matter of fact," James said politely, "we are." After a pause he added, purposefully failing to explain the outcome, "and we too have discussed our programme with the colonel and, indeed, it was he that took me to Brač."

In recent memory, Demetrios Pagonis could not recall having his orders contradicted, now he sat glowering in angry silence as James explained further, purposefully declaring his hand, "So, we will continue to monitor Ploče on a regular but unannounced basis and we will keep an eye on the islands. Something odd is going on but precisely what, I have no idea…"

An urgent knocking stopped James. All looked towards the door as Matea swung it open, before disappearing into the corridor from where intense whispering could be heard. When she returned she was ashen-faced and trembling. James stepped towards her, suddenly protective. "What's happened?" he asked.

"Very early this morning a Croatian army helicopter crashed into a house on the outskirts of Bol. On the southern coast of Brač."

James swore, "I've never trusted those bloody Russian MI-8s."

Matea, close to tears, mumbled, "It killed five Croatians on the ground. The Americans have offered to help clear the mess."

James turned back to Pagonis, "You see, something is going on and it is our duty to know what."

"A Croatian helicopter crash is not our business."

"Sadly, Demetrios, I think you may be very wrong because…"

Pagonis stood to face James, cutting him short, "I was warned by Guillaume Larouche that you are inexperienced and now I know, first hand, that you are also impertinent. Right now I am suspending you." He turned for the door, dragging Karla after him by an arm, "Come, we need spend no more time here."

Finding it difficult to supress a sardonic smile, James shouted at their backs, "I suggest you use the stairs." His words followed them down the corridor as they made their way towards the lift.

James shut the office door. "I'm not sure that went quite

according to plan," he laughed then, remembering Matea's news, said. "Sorry. That is a terrible thing to have happened. Do you know any more?"

"Nothing."

"Callous as it sounds let's analyse what has just occurred before we work out if the helicopter crash should concern the ECMM."

"Personally," began Patrick, "I think Pagonis deserved what he got. It is best to start off as we mean to go on rather than having to sort things out once they have become established." His tone changed as he turned to James, "I suggest we contact your Consul for he may have news on the accident. We should also ask Slavić, although I can guess his reaction."

James dialled Slavić's number not expecting an answer.

"*Da. Slavić govoreći.*"

"Colonel Slavić?" confirmed James.

"Yes, Slavić speaking," the Chief of Staff repeated in English.

"It's James Laidlaw here."

"I am busy this morning."

"We are very sorry to hear of the helicopter crash. If there is anything the ECMM can do please say so."

"Thank you," replied Slavić pleasantly enough before reverting to form, "but this is an internal matter."

"I am sure it is, colonel, although we are bound to be interested to know what a Croatian helicopter was doing over Brač at that time of the night."

"That is my concern. All right?"

"Not really."

"Keep out of something that is not your business," Slavić almost shouted before adding less severely, "It is a tragedy for the army."

"And the civilians too I would have thought."

Yelling, "Incompetent bastards," Slavić thumped the telephone down leaving James wondering which bastards were the incompetent ones. He stared briefly at his own handset before replacing it slowly on its cradle. "You're right," he said to Patrick, "we'll get more from the consul."

James dialled Milna's Brač number.

"*Zdravo.*"

"Good morning, James here. Sorry for bothering you over your Christmas holiday."

"That's not a problem, how can I help?" replied Augustin. "I expect this is to do with the crash?"

"We only know the basics."

"Well," Augustin replied, "it seems that a Croatian helicopter suffered some form of mechanical failure in the night and crashed into a house near Bol."

"Any idea where it was from and where it was going?"

"None. Within the hour, almost before our own emergency services had arrived, the place was swarming with helicopters from the American Sixth Fleet shuttling the dead to Split hospital..." Augustin hesitated, "When I drove across at dawn there were dozens of police and US soldiers already sifting through the wreckage and removing great chunks. All behind a tight security cordon."

There had to be a reason for such a helicopter to be flying over Brač at dead of night. "Augustin," James said, "Since before I arrived in Zagreb I had heard rumours of suspicious goings on in the islands and ports but they were, until, this day, just that. Rumours."

"They may still be rumours."

"You are probably right, but something is happening and even if it turns out to be nothing to do with us I still think it deserves investigating."

"James," argued the Consul, "I have to ask whether or not what the Croatian army is doing is covered by your monitoring guidelines?"

"If it is all entirely innocent I'll drop it right away but night time helicopter flights over the islands, if not over the mainland, are suspicious. For my own peace of mind, never mind that of the ECMM's, I would like to know, first hand, what is happening."

"I understand, James," Augustin replied, "but it might involve considerable personal risk."

"Tough," laughed James, "Will the ferries be running this close to Christmas?"

"Of course," Augustin paused, frowning to himself, then asked, "You mean you want to come across now?"

"Yes, before all the evidence is removed."

"They were doing a pretty good job of it when I was there earlier and, anyway, the crash-site is so well guarded that you would be wasting your time."

James looked across at Matea. Putting the telephone's handset aside, he mouthed, "Will you come with me?"

Matea gripped his arm, "This is beyond monitoring, James." she replied, "It might be awkward for me."

"That's not the question."

Matea did not reply. She, too, felt, that there was something wrong, something very wrong and she wanted no part in it.

"Why should it be difficult for you?" James prompted, "We will, perfectly legally, be visiting a crash-site that will have been secured and made safe."

"James!" Augustin, listening to this latest exchange, shouted down the line.

"Sorry, Augustin."

"Go nowhere near the ferry. I'll meet you at the Split

moorings in my boat in two hours time. Then we'll drive to Bol. I'll think of a reason why you are with me if we are spotted but Slavić has already visited and left on the ferry back to Split."

"That was quick."

"He was lucky with the timings," explained Augustin, "which is fortunate for you too as he would have been your major headache had he seen you here so soon after the crash."

James was anxious to get going, "I'll see you in two hours."

"Done!" They replaced their telephones.

James turned to Matea, "Coming?"

She paused then slowly answered. "Yes," she said, "but not as your interpretress. As a friend!"

"I suggest we use your car."

"Its only got two seats," she giggled, "and I'll need to change into sensible clothes on the way to Augustin's boat and check that Dino can be collected from school."

James turned to Patrick, "You coming too, Paddy?"

"Not if the car is a two-seater! You go. With a bit of fast talking and a girl by your side you might be able to pass it off as a private visit. Anyway," he laughed, "there'll be even more olives for lunch."

Matea drove to her house, the far side of Split harbour, from where, eight minutes later, she emerged in red jeans and a large blue jersey beneath a waterproof jacket.

"Dino's fixed," she said slipping into the driver's seat. "I'll collect him from friends when we get back."

At the western end of the Riva waterfront Augustin was pacing along the quay, mobile telephone in hand.

"James," he began, "and Matea, how nice to see you again although I am sorry for the reason."

"This is very good of you…" James replied but he was cut short.

"Nonsense," Augustin said, "It is my sad pleasure. Did anyone see you coming?"

"Not been here long enough to identify cars but I don't think so." James turned to Matea, "Did you recognise any one following us?"

"No," she said firmly.

"Hop in," commanded Augustin. "We'll be there in twenty minutes. Flat calm. Beautiful afternoon."

James stepped down into the speedboat to hold up a hand for Matea. Delighting in its unexpected warmth and suppleness he held it for a fraction longer than necessary as he guided her to the padded bench across the vessel's stern, then sat down beside her.

Augustin unhitched the warps, slid behind the steering wheel and pressed the engines' starter buttons. One after the other the still-warm, twin, inboard petrol engines screamed into the still air. "Hold tight!" he shouted over his shoulder. True to his word the crossing took twenty minutes during which the noise of the powerful engines, the rush of the sea and the wind in their ears prevented any conversation.

James was uncertain what he was going to do when he reached Brač. They knew the crash site was sealed off by American servicemen and Croatian police. Then what? He would return to Hotel Split and the uneasy conclusion that by being present he may have played into Slavić's hands. And for what purpose? He had no idea.

Once he had moored the boat Augustin led his passengers to an elderly, much-battered Citroën. "No point in having a good car this side of the water," he explained as James and Matea nodded their agreement. "Its about 40 kilometres and will take us at least an hour. Single-lane roads for much of the route, winding through the hills."

They twisted among Brač's wooded slopes and valleys until at last the road turned south towards the coast. "See," explained Augustin, "we have had to drive well to the east of Bol before we can reach it. Now we will come to the place where a large part of the helicopter came to rest on the road, before we reach the town."

As the Citroën rounded a tight left-hand bend, contouring a steep-sided valley, two stationary police cars, blue lights flashing blocked the road. Security tape extended away on either side. Augustin pulled over and switched off the engine. Brač was a peaceful place, unaffected, physically, by events on the mainland. No longer.

Beyond the road-block two American Sea Knight helicopters were perched on the tarmac, their rotors turning, while a third was lifting away, a bulging cargo net slung below. All around men, sweating despite the cool air, thrashed their way through the undergrowth and rubble, occasionally dragging jagged pieces of aircraft to the roadside. Further up the hill wisps of black smoke rose from what, a few hours earlier, had been a stone-built cottage surrounded by well-kept gardens. Men in white face-masks sifted slowly though the burnt remains of aircraft, buildings and scrub. Following behind, a second team wearing light-blue overalls and carrying body bags investigated each grim discovery that their colleagues in front had marked with sticks prodded into the rough ground. Body parts were still being recovered.

Scattered untidily across the hillside, some gleaming in the pale sun, others blackened by fire lay dozens of eight foot long, narrow aluminium planks. The smell of burned aviation fuel and scorched wood floated through the Citroën's open windows. It was a desolate and forbidding scene. Matea shivered and looked away.

"What on earth are those?" asked Augustin.

"The makings for a portable airstrip. One helicopter could not have brought in enough for a fixed wing aircraft but sufficient to make an all-weather helicopter pad. Maybe with the idea of lengthening it." James thought for a moment, "But it would take hundreds of loads, so probably not."

"All I know," Augustin said, "is that some years ago the army was excavating a new quarry beyond the top of the escarpment."

"Maybe that is where they want to base their helicopters. Safer here than close to the confrontation line."

"Which could be why Slavić does not like you monitoring Brač," suggested Matea.

"And even more reason to do so."

Matea not only felt sick but she was distrusting of all that she had been told, "If the Americans are helping my government then there has to be only one reason."

"This is humanitarian work. Even the Yanks like to help when there has been a disaster."

"Of course," Matea was contrite, "I'm sorry."

To the left, down the hill, a slight movement, a flash of reflected light, caught James's eye. The wind in a bush perhaps? What ever it was had to be unnatural. He opened the door, "I must have a pee," he said over his shoulder and stepped out.

"The last time he did that it saved his life," Matea murmured to Augustin.

"Well let's hope he doesn't lose it this time," the British Consul replied as an armed policeman strode towards the car, drawing his pistol. He knocked on the driver's window. Augustin unwound it, *"Da?"* he said.

"You were here earlier. You know you cannot pass through so why this second visit"

Augustin thought quickly, "My secretary thought she might

have relatives in the house up the hill. I had to bring her, but it is the wrong house."

"Understood. Where has your friend gone?"

"To relieve himself. He couldn't wait."

"Fair enough. As you already know we have a major incident. The road will be closed for some time. Do you live in Bol?"

"None of us do," Augustin replied.

"When your colleague returns you will have to go back the way you came," the policeman ordered pleasantly, returning his pistol to its holster, "This is a secure area right now so, please, no more toilet stops till you reach the top of the escarpment. And no more visits."

"I have no desire to return. It's a ghastly sight."

Eighty yards away James reached the spot that had caught his eye. Two oblong, stainless steel identity tags, joined by a small, broken chain hung from a low bush. Masked from the road by the trees and scrub, he swiftly snatched them and, in the same movement, stuffed them into a trouser pocket with his left hand while his right unbuttoned his fly.

Satisfied, he sauntered back.

"Better?" asked Augustin.

"Thanks," James said opening the rear door to slide in alongside Matea.

"I would sit in the back with her too," laughed Augustin, "but we have to turn round before the police decide we have overstayed our welcome."

"Quite agree but I have found something that I should not keep." James felt in his pocket. Handing the tags in later would lead to questions, "Got a piece of paper and a biro?" he asked.

Matea searched her handbag.

"Thanks," James replied. "Please can you hold these steady

while I read what's on them."

James scribbled on the paper. "Well done," he said handing back the biro and turning to Augustin in the front, "These had better go back to where they belong but it might be best if a Croatian gave them in."

Augustin strode to the police car where, after some moments of earnest conversation, James watched him pointing to the gutter by the Citroën, grimacing. As he was doing so an elderly grey, dusty Opel saloon braked sharply to a halt alongside. The driver jumped out then, pushing Augustin aside, began arguing animatedly with the police while waving a hand towards Augustin's car then at the aluminium debris still littering the hillside.

The British Consul smiled and walked back, glancing occasionally over his shoulder.

"What's the commotion?" James asked, back in the front passenger seat.

"I was making a serious point about debris being scattered way beyond the cordon when that car turned up with an American driving."

"I got the impression nobody was amused."

"The American particularly, which is why I left. You were right not to have taken those tags yourself."

"Did the police not recognise you?

"They are from the mainland."

James thought for a moment. There were a number of anomalies that he need to get straight in his mind but he had no idea whom to ask for help. Certainly not Slavić. Perhaps Augustin could make some discreet enquiries after Christmas but he was anxious not to place him under suspicion with the authorities. He would have to find out for himself: when the time was right.

"I just hope you don't feel that it has all been a waste of time," James said apologetically.

"Certainly not."

"And you Matea?"

"I know it means something to you and your work but now I would like to go. Please." Matea had been staring out of the window. This was not right and she felt tears welling. She could say nothing more for fear of choking, other than to repeat, "Please."

"Of course," replied Augustin as he watched the Opel driver running up the hill towards them. "In a moment." Then, out of the side of his mouth, he whispered, "James. Don't say a word!"

The Opel driver snatched open Augustin's door with his left hand, his right reaching inside his coat, towards his shoulder holster.

Augustin smiled at the intruder. Calmly, he said in English, "I wouldn't do that if I were you." The American moved his hand away from the pistol. "Thank you, "Augustin responded, "I feel safer now. How can I help?"

"I am told that this is your second visit here today. Why?" The American was bellowing now, "And what else did you pick up that doesn't belong to you?"

"I have relatives in Bol and, thankfully, there is still freedom of movement across Brač so why I am here is no business of yours." As Augustin was determined not to let the American butt-in, he continued swiftly, "And as far as those ID tags are concerned they were lying in the gutter, outside the cordoned off area."

"Did you see what was written on them?"

"No," Augustin lessened his smile.

"Thank you," the American replied harshly, glaring into the car. "If I had my way I would have all of you searched."

Still smiling, still calm, Augustin continued, "Thankfully we are not under your jurisdiction, whoever you might be but, if you insist, why not ask that policeman to come and search us."

"That will not be necessary," the American snarled without grace.

"Good, because we use this road often and have no interest in souvenir hunting. And," Augustin paused, pointing at the American helicopters, "if I had my way you would be told to pack up your war machinery and never return. Your presence will only bring yet more problems."

The American, desperate to respond, said simply. "We are helping to clear up the mess after a Croatian helicopter came down." He could not tell civilians what he had failed to tell Slavić.

Augustin slammed the door shut and engaged reverse gear leaving the hapless American with his right hand twitching near his left armpit. With a friendly wave to the police the British Consul then accelerated up the hill.

Two hundred yards further on, as the road levelled to contour around the valley, James suddenly ordered, "Stop! Stop, Augustin. Just there," he pointed ahead, "by that scrap of paper."

As the car slowed to a halt James opened the door a crack, bent down and grabbed the paper from the road's surface. "Thanks," he said, "just a hunch. Now we'd better move on."

"I hope the American didn't see you do that."

"Who was he? His face seemed strangely familiar."

"I pretended not to recognise him but in fact he is the US Defense Attaché."

"Of course. Magnus showed me his photograph."

In Augustin's house James laid out the scrap of paper

alongside his own scribbled notes and stared at his finds. Eventually he looked up, his mind still half way up the Bol escarpment, "I think these could be useful clues but I will need outside help."

"What makes you say that," asked Augustin.

"Those 'dog tags', as we used to call them in the Royal Navy, were clearly torn from the body of a US marine. I have his name – Joseph P Martinez – nine-figure regimental number – his religion, Christian – and his blood group, A Rhesus Positive. The loop of metal links had been stretched until it broke so I have no doubt the owner was in the crash and thrown clear. At the same time his body probably disintegrated into..." he paused, "...sorry Matea...into individual parts which, we must presume, are still being recovered."

Matea looked away. Until a few hours ago, the 'necklace' she had handled in the car had been around the neck of a living being. A son certainly, a father perhaps.

"Any idea why a US marine should be in a Croatian helicopter?" James asked.

No one answered.

James mulled over his other find, "This page, a good two thirds of which has been destroyed by fire, may be unimportant but," he pointed to the letters ..CRET printed across the top in red above the words ..or US Eyes Only. "That classification is there for a purpose. The remaining torn perforations down the left-hand side suggest that it may have been ripped from a note book. A manual of directions possibly for something called an ... edator. Instructions for the assembly of the starboard ... As you can see, the rest is missing."

"What is all that about do you suppose?" asked Augustin.

"Not a clue but I think I know someone who can find out."

"Magnus?" questioned Augustin.

"Magnus," James confirmed, "and I think we are just about to disturb his Christmas."

Back at Split's Riva waterfront James helped Matea ashore.

"I'm off to my office," the Consul explained, "to fax through the burnt page and Martinez's details. Magnus's line switches through to wherever he is."

"Thanks so much for today. Really helpful."

"My sad pleasure," replied Augustin, turning for his office.

"Magnus?" asked Matea when they were alone by her car.

"A mutual acquaintance in England," James answered, "A wizard at amateur detective work."

"He will have to be."

James opened Matea's car door for her, "You must collect Dino from his friend's house so I'll walk back to Hotel Split."

"Sure?"

"Sure."

When the punch came from behind James tried to turn but he was already falling down the low cliff towards the sea-washed rocks. He remembered a flash of disruptive pattern uniform before his right arm snagged on a branch. The fall below the branch lasted a further three seconds while his hands and feet clawed subconsciously at non-existent holds, vainly attempting to arrest his downward progress. In a fading blur of red and black, his mind turned blank.

The stagger back to the hotel with blood-matted hair, clothes torn, arms, legs and stomach cut and bruised while nursing a badly twisted ankle, took James over an hour. He remembered nothing. Nor had he any recollection of the ladies at the reception desk asking if he needed help. He had no idea whether or not he took the lift or a 'time passing' climb up the stairs.

His first sense of awareness since seeing the cliff flashing past his face was now and he was in a bed.   Whose bed? Someone's hand was stroking his arm. Whose hand?   Voices… He could hear voices. Whose voices?

James lay still, not daring to open his eyes which would be difficult enough anyway as both lids were swollen into massive, puffy, black semi-circles. His head hurt, he had no feeling in his left foot or his right arm. Numerous cuts and bruises stung and ached. It was easier to lie back, cocooned in his own ethereal 'time passing measure' over which he had no control.

He would wake. All in good time he would wake. When nature decided.

Subdued voices still surrounded him.   A soft hand continued its stroking.

Time passed. James drifted in and out of awareness until…

"James, you silly old sod. Can you hear me?"

'Bugger off, Patrick,' his internal voice replied. 'Can't you see I'm tired.'

"James," a different voice, a woman's voice, joined the conversation, "Don't listen to him. Wake up in your own time."

In my own time. When will that be. Time is what we may not have.

Struggling to move his swollen eyes James lifted one painful lid. He tried the second. That didn't work either. He squinted through both together. Agonizing but possible and he could live with that while he assessed his situation, focussing desperately slowly on a far wall and a picture he recognized. Dubrovnik. Above his desk. Thank God he was not in a Croatian hospital.

He looked to his right. Matea was gazing down at him, "Hello, James," she smiled, fondling his battered arm.

CHAPTER SEVENTEEN

Wednesday 22nd December 1993
Headquarters, 4th Guards Brigade, Hotel Resnik,
Put Resnika, Kaštela, Croatia.

Without waiting for an answer to his knock the United States' Defense Attaché strode into Colonel Ante Slavić's office. The Croatian stood quickly, his left hand spilling a glass of white wine down his wrist.

"I left Zagreb as soon as I heard the news," Dwight Anderson said, by way of a greeting.

"I have only just returned from Bol myself," Slavić replied. "I assume you are on your way."

"The ferry leaves Split in an hour. I've booked into a hotel there for the night."

"Do you know what happened?" Slavić asked, suspecting that as the American had not been straight with him before he was not going to be straight with him now. It was as good a time as any for some direct questions: whether he would get direct answers was another matter entirely.

"Before I answer that, has anyone visited the crash site other than the police and the press?"

"There is only one road into the village and the same one leads out of it and that is also the one that your guys are using as a helicopter landing zone. One police road block is well down the hill from the crash while the other is up the hill. A number of locals have tried to get in and out but there is no movement through in either direction."

"No one else?"

"Not that I am aware of. I had the Chief of Police check all ferry passengers since dawn. No one untoward has travelled to or from the island. A few holiday makers going to the island for Christmas but that is about all."

"No one will have seen the aluminium planks that must be scattered all over the place?"

"I can't swear to that," Slavić repeated, "Certainly not if they were coming up the hill as I've said. Possibly, if they were coming down towards Bol. It is not so easy to hide the crash from that direction and certainly not the planks littering the hillside."

"You could try!" Anderson was tetchy.

"My military police are doing their best, but their job is to secure the area while the Americans tidy the place up and that includes the planks. Yesterday you said it was to be a recce flight. So why all the aluminium?"

"I keep telling you, Ante. Need to know."

"Well I bloody well need to know."

"All in good time."

"I would have thought that now was as good a time as any. You say you are keen to help us and of course we are more than grateful for that but you can only tease the system so far. If I don't know the truth how can I lie to the Croatian public with conviction."

Recognising the beginning of a Slavić lecture Anderson sat down. His long drive had begun before dawn. Right now he would have preferred a cup of coffee, even one of Slavić's plastic cups of instant coffee, rather than a harangue but none was offered.

Slavić continued, "I will deal with the public relations aspect of this incident while your teams clear the evidence. We can't hide what has happened so we can at least try and calm everybody while helping them believe it was one of ours. We are used to helicopter disasters but all occur inland, in daylight and usually with a convincing cover story. Now I have a night-time crash on an island, hundreds, if not thousands, of aluminium planks strewn across the countryside and a large number of casualties. I have got to be able to tell the press something that they can swallow."

Anderson stood, "Thanks for the coffee," he said sarcastically, "Don't forget, you need me more than I need you. When I get back this evening I'll give you a full brief over dinner."

Anderson knew well that his President could not give a damn for Croatia's reputation. All he cared about was re-election for a second term of office in 1996. If the White House could help prevent further Serb atrocities, through the re-arming of Croatia, then so be it... and sod Croatia's status.

Glad that the Defense Attaché had gone Slavić sank into his chair. He was not looking forward to his return and he had good reason for his trepidation. He had offered the Americans an unused airfield, an airfield that did not officially exist. Now the whole of Croatia would know that something was going on. He began to compile a list of questions.

The hours passed slowly until, towards the end of the afternoon, the telephone on Slavić's desk rang.

"*Da.*"

"Colonel," the southern American accent said, "the English monitor, Mr Laidlaw, has had an accident,"

Slavić's cold blood ran a little cooler. "What sort of accident?" He hesitated then asked a more sensible question, "Who are you?"

"I followed Laidlaw from the Riva moorings where he had just arrived from Brač."

"And…?" Slavić prompted.

"A jogger bumped into Laidlaw as he was walking back to his hotel. The cliff where it occurred is about twenty feet high as I expect you know."

Slavić did not know. He never walked if he could drive. He took the caller at his word.

"Where is Laidlaw now?"

"No idea," the voice answered.

"You dumb bastard." Slavić was not happy, "all I asked was that one of you guys, I assume you are in my brigade, kept an eye on him not bloody well kill him." He slammed the telephone down.

The caller, staring at the mute handset slowly rubbed the right side of his neck, stroking the feathers of the American bald eagle tattooed there. He would not be sorry if the Limey bastard, that had identified him to the police, was dead.

Slavić, irate before the call, was now angry. This was not in his plan. He needed Laidlaw as an ally. If the Brit commander was now to become inquisitive and suspicious… But that was not today's problem. Anderson was today's problem. Slavić's trepidation remained.

The telephone rang again.

"It's Dwight. I'm back."

"Good visit?"

Anderson did not answer but gave the name of a hotel near the ferry port. He suggested Slavić joined him within the hour.

The American was waiting in the hotel bar overlooking the

harbour and, being in no mood to hang around, had already booked a table in the dining room towards which he led his guest. It had been a long day and, apart from the underlying tragedy, it had also been an unsatisfactory one.

Once settled, Anderson began, "What I am about to tell you is for your ears only."

Receiving a firm nod from Slavić, the Attaché continued.

"This morning we lost a helicopter with three crew, twelve passengers and some logistics. At the same time you lost five members of the Brač community. Currently we have no idea what caused the crash. A brief Mayday call was sent but it was too late. We will be ruling out foul play as no one could have known the helicopter was going to be where it was and at that time."

Slavić took a deep breath to speak.

Anderson silenced him, "No, Ante. Hear me out."

Slavić took a deep draught of wine instead.

"The Super Stallion, in its various forms, does not have the best safety record so I expect the experts will be looking into some form of mechanical failure."

Appreciating that he would learn more if he remained silent, Slavić nodded.

"It is now no secret that the aircraft was carrying a number of aluminium planks. So far we have removed all US bodies back to the Sixth Fleet. The five civilians were flown, individually, to Split hospital throughout the night. The aircraft itself, in three major sections and dozens of smaller segments, is being removed for the air accident investigation guys to start their work.

"Clearing up will take a few more days. We have removed all debris from the road itself and by using some of the planks, have laid an area of hard standing for the helicopters so the road is now open."

Anderson stopped but before Slavić could respond he began again. "The downside is that while we cannot stop people using the public roads I am worried that people are now alerted to something happening at the top of the escarpment."

"Everybody thinks we were excavating a quarry."

"Sure, but it's still a large piece of real estate to keep hidden."

"We've opened up the original approach in an attempt to allay suspicions but have had to place armed guards and a road block at the quarry's entrance."

"I saw one car today which did not strike me as being a sightseer's. The driver handed in some ID tags to the police that he said he had found by the road."

"Did you look into the vehicle?"

"Two men and a girl in the back."

"It's just a hunch," Slavić said, pulling out his wallet and removing a well-thumbed snap shot. "Was this one of them?"

Without hesitating Anderson replied. "Yeah. The one in the passenger seat."

"That, my friend, is Commander James Laidlaw."

If the blood did not drain from Anderson's face it was because he was used to such surprises, instead he asked, "Why the hell do you carry his photo?" and then, "More importantly, what the hell was he doing at the crash site?"

Slavić, still smarting at being kept in the dark, decided, for the moment, to support Laidlaw's presence. He needed the Englishman 'on side' especially now that the Greek, who had been pestering him with incessant phone calls from Zadar, was beginning to throw his weight around. Until Laidlaw actually refused to assist Slavić he was not going to expose him.

"Well," he eventually said, his wine-befuddled brain taking time to decide how to handle this news, "although I do not approve of the monitors visiting the islands it is in their remit. I guess that had I been a monitor I would have been at the scene too."

"It's your bloody job to prevent it. Your brigade is responsible for security in this area and you, as Chief of Staff, should be enforcing that security." Anderson knew he was tinkering with the truth, but took the risk.

Chaffing at the insults, the Croat stalled for time. There were still questions to be answered by the American who had been playing fast and loose with the truth since they had first met, now he was not going to have his work impugned by anyone, let alone a Yank despite hoping for the American's help. Bugger the next Presidential election campaign, even if Croatia could not rid itself of the Serb threat alone!

"OK," Anderson persisted, "we now know the Brit saw the planks…"

"So would every one else who tried to reach Bol."

"The Brit will have done some educated guessing."

"Actually," Slavić, was not going to give way, "I don't see the problem with that. We are all-but at war with Serbia. We ask for help. We get a load of aluminium planks."

"He will work out what they are for."

"Even I have no idea and yet I am closer to the operation than he is."

Anderson nodded. If his Operation Stakeout was not going to go 'pear-shaped' before it got underway – and it had already begun badly – he had better come a little cleaner with the Chief of Staff of Croatia's 4th Guards Brigade.

But Slavić had not yet finished, "We need your help, you know that, and we are getting it but too many bubbles of American security are hindering our working relationship. If I don't know what help you need I can not supply it and, up to now, I have gone as far as I can while remaining in the dark."

As Anderson glowered across the table, Slavić continued, "We need arms, we need men, we need armour, we need aircraft and we need intelligence. What we don't need is suspicion. Now that part of your plan has been exposed to the public, perhaps you will be more open with me."

Anderson leaned back in his chair. If he was to help his President's re-election plans then the Serb atrocities had to end and the only way that would happen was if Croatia rearmed. He had, though, hoped that events might have progressed further than they had before he would feel obliged to tell Slavić the whole truth. Slavić was unreliable, he was mercurial, he was unstable... but he was the only contact who was wholly, almost fanatically, willing to help: he held the right military appointment and had the right attitude. Colonel Dwight I. Anderson made up his mind. He would tell Slavić the truth, but not quite the whole truth;' not yet anyway and, perhaps, never.

"Ante," Anderson began pleasantly, "while you study the menu listen to what I have to say."

"Thank you," Slavić replied uncertainly, determined to listen rather than read.

Anderson continued, "My President believes that the only way to achieve peace is to defeat the Krajina Serbs through a military offensive."

Slavić nodded. So far so good... but nothing new.

"Our Department of Defense sees three ways in which it can help. First, it can assist in breaking the embargo through the ports of Ploče in the south and Pula in the north. Second, it can supply intelligence with which, once it has rearmed, your army can plan its attack with growing confidence. And third it can assist those Americans who wish to enlist in your army as mercenaries, to return stateside with no questions asked."

The first and third proposals were no surprise but the second most definitely was. "Go on," Slavić said putting down his glass, "Tell me how your DoD can supply intelligence."

"When we first thought of how we can gain information from across the confrontation line we were a little stuck. We considered infiltrating one of the ECMM teams in the RSK but that was never going to work so we decided to use a Cessna L-19/O-1 for aerial reconnaissance. The Bird Dog, as we call it, is a fixed-wing, light spotter aircraft that we will bring out of retirement. It can be lifted, with its wings detached, in a C-130 and is slow enough to fly into some very tight places. Uniquely it has a large rear-facing window and is better for our purposes than anything else in service, including helicopters. As it looks like a private aircraft we will paint it in civilian colours with false markings.

"We thought of using Split airport but met difficulties. We needed hard standing set aside from the main airport but adjacent to the runway and we needed security as we would only operate at night. Here we encountered a snag in the shape of the ECMM's airfield monitor, an Englishman called Roger Sampson. He may only have one eye but he misses nothing.

"In the absence of anything better it was decided to fly in aluminium planks for the hard standing and a large portable, canvas hanger in which we could re-assemble and maintain the Cessna in a distant corner of Split airport, far from prying eyes. Then you suggested Brač and I had a look myself but you never told me at the time that getting there would be such an obstacle course. A day or so later we had a C-130 fly across the islands as you know. In due course they will use the runway to bring in the Cessna then resupply fuel and logistics direct from the Sixth Fleet.

"By now, though, we did not need the planks or portable hanger as the concrete apron, dispersal and hangers at Brač are big enough and of course there are no prying eyes. But they were half way across the Med and we reckoned that they might still have a use."

Anderson pointed at the menu. When they had ordered he added, "So you see why we need a runway..."

"Why didn't you tell me in the beginning?"

"I wasn't prepared to trust you until after the operation – we've named it Stakeout – had begun and could not be reversed. It was easier to hint at a helicopter. Which was, of course, partially true for the initial insertion."

"But the need for security still exists?"

"Obviously," Anderson snorted, "What we are up to is in contravention of the embargo but once you have thrashed the Serbs who but they will care how we achieved it. Until then we must ensure that the likes of Laidlaw and Sampson are themselves monitored very closely. At the slightest sign of them discovering anything," Anderson looked directly into Slavić's bloodshot eyes, "you will know what to do and it will be done with my President's unwritten blessing. The defeat of the Serbs will mean a lot to him while the inevitable slap on the wrist from the UN's Security Council will count for little."

"Thank you for telling me all this." Slavić was pathetically grateful but he still had questions. "Now that you have lost many of the planks and, presumably, the portable hanger and the men to build it all what happens next and how long will the delay be?"

"We can live without the planks and hanger at Brač," Anderson replied, "the problem is replacing the men as they were specially trained."

"Can't be that difficult replacing men to fly and maintain a

Cessna?"

Anderson was wary. Slavić was close to asking an awkward question and he would not be able to answer it, at least, not truthfully; but then telling the truth to Slavić had always been the least of Anderson's concerns. "No, of course not," he replied, thinking quickly, "We have plenty of others qualified. Forgive me. I wasn't thinking. I expect they will start again within a day or two. As soon as a C-130 can be made available." He did not need to explain that five members of SEAL Team Six sent ahead to prepare the landing site were now stranded on the Brač airstrip with limited food and water.

"So no real delay then?"

"No."

"Good," Slavić repeated and changed the subject, "Did you know that Laidlaw was pushed off a cliff last night?"

Anderson looked genuinely surprised. "No. By whom?"

Slavić's reply was as devious as he intended, "I thought you might be able to tell me as my informant spoke with an American accent over the 'phone."

"There are a great many American mercenaries enlisting in your army."

"If Laidlaw knows it was not an accident then that would double his suspicions."

"I take it he is still alive."

"D'you know what, Dwight? I have no idea but I hope so."

"Hope so?"

"He may still be helpful."

Anderson looked into his wine glass with a stony face.

CHAPTER EIGHTEEN

Thursday 23rd December 1993
Room 519, Hotel Split, Put Trstenika 19,
21000 Split, Croatia.

With his eyes open enough to take in more of his surroundings James confirmed that he was not alone.

"Matea," he murmured returning her smile and reaching for her hand, "What on earth are you doing here?"

"Welcome back, James," Patrick's voice boomed from the opposite side of the bed. "You had a bit of a fall walking back from Augustin's boat. Reception called and between us we got you into the lift…"

"I thought we agreed to use the stairs as a TPM!"

"Take this seriously will you. Apart from some cuts and bruises, a damaged ankle and a torn shoulder muscle you are also suffering from concussion. Not badly but the hotel doctor looked you over once Matea and I had undressed and washed you. He has ordered complete rest for three days."

"Matea," James swivelled his head on the pillow, "You undressed me?"

"Yes," she smiled, looking away, blushing.

"And washed me?"

"Yes," Matea's blushing increased, "Patrick asked where

you were and as I became worried too I drove to the hotel with Dino to see if I could help by contacting the police and so on. I was in your office when reception rang to say that you had just staggered through the swing doors and were bleeding all over the floor."

"That's more of the carpet they will have to hack away!"

"Thank you, Paddy. What time is it?"

"Eight in the morning."

"Have either of you slept?"

Matea answered, "Patrick and I have taken it in turns to rest on the other bed. Dino is tucked up in an arm chair in the office."

"What a bugger!"

For James, the Christmas period passed in an idle haze. Able only to get up to wash and have his dressings changed he was conscious of little more other than the almost continual presence of Matea by his bedside.

"Matea," he said on Boxing Day, propped up by pillows, finishing a small plate of keflika that the Greeks had persuaded the hotel's Croatian cooks to prepare for everyone's lunch the day before, "you were kind to help Patrick in his nursing duties and I want to thank you."

Matea looked down.

"Don't look down. I mean it."

"Patrick couldn't do it by himself," she argued.

"Maybe but I have ruined Dino's Christmas and that is unforgivable of me."

"Rubbish! He has been so spoilt by the hotel that he thinks it is the best ever. Not that he has had many for comparison," she laughed.

By the 27th James's recovery was accelerating. His headache had left him, his eyes were opening wider, the cuts and grazes were healing and his ankle was noticeably stronger.

"As your accident was not an accident," Patrick offered, "I am pretty sure that Slavić has to be behind it… but why?"

"Probably because of what we saw."

"What did you see?" asked Patrick. "You haven't debriefed me yet."

James recounted the journey to Brač, leaving out nothing, ending with their arrival at the Riva. After that Patrick knew the story better.

"So," Patrick was fishing, "Much as expected?"

"Very much so. No idea what type of Croatian helicopter it was other than that it must have been a large one. Possibly a Russian built Mi-17. I found the ID tags for a Joseph P Martinez of the United States Marine Corps. No rank given although the regimental number might give a clue to those who understand these things. Someone might know if he was attached to the Croat army and if so why? I also picked up a piece of burnt paper which I had faxed to a contact in London."

"And?" asked Patrick.

"I have no idea where the aircraft was heading of course but Augustin said that some time back they were excavating a quarry on the flat ground above Bol. That might tie in with the planks. Not enough to build a runway but certainly enough for a helicopter's hard standing."

"Why use Brač?" asked Matea.

"We won't know that till we have seen what is at the top of the escarpment."

"Please, no monitoring of the arms embargo," Matea pleaded optimistically.

"Of course not! NATO's Standing Naval Force, Mediterranean, does that," James argued. "What Croatia is short of is armour and aircraft and those have to come through the sea ports, not by helicpters. In due course they will have enough men, even if the majority will be mercenaries."

"So," Patrick summed up, "Although we may be a little wiser, we now have a damaged monitor and more unanswered questions."

Three days after Boxing Day – a Tuesday – James dressed fully for the first time. The previous evening Matea had returned home and Patrick ceased his nursing duties following the doctor's pronouncement that James could return to 'light duties'. The bruises and sprains would improve in their own time.

Before leaving Matea brought Dino to say good bye. "Mama say, brave man," Dino said, echoing his mother's words. "*Hvala*," he continued and gave James a wet kiss on a cheek.

"You were the brave one. Now you look after Mama as she is very, very special. When I am better I'll take you fishing off the rocks."

Dino thought for a moment. "Does that mean you will be my tata?" he asked.

"If you want."

"Does anyone else call you tata?"

Now it was James's turn to think back to what might have been, to the son he never quite had, to the father he never quite was. "No," he said at last. "You will be the first one."

"I would like that."

"His English will improve," Matea promised, "I'll see you tomorrow." Then, without a hint of hesitancy she bent and kissed James on the lips.

"Thank you, Matea," he managed, "Thank you so very much." It was only after she had left that he realised he was thanking her for the kiss not for her patience and diligence.

On Thursday, the telephone in Team Split's office was

ringing as James limped past, he snatched up the handset.

"Team Split."

"It's Augustin. I have waited until you were better to give you some news."

"From Magnus?"

"I will bring his cypher messages in person. I can then also see for myself if you really are better."

Half an hour later the British Consul strode in clutching a Foreign Office black, leather brief case with its familiar EIIR initials stamped in gold leaf above the side lock. While Patrick made coffee Augustin laid out sheets of paper across the office table.

"I have here," he explained, "a number of tele-printer messages, some line drawings and faxed letters from Magnus. All are marked 'secret' but I am not sure what your security classification is."

"Mine was Cosmic Top Secret but is now lapsed. Paddy, being an Irishman, is probably classed as an alien," he winked at his friend, "while Matea, who will not be in for another hour, is… well she is not classified at all, rather obviously."

"Magnus?" Patrick queried.

"A friend."

"I'll ask no more."

Augustin continued, "Either way Magnus gave me clearance to pass on everything that I have on the understanding that you will know who to discuss it with and who not to discuss it with."

The British Consul picked up one set of papers, "Let me guide you through them," he suggested. "But before that I must relay to you a conversation I had with Magnus last night."

"I can guess," James laughed, "he had to work over the holiday?"

"Close. What he said was, 'Tell James that although one

of our unofficial mottos is 'Intelligence Never Sleeps', can he please try to avoid Christmas next time.'"

"He should discuss that with the Croatian helicopter pilots."

"I'm sure he will," responded Augustin, laughing, as he handed two pages across the desk. "Now, here is a report on the late owner of the ID tags."

James read it first in astonished silence then picked out the salient points for Patrick. "Joseph P Martinez was a lieutenant-colonel in the United States Marine Corps and, until his death, was the commanding officer of the Sixth Fleet's Special Operations Flight." He read on, paraphrasing the closely-typed document in order to simplify the American Special Forces order of battle and acronyms. "It would appear that he'd been assigned for a four month tour in support of a squadron of SEALs attached to the Sixth Fleet."

"I feel as though I should have heard of them."

"Yes, you should have," James teased good humouredly. "The name is a left-over from 1980 when a US Navy special forces team was established following the United States' failed attempt to rescue American hostages in Tehran during the disastrous Operation Eagle Claw."

"I've certainly heard of that cock-up."

"Then, in 1987, the name was changed to the Special Warfare Development Group or," James elaborated, "in line with the American love of abbreviations, as Devgru but SEAL Team Six is how they are still known." He looked up, "Sadly, it seems that Martinez's luck finally ran out as he had been a junior Sea Stallion co-pilot during Eagle Claw and was lucky to escape intact from that mayhem."

"Poor bugger," Patrick said before asking softly, "What's the link?"

"That was not a Croatian Mi-17 that crashed but a USMC

Sea Stallion piloted by Martinez."

"Perhaps you had better tell me more about SEAL Team Six."

James continued his explanation, "Devgru is the US Navy's counter-terrorism unit. Currently based at Dam Neck in Virginia it consists of about two hundred personnel and is one of only two, Tier One counter-terrorism and Special Mission Units, the other is the US Army's Delta Force…"

Patrick, listening carefully, felt James was offering too much detail of a counter-terrorism unit when they were not about to face a counter-terrorism situation. He butted in, "Sorry, James, but why is all of this important?"

"I am coming to that. These are the only two Special Forces units whose operations are sanctioned directly by the US President and," he paused momentarily to highlight this morsel, "only by the US President."

"Wow," exclaimed Patrick, "I guess that that really is relevant!"

"Probably but I can't tell quite yet. Let's see what else Magnus has for us."

James picked up another sheaf of papers and, again, read them through to himself first. As he did so both Patrick and Augustin watched his eyes widen until he placed the papers back on the desk.

"Now we know the future," James said simply, "and I am not sure that I like it. I can also tell you precisely why Slavić does not want us anywhere near Brač although it does not answer why Pagonis does not want us there either. In that respect the plot is certainly thickening."

"Don't keep me in suspense."

"The scrap of burnt paper we picked up off the road had been torn from a manual for the assembly of a remote controlled aircraft called, apparently, a Predator. It is still in the experimental stage and, when ready, could be sent to Brač for what Magnus describes as operational trials."

"It wasn't in the helicopter that crashed?"

"No."

James paraphrased further as he laid two pages of line drawings of the pilotless, 'unmanned aerial vehicle' on to the desk. "Magnus believes this UAV will be used in surveillance tasks operating out of a secure base but he offers no prognosis on when or even if this could happen. His understanding seems to be that it depends on the success or otherwise of the continuing trials in the Mojave Desert in southern California, the availability of such a forward base here in Croatia and the extent to which the President is prepared to flout the embargo.

"Also," James continued with Magnus's explanation, "A memo that crossed his desk recently, stated that the US President is determined to increase his popularity at home by taking decisive action to halt Serb atrocities."

"No mention of Croat atrocities?"

"None!"

"Magnus," James continued, "has no idea what the aluminium panels were for although a Royal Naval Liaison Officer on the Sixth Fleet Admiral's staff, reported that USS Drake had collected an unidentified cargo – even the Admiral did not know what it was – from Newport Virginia, then crossed the Atlantic to join the Fleet on the day of the crash.

"As it happens," James summed up, "the two exhibits we picked up have told us far more than I expected but they have also left a fair amount for us still to discover. For instance, the involvement of SEAL Team Six, under orders from the White House, needs to be investigated although it is possible that, despite his qualifications, Martinez was being employed on a reasonably routine insertion that simply needed the largest helicopter available."

Patrick chipped in, "His cargo would suggest not."

"An alternative assumption that Magnus makes is that the Predator manual was not on board the Super Stallion on purpose but had been left behind from a previous, unconnected, mission."

"In which case someone was playing pretty loose with a classified document."

"I agree, Patrick, so I am not inclined to believe it was on board by mistake. Magnus goes on to mention that the Predator, assuming that it is central to this saga, needs at least a 3,500 foot runway. It can land and take off in far less but that is the safety requirement.

"And it will have to be lifted in by a much larger aircraft such as a C-130 and while I know that a Hercules can land and take off in well under 2,000 feet using Military Operating Standards, they prefer a runway closer to 6,000 feet for normal day-to-day operations."

"That will take a very long time to build if the planks come in such penny packets by helicopter."

"So, are you thinking the same as me, James?"

"I saw a C-130 the other day. Not actually landing but looking as though it was checking-out somewhere suitable to do so."

Augustin, sensing that his part in the growing saga had run its course, put down his empty coffee mug. "When you have a reply let me know and I will collect it at a place other than either of our offices. In the meantime I'll let you two get on with it."

When the British Consul had departed, clutching his now-empty brief case, James and Patrick drew their chairs up to the table ready to list any outstanding questions. Although further on in their knowledge there remained gaps.

Before they had time to begin their summing up the telephone rang once more. James grabbed the receiver.

"James, it is Gaspard. How are you?"

"Recovering."

"Good. Patrick told me what happened."

Something in the Head of the Reginal Centre's voice suggested that this was not a social call. James listened.

"I have been chatting with Pagonis," Gaspard began. "He is not happy with his first visit to Team Split."

James, expecting this call, waited to hear the evidence before putting the case for his defence.

"He tells me that you refused to listen to his orders and that you would be deciding your own programme. He wants you to monitor the confrontation line but you said you had better things to do."

James continued to keep silent until Gaspard was ready to hear him. "He says you have a fixation about Croatian re-armament and are only interested in monitoring the arms embargo. Is this true?"

"Gaspard," James began, "we had a very difficult time with Pagonis who demanded that we ignore the coast to concentrate solely on what is happening along the confrontation line. While I agreed that that was an important part of our work it is, in large part, covered by the United Nations Military Observers. You also know that the Dalmatian coast is the power house required for any re-generation of Croatia. You know, too, that with the RSK's stranglehold on the immediate interior there is no railway link with the outside world and that there is precious little road traffic to or from further east. Dalmatia is being throttled and there is nothing anyone can do about it..."

"I was merely repeating what Pagonis has been saying."

Realising that he had been pushing at a door that was already wide open all James could say was, "Sorry."

"You have my full support but whether or not you will have the full support of my relief I cannot tell."

"Sublette?"

"Very soon I will be handing over to him in Hotel Betonska and had hoped to say goodbye to you both in Split on my way there but the shuttle will take me direct to Zadar and then on to Zagreb."

"We could meet you in Zadar."

"Good idea. I'll let you know when."

They each said *au revoir* and put their receivers down. James turned to Patrick. "Fancy a day trip to Zadar, Paddy."

"When?"

"He'll let us know. Now these lists."

The telephone rang.

"Blast! Your turn Paddy!"

"Team Split," Patrick barked.

James watched his colleague's face grimace, then smile… then he nodded.

Eventually Patrick said, "Thank you. We will look forward to it," and put the receiver down.

"Who was that?"

"Captain Demetrios Pagonis of the Hellenic Navy," Patrick imitated the Greek's voice. "Offering an olive twig."

"Not a branch?"

"Not yet. He wants to apologise…"

"You're joking…"

"…and said he would welcome us to lunch with Gaspard on Monday."

"Gaspard did not mention the date."

"That's Demetrios trying to run the show."

On Monday James, Patrick and Matea, accompanied by Dino, headed north-west for Zadar.

Didier Levesque was standing on the hotel's steps clutching a mug of coffee. "Great to see you Matea and Dino," he shouted as Patrick pulled the Land Rover to a stop. "And you James and Patrick."

James, looking around him, asked, "How's the new Head of the Coordinating Centre?"

"Not like the last one," was all Didier was prepared to say, "Got off to a bad start. Threw his weight around. Brought a girl friend as his personal interpreter and lives privately with her somewhere in town. Never wears white uniform and so on."

"We had that in Split," James observed.

"Yes, we know." Didier laughed, "He came back the next day. Fuming."

Matea excused herself and took Dino a few hundred yards to a friend's house leaving the monitors to settle onto bar stools, pouring cold Ožujsko beer into tall glasses.

"Welcome to my headquarters," a now-familiar voice called from behind. The trio turned, wiping their mouths to watch a smiling Pagonis striding towards them with Karla two paces to his rear.

James grinned. Unsure what catalyst, what hidden spur, had brought about this sudden outburst of overt friendship, he had only a few moments to wait.

"Before Gaspard arrives, I want to ask that neither of you mention our meeting the other day…"

"Bit late for that," James said.

"Well," Pagonis replied, trying to look composed, "Maybe after Gaspard has gone we can talk about what went wrong. Right now there is something else you should know," Pagonis was still smiling. "Guillaume Larouche is no longer with us."

Without looking relieved James asked, "Was he pushed or did he jump?"

"Pushed!" was the curt answer, uttered with the hint of a smile.

James, keen to inquire further, was interrupted as the hotel's front door swung open and in walked Gaspard. Pagonis, exercising an oily charm, swiftly excused himself to usher the French diplomat, via brief handshakes, to the Operations Room where he faced his monitors and members of the Zagreb staff. "I want you to know," he began his valedictory de-brief, "that when I get to Zagreb I will be advising my relief, Jean-Claude Sublette, what I believe should be the route ahead. It is only correct that I tell you too."

James looked sideways at Pagonis's expressionless face. Patrick was smiling, so was Didier.

"I have yet to be convinced," Gaspard continued, "that Croatia is breaking the arms embargo but I am equally sure that the country is desperate to rearm. By any means. Thus I believe that the monitoring of the ports of Pula and Ploče must continue. The NATO flotilla at sea should ensure that the embargo is watertight but I am not so certain. Although," he added carefully, "I have no specific reason for saying that."

Gaspard looked around the room, inviting questions. There were none. "Embargo monitoring," he continued, "is not our direct concern. On the coast, unlike inland, the commercial monitoring, including the defunct tourist industry, is vital so that when peace does come the EU will know where financial help is needed. The welfare of the refugees needs watching while plans for their eventual repatriation need to be considered. All cease-fire violations must continue to be recorded although the UNMOs are here to lead on that. The appearances of swastikas and Ustaše symbols is deeply regrettable and this, too, needs to be reported. The build up of Croatian Forces, if that is happening, and their activities on land and in the air both need monitoring. It is not, therefore, a single-issue task that we face."

Pagonis broke Gaspard's monologue, "I concur but I would also like to add that the crash of a Croatian helicopter, which I know has occupied the thoughts of many of us, is a local tragedy. Nothing more." He glanced at James and Patrick in turn. James looked at his Irish friend and, very gradually, shook his head. Patrick said nothing.

"I tend to agree with you Demetrios," Gaspard said, "but it was an odd place for it to have been. And at an unusual hour."

James decided it was still best to keep quiet. He did not want anyone to know that he knew the truth and he certainly did not want anyone to know how he knew the truth.

Gaspard explained further, "When I called Colonel Slavić to express my condolences he was grateful for my concern and confirmed that it had been an army Mi-17 but he didn't say why it was flying over Bol in the dark. Then was not the time to ask. I took his word that it was simply a catastrophic accident."

Slowly the conversation died allowing Gaspard to leave the room and return with a tray of champagne and glasses. "This is my way of saying thank you and good luck with my successor."

"Will we need luck?" quipped Patrick.

"I have a feeling that you might!"

The impromptu party ended with the mini-bus driver banging on the door prior to announcing, "Time to go, boss."

Gaspard's departure, following handshakes and the occasional Gallic hug, brought James an unwelcome premonition: a prescience that all would not be well with Sublette's arrival, gloomy thoughts that were interrupted by Pagonis cheerfully proclaiming, "Lunch! Since some of you were last here the hotel has repaired the dining room."

With all seated according to the Greek's hastily thought out plan – Karla on his right, Patrick on his left, Didier and James opposite and with the staff further down the table – Pagonis poured glasses of local white wine. "*Žjivili,*" he said in Croatian, then in his own language, "*Yasoo.*"

"Your good health," replied James, unconvinced that he meant it.

With the meal underway Pagonis began his promised apologies, "I've come from Greek Special Forces and have not adjusted as quickly as I had hoped. Perhaps we can start again and if you are happy with that I'll ask Didier to explain what the Zadar coordinating team will be doing. Then I will ask James how he sees Team Split fitting in to the overall plan."

When at last Pagonis motioned to James to offer his thoughts he tested this new sense of reconciliation by sticking to his original line: but with the added conviction that he knew now that he was on the right track.

At the end Pagonis was almost appeasing, "Please pay as much attention to the confrontation line as you can. That's all I ask,"

"Of course," replied James, "but I do remain concerned about the helicopter crash."

Pagonis challenged James's suspicions, "Gaspard did not seem worried."

James thought it safe to share some of the mystery, albeit a little doctored, "Ah," he said, "but what Gaspard did not know is that the Croatian helicopter was carrying aluminium planks to build a landing pad."

Astonished, Pagonis looked at James, "Slavić didn't tell me that."

James, detecting the 'old' Pagonis close beneath the surface and wanting that persona to remain there, said, almost apologetically. "I would have told you earlier but by the time I had recovered from my fall I thought it could wait until you were in a receptive mood."

"How do you know?"

"I saw them myself."

"I haven't seen the patrol report."

"It was another private visit."

Pagonis, realising that he would get more if he let James have his head, encouraged him further, "If it helps the ECMM I am all for those."

"That is all I know. Probably an innocent reason, but," James was not going to elaborate, "there is still something that bothers me and I can't tell what it is quite yet."

"I'm not pushing you to go snooping around the islands as I told Slavić we would leave them alone but if you hear anything I am sure you will let me know. Officially."

"I'll do that," assured James.

Outside Matea and Dino were waiting by the Land Rover. "Good lunch?" she asked, "How was Pagonis?"

"Oddly charming!"

CHAPTER NINETEEN

Monday 10 January 1994
Team Split Office, Hotel Split, Put Trstenika 19,
21000 Split, Croatia

James closed Team Split's office door behind him. "We need to finalise our plans for Jean-Claude's visit later this morning," he declared. "As he is a DGSE man I suggest we give him a full operational presentation."

"I have roughed out an aide memoir rather than a strict script. That map," Patrick pointed to the wall, "is all we need. Nothing else to a better scale."

James read through Patrick's draft, noting the division of subject headings they each would cover. "Anyone would have thought you were staff trained," he teased.

"Thankfully, I managed to by-pass the Irish Command and Staff School."

"You could have fooled me. What time is JCS due?"

"Eleven thirty. In an hour. Time for another run-through?"

With no distractions Patrick and James rehearsed their presentation. Assuming that a member of the *Direction générale de la sécurité extérieure* would expect perfection and, anyway, not prepared to offer anything less, the two monitors covered every aspect in as chronological an order as they could. They covered the background to Team Split's existence, its geographical limitations and boundaries. They aired the perceived areas of concern, including the possible use of Ploče as a conduit for illegal arms imports. They agreed not to mention the islands and the helicopter crash. They would cover social concerns such as the eviction of civilians from their own homes to house Croatian soldiers returning from the confrontation line; they would explain their views on the local industries and finally move on to the absence of tourists and the influx of refugees.

They would end the briefing by reiterating Gaspard's views that two teams, if not three, were needed and they would paraphrase Pagonis's acceptance of the overall monitoring plan for the coast.

"That should satisfy JCS," James declared after their final practice. "Now for some coffee." He looked up at the wall clock, "Blast!" he declared, "It's 1130 already."

On cue, Jean-Claude Sublette entered Team Split's life.

"Good morning," the monitors pronounced together, "Welcome."

"Hello," the new Head of the Regional Centre replied, pushing past, ignoring outstretched hands.

Sublette, hoping to appear masterful and in charge stated, "I intend to listen to what you have to say before telling you of my plans."

"Good," James declared, raising his eyebrows, "I am sure they will be the same as ours. As soon as the coffee is ready Patrick and I will crack on with the presentation. We can then discuss the future over a glass of wine and lunch."

"I do not drink wine."

"Then I'm sure the hotel will find some tap water," James

taunted, already acutely aware that the next two hours were not going to be easy. Pagonis had been bad; this could be far worse.

Ushering Sublette to a seat James took up his position to one side of the wall map, opposite Patrick. "We will offer you a formal presentation," he began, "so that everything is covered in a logical and easily understood fashion. At the end there will be time for questions."

"Please get on with it."

"Right. Situation…"

Less than five minutes into the briefing Sublette stood, shaking his head. "Stop. I have heard enough. I do not like this military style. Answer me this instead. Have you visited the chamber of commerce?"

"Not yet."

"Then I order you to do so immediately."

Un-phased Patrick said politely, "If we may continue with our briefing you will understand our priorities."

"I decide what your priorities are."

"I assume," James felt obliged to argue, "that when you took over from Gaspard you listened to him. In which case, may I suggest that until you have been here long enough to make up your own mind you let us get on with monitoring as your predecessor has laid down." Not prepared to put up with a repeat performance of Pagonis's visit, he continued his pre-emptive assault, "In case you have not heard there is a possibility that arms are being illegally imported into Croatia with a view to attacking the RSK."

"I do not believe these rumours," Sublette half shouted, "you are to concentrate on humanitarian affairs and commercial monitoring."

Sensing the beginnings of a rift, James countered, "If you believe that is the correct way to carry out our work so be it but it would be a dereliction of our duties within the ECMM."

With their briefing in tatters and with Sublette issuing a stream of orders, and at times contradictory orders, James and Patrick let the Frenchman's ill-thought out instructions cascade on. And on. It was, by any stretch of James and Patrick's imagination, a farcical two hours that had not included lunch.

At last, with the Frenchman's back disappearing through the hotel's front doors, James silently took Patrick by the arm and led him back to the Foyer Bar, stepping over the holes in the carpet like children avoiding the gaps between a pavement's squares.

"I really don't believe what we have just been through. It was bad enough with that Greek buffoon but this is far more serious."

"James," Patrick began, his Irish accent pronounced, "I really don't know what we are doing here other than wasting our time. The only way ahead is to carry out our own, possibly unofficial, monitoring. Once we have proof we lay it at JCS's door, copy it direct to Zagreb, and see what happens."

"We'll have to be bloody sure we get it right or we might make real fools of ourselves."

CHAPTER TWENTY

Tuesday 8th February 1994
Headquarters, 4th Guards Brigade, Hotel Resnik,
Put Resnika, Kaštela, Croatia.

Colonel Ante Slavić looked over his left shoulder towards the office door. It was nearly lunchtime and he was expecting the recently appointed head of the ECMM's Regional Centre from across the Confrontation Line in Knin. He turned towards the window and the outline of Brač beyond Split Harbour.

Jean-Claude Sublette's personal hygiene was certainly suspect but Slavić was so used to the scent of Old Spice aftershave in his bunk on board *Helena* that perhaps he was becoming a little sensitive to other odours. Maybe he should buy the Frenchman a bottle... Anyway, right now JCS was late despite Slavić having ordered his border guards to give him an easy passage. This was a nuisance for he had planned lunch and a long afternoon with his boys on board *Helena*.

He stared towards the islands. The Englishman was in danger of discovering the truth while the new Greek Head of the Zadar Coordinating Centre had yet to declare his hand. They had met, briefly, but even Slavić's own bombast had been outmatched by that of Captain Pagonis and so he had learned little.

Now Colonel Anderson was asking for more security around the Brač airstrip, even though all the debris from farther down the hill had been removed, while those demands were not being paid for with any more information.

From what little he knew about Sublette Slavić had hopes that he would become as useful an ally as the American colonel. He also harboured a faith that the Frenchman might become more than a friend. The boys were mere boys and useful as long as they kept his boat ready for sea for the day that he… he thought no further of the possibility of escape but the longed-for, national fame. Just suppose the Chief of Staff to the Guards Brigade, with a little help from his American and French friends, was to be the architect of a Croatian victory over the so-called Republic of Serbian Krajina, then who knew what honours would lie in store...

A timid knock on the door had Slavić easing his portly frame to its feet. His heart increased its beating. He began to sweat.

"Ah, Jean-Claude," Slavić reached forward, his sticky hand ready to grasp JCS's clammy palm, which he held for a little longer than might have been necessary, while looking directly into the Frenchman's eyes. "It is very good to see you again," the Croat declared.

An instantly-cautious Jean-Claude Sublette pulled back. He was not ready for such liaisons, especially while his director's words still resonated through his head. If he did not make a success of this mission his career in France's intelligence service would be over. He had to continue stamping his mark by outward displays of what he liked to think were signs of strength.

"Colonel, it is kind of you to invite me," he answered,

pulling his hand free.

"Not at all my dear Jean-Claude. My pleasure. Do sit down and have a glass of wine." Slavić knew he didn't drink but tried anyway. People who didn't drink had something to hide and he wanted to know what JCS was hiding.

"Thank you but, as you know, I don't drink." Sublette did not dare to do so anymore. Two glasses of weak wine made him irrational if not downright foolish and the innocent-sounding Koutoubia red wines during his previous posting in Algeria had been witness to that.

"I am sorry for you."

"*Ce n'est fait rien,*" Sublette replied in French without thinking.

Slavić, watching Sublette closely and considering how to approach the subject without frightening him off, decided that a blatant statement might do the trick. "I am concerned about one of your monitors," he declared.

"Laidlaw?"

"Correct."

Sublette had not yet carried out his reappointment of the monitors, deciding that he needed a little more time and thus a little more rope with which Laidlaw would hang himself irredeemably. Now Slavić, he hoped, would be offering him the perfect excuse to rid Split of the Englishman.

"He is becoming too concerned with the arms embargo and I suggest that this is overshadowing his normal monitoring duties."

"Do you have evidence?"

"Yes and no. As you will remember from our previous discussion, the first time he visited Ploče he was observed pacing out various marks in the dust. Then he and his interpreter visited the crash site almost immediately after one of our Mi-

17s ploughed into the hill. Now, which is why I wanted to see you, he is planning to return to Ploče."

Unwilling to declare his hand quite so soon Sublette muttered, "All within his remit."

"I'm not happy with him going there."

"If you insist."

For the next half an hour the two discussed the general situation on the coast, neither mentioning the embargo. All the while Slavić took every opportunity to study the Frenchman: he didn't like the way he smelt but he did like the way he was beginning to assert his position as the chief monitor for Dalmatia and the adjacent section of the Republic of Serbian Krajina. He began to warm to him more than he should, despite knowing that the ECMM as a whole was a damned nuisance to his personal aspirations. Nor was it taking Slavić long to appreciate that Sublette, far from his outward appearance, was a weak man, easily influenced: especially if he, Slavić, could offer some – he would have to think how to put it – some little personal inducement.

As they stood to say goodbye Slavić lent forward in a conspiratorial manner to speak softly in Sublette's ear as though they were in a crowded room, "If I hear any rumours about the breaking of the embargo would you like me to let you know?"

Sublette, keen to seize any opportunity that might gain him favour with his boss at 141 Boulevard Mortier, did not hesitate. "Yes," he said, "I would like that very much but I would not want Captain Pagonis to know."

"That will depend on how well you control Laidlaw."

Sublette did not like the reply but knew that it was the best he would get.

Ten minutes later, and with his office at last free of French sweat, Slavić picked up the telephone and dialled Colonel

Anderson's number in the United States Embassy to ask for another bottle of Old Spice. Then he drove to Split's yacht marina... and lunch.

CHAPTER TWENTY-ONE

Having lost the toss for 'duty driver' Patrick negotiated the final twists and turns as the road to the port of Ploče wound down the coastal escarpment. He turned to his front seat passenger, "James, we know Slavić's views but I doubt that JCS will approve of today's patrol either."

"Which is another good reason to be doing it! Anyway, he saw our weekly schedule and made no comment which is as good as a nod. Apart from that, Pagonis seemed to like the idea. After all, we all agree that monitoring the embargo is not part of our duty but that monitoring a commercial port most certainly is."

In the back of the Land Rover Matea, trying to stay awake on the long journey, pricked up her ears. She leant forwards. "Remind me please. Why are we going to Ploče again?"

"Normal monitoring duty," James was non-committal.

"And do you hope to find anything?"

"It will be interesting to see what commodities are being imported into a country with no money and at war with its neighbour."

"James!" exclaimed Matea, her head now between those of the two men in the front, "I know perfectly well you're keen to see if the embargo is being broken."

"Actually, I'm keen to see that it isn't being broken because that would save everyone a great deal of heartache."

"You know I once wanted that too."

"You must be alone among your countrymen," James replied then, thinking for a moment, unsure that he heard correctly, asked, "What was that you've just said? Have you changed your mind?"

"Probably! But I have been thinking, which is why I now want you to discover if the embargo is being broken because, if it is, you can then tell the UN and they can prevent it and Croatia will then be unable to wage a war. If it is not being broken or if it is and the UN stops it the the result will be the same. No more bloodshed and the politicians will be forced to negotiate."

"If they will listen to us. Also assuming our reports get past the Greek in Zadar, then the Frenchman in Knin and finally the Greeks again in Zagreb. Even so, Matea, simply and honestly put but why the sudden change of mind?"

"It will be a risk. I know that but I would like to think that the UN is more powerful than the US and the rearming would stop."

"We can only hope, Matea, we can only hope."

Dougal Macgregor greeted them. "How nice to see you all again," he began as they moved, clutching mugs of coffee, towards a low table in front of the wide window that faced the quaysides. "Not much has happened since you were last here. Mind you, I've been away myself for a week or two."

Matea made an excuse to leave, suggesting an interpretress was not needed between an Englishman, an Irishman and a Scot. "Actually," Patrick joked, "it is now that we probably need you more than ever."

They laughed as she made for the door, stopping briefly to explain her absence, "One of Mr Macgregor's secretaries is a girlfriend of mine."

As Matea left the room James looked past MacGregor to watch a 10,000 ton general cargo ship being unloaded by a large mobile crane. This ship was not registered in Monrovia for a faded Ukrainian flag hung limply from a rusty metal flagstaff at her stern. As his eyes adjusted to the dim afternoon light they were able to focus more closely on tracks scoured into the sand and dust between the crane and the secure compound they had noticed before. These were fresh imprints.

James turned back to the port manager, "Do you check the manifests of all cargoes against what is actually landed?"

"You asked that last time and the answer is still the same. No."

"Why?"

"There are risks." MacGregor replied simply

"You told me that you're not here all the time?"

"I have come back from a brief holiday and when I am here I run a shift system with my Croatian deputy."

"Do you prevent any illegal arms from being landed?"

"I would but I am not aware of any that have landed."

After half an hour of polite chat James needed to hear no more and with Matea already sitting in the Land Rover, the monitoring party left Ploče.

James, now driving, turned to Patrick. "Not much new there, Paddy," he exclaimed.

"I saw you looking at those tracks. I guess they were made by the same type of vehicles as before."

"Not surprising, if the deputy manager is in charge for much of the time," James said.

In the back seat Matea scrabbled through her large

embroidered handbag before piping up. "You might be interested in these," she said handing a small packet to Patrick in the front. "My friend thought you should see them."

While Patrick drew out half a dozen grainy black-and-white photographs James pulled the Land Rover onto the grass verge. "Careful with those," he said after a brief sideways glimpse at the top one, "we may be stopped again and I have a suspicion that they may not let us go so easily if they see what I think Matea has found."

"You're right there, James. Dynamite!"

After studying each one for ten seconds or so Patrick handed the prints, one by one, across to James and as the photographs were passed between the monitors a picture of systematic embargo-busting became more clear. The black-and-white images had been taken in the dark, with only the deck lights of the offloading ship offering any illumination yet it was clear that main battle tanks had been landed directly onto the dockside, using a ship's crane. The rest of the wharf was in darkness.

"They were taken," Matea leant forwards, "by my friend. One evening she found some excuse to stay late as she knew that a ship was due in in the dark. By coincidence the area suffered a power cut as the ship was docking and so the only lights available were those from the ship. And the only crane available was the ship's."

"I don't know about you Paddy," James said, "but that is not steel plate for the Brodosplit shipyard. Pity we can't see the vessel's nationality, nor her name, but this is not normal."

"I wonder who decided to turn the lights out while the ship was unloading. I know blackouts are happening all the time but even so…"

"What it confirms," said James, keeping a watchful eye on

the road ahead for military vehicles, "is that, next time, we shall have to pay a less overt visit. And one that is most definitely not part of our monitoring schedule." He turned to Matea, "Is your friend prepared to tell us when she hears of another ship coming in in the dark?"

"She is and thinks it may be during the next full moon."

"Good lass. And well done to you too, Matea. This could be invaluable."

Team Split now possessed irrefutable evidence that main battle tanks were arriving on Croatian soil and, although they knew they could have been adding two and two and probably making five, the monitors were certain they were arriving in Ukrainian-flagged ships.

In the Split office, with all the photographs laid across the desk, James turned to Matea, "Bravo, again," he exclaimed, taking hold of both hands and looking closely into her eyes. "Bravo."

Matea gently squeezed his fingers before she turned away and walked to the balcony's French windows muttering, "Now we know… now we know."

James, an unexpected thrill running through his tense body, looked across the room towards Matea's gently shaking shoulders.

"James," Patrick said softly, "Over to you, I think. I'll see you later."

Once the door had been shut as gently as possible, James stood behind Matea clasping her shoulders lightly. Without turning she whispered between shallow gulps, "I think this is the watershed. I don't know what you're going to do but I will be frightened if you do it and I will be frightened if you don't." She leaned back against his upright body, the back of her neck resting on his left shoulder.

They stood like that for a length of time that neither could remember, but long enough for James to realise that he needed her, not as an interpretress, not even as a friend but as a long-term companion... and damn the ECMM's un-written rules. He would never know what finally sparked this change in his fortune nor would she ever know what caused the same alteration in hers but, for this moment, they stayed still.

"James?" Matea finally turned to face him.

He stopped her with a finger placed lightly on her lips then said kindly, "I know why you are frightened. Don't make it worse by explaining."

"I don't want you doing anything that means you will get you hurt."

"That might be asking rather a lot. If I have this correct you will now be happy for me to report what we have found to the UN."

"Yes and no. I want my country to be strong enough to beat the Serbian Krajina army but not strong enough to evict all the civilians."

"That might be difficult to stop."

"I know that too but sadly the politicians will want to be rid of all Serbs. I just know it. I just know it," she repeated.

"You tell me. It's your country."

Wiping her eyes, Matea asked despondently, "If they do know about the embargo breaking what can the UN do?"

"In theory everything but in practice nothing without the US's agreement and that is the true conundrum. If Croatia doesn't rearm, your country will remain weak and the RSK will seek the help of greater Serbia and, one day, launch a full-scale, properly coordinated attack that would – could – destroy Croatia for ever. Do you want that?"

"Of course not but surely the European Community will

help us. Surely?" she questioned optimistically.

"I'm not so sure about that," James replied, not unkindly. "Croatia may be independent, thanks to support from some members of the EU, but it is not yet a member and with all its current problems the Europeans may not want to take on yet another responsibility. Apart from that, Europe does not have its own army, and is never likely..."

"It is not for us to decide the future," Matea argued, "It is for us to try and manipulate the present which is why I now believe we must expose the importing of arms to the UN or my worst fears will come true."

"They may well still come true," James replied, "If the Croatian army is illegally rearmed then it will do exactly what you fear and would not stop once it had beaten the Serbian army. It would want all the Krajinas cleansed of every Serb civilian. That's the stark alternative especially as, sadly, I don't see the USA bowing to any UN ultimatum. And anyway," he added, unsure that it would help, "we haven't reported it to the UN yet and I doubt that the ECMM will."

For the second time in their short conversation Matea did not know how to respond.

They had been standing facing the window, looking out across the nearby slums and towards the harbour entrance, now tinted a pale yellow as the sun began its descent beyond Brač island. Very slowly, for she was afraid of the response she might get, Matea took James's hand and held it tightly. He did not remove it.

Plucking up a courage she was not sure that she had Matea said slowly and softly, "I want to look after you more than I can tell but I also want you to look after my country," then she straightened her back to face James squarely. "Now I must go and collect Dino," she said.

James, surprised by this unexpected confession said nothing as Matea kissed him firmly on his cheek, picked up her bag and walked out of Team Split's office. Elated and yet anxious, he stood for five minutes, watching the light fade over Split. He hadn't responded to her last words for they might have been very much his own words... and he felt that any relationship, if there was to be one, had to evolve slowly.

He locked the office door and took the stairs down to the Riva Bar.

"James I bought you a beer. Drink it before it goes flat."

"Matea is a little mixed up," James declared, determined to mask his excitement, "she wants the Krajina business to be solved but does not want it to be solved militarily unless the Croatian army can guarantee that it is only the Serbian army it defeats."

"We are merely monitors James. Our job is to expose the breaking of the embargo while others, way beyond our level, pick up the pieces."

"We need proof. Grainy black-and-white photographs and tracks in the sand are only a start."

"Which is why we should establish, for one night only if necessary, an observation post overlooking the port. If Matea's friend is as good as her word and if the next ship," James opened his pocket diary, "is due during the coming full moon, which I see is not until Sunday 27 March, we have a little time to set it up."

"Without telling anyone?"

"No one!"

Team Split's Daily Report that evening mentioned the visit but not what had been seen.

The following morning, Friday 4 March, began normally ... until the telephone rang.

"Laidlaw speaking."

"Laidlaw?"

"Yes," James replied, instantly on his guard.

"It is Monsieur Sublette that is speaking and you are to listen very carefully."

"Ah, good morning Jean-Claude," James replied as sweetly as he dared. "How can I help you?"

Over the previous weeks the only messages to come from Knin had been a stream of confusing orders that even Pagonis had been unable to decipher. To suggest that the Greek was becoming an ally would, James knew, be putting gloss on an awkward situation although both, privately, acknowledged that they faced a common foe.

"You were yesterday at Ploče?" accused Sublette.

"Absolutely right we were," James began the fight back. "It was on our patrol schedule which you must have seen before we went. By your silence, we presumed you agreed it." Keen not to let Sublette get a word in until James was ready he continued swiftly, "I'm not happy with the way that the port is being managed. The casual manner in which imports are checked, or not checked, means that there is no control over cargoes either in or out and certainly no records. And another thing…"

"No 'other things', Mr Laidlaw." Jean-Claude Sublette's voice was at its highest pitch, "I hereby forbid you, absolutely, to visit Ploče until I say so. Which I will not do. And that includes the islands. You are to patrol daily the confrontation line. And," Sublette played what he hoped would be his trump card, "you should know that I am moving you to another post."

James ignored Sublette's last remark, "Well, Jean-Claude," he said with exaggerated politeness, "you have raised two important points. First, as it is within our mandate to monitor the commercial aspects of the port I must ask why you are forbidding us to do just that. Secondly, while we already patrol the confrontation line on an irregular basis it is the UNMOs job to report ceasefire violations. All we are required to do is pass on their reports. Shelling on both sides, as you well know, occurs so regularly it would make more sense to report the days when there is none."

"Are you telling me my job?" Sublette screamed.

James thought for a long moment, before saying quietly, "It is high time that someone did."

With a loud click the telephone went dead.

"I could have heard that Frenchman from the dining room," Patrick laughed.

"He has ordered us to stop…"

"I know!"

Before James could continue the telephone rang again. "Oh bugger it," he swore and picked up the receiver.

"James, this is Demetrios."

"Good morning…"

"I have had Jean-Claude shouting at me and thought I had better pass on the message."

"Don't bother, I've just had him on the telephone too. What do you make of it?"

"I cannot talk. Please meet me at the Sibenik Bridge layby in two hours time. Alone and in civilian clothes."

"I'll be there."

Putting down the telephone James looked across the room at Matea and repeated the brief conversation he had just had ending, "That's it for the week Matea," he smiled. "See you on Monday."

"Are you sure you don't want me to come with you?"

James surprised himself with his answer but, once said, it was too late to retract it, "I would give everything for you to come with me but Pagonis made it clear I was to be alone so I had better stick to that."

Matea, equally surprised, kissed his forehead, muttered goodbye, picked up her bag and left. Had Patrick not been watching she might have kissed James on the lips.

Two hours later James parked in Sibenik Bridge's dusty, gravelled layby. Ahead of him Pagonis, a cigar clenched between his lips, was opening his black Toyota's door.

The Greek was nervous, his hands twitched and his eyes shifted. "Come with me. I don't think we should talk in our cars," he said and led the way to the middle of the bridge where he leaned over the metal parapet staring at the river eighty feet below, his fingers tapping on the metal guard rail.

"You seem to have a problem?" James ventured.

"Well," began Pagonis, "you have the same problem..." Then he paused to study his still unlit cigar.

James was not sure whether this was for effect or whether he really did have a problem that could only be discussed over a cigar in the middle of the Sibenik bridge.

"Your recent patrol to Ploče has sparked a storm..."

James interrupted him, "Unlikely considering part of our remit is to monitor the ports and airfields."

"Let me state," Pagonis said unexpectedly, "that I, too, now believe that we should be monitoring these places rather than spending much time on the confrontation line."

Unsure where this was leading James asked, "Until you tell me what it is, I'm not sure where the problem lies especially as the port of Ploče is a commercial enterprise and so well within our terms of reference."

"The problem is Jean-Claude Sublette."

"That doesn't surprise me."

"What I'm about to say will surprise you..."

"I doubt it," James laughed softly.

"He has now forbidden all monitoring other than along the confrontation line. No monitoring of tourist areas, no monitoring of commerce, no monitoring of trade or, rather, the lack of it."

"We can't spend every day along the confrontation line. For a start it's mined and not marked properly, if at all, and from my brief experience the Croatian army is just as likely to fire at us as on the Serbs."

"I agree."

"Sublette may be the Head of the Regional Centre but even he has to answer to the Head of Mission who, as you are aware, is a countryman of yours."

"That's why I have asked you to meet me. I want you to continue monitoring the port and, when you think necessary, the islands. We are of course not looking for signs of anyone breaking the embargo but we are required to study and assessing the overall economic future and the eventual regeneration of tourism."

"Fair enough. I take it you will sort this out with Jean-Claude."

"Sadly, James, it is not that easy."

"Seems straightforward to me."

"Jean-Claude need never know," Pagonis said quietly, staring at his cigar.

"He will read our Daily Reports."

"He will read your Daily Reports but, from now onwards, they will not be a true account of what you have been doing."

James, sensing the beginnings of a chill invading his spine, stalled for time. Deciding on a straightforward approach he eventually said, looking directly at the Greek's right cheek, "Demetrios, are you suggesting that I falsify my daily reports?"

It took Pagonis some time to reply, "You will continue patrolling as you have been doing, but you will deny going anywhere near the ports and islands. Instead you will fabricate your patrol reports in a manner such that Jean-Claude is not likely to know where you have actually been. I'll leave that up to your ingenuity... while you send me the truth of where you go and what you find," he paused momentarily, "...or what you don't find."

Appreciating that this was yet one more watershed in his short career with the ECMM there was no question of James 'falsifying' anything. He would not, in all conscience, risk his reputation by resorting to lies. He also knew that it would take some time to conceive a way round this impasse: short of a swift resignation.

Choosing his words with care he retorted, "You're asking me to do something that is totally against everything I understand." He faced Pagonis, now glaring at the river below. Resisting an urge to smash his fist into the Greek's head James grabbed a shoulder firmly and physically forced him round. "Do you really think," he was almost snarling with indignation, directly into the Greek's face, "I can fake my official reports as a monitor of the European Community Monitoring Mission? Do you really think you can ask me to do that with a clear conscience?"

"The French do not want to know the truth or they might have to act on it which is why Jean-Claude is making this rule. But the rest of us do need to know what is happening."

"Why?" James was not sure that his shaking hands were due to a rising anger or a rising desire to push Pagonis over the parapet. He thrust them into the pockets of his jacket before they did something he might regret. He asked again, "Why do the French not want to know the truth."

"If they know what is going on, if it is going on, they will have to prevent it. And that they do not want to do."

"And the Greeks do I suppose."

"What the Greeks want is not your business."

"It bloody well is if I'm the guy who is going to do your dirty work for which I will then get the blame."

"I had hoped you would not see it like that, James."

"A forlorn hope because that is exactly how I do see it. What I don't understand is that all you had to do was ask me to send my Daily Reports direct to you without copying them to Jean-Claude, as we do at the moment, and then you could doctor them to your heart's content. Without involving me."

"If Jean-Claude asked you about something he thought you had done and you hadn't known that that had been in your report you would smell a rat."

"Not as big a rat as I am smelling at the moment," James spat, barely controlling his disgust, "He doesn't speak to us monitors and as you probably know he is trying to move me so I am still not sure why you have asked me to do this."

"I thought I could trust you to help."

"Help who, you scheming bastard."

"So you won't do as I ask? Indeed I order you to do as I ask since you are working under me as an ECMM monitor."

"We'll see about that. In the meantime I will speak to my Head of Delegation and see what he thinks, although I will have no trouble in guessing."

What little colour was left in Pagonis's face drained away. His tanned skin turning a cadaverous and ghostly shade of chalky yellow. "Will that be necessary?" he asked quietly in a voice close to breaking, "Will that really be necessary?"

Unexpectedly and unknowingly, James had hit the most raw of the Greek's sensitive nerves.

Realising that he had misjudged his erstwhile colleague,

Pagonis changed tack, "Suppose we forget this whole meeting as your Head of Delegation is the one person who I must keep as a friend."

"You have a bloody funny way of going about it."

"I am not used to people disobeying my orders so I will repeat my question but in a different way."

"Ask it in anyway you like, Demetrios, but the answer will be no."

"You could always say you have been to the port but seen nothing. As you have already done!"

"Comes to the same thing." James was not in a conciliatory mood. If this was how the Greeks were going to run the mission for the next six months he wanted nothing to do with it. It was time he left the bridge over the Krka river, retired to Hotel Split and re-entered what passed for a saner world.

"Sorry, Demetrios, I can help you no further. I'll continue monitoring – and reporting – as we have been until someone more senior tells me to stop."

"Were you not trained to obey orders in the Royal Navy."

"Not illegal ones as clearly you are happy to do in your navy."

Unable to search for the correct words Pagonis stepped back from the parapet.

"I hoped we could have been friends and worked together," he glowered sideways at James as they walked back along the narrow pavement towards the layby then, throwing his unlit cigar into the river growled unpleasantly, "but your bloody British principles seemed to have got in the way."

"My bloody British principles, as you call them, are what keeps us on the correct track."

"Not in this part of the world they don't. A part of the world that you have no interest in and should have no influence over."

"I don't accept that," James retorted quickly, "Honesty and straight dealing might have prevented this whole dreadful business from getting to the impasse that we are in today."

As Pagonis made no reply, James continued until they stopped by their cars. "And you haven't explained why it is so important that Greece knows what is happening and why it is equally important that France does not."

"I would have thought that was obvious."

"It may be obvious but I would still like to hear it from your lips." James was not going to let Pagonis off the 'intelligence hook' but the reply he received was a car door being slammed shut and the screech of tyres as the Greek accelerated west across the bridge leaving a fleeting glimpse of a second head silhouetted behind the tinted back window.

James turned his Land Rover for home and, in deep thought, drove slowly. Pagonis had to have guessed that James could not, would not, accept his instructions while Sublette, too, should have predicted that any such restriction to his monitoring duties could also lead to a resignation. He might call both their bluffs, together, at the same time but whatever his decision, he could not continue under Sublette's present rules or Pagonis's current demands.

It was March, his contract ended in May yet, away from the coast – the only alternative to resignation – he would be of no use to Magnus Sixsmith. But, and he knew it was becoming the largest but of all, he was attracted to Matea and, it would appear, she was beginning to look to him for stability in her own troubled life. He needed time to think things through, calmly and methodically.

Patrick was in the office, his feet and a plate of biscuits on the table, a cup of tea in his hand.

"You look pretty relaxed," James began.

"With you away and Matea away I decided to read Team Pula's patrol reports."

"We are not on their distribution list."

"Your friend Roger Samson called in while you were with Pagonis and seemed to think they would interest you. And they will," Patrick tossed the papers onto the table with a chuckle.

"What have they discovered?"

"Pula's monitors recently watched three suspiciously large, wooden crates being unloaded from a Ukraine-registered ship using its own derricks, at dusk after the stevedores had gone home. They demanded to see the ship's manifest." Patrick stopped to take a swig of tea.

"Go on, Paddy," James was impatient. "Something so significant should have been disseminated around all the teams. It's crazy that we are not allowed to see other reports until they have been sanitised by the various HQs."

"According to the paperwork," Patrick continued, "the ship was carrying general goods dispatched for the benefit of refugees by one of the non-government organisations in Estonia, although she then called in at Bremerhaven after passing through the Kiel canal. The Pula team were not convinced so asked to see inside one of the containers. The ship's master, unaware of what he was carrying, agreed. The sight of a fighter aircraft's wing was all the team needed to know."

"Under normal circumstances, that should be enough to convince Sublette that we must continue monitoring Ploče but after what I have heard today it will probably strengthen his view that we should go nowhere near the port..."

"I was going to ask," Patrick chipped in, "how did this afternoon go?"

"Let me just say it was a crunch-time meeting best discussed over a proper drink."

"If you mean a gin and tonic. It must be serious."

"It is."

In the ECMM dining room they chose a table away from the Forward Logistics Group then, settled with plates of cold chicken legs and olives, James explained his meeting with Pagonis in precise detail. Patrick did not interrupt until, at the end, James suggested that the Greek had not been alone.

"Who else do you think was in the car?"

"No idea but I suspect it wasn't male!"

"Par for the course. Whoever it was will also know what you have just described to me."

"His so-called interpreter is not a valid member of the ECMM and thus has no loyalty other than to Pagonis."

Passing various ideas between themselves throughout the meal helped James to make up his mind. He would start by challenging Sublette with the suggestion that it was now imperative that the southern port was also checked. It was his duty to do so, he would argue, and if Sublette did not see it that way it would need to be discussed with the Greek Head of Mission in Zagreb.

Before that, though, he would ask Magnus Sixsmith for a breakdown of the international naval flotilla responsible for enforcing the arms embargo at sea. If he was to face down Sublette his facts had to be meticulously correct and up-to-date. He would telephone the British Consul first thing in the morning.

James slept well despite a niggle deep in his consciousness. Whatever decision he might make towards resigning or demanding an inland posting for the remainder of his current contract might affect Matea. These thoughts began as mere wisps drifting through the back of his mind but by the time sleep enveloped him they had hardened into a resolve that most definitely would involve Matea.

"Augustin," James called on the British Consul the next day, "would you be kind enough to ask Magnus a few simple questions. Despite it being a Saturday." Laughing, he handed across the table a piece of paper with his queries written in longhand.

"Certainly," Augustin replied, "knowing him I'll have the answer by the end of the day."

"Brilliant. Now one for you. What range does your motorboat have at its top speed?"

"Two hundred and fifty nautical miles with two persons on-board and at 35 knots. Less of course with four up and stores but greater at, say, 25 knots."

True to his prediction Augustin telephoned Team Split's office that evening, not with Magnus's answers but with the suggestion that they met somewhere different.

"Not Sibenik bridge I hope?"

"Whatever made you think that?"

"I'll explain when I see you."

The meeting took place in a café James had not visited, well back from the crowded waterfront, where Augustin took out a slim white envelope from an inner pocket. "I think you'll find all you need is in here," he said. "Open it if you like, you may have some supplementary queries."

James pulled out the single sheet of paper and read a précis of the duties of the international fleet, together with a list of the warships involved, their operating schedules and specific patrolling 'boxes'.

By the next morning James knew that he was at a crossroads, nevertheless, relaxed and composed he dialled Sublette's telephone number.

JCS answered immediately. "*Qui*, Sublette."

"Good morning Jean-Claude."

"What do you want?"

"I've been reading the most recent patrol report from Team Pula and it seems that they have discovered a serious case of embargo-busting." James then added for good measure, "Fighter aircraft."

"How did you know? I demand to know who handed you these informations."

"That is immaterial. The important fact is that if it is happening in the northern port it is, as sure as hell, happening in the southern port. And another point is this, the ships seem to be operating under flags of convenience and yet no matter what flag they are sailing under they avoid the coalition fleet offshore, for which France, Germany and the United States, among many others, supply warships to the Standing Naval Force Mediterranean engaged in what is called Operation Sharp Guard. I will be surprised if a member of the French DGSE has not heard of this."

Sublette had not heard of Operation Sharp Guard. "Of course I know of this… this operation," he stuttered, horrified that not only had he no idea of French participation but he had no idea either that anyone knew that he was from the DGSE and not the Quay d'Orsay. Sublette did not enjoy one of his monitors knowing more than he did.

"In which case," Patrick rubbed it in, "you will know that two of the four French ships, the *Jean Bart* and the *La Fayette* carry helicopters which are ideal for landing inspection parties on suspect vessels."

From the silence at the other end of the telephone James knew that he had scored an important hit if not exactly a bullseye. Riding the silence he continued, "And I have a sneaking suspicion that if I find out which warships are on patrol off Pula and Ploče each time the embargo is breached I will lay you a bet that they will be either French, German or American."

"I have already forbidden you to be involved in Ploče. You will obey me. It is not your remit to do these things."

James thought for a few seconds. "Jean-Claude," he began again, his voice now suggesting a degree of menace, "It is, precisely, within Team Split's duties. As you very well know. And unless I hear from the Head of Mission himself that we are not to visit Ploče I shall continue to do so."

"You will not speak behind my back."

"Will you allow the patrolling of Ploče to continue?"

"I will not."

"That settles it."

Incensed by this attack Sublette made a decision he had long delayed. "You are sacked. As from this moment you are sacked. I will hear no more from you. Do you understand."

James, half expecting this pronouncement, replied, carefully enunciating each word so that Sublette would not be mistaken. "You cannot sack someone who has already resigned."

After a pause the Frenchman replied, "You will not retire. You English are here for the money."

"Sacked. Retired. Resigned. All adds up to the same thing financially and, since you mention it, I do not need the money."

"You all do," Sublette screamed at the man likely to be responsible for his final dénouement as a DGSE officer unless he could disgrace him or have him removed first. Preferably both at the same time, *avant de la chaussure était sur l'autre pied.*

"I mean what I have just said." James spoke as though to a child unable to listen to reason. "I have resigned and in my resignation letter I will describe the reasons very carefully." Then, playing a card he did not believe he had but was prepared to risk, James continued, "And I will make sure that a copy of my resignation letter is sent, personally, to the head of your DGSE."

For the second time in as many telephone conversations with Sublette the line went dead.

James had not meant to resign quite so quickly or so peremptorily and certainly not before discussing his decision with Patrick, CC and – especially – Matea. He would tell Patrick immediately: CC and Matea could wait until Monday by when he would have decided how to explain his decision.

CHAPTER TWENTY-TWO

Sunday 6th March 1994
Headquarters, 4th Guards Brigade, Hotel Resnik,
Put Resnika, Kaštela, Croatia.

By Sunday lunchtime Slavić had had his office in Hotel Resnik rearranged into an impromptu dining room. The weather, too, was playing its part with light winds and a warm sun reflecting off the calm waters of Split's outer harbour. The colonel's ulterior motive was simple. He needed, once more – this was becoming tedious – to make it plain, but not so plain to alert that suspicions, that there was no need for the ECMM to monitor the ports and islands. He had failed with Monsieur Gaspard, now he must work on the Frenchman's weaker successor whom, he hoped, would be more accommodating. As for Matea, Team Split's only interpreter, she would do nothing that would endanger her Croatian parents in Drniš: Serb apologists who had not escaped back to their home country, the breaking of the embargo would certainly place them in jeopardy. He wasn't yet sure of the Greek, despite Sublette at their last meeting stating that Pagonis would do as he was told... but, from the few telephone conversations they had had, Pagonis appeared a powerful man not likely to acquiesce to a Frenchman.

The wine was chilled – Slavić had already tasted two glasses to make sure – and the simple hors-d'oeuvre of grilled sardines, sent across from Hvar island, equally delicious. As the weather wasn't yet warm enough for something lighter he had asked the hotel's chef to produce a goat stew.

Now all he had to do was persuade the ECMM's new coastal monitors to stop watching Ploče – Pula was not in his bailiwick – keep them away from Brač and, if successful on both counts, he would be heading for national fame and, of more importance, personal fortune.

He poured a third glass of wine then looked towards the door as a timid knock announced the arrival of the Frenchman. Slavić glanced at the window to make sure it was at least half open.

"My dear Jean-Claude, welcome yet again." Slavic advanced towards him, hand stretched further forward than might be considered normal for he had yet to receive the extra bottle of aftershave from Zagreb. "No trouble at the border I hope."

"None, thank you," Sublette said looking past his host at the table set with five places. "We will not be alone?" he observed, abruptly nervous.

"I want you to meet the American Defense Attaché. Another guest is Matea Marković, whom I believe you may have met as she is Team Split's interpreter. Then there will be Demetrios Pagonis who, as I understand it, is responsible to you for the monitoring in southern Dalmatia."

"Why is the girl important?"

"She has many reasons to hate the Serbs and, because she has an entrée direct into Team Split, she may well be persuaded to exercise her feminine wiles and thus influence the team's day-to-day decision-making."

"That is my job," Sublette answered prickly.

"Of course my dear Jean-Claude," Slavić was quick with his reply, "but she is an attractive widow and is Laidlaw not also a widower?"

Before Sublette had a chance to explain Laidlaw's latest position the door opened and Dwight Anderson walked in dressed in the day uniform of an officer in the United States Army with the spread-eagle badges of rank on his shoulders and shirt collar, indicating that he was a full- or 'bird-colonel'.

"Bravo, Dwight," Slavić gushed, "sorry you had such a long journey..."

Anderson cut him short, "Not long. I stayed in Makarska. Down the coast from here, opposite the east end of Brač."

"There was room in the hotel?"

"Not until I waved a fistful of 'greenbacks' in the landlord's face," Anderson laughed coldly. "Always works. Who's your friend?"

Turning to Sublette, now clutching a glass of water, Slavić introduced him by name and appointment. As he finished Matea, in a light coloured, woollen dress, heavy cotton jacket topped by a striking dark red and blue, paisley-pattern scarf tied loosely around her neck, was standing in the entrance shaking off her coat.

Unable to guess why Colonel Slavić had asked her to join him for Sunday lunch she had accepted for the simple reason that she still held a residue of loyalty towards one of her country's more senior army officers. She didn't like his openly-expressed desire to see the extermination of the Serbs but... well maybe even he could change his mind.

It was inevitable that Captain Pagonis would make a late and swaggering entrance, nodding curtly in Sublette's direction he then smiled at Matea for a little too long. She turned away as the Greek faced Dwight Anderson, angry at himself for not also appearing in his own national uniform. He said, without offering a handshake, "I am a captain in the Hellenic Navy.

Maybe we have something to talk about."

Anderson muttered, unconvincingly, that he hoped so too.

To his host Pagonis simply said, "I am glad we meet face to face and not on the telephone." Then, pointing to the table, added, "If that is Croatian wine please may I have a gin and tonic."

Slavić led the way to the dining table that had been placed across the French windows. Sitting at the head he placed Anderson on his right with Matea opposite. Next to the American was Sublette while, opposite him, Pagonis sat on Matea's left side.

"Now," Slavić raised his glass, "I would like to praise the work of the ECMM's monitors."

"Quite so," muttered Anderson, not sure where the charade was heading, but grateful to have had the excuse to watch Brač from the mainland. He had seen nothing and had hoped to see nothing. Right now, and apart from the helicopter crash, it was 'so far so good' with the first of the C-130 Hercules and their sensitive cargos due shortly: he certainly did not want any monitor in the way when that happened and he would have to rely on Slavić to make sure there were none.

"Jean-Claud," Slavić looked towards the Frenchman, "We have already discussed your monitoring of Ploče and the islands. Remember that you agreed that you would concentrate instead on the confrontation line."

Sublette had no difficulty answering 'Yes' with a clear conscience, hoping that Pagonis was listening: but Pagonis was not listening for his right hand was creeping closer to Matea's left thigh beneath the table cloth while his brain pondered the unlikely event that she would resist a captain in the Hellenic Navy.

"I have instructed my teams not to monitor Ploče and

the islands," Sublette droned on, "As you asked when we last met, Ante. But you must continue to assure me that Croatia has nothing to hide for if we hear it has then we might have to reconsider our plans."

Slavić looked hard at the Frenchman. Pagonis, briefly disregarding what his right hand was up to, looked even harder at Sublette.

"And you Captain Pagonis," asked Slavić, "I have no right to ask this in front of your boss," Pagonis flinched at the description, "but it is my country. I take it you will be telling your Team Split to do as Monsieur Sublette commands."

"I will follow orders," Pagonis smirked, without clarifying whose.

"Well this is all good news I must say," Slavić announced cheerfully, then turning to Colonel Anderson he said, "And you Dwight. Do you have anything you would like to add?"

"The United States is complying fully with the terms of the UN embargo," he lied, certain that such incompetents that made up the ECMM monitoring teams would not discover the truth. "Rest assured that any ship caught carrying arms will be turned away. Added to that, my intelligence reveals that you, in Croatia, should concentrate all your energy onto the border. Look east and continue looking east would be my strong advice. Or," he tapped the table, "you may miss a Serbian trick."

Pagonis, ignoring Anderson's advice, asked, "And those ships that are not caught? May I rely on Mr Laidlaw to do his duty?"

"The world's most powerful navy," Anderson replied mischievously, "is patrolling offshore with the prime aim of ensuring Croatia's security so I don't think you need bother Mr Laidlaw with that task."

Sublette, equally roguishly, countered with a bombshell,

"Laidlaw would have done as I ordered him had he not resigned from the Mission yesterday.

Matea, shocked, looked up from her sardines, hardly daring to speak, "Are you sure? I didn't know that."

Quick with his reply, the Frenchman asked, "Why should you need to? You are only a civilian employee."

Sensing an opportunity to speak in her defence Pagonis butted in. "As you will learn, Jean-Claude," his comment was waspish, "the interpreters know more of what is happening than the monitors themselves for they hear both sides of all conversations. That is their job." His right hand, now on top of the table, reached for Matea's to give it a supportive squeeze in public but she jerked it away violently, accompanied by such an intense scowl that even Pagonis – well used to such rejections – looked surprised.

"Good," said Slavić, not believing his own words, "that is one of my worries removed…"

"…and mine…" Anderson confirmed.

"…when did this happen?" asked Pagonis.

"Yesterday. I told him not to monitor Ploče and as that was unacceptable to him he resigned on the spot."

Pagonis, regaining his calm added, "He was an honest monitor and there are not many of those here."

"Perhaps," Anderson suggested with a grin, "you can be too honest in this game of yours."

"And your part, in this too-honest game of ours," parodied Pagonis, "is what?" Answering his own question he continued quickly, "Making sure that the UN's embargo remains intact I trust."

"The US will always support UN embargos."

"Lady and gentlemen," admonished Slavić, "may I bring us back to the point of this meeting which is to ask that you," he looked at each ECMM member in turn, "trust the Croatian army to ensure that no illegal arms pass through Ploče while my soldiers ashore in the ports back up the work of the US-led, international fleet offshore."

Sublette raised a hand, "In that case I will not stand in the way of the army's duties."

Matea, looked hard at her companions through eyes clouding with disbelief that a more positive attitude towards monitoring the arms embargo was not being taken by the very organisation empowered to do so. To her it was obvious – the body language, the over-firm assurances – that the Mission was being expected to turn a blind eye to something that was already happening. It was time she entered the discussion, "My country will never be strong enough to beat the RSK army unless we re-arm," she said while Slavić nodded his approval, "but if we re-arm there will more killing..." Slavić's nodding slowed down, "...and we can only re-arm by breaking the embargo."

Slavić began to scowl now as Matea spoke to the quiet room, "If the embargo is broken the UN will be powerless, because of the influence of those who will be doing the breaking." Slavić nodded again but less enthusiastically as Matea came to her unexpected conclusion, "Therefore, it is far better that the ECMM, as the only unaligned and impartial party, tries to ensure, by aggressive monitoring, that the embargo remains intact. In the long term that has to be the best way forward for the Mission for the Mission carries more clout than the UN in this part of the world and the last thing anyone should want is more bloodshed."

Slavić now shook his head vigorously, as it was the shedding of Serbian blood that he very much had in mind, "Unless, of course" Matea ended enigmatically, "my country can promise that any arms imported, from whatever source, will only be used to beat the Serb military and not subjugate the Serb people..." she paused before driving her point home... "Except that even that would be illegal."

Following this outburst of morality the two ECMM men stared at Matea with barely supressed admiration. To Slavić, though, this was a morality verging on treason. "Who has been putting these ideas into your head, my dear," he said silkily, adding with more menace, "I hope it isn't your parents in Drniš for we need to teach those Serb bastards, among whom they live, a lesson and if the embargo is broken then monitoring of the coast will become a waste of the ECMM's precious time as the UN will be powerless to do anything about it," he paused before adding chillingly, "But I think you have already established that."

"Colonel Slavić," Matea was quick to pounce and her repost was direct, "If I have this right, you expect the embargo to be broken so," she paused to add emphasise to her final words, "... and so it will be broken and..." she paused again, uncertain whether or not to declare her hand and, by inference that of the man with whom she knew suddenly – in this instant – she was falling in love, "...is almost certainly being broken." In the hostile silence that followed Matea added firmly but sweetly, "Surely?"

"How the hell can you say that young lady," Anderson butted in, his face and head already reddening, the deepening colour showing through his thin crew-cut, "Do you have proof?"

"None... yet!" Matea replied with an honesty that verged on the dangerous for she knew that even that simple last word, added deliberately as an apparently-innocent afterthought, could stand her into to danger, yet the hypocrisy and deceit to which she had been listening had forced her to, as it were, imply intent.

She knew this was hazardous territory not only for herself but also the Defense Attaché who, without thinking, attacked immediately while barely controlling an underlying anger. "What are you implying, miss? If you are suggesting that all you need is hard evidence when we all know there isn't any then you'll be in real trouble if you start spreading unsubstantiated rumours." Anderson turned to Sublette, himself motionless with astonishment, and snarled, "She works for that warped organisation of yours so take control of the bitch or, by Christ, I'll get Colonel Slavić to do so instead!"

In the stunned silence following this unexpected outburst of vulgar anger, and conscious that his agenda was in danger of collapsing, Slavić changed the subject, fearful that further discussion might lead to an open reversal of all that he sought. He would, though, have to speak to Anderson as soon as the other guests had left.

Outside, as Matea was opening her car door, Pagonis approached noiselessly from behind and gently placed his hand on hers as it gripped the handle. She jumped instinctively, turning on her heel as she did so.

"Now that James is no longer with us," the Greek naval captain leered, uncomfortably close to Matea's face, "and as you seem to know more than any of us I want you to be my personal interpreter." He hesitated then added, "I'll tell Camille tomorrow that you have agreed."

Pagonis pressed the length of his body against hers, pushing her against the side of her car, as a hand started to stroke her upper thighs through her woollen dress. If she didn't act quickly it would be too late, or could even be taken as acquiescence, especially as she was conscious of Pagonis's growing excitement.

With every ounce of strength she could summon her free hand smashed into his face. It was not a slap, and not intended to be one, but a full-bloodied, clenched-fist, sideways swipe designed to hurt. And it did. The Greek naval captain would soon be sporting a black left eye, a bruised nose and lips that would remain swollen for days.

"You bitch," Pagonis bawled as blood streamed from his nostrils, staining his cream-coloured, silk shirt, printed tie and suit. "My God I'll make sure you never work for the…" He staggered backwards towards his car, anxiously digging in a pocket for a handkerchief, unable to say more as his mouth and nose filled with gore.

"If it's full of people like you then I don't care." Free of the threat, Matea spoke with disarming coolness.

Pagonis, furious, stunned, embarrassed and blood-soaked, stood in the near-empty car park as Sublette drove slowly past, grinning broadly.

In Slavić's office Dwight Anderson was also trying to say good bye. "I've no idea what the point of that meeting was, Ante, but to begin with I thought they were off the scent. Then that goddam girl hinted that it was only a matter of time before they have the proof they need, and that can only have come from Laidlaw. With him out of the way I thought we could relax but now I worry what she might discover."

Slavić was quick with his response, "I think it wise if I issue an innocent-sounding press release that will pre-empt anything she might say. We can state that we now know that it was an American aircraft that had an engine malfunction during a coastal navigational training exercise and that the US Embassy has been doing all it can to help repair any damage and support the bereaved."

"Fine, do that Ante but I would also hope that you will silence that blasted interpreter before she does any harm."

Slavić, who had more than his reputation to lose if the

embargo was to be enforced through the public accusations of a 'mere ECMM lady interpreter', needed no orders from Anderson to stop Matea. "I'll get my people to take care of her," he assured the American. "You can be certain that your project, what ever it really is," he added with a sheepish smile, "is safe while I will also take care of the embargo issues. You needn't worry about that side of things."

But it was precisely 'that side of things' that worried Colonel Anderson most.

CHAPTER TWENTY-THREE

Monday 7th March 1994
Team Split Office, Hotel Split, Put Trstenika 19,
Split, Croatia

"Colin? James here." The telephone line to Zagreb was unusually clear, thus less secure than normal.

"How's Team Split?"

"No idea. I'm no longer a member!"

"You had better explain."

"I will, face to face."

"Roger!" CC replied in acknowledgement, "I'll take no action and in the meantime assume there is a good reason."

"There is," assured James, "a very good reason." He replaced the handset.

Before James could rise from the desk a firm hand grasped his shoulder. Without turning he knew that its owner was crying. Matea, arriving for work, had heard his voice from the corridor and crept in.

"You can be a bastard, James," she gasped. Then, without thinking of the long term consequences that might follow such admissions, blurted, "If I didn't love you so much I would hit you harder than I hit Pagonis yesterday."

James, unexpectedly confronted with two opposing emotions, one of love and one clearly of hate, stopped. He was not expecting either although both were more than welcome. "Matea, you're crying and I can't take that?"

"I said I loved you but I think it was wasted…"

"Never!"

"I also said that you can be a bastard for planning to leave the ECMM without telling me." Matea, appalled at admitting her feelings in such an unsubtle manner – even before she had analysed them herself – knew that the thought of James leaving the ECMM within days had forced her hand: it had to be now or never. Over the previous weeks she had felt a growing strength each time he was near and understood, too, that this was not a deliberate act on her part: it was happening subconsciously to the point that she now, quite intentionally, hoped that he might feel the same.

James, not expecting these revelations, had no idea how to react… he knew his first duty was to explain his current predicament to Matea's satisfaction, the second was to ask what caused her to hit Pagonis, although he could guess, and his third instinct… well his third would have to wait a moment longer.

With his mind still reeling from the suddenness, and directness, of Matea's statements, James stalled for time, "If you tell me why you hit Pagonis I'll bring you up-to-date with developments."

"He tried to rape me," an exaggeration but it would do for the time being. It also dragged James's subconscious feelings crashing into the open. He turned from his chair and stood to face Matea, now stepping back, dabbing her eyes with a handkerchief.

James, uncertain how to respond to this second admission, coming so soon after her declaration of love, said lamely, "I don't want you to relive the details now but one day I'll make him bloody well pay."

"It was after Slavić's lunch party. In the car park Pagonis launched himself at me. It was over too quickly to be frightened as the moment I hit him he backed off. Made his nose and mouth bleed and with any luck he will have a black eye… and I have sore knuckles!" She then added with delightfully malicious pleasure, "Kissing his girlfriend should be painful!"

"Good for you but why did he do it at that precise moment?"

"Sublette told everyone present – and it was the first I knew too – that you had resigned from the ECMM so I suppose Pagonis thought he could stake a claim."

James took both of Matea's hands in his, looked directly into her eyes and said, "I am so sorry that you heard that way. Most definitely not part of the plan."

"Careful of my right hand," she admonished then, serious again, said more softly, "Is it true? That you have resigned."

"It is true but whether or not my resignation will be accepted is another matter. I'm sure JCS, who started it all by sacking me, will be thrilled. As it is not actually up to him to make those decisions I've booked myself onto Wednesday's shuttle. In Hotel Betonska I may be able to sort things out."

"And if things don't get sorted out, what then?"

"I guess I'll be sent on my way."

Matea's knees weakened. She sat down. James sat facing her, their knees touching.

"James," it was now Matea's turn to take his hands. After a long pause staring at their fingers, clasped together, she said softly without looking up, "I don't want that. You now know my feelings for you. And if you didn't before you do now and yet you still make no comment." She stopped before adding, almost in desperation, "Perhaps I mean nothing."

James hesitated. His desire for Matea's companionship was growing faster than his desire to see honesty prevail and yet the Mission would mean little to him if he could not follow his suspicions. If he did nothing and the RSK's army was defeated then 200,000 Serbs, plus those Croats who remained in the RSK – including Matea's Croatian parents – would be forcibly deported from their 500-year old homeland. It all boiled down to what Matea wanted for her country and whether or not he could help satisfy that desire. It also depended on the UN having the courage to face up to the Americans and Germans.

At last, and while he too looked at their hands resting on his knees, James said slowly and firmly, raising his eyes to meet hers with an intensity that almost hurt, "You mean a very great deal to me and have done ever since Hotel Adriatica was shelled but," suddenly unsure of himself and how to continue he managed to stumble on, "I came out here to do a job while taking my mind off affairs at home. Perhaps I have been pursuing the monitoring programme too rigidly, at the expense of..." he hesitated, considering his next words, "my private life."

Now it had to be all or nothing if his love of Caroline was to be matched as she deserved... and that certainly could not be forced, but before Matea could respond, the door crashed open. "Oh, Sorry," muttered Patrick, not looking sorry.

"Not at all, Paddy. As a matter of fact I was about to tell Matea why I have resigned from the Mission. Why don't you continue with the patrol by yourself. At least you'll get a good lunch from the UN Military Observers on the border."

"Good idea. I'll leave you to it," Patrick disappeared, grinning to himself.

James, still holding Matea's hands, explained what had been discussed at Sibenik bridge and how he had considered resigning then on a matter of principle – and disgust. At the time he had felt it necessary to seek a way that would not only satisfy his conscience but also produce the intelligence he sought… and if there wasn't a way it was back to St Mawes as soon as this Wednesday. He knew, though, that that would mean a clean break with Matea and he knew, too, that that was not what either wanted.

"Matea," James continued, "I may have been a bit hasty in resigning but I really did not have an alternative."

"I don't blame you but you must excuse me if it is my turn to be a little direct."

"Totally understandable."

"We are both suspicious that Croatia is rearming."

"Yes."

"And the helicopter crash has to be part of that rearming?"

"More and more I am thinking so."

"And if the UN does not react then Croatia will one day crush the RSK. Including my parents?"

"Including your parents."

Apprehensive and scared, Matea squeezed James's hands as tightly as she dared, looking into his eyes with as deep a passion as she could muster. "That cannot happen, James. That cannot happen."

"It will happen if we don't expose any wrong-doing."

"And we can't do that if you have resigned. Don't do it James, Please don't do it!"

"If I don't resign it means I will have to live a lie and I am not sure I can do that for Croatia."

"But can you do that for me, James? Can you do that for me?"

James didn't answer Matea's plea. Instead he kissed her lightly on her lips, for the first time, then lifted the telephone.

Frustrated she asked bluntly, "Who are you calling?"

"Augustin Milna," James replied dialling the British Consul's number, "With your help I will do it for you."

"There is one other confession I have to make," Matea feared that her earlier indiscretion could be an unwanted obstacle to what ever plans James was hatching and she had to tell him.

Before the telephone had time to ring in Augustin's office James replaced the handset and looked directly into Matea's eyes. "Yes?" he responded with a touch of unease.

"I hinted at the meeting that we now have reasons to be suspicious about the embargo but that we haven't established any proof. Yet. I had to tell them, James, I just couldn't go on listening to their subterfuge, their lies. I had to force them out into the open." As James said nothing, trying to consider the aftermath, the impact, of such a revelation, Matea added quietly, "Did I do wrong?"

Alleviating her obvious fear he was swift with his reply. "No, Matea. You did the right thing. We are close to discovering the truth and, when we do, it will become public soon enough. My only worry is that you will no longer be considered as a mere, impartial interpreter but as an ally of the ECMM and, worst still I suspect, of the British."

"I know, Anderson told Slavić to, in his words, 'take care of that bitch.'"

"Well, my reply to him would be that he needn't bother for it will be me that will do the caring!"

Suddenly Matea had the response she had dared to dream of, the only response she wanted to hear. She leant forwards until her lips were tantalisingly close to James's. She could smell the shaving soap he used, she could feel his soft breath on her cheeks, she could feel a passion rising within her own body and was, suddenly and excitingly, aware that he felt the same. They didn't kiss but for all the emotions that passed between them they might have done...

James picked up the telephone and re-dialled the British

Consul's number.

That evening James and Matea stood on a darkened, deserted and crumbling concrete jetty jutting from the foreshore below Hotel Split, looking down at Augustin, perched at the wheel of his speedboat. The Consul was dressed in sea boots and warm clothes topped with an oilskin. Matea and James, also in warm clothes, wore stout walking shoes. Both carried light rucksacks while a communal canvas bag containing sandwiches, spare jerseys, a thermos of hot soup and a bottle of whisky was lowered into the vessel. To a casual observer Augustin was setting off on a night-time fishing expedition, confirmed by the assortment of fishing rods that poked, ostentatiously, from the stern.

Transforming an idea into a firm plan James had known that he was going to have to walk alone into the 'hidden valley' above Bol and that he would have no excuse if caught but when he put this to Matea she had been adamant that he would need a Croatian speaker.

James was equally obstinate, "There might well be danger once I leave the road for it will be obvious that I am not a simple traveller. Anyway I am not expecting to meet anyone so I won't need an interpretress."

"And that is why I should be with you so that I can argue that we are simply," she thought momentarily before continuing, "lovers out for a stroll. A single person would be bound to attract suspicion."

"Bit far off the beaten track for a stroll don't you think? Even for lovers intent on privacy." James responded without blushing.

"Isn't that what lovers want?"

James gave in gracefully, "You had better come dressed for the part."

"Which part?" she asked with a smile.

Before setting off James had considered his position further. Officially he had been sacked by Jean-Claude Sublette and he had also resigned as a monitor but until either position was ratified by the Head of Mission in Zagreb he would still be covered by the diplomatic immunity accorded to the ECMM by the Croatian government. Nevertheless he knew that the self-imposed task upon which he was embarking straddled the fuzzy line between monitoring and intelligence gathering. Of far more importance to him, though, it would also satisfy the two promises he had so recently made to Matea: he would take care of her by keeping her close at all times while, at the same time, exposing the breaking of UN Arms Embargo 713: assuming that what was going on beyond the escarpment's lip was far from the innocent quarrying of stone.

Augustin had suggested that a visit to Brač by ferry would set tongues wagging so he had proposed taking James and Matea in his boat to a secluded spot to the east of Bol. Ashore, his eldest son, Filip, would ferry them halfway up the escarpment via a rough gravel-track from where, a quarter of a mile from the summit, they would face a further climb of just 300 feet.

Once aboard, Matea huddled on the now-familiar stern thwart with the engines idling quietly beneath her feet while James sat beside Augustin. "It's a dark night but thankfully the visibility is good at sea level so we should be able to pick up the lights as we go along," he explained, "Providing the cloud base doesn't lower much more. Right now its about 2,000 feet."

Augustin handed James a chart encased in a thick polythene cover. "This is the largest scale that I have covering our whole journey on a single sheet," Augustin explained, switching on a small red light at the end of a long flexible metal tube that allowed James to recognize British Admiralty chart 2712. The navigational brief continued, "I'll rely on you to keep track of our progress in the dark while I keep a lookout ahead for any unmarked obstacles. The initial course should be about 195 degrees by compass then, when we identify a green light flashing once every three seconds on a small island, we will be off the entrance to Milna. Where I live remember." James remembered and nodded in the dark. "By then we should have already seen the white flashing light that marks the western end of Brač. We must leave that on our port hand," he laughed, "or we will be walking to Bol!

"The channel," Augustin confirmed, "between Brač and Otok Šolta island to the west is less than half a nautical mile wide. We must be careful there as the coast either side is sparsely populated so not many shore lights to help fix our exact position. Clear of the headland we'll come round to about 210 degrees for five or so miles but you'll need to check that at the time. Then we should soon be in sight of Bol's lights and a buoy that marks the end of the spit of sand called Dugi Rat."

James squinted at the chart, identifying the lights and landmarks as Augustin continued, "Plan on travelling at 30 knots," he ordered then turned to face the stern, "Ready my dear?" he whispered loudly.

Matea was nervous and, with no idea what James's detailed plans were, was experiencing more than a hint of jumpiness. The man to whom she had now admitted her love had vaguely suggested looking at the quarry and, if it existed, the rumoured helicopter landing pad. And if there was a pad... why not? Helicopter pads by themselves do not break UN embargoes: nor, usually, do quarries.

"Right, hold tight everyone," Augustin cried, sliding the twin throttle levers steadily forwards. Accelerating away from the shore the vessel's stern sank until planning speed was achieved when the hull was able to level-out across the water's still surface rather than ploughing through it. The air was cool and with no sea running the spray burst well astern.

Settling onto the correct course they crossed the Splitski Kanal in the projected twenty minutes and as the light on Mrduja island slipped quickly past, half a cable to port, their faces were lit every three seconds by its ghostly green glow. Ahead lay the narrow channel between the islands through which they sped at a reduced 25 knots, the shoreline on either side barely visible. Reaching clear water Augustin again opened the throttles, peering ahead, concentrating hard for flotsam.

Confident of their position, James ordered. "Come to port and steer 105 degrees. The Dugi Rat buoy is about five miles ahead."

Two nautical miles beyond the dramatic spit of sand and abeam of Bol's red and green harbour lights Augustin altered course for their destination... then he suddenly brought the vessel to a complete stop. "Look at that James," he said pointing towards the shore as they wallowed uncomfortably in their own wash, "that slight glow in the low clouds above the escarpment. Never seen it before."

"The quarry?" James hazarded a guess.

"I didn't know they worked at night."

At dead slow speed Augustin manoeuvred his speedboat towards a concrete jetty. "Grab a line, James," he commanded.

With the vessel securely moored the three of them piled into the small Citroën that Filip Milna drove carefully into the village. "I'll drop dad off with some friends then we'll head for the hills. We'll turn off the main road roughly where the crash happened and see how far we can get up that track. Then you're on your own. How long do you think you will need?"

James, who had photocopied the Brač portion of the

1:100,000 map, had no idea. Although the main road was shown, marking the sharp bend close to where they had observed the aluminium planks, the map did not mark the track that Filip had mentioned.

"It's nine o'clock now," James said, "Probably an hour to complete the climb, an hour there and less than an hour to descend. Let's say three hours."

Filip thought for a moment, "I'll be back at eleven o'clock in case you are early. If you are not there by one o'clock I'll drive along the main road, past the quarry's entrance. If you see a car with its right indicator flashing that will be me."

"Filip," James was determined, "We'll be back!"

"What excuse will you use?"

"Do I need an excuse to walk at night?"

"With your lover," Matea chipped in.

"With my lover!" James happily repeated.

On reaching the sharp right-hand bend Filip swung left onto the rough track, switched to sidelights, engaged a low gear and began the climb through the scrub. After half a mile they entered a small clearing with just enough room to turn. Filip swivelled in his seat, "Can't go any further," he said.

"That's fine," James squinted in the dark at the luminous dial of his watch. "We'll be here at midnight, if not a little earlier."

"Good luck."

"Thanks. Come on Matea. Let's see what we can find."

As the rear lights of Filip's Citroën disappeared down the hill Matea and James stood still and alone. But for the glow above them, beyond the escarpment's edge, it was pitch black beneath the low cloud cover. The smell of burnt undergrowth still lingered.

"Matea," James said taking her hand, "This may not end up as planned. I have no idea what is going on here and I don't want you getting hurt."

Matea stopped him, "I don't want you getting hurt either."

"That's not the point. This is my job. It's not yours."

"As your ECMM interpreter it is my job too."

"I am not here as a monitor. This is a private matter."

"I don't see how it can be anymore."

Unable to match her logic he said simply, "Right. Let's go."

The ground was rough, the danger of a twisted ankle uppermost in their minds, but James had brought a small torch onto which he had fitted a red, glass disc. It lit about three yards in front of each footstep, far enough to find a way between the boulders and bushes yet, he hoped, not far enough to alert anyone ahead. He knew that, in theory, what they were doing was innocent but these were not normal times. He had considered blacking their faces but Matea had giggled saying that even lovers wishing anonymity did not go that far!

"As long as we keep going upwards we can't get lost," James was cheerful and, back in a familiar element, he was enjoying the dare of the unknown; enjoying the challenge of an 'operation' and enjoying it in the company of a woman whom, he knew deep down, was now a permanent part of his life. He had been hesitant to make the first move for fear of rejection, a second loss that would re-awaken the long string of memories that led all the tortuous way from Treliske's hospital to the Adriatic.

James guessed the evening would be beyond Matea's experience but it had been she that had insisted on coming. He knew nothing of the dangers towards which they might be heading especially as he puzzled why, in this time of extreme austerity, there was the need for crushed stone or rock... or whatever the quarries of Brač produced.

They climbed gingerly at first, picking their way carefully upwards towards the sharp edge of the escarpment, silhouetted clearly against the soft glow in the cloud that James estimated to be a further three hundred feet above the plateau. Behind him, her hand occasionally grasping his coat, Matea gamely kept pace. Every so often they stopped to listen and, as she stood beside him catching her breath, he leaned towards her to ask in a whisper if she was all right. She always was. As they progressed up the steep, stony incline James's confidence that she would not let him down increased.

Fifteen minutes later, scrambling forwards on his hands and knees, James sensed rather than saw that he was close to the escarpment's edge. Then the dim red beam of his torch glinted on something solid, man made, six feet ahead. He stopped immediately. Matea stumbled into his side and held his arm tightly.

"Wait here," James whispered, "There's something I don't understand."

Crawling the last few feet upwards, his legs complaining at the hard shale pressed into his knee caps and shins, he felt into the darkness not daring to use the torch now for fear of …? He did not know other than that his deeper senses were alert.

In the darkness his finger tips brushed lightly against an upright stake. He was sure it was metallic and explored further to make sure. His first, but fleeting, thought was that it was a left over from the helicopter that had crashed 300 feet down the valley. It was out of place on the mountainside and yet it felt as though it had been deliberately placed and, as his hands reached the earth, he knew that it was embedded in cement and was supporting a wire mesh fence.

Running his fingers up the lattice he felt a single strand of highly tensioned wire that stretched away either side. Moving his hands higher he leapt back clutching his fingers, trying hard not to yelp! The electric shock was not only harsh but it was a surprise and immediately confirmed his suspicions. The glow in the cloud base, now almost above them and slightly to their left, was bright, emanating from something the Croats, he assumed it was the Croats, did not want seen. He sat down beside Matea, already feeling for him in sympathy.

She leant her head close to his, "What happened?" she whispered.

"They don't want us any closer."

"How do you know?"

"Firstly, this fence is electrified and secondly it is on the far side of the hill from the quarry so they don't want anyone to see anything either."

"Are you all right?" Matea was nursing James's hand, stroking it softly.

"It caught me by surprise. That's all."

"What do you think they are hiding?"

"If it really is a quarry then it is wise to keep people from falling in – but I would have thought any perimeter fence would be closer. Not over the hill in dead ground."

They sat together for some minutes while James's mind pondered their next move. Matea rested her head on his shoulder, pulling his hand into her lap, massaging it between her thighs. James felt the warmth of her cheek and smelt her now-familiar scent as her head rested against his, her hair gently drifting in wisps across both their faces. This is no time for seduction he thought before deciding that in this new life there was probably never a perfect time for flirting – if that was what Matea was up to. Anyway, were they not supposed to be lovers out for a night-time stroll! Some stroll, up the steepest escarpment on Brač's south coast. He did not push her away and while his mind hopped from Matea to what was beyond the fence it also kept returning to his right hand squeezed between her thighs. He said, more seriously than he meant, "We're on an operation and while I would love to sit here all night with you we must find out what it is they are hiding from us."

While pondering in which direction they should follow the fence, the lights, reflected off the base of the low stratus, suddenly brightened alarmingly. Instinctively James collapsed to one side to lie prone on the slope, dragging Matea with him, hugging her close.

"James!" she exclaimed as he smothered her.

"Don't move," he was blunt. "Something's happening." Without any idea why other than that it seemed sensible, James tugged a small pocket compass from a trouser pocket.

Matea did as she was told. She, too, had seen the light's new intensity but had thought nothing of it, now she flattened herself further into the scrub and shale, terrified yet determined to evade what ever it was that was approaching and making the strangest noise she could recall. As this unknown threat – she was certain it was a threat – increased swiftly in pitch and volume she wriggled herself sideways, even closer to the safety of James's torso as a massive, dark shape overhead blacked out, fleetingly, the cloud three hundred feet above them.

While the muted roar from the object subsided James pushed Matea aside. Standing as high as he could, he sensed rather than watched an aircraft's unlit, but silhouetted, form sink below the near horizon and aimed his compass in the same direction. As the din of four propellers, pulled into reverse thrust, reached him he had no further doubts. The Alison T56 turbo-prop engines were more deafening now than the earlier muffled-whistling of air flowing past wing flaps set at 100 per cent and throttled-back engines. James knew that he had just witnessed a variant of a Lockheed Hercules C-130 transport aircraft landing into Brač's quarry.

"Bloody hell," he said, "Bloody hell."

"What is it?" Matea stood alongside him now. Scared. He could feel her body shaking with fear or cold… or both.

Now it was James who felt for Matea's hand. He pulled it close to his chest. "I think this is beyond my monitoring duties. No wonder Slavić does not want us or anyone else anywhere near here."

"What was it?" Matea asked again, "It can't have been an aeroplane."

"That was a heavy-lift transport 'plane coming in to land."

"You mean the same type that we saw," she corrected herself, "you saw, at Supetar the other day with Slavić?"

"The very same."

"But there is no airport here. The colonel told me."

"Well, there is now and we need to know what it is being used for. Hold the torch while I look at the map."

Sensing him switching to a mood she did not recognise Matea said, "James this isn't for us. You are supposed to be monitoring the Croats not the Americans."

"I'm no longer in Team Split and, anyway, I now think they are one and the same."

As they spoke, the lights above, still bouncing off the clouds, dimmed leaving them in the same near darkness they had known before the C-130's arrival. James knelt with the map across his knees, guiding Matea's hands to where he wanted the red light to be shone. As he did so she felt a pleasant shiver ripple through her arms and into her breasts. James remained still for a minute, his brain calculating distances, heights and speeds. Then he broke the silence, "We are as near as dammit at the top of the escarpment and the aircraft was roughly 150 feet above us so, if it had been a British RAF Hercules from the Special Forces Flight of 47 Squadron conducting a special forces operation it would be a quarter of a mile from touch down at a landing speed of about 96 knots. When the radio altimeter, set for 17 feet, bleeps the pilot will ease back on his control column, pull back the four throttles and," he gave a little laugh, "wait for the bump. If he's happy he will then engage maximum braking and reverse thrust until it stops. The USAF with their heavier aircraft do things slightly differently but, either way, it means I can calculate that we are to the right of the glide path with the runway's threshold about 500 feet away and slightly to our left."

"And the extra lights?"

"Runway lights. A rare luxury for special forces operations. These were switched on at the last moment then switched off once the aircraft had stopped. Bloody clever approach with this low cloud." He was thinking aloud, "Terrain following radar. Probably infra-red, forward-looking television as well."

James's thoughts were three quarters of a mile away in the cockpit of the taxiing C-130. Closer to home he was still, subconsciously, holding on to Matea's hand. A hand that remained resting on his thighs, holding down the scrap of map he had unfolded.

"Even laden the Hercules can land in under 2,000 feet and take off in slightly less but I would guess that the runway would never have been built under 4,000 feet. Of course I have no idea why it was built in the first place but it must have been before the Yanks became involved. So it is probably between 4 and 6,000 feet to cater for most short-haul or small, local civilian aircraft."

He took a biro from an inside pocket and scored the rough alignment and his estimated length of the runway on the map then looked up at Matea in the pale light, "I'll award you a prize if I am right." He pressed her hand, forcing it deeper into his thigh with no sign that this was on purpose rather than because he needed to push himself onto his feet.

"I'm sure you will have got it right so what's the prize?"

"Dinner alone. But not in Hotel Split."

"I'll be there… but," Matea came down to earth, "what now?"

James wasn't sure. Privy to a tantalising piece of information, aircraft coming and going, even in the dark on a 'secret' airfield, wasn't proof of very much. They had to press on in the hope that somewhere the fence was not in dead ground from the airfield. He explored further with his torch. The ground either side of the barrier was beaten flat and without obstacles. On the inside it was compressed into a wider, more formal track. On the outside the ground was roughly trodden as though mouflon walked along it, but not often.

"Matea," he turned to face her, "Have you a scarf I can borrow?"

"James, really! Are you not so hot after that climb."

"I need something to mark this spot. Something dark and large?"

Matea wriggled her small rucksack off her back and produced her red and blue, paisley-pattern scarf which James tied low down on the metal fencing pole, careful to avoid the topmost strand as he tied the knot. "Now," he said, "which way to go? That is the question."

"Your decision."

"I thought I heard the aircraft move off to the left after it landed so towards, presumably, any hangers or control tower. We'll go in that direction especially as the light reflecting off the cloud base is also from there."

The going was easier on the flat but both remained warry in the dark of stumbling against the top, electrified strand. Only six feet off the ground it would have been no obstacle had it not had a significant, even excessive, voltage running through it at one-second intervals.

After a few hundred yards the fence unexpectedly angled away from them, through ninety degrees, towards the north.

James stopped, listened and checked his map. "We may be in luck," he whispered. "The land actually rises for a mile to the west across a deeply wooded slope from which the airfield will be visible. They must have bargained on no one bothering to fight their way through the undergrowth on this side whereas to the east, towards the road from Bol, the dead ground is much closer."

Matea followed his finger on the map as it traced its way around the runway that James had etched onto the paper. With the reflected light now almost above them she sensed that their journey was reaching its second climax. The aircraft had been one surprise now, she felt, they were closing in on the second.

Heading north-east and parallel with the supposed direction of the airstrip there was no doubt that they had chosen the correct side of the fence to follow. With every step it was not the lights reflected off the cloud base that were now beckoning but the increasing hum of electricity generators.

Then, almost as suddenly as the aircraft itself had appeared over their heads, a rudimentary control tower faced them through the bushes, lit by security lights, lights that also illuminated a row of low hangers. To the right, on the airfield's apron, the Hercules, with its stern ramp down, was being unloaded. James pulled a pair of mini-binoculars from inside his jacket and focussed them on the rear of the aircraft, four hundred yards away and slightly below them.

He sank to his knees, gently tugging Matea down beside him. "If you could turn round and face the action then I can rest the binoculars on your shoulder," he asked. Matea did as she was told, kneeling on the ground with James close behind her, his breath warming her right ear.

"Steady," he said, "steady. Whatever the 'plane brought is being lifted out now. Slowly does it," he encouraged the ground crew ahead of him, "Slowly does it."

Matea leaned back as lightly as she dared to feel James's chest down the length of her back while he watched the fuselage of an American, intelligence-gathering Predator, un-manned 'aerial vehicle' arriving on Croatian soil.

James swung his binoculars towards a group of three men standing at the base of the control tower's external, metal ladder. He wasn't sure and re-focussed the lenses until there was no doubt. Colonel Slavić, Colonel Anderson and a third man were engrossed in conversation with the occasional arm waving towards the scene in front of them.

"Bloody hell," he said for the third time, "Now I've seen it all. No point in hanging about once I have a picture or two. You will have to stay very still indeed as there is not much light." James replaced the binoculars with a small camera fitted with a zoom lens."

Satisfied, he tapped Matea on her shoulder. "Right, let's go home."

Matea turned. The artificial light was casting well defined shadows across their faces. The adrenaline, the excitement, even the thrill of the chase made her want him now, physically, emotionally, passionately more than she ever had… and to hell with the Americans and their war games. But now was not a good time. She knew that. James would need all his military training to assess what was going on while helping them both back to safety. Reluctantly she pushed herself away, whispering, "What have you seen?"

"I'll tell you as we go down the hill. Right now I think we should make ourselves scarce. Quickly and quietly."

As they turned to retrace their steps along the outside of the fence James froze. Not expecting such an abrupt halt Matea bumped into his back. Tripping sideways she grabbed at his coat. James hauled her up slowly until her head was alongside his.

"Lights ahead. On the move. Coming this way from where we met the fence. Can't yet make out which side of it they are on." He paused, then, "Hold tight," he commanded and began stumbling his way down the slope into the bushes pulling Matea after him. He stopped and turned, sinking to his knees as he did so. Matea followed as two small, electric-powered, moped-style 'bikes drove slowly, almost silently past on the far side of the fence, heading towards the control tower; the sound of their purring motors not carrying far. Each bore a pillion passenger waving a powerful lamp either side of their track. As they neared the hangers a passenger shouted in a voice heavily accented with a southern American drawl. Individual words, drifting back on the light northerly breeze towards them were difficult to identify, "...shoot to kill... Croat colonel... no locals... night... waste of time..."

James tugged on Matea's arm, "We must crack on in case they decide to turn round. Right now they don't know we are here." They half walked, half ran with the fence as a guide until, without turning James knew that they were being followed. He did not know how or why he knew, he just knew. He stopped to look back along the route they had covered. There was nothing there.

"Come on," he whispered loudly, "No time to waste." At the fence's right angled bend he quickened the pace. "Got to find your scarf or we'll miss the way down," he muttered between breaths, grabbing Matea's hand to make sure she kept up. Further from the airfield's buildings there was, once more, less light forcing James to risk the occasional flash of red, low down along the fence, as they passed each upright.

Unexpectedly the increasing noise of moped-mounted voices began to catch up with them. One hundred yards away, fifty yards away in the darkness. No lights this time. Just the sound of voices coming closer. James dived for cover to his right once more dragging Matea with him, wrenching on her arm.

"James!" she squealed.

"Shush!" he snapped, smothering her face with crook of his elbow.

The mopeds stopped. "All right," a voice shouted in their direction, in English. "Who the hell are you?"

James kept a hand across Matea's mouth.

Silence.

"Stand up or I'll fire."

Silence.

"One last chance. I can see you down there. You can't hide."

The second voice joined in, "Goddammit man, they're on the other side of the wire."

James felt Matea shivering, this time he knew it was a deep-down terror that was shaking her so much that the leaves on the bushes, their camouflage, began to rustle as though shouting 'over here, over here'. The only way he knew to keep her still was to roll on top of her, pinning her to the shale, facing downhill but he needn't have bothered thinking about it. Nothing was going to be heard above the sudden staccato cracking of semi-automatic gunfire that followed, the rounds smashing, zipping and whinnying through the undergrowth, ricocheting of the larger branches and zinging past their motionless bodies. The sharp report of the shockwaves – CRACK-CRACK, CRACK, CRACK, CRACK-CRACK, CRACK – close to their ears was more than deafening; numbing their ear drums, sending a high-pitched whistling deep into their brains' receptors.

"Oh God," Matea prayed, "Please let it be quick."

Rigid with dread and with every artery, vein and tiny blood vessel in her body filled with icy adrenaline, Matea could only lie still. Her body had stopped shaking. She was now too petrified for that as the rounds smashed and cracked through the undergrowth, around her arms, around her legs, around her body, around her head: the head that James was clutching to his breast for protection. How were they missing her? What would it feel like when they didn't miss her? Would it be over in one painless instant? Pray that she would not slowly fade away as her vital fluids were pumped into the dry Brač earth. Pray that someone would look after Dino.

Despite his crushing weight Matea was certain that every bullet in the long burst was meant for her but knew too that they would hit him first. An uncountable number of random images flashed through her brain, a brain that expected at any moment to be smashed to a grey pulp before itself also oozed into the Brač mountainside. If it wasn't quite her whole life that rewound past her mind's eye it was pretty damned close.

But who were the gunmen? They had spoken with American accents. Many foreigners and even some Croats spoke English with American accents. 'Colonel' one had shouted. There were many colonels. Slavić was the only one whose name came racing into Matea's consciousness. 'Shoot to kill... waste of time... only locals... must mean something to someone but not her and, anyway, it didn't sound right with James shielding her... and that was not right either. Why should he die for her country and not her? It was she that should be protecting him.

Wasn't that why she asked to come along? They were in this together and must take their chances together... but... he had saved her life once before, and that of Dino, now it had to be her turn to do the same for him. She tried to wriggle out from under but his weight was too much and she knew that any movement would help the enemy.

They lay still.

"Reckon that got them. Bang on target." The voices spoke again.

"They're outside the bloody fence."

"Don't worry Mac. I'll try another burst for good luck. I think I can see something through the night scope."

A second cacophony of noise crashed around James and Matea – CRACK-CRACK, CRACK, CRACK, CRACK-CRACK, CRACK – forcing them to brace, mentally and physically for the anticipated, intense, searing, flesh-exploding, bone splintering pain that, sometime during the next split second, would ruin their lives, perhaps even for eternity. Impotent, they could do nothing but lie as rats cornered in a barn, inert, apparently lifeless... waiting... waiting...

And then a full-metal-jacket 5.56 mm round, found a target.

Matea felt the stinging pain that came half way through this second, continuous shockwave, as the round sliced cross the outside of her left thigh. James, too, heard rather then felt the impact as the spent round spun away past his head. He felt her body writhe with pain and heard her tortured breath hiss in his ear. They were no identifiable words, just a sharp exhalation of air, making a sound so terrible that he knew it would be unforgettable.

His first instinct was to roll between her and the gunmen but a second instinct told him that to lie still was the more sensible action… and yet he would never forgive himself if it was her body that took the next, fatal, spray of lead. In that briefest of moments, and for the second time since he had first met her in the hotel, an overpowering need to protect Matea surged through his motionless body.

Determined they stayed alive James was equally determined they should play dead. Desperate to sooth her wound – he had no idea how badly she had been hit, or where – and anxious to staunch the blood that he could sense would be flowing freely, absorbed by her clothes… yet even the slightest twitch would be lethal. They were hidden from sight, even from eyes aided by second generation night vision goggles, by thick acacia bushes, but they were not hidden from 5.56 mm rounds: no respecters of subterfuge or camouflage.

Mercifully a third shock wave did not materialise, instead more words were shouted through the fence and down the mountainside.

"C'mon Mack," a voice called through the darkness. "They're outside the bloody wire."

"I know. I had a bead on the bastards. Job done. What idiots."

"They were outside the wire. Could have been anybody."

"So?"

"Nothing. Let's hope no one finds their bodies before we do."

James waited, listening to the receding mopeds' tyres softly crunching away across the shale and dry earth until there was silence once more. Cautiously he shone the red light onto Matea's pain-contorted face, "I've been hit, James. I've been hit."

"I know. Where?"

"Left thigh. Have they gone?"

"For the moment," James replied, fumbling for a knife.

Using touch rather than sight it was easy to find the blood-matted, slippery tear in Matea's trousers. He cut the cloth wider and pulled the edges apart. By the torch's red light, held between his teeth, he inspected the gash. The wound was draining blood swiftly but not pumping it. Bad but better than he had first feared. Nevertheless, it needed staunching. Quickly.

"Bloody brave of you," praised James, probing Matea's injured leg with a handkerchief, assessing the depth and length of the laceration.

"Being hit isn't brave, James," Matea's voice was soft.

"Not shouting was!"

"Careful. That hurts."

Matea, her mind drawn back to the present by the sudden agony and with her body verging on shock, murmured, "How bad is it? Tell me the truth, James. Please *duša*."

"Not as bad as it could have been but I must get a bandage on it."

"You haven't got one." Matea was matter of fact.

"I will have if I can find your scarf."

"We must be close."

"Stay here," he ordered without thinking. Then, to make light of his tactless instruction added, "Don't go anywhere till I get back."

"Be quick. My leg's going numb and cold."

James returned within a minute, clutching Matea's scarf then, using it as a deep, thick pad of a bandage, kept in place by the tightly tied arms of a jersey recovered from his rucksack, the flow of blood stopped.

With her leg roughly bandaged and using James as a crutch Matea experimented with a few steps. "Not bad," he encouraged as she sat down again. "Now we had better get off this hill. Do you think you can manage if you use me as a prop."

"There's no other way."

"True."

James stood and, in the dark, felt for Matea's hands. He slowly lifted her up allowing her right leg to bear all the weight.

"Good girl. Now see how much use you can get out of the damaged leg."

"If I sort of hop while you steady me. That way I think I can make it."

Slowly they made their excruciating way down the hill, sometimes slithering, sometimes sliding down the steepest sections with Matea lying on her back while, raised in front of her, her right leg took the weight of the left. At some point James held her under her arms, controlling their descent of the escarpment until, as the ground began to level out, he pulled her to a stop.

"From here onwards I'll carry you."

"You can't James. Let me lie here till dawn then we'll get help."

"Not on your bloody life. By then those bastards will be scouring the hillside removing the evidence. We don't want to give them any more proof than they probably have already."

"It hurts James. At least it would if it wasn't so numb."

"If I kneel in front of you do you think you can climb on my back? Don't hold on with your legs. Let them hang loose and I'll get both hands under the backs of your thighs, higher up than the wound."

A hundred yards from the track Matea asked to be put down. James shone his torch over a rock on which she perched, clutching her thigh. "I need to catch my breath before we meet Filip," she explained, "I'll be alright then…" She paused then let out a brief exclamation. "My God…"

"What's happened?"

"The bandage, James. The bandage. It's gone."

James switched on his torch. The jersey was in place but was now hanging loosely with nothing beneath it but the bare, bloodied flesh of Matea's left thigh.

"Bugger," James swore then, looking at the wound more closely, added calmly. "Well at least the worst of the bleeding has stopped. Probably because of the pressure when you were sitting on my hands." He stopped before repeating himself after a moment of thought, "But it is still a bugger."

"Do you want to go and look for it?"

"And leave you here, alone," he answered, "Not bloody likely."

They sat in silence, both assessing the scarf's loss, knowing that it would be found but praying that it's owner might not be traced.

"Here, this will help," James said unscrewing the lid to his thermos. "You need liquids." The soup was good and, against all his training, the tot of whisky that followed it was better.

Setting off across the last yards James asked, "Is there a hospital or medical centre on the island? Better it is cleaned up here than in Split."

"There's a small clinic in Supetar," Matea replied, "but people will still gossip. I'm sure I'll be OK if you can get me home."

"It's quite a journey."

"I know a doctor who will look after me. One who won't talk. A trusted friend."

"You're a brave girl," James repeated but this time with more feeling.

As they reached the clearing at the end of the track, Filip's car was approaching.

"That was good timing," he said through an open window.

"Did you find out anything useful?"

Matea let James do the talking. "Not really. I hope we haven't wasted your and your father's time."

"Father's fine," Filip said cheerfully, "He's had a good dinner and a game of backgammon or two. Jump in."

James helped Matea shuffle onto the back seat of the Citroën then, as soon as Filip had turned the car, she rested her head on James's shoulder and shut her eyes. She was faint and she was cold.

Reaching the outskirts of the coastal town Filip turned to Matea over his shoulder, "We'll wait for father at the boat," he said, "Is that OK?"

James answered the question, "If you know where he is I think it might be a good idea if we went there instead. We need to get back quickly."

"Sure. Is there a problem?"

"Don't know," James replied and felt for Matea's forehead. It was clammy and cold. "Possibly."

Filip drew the car to a halt outside a white villa, set back from the road behind a neat stone wall along which recently pruned grape vines, now just beginning to bud, were draped. "He's in there," he said.

"Please wait while I have a word with him," James ordered, gently lowering Matea's head on to the inner arm rest, before sliding out and closing the door softly behind him. Filip looked over his shoulder again, this time hoping for an answer from Matea but, in the gloom of the dim overhead light he could see that his passenger's eyes were shut, her face was waxen and her breathing was slow through violently chattering teeth.

Within a minute Augustin was also peering into the back of the Citroën.

"How much blood do you think she has lost?" he asked

James.

"I got the bandage on pretty swiftly although it eventually fell off."

Augustin pushed himself away saying firmly, "I'll be back." Three minutes later he reappeared clutching a pad of sterile gauze, two thick blankets, a pack of analgesic pills, a plastic bottle of water and a canvas bag. "Now," he said after applying the fresh bandages and selecting two pills for Matea to swallow, "if you think she can manage the boat trip we'll soon have her home. What caused it?"

"I would think a 5.56 millimetre bullet," James replied shortly. No need to elaborate quite yet.

At the quayside the three of them lifted Matea over the water-gap, stretched her out across the stern seat then tucked the blankets around her sides. A fender wrapped in a towel made a passable pillow.

The twenty-five nautical mile run back to the Riva waterfront took fifty minutes with James sometimes studying the Admiralty chart but, more often, checking on Matea. The sea was still calm.

With the boat secured Augustin and James helped Matea into the Consul's car. As Augustin switched on the ignition a Croat voice was speaking on the wireless. Augustin leant forward to turn it off and then stopped, his fingers poised over the button.

"Wait," he said loudly to himself. "I'll translate when it is finished."

Listening intently James managed to pick out the words Brač and even *kamenolom* – the Croat, he knew for quarry – but nothing else. When the bulletin was replaced by light pop music, Augustin explained, "That was a statement by a Croatian army spokesman saying that one of their patrols had frightened off some petty thieves trying to break into a quarry on the island of Brač and wanted to warn people that armed guards patrolled the perimeter fence."

"A straightforward warning I suppose in case anyone heard the gunfire," James commented, "although people might wonder why a quarry needs an armed guard."

"Interestingly," added Augustin, "the spokesman said that as the quarry was producing stone for the war effort it was considered a military facility and was being treated accordingly. The bulletin ended with the announcement that the public must stay away for their own safety."

As James grinned quietly to himself Augustin was parking outside Matea's house on the 'promenade' Ivana Meštrovica, overlooking the coast to the west of Split Harbour. He had been here before, when Matea had changed for their trip to the helicopter's crash site, but had not left her car.

The two-storied, red-roofed house was set back, on its northern side, from the 'promenade' itself. Separated from its neighbours by wide paths overhung with native plants James remembered that in daylight the honey-coloured stone villa enjoyed a magnificent view of the Adriatic and the near islands including Šolta – and Brač. Matea, curled up on the rear seat, handed James the front door key. As he made his way round the villa's left side a safety light automatically switched itself on over the pillared porch.

With the front door already open it was easier for Augustin and James to carry Matea straight indoors and, under her instructions, lie her out on a sofa. Before the Consul's departure for his Split apartment James, again under Matea's instructions, poured generous measures of whisky while giving him a brief summary of events; leaving nothing out. Before he left, Augustin excused himself and returned from his car with the small canvas bag he had brought from Bol. "Here," he said to James pulling out a limp bundle wrapped in damp newspaper, "put this in her fridge. It is a get-well present from me. She'll know what to do with it."

By the front door Augustine turned, "Well done James, getting Matea back in almost one piece. From what you say it could have been far worse all round."

"We were very lucky to begin with then very unlucky to end with. Now I have two last requests, Augustin. If I may?"

"Go ahead."

"Here is the roll of film I took at the airfield. I hope you may know someone you can trust to develop it. Secondly, I'll need to use your secure mobile to talk to Magnus. Not quite yet as Matea's health comes first right now. I'll let you know when."

"When you have contacted her doctor, I expect you will be compiling a detailed report."

"I most certainly will, just as soon as I have worked out who needs to know what and who most definitely does not need to know what!"

They laughed. Augustin waved goodbye and James closed the door.

CHAPTER TWENTY-FOUR

Monday 7th March 1994
Veško polje airstrip, Brač Island, Croatia.

The track that led from the public road to the airstrip at Veško polje was not marked on any map, nor was the 4,724 foot runway itself. The only indication that anything at all happened above the escarpment, one and a half miles to the north-east of Bol, was a newly painted road sign that read:

Veško polje kamenolom
Vlada nekretnine
Opasnost
Ne ulazi

Beneath this indication that the quarry at Veško field was *Government Property*, that it was a *Dangerous Area* and that everyone should *Keep Out* an additional, unequivocal statement warned that:

Uljeze će biti snimljen!

At the very bottom of the notice was an English translation of these last four words for the benefit, Colonel Ante Slavić smiled as he read it, of any ECMM employee foolish enough to try a spot of monitoring. This version declared, equally unequivocally, that *Trespassers Will Be Shot!*

The notice had not been there on Sunday, the day before.

Shortly before sunset Slavić manoeuvred his Zastava AR-51, four-wheel drive 'jeep' between a stone chicane that marked the beginning of the gravel track to the quarry and halted, around a blind bend, at the checkpoint. He needed to offer no identification papers for the sentries, American mercenaries now in Croatian army uniforms, knew the Colonel well and his second-hand 'jeep' with its canvas roof. The distinctive vehicle was not in the army's inventory for it was Slavić's own and far more 'macho' than anything the Croatian government could offer. It made him look good, more in line with the image he wished to project rather than the one that his flabby, over-fed, over-wined features suggested. He had had the Zastava painted in a disruptive pattern, dual-colour camouflage scheme and fitted with the 4th Guards Brigade's tactical formation signs. The Brigade even kept it full of fuel with no questions asked. There was no point in being a Chief of Staff without perks.

The barrier was lifted, small arms replaced into holsters and the 'boss' waved through at the start of the two and a half mile circuitous route to Veško polje airstrip's rudimentary control tower.

Slavić had no idea why Dwight Anderson had suggested they meet at the control tower, especially as he had no interest in the United States' Defense Attaché's supposed administration teams stationed there. Unconvinced that Anderson was 'on the level', as he claimed, Slavić only agreed to come as he still needed to know the truth behind the aluminium planks. Maybe at last, at long last, he would learn what the Yanks were doing in his country: helping to beat the Serbs was what he hoped to hear but he was far from sanguine.

"Ante!" Anderson's greeting was effusive. Too effusive. "Welcome. I'm so glad you could come this afternoon for when it is dark I hope to have a surprise for you."

"A surprise?" Slavić questioned through his 'jeep's' open window.

"Sure thing, Buddy, but before that come into the Operations Room and listen up."

Slavić parked his vehicle and followed Anderson into what had been a hanger; but that was in the era when the airfield had been built from which sorties would have flown against Serbia. The place had become deserted since those heady but unproductive days: the control tower had lost its electrical supply thanks to the mouflon and their inquisitive teeth and the single approach road overgrown and, eventually, physically blocked – as Anderson had discovered for himself. When Slavić entered through the wide double doors, whose rusty hinges were only just supporting their weight, he was astonished to find himself at the hub of a military operation whose focus was obvious. The whole of one wall was covered with a large scale map of the Republic of Serbian Krajina and the land beyond it's self-imposed borders. Computer screens flickered. What looked like a mock up of an aircraft's cockpit was half curtained off in a near corner.

"*O moj Bože!*" Slavić exclaimed, then more softly and in English, he repeated himself, "Oh my God!" Overawed yet put-out that such an undertaking had been conducted without his knowledge, Slavić accepted that some things that were happening were best left un-questioned. Instead he smiled admiringly, taking in the technology and the industry that surrounded him.

"I thought you would be impressed," gushed Anderson.

"And before I forget, thanks for the guards. As agreed we have supplied them with Heckler and Koch .45 cal pistols fitted with silencers. Let's just say they are on loan from the US Special Operations Command. One day we will need them back."

"I'll make sure they are returned," lied Slavić.

"And the wandering patrols are equipped with Russian Izhevesk AK-102, 5.56 cal carbines with folding stocks and fittings for night vision sights," Anderson paused for effect before adding, "And no! Don't ask. My supplier will want them back as well."

"I'll remember that too," Slavić repeated his deceit.

"We have a little time so let me introduce you to the map. I appreciate that you know the local countryside but my concern is how little you probably now know about the area beyond the present confrontation line."

For the next ten minutes Anderson pointed out key geographical features and the latest military dispositions on both sides of the border. Slavić was embarrassed to acknowledge that the Yanks knew more than he did about the locations of not only the whole Croatian army but, more specifically, of his own brigade.

Noticing that his guest could not keep his eyes away from the near corner and its extra large, but currently blank, screen Anderson broke off from his military brief, "Don't you worry about what's going on there," he admonished lightly, "All will be revealed shortly."

Anxious for the first of his evening's glasses of wine, the anticipation for which was turning into a pressing need, Slavić continued to look around him. All these men must eat and drink somewhere.

"I know what you must be thinking, Ante," Anderson guessed wrongly! "Since the crash we have been busy ferrying men and supplies ashore by night from the fleet. We've built up quite a strong admin and support facility and shortly we will have the operational aspects in place. We've beefed up and repaired the perimeter fence you guys built all those months ago and we now have a good security track around the inside patrolled by men on electric motor bikes. We've installed generators and have rudimentary sleeping quarters and a galley so we are self contained and supplied by helicopter. No one needs to leave the base, not that I would let them anyway."

Slavić could only grin in silent admiration.

"As you know we are supposed to be a quarry and so must appear to have an entrance which is why I have had it opened up again. Otherwise I would close the whole place off from the outside world altogether! And that is the way we must keep it. It is vital that not only our work here is kept secret but the fact we, the United States, are here at all must be secret too. Absolutely no one, apart from you," Anderson smashed a fist into a palm in violent emphasis, "knows we exist. Got it?"

"Got it," replied Slavić hesitantly. "But, we know the girl is suspicious and that means that Laidlaw will be too."

"I don't agree, buddy. They may know the true nationality of the crashed heli but these things happen and, anyway," Anderson had convinced himself, "even they will know that a single helicopter is hardly likely to endanger an arms embargo."

Not wishing to argue with the man who was the key to his future national fame Slavić could only mutter, "I am sure you're right," while already forming a plot to silence the one person – a fellow Croat for God's sake – who could jeopardise his long term aspirations.

"Good. We have an hour or so to fill in so let's get some chow."

Slavić nodded vigorously as Anderson led the way through

a far door into an adjoining hanger that had been partitioned into various domestic functions. The hamburgers and chips were expected but the bright mauve 'bug juice', an artificial-fruit drink ubiquitous in all alcohol-free American warships, was not... and it certainly was not to the Croatian's taste. Nevertheless, even Ante Slavić appreciated when it was tactful to refrain from complaining. He knew he was witnessing something... something... he had no idea what, other than it was something extraordinary.

Later, as they sipped black coffee from paper cups, a soldier in pressed fatigues stood by their table and saluted smartly.

"Colonel Anderson, sir."

"Yes, soldier?"

"Yes sir. The aircraft is due in five minutes, sir. May I suggest you come to the foot of the control tower."

"We're on our way."

Outside Slavić was introduced to the base commander, a US Army major. "What you are about to witness, colonel," the major began, "is the first operational landing onto this airstrip of a Hercules MC-130E Combat Talon I aircraft. Tonight is the real thing. We wanted to wait till the full moon in two weeks but the United States Air Force Special Operations Command guys said they were happy and as we are ready to go we had no reason to delay."

Apart from the floodlights surrounding the hangers Slavić could see no sign of lights to guide such a large aircraft to a safe landing. Glad he had come by jeep he asked lamely, "How will the pilots see?"

The major explained that the only guide the USAF Special Operations C-130 Talon pilots normally needed were what he described as a 'box and one' formation of hand-held lights. "Two across the threshold of the runway, two more 500 feet from it to form an elongated box with a single light placed at the centre of the far end of the runway. However," he continued, "as the facility exists here at Brač – thanks to a major re-wiring project – we will switch on the full runway lights at the last moment. The 'box' of handheld lights will remain in place just in case of a power failure. The aircraft," the major finished, "will come in low using its terrain following radar and infra red television, planning to be over the threshold at about 105 knots and at a descent rate of 300 feet per minute. The pilot will then pull back on the control column and wait for contact with the runway."

Slavić was further convinced that jeep travel was preferable.

An airman now saluted the American officer who excused himself, "The aircraft is on finals," he said turning for the control tower's ladder from where, less than a minute later, the runway lights were switched on.

Slavić watched, engrossed, as the large aircraft landed exactly as had been described, then, instead of taxiing the remaining 2,000 or so feet to the turning area at the far end of the airstrip and still using reverse thrust it moved backwards to the single exit taxiway that it had passed during its landing run. Moving forwards again it came to a halt 100 yards in front of the operations hanger. The runway lights were switched off.

"Bravo," was all the Croatian colonel could say, now even more anxious to discover what it carried that required such a complex support team. His unspoken question was answered as the C-130's rear ramp was lowered to the ground allowing him to watch, open eyed and open mouthed, as the fuselage of a small aircraft slowly emerged as though the Hercules was giving birth to a tiny incarnation of itself. Mesmerised, Slavić could only guess at what he was witnessing: the arrival of a Cessna Bird Dog reconnaissance aircraft that Anderson had once mentioned.

Anderson took his arm, "Come back to the Ops Room and I'll enlighten you."

Still clutching their paper mugs of coffee Anderson was as good as his word. What Slavić had just been watching, he explained, was the arrival on Croatian soil of the first of two Predator RQ-1A, medium-altitude, long-endurance, unmanned aircraft systems or, as he would learn to call them Unmanned Aerial Vehicles or, even more simply, UAVs. The second UAV would arrive shortly and another two 'drones', once further development had been completed, would be delivered to the airfield at Gjader in Albania.

"They are still experimental. The first official, public flight is not due to take place until the summer in the Mojave Desert. But," Anderson lowered his voice, "the Commander in Chief himself, our President, ordered these to be flown here as part of their Advanced Concept Technology Demonstration."

"That's obviously good news for you," Slavić intervened not quite understanding the jargon, "but is it good news for us?"

"Intelligence." Anderson replied shortly, "Pure and simple. One day the designers hope to have these UAVs armed with missiles but right now their on board sensors will be used to supply your army with all the up-to-date, real time 'intel' on the RSK that you could possibly want."

"So that curtained off area with the two smart-looking seats over there? The pilots presumably?"

"Yes." Anderson confirmed. "Currently it is an army-run operation but with civilian pilots supplied by General Atomics Aeronautical Systems, the manufacturers. That, too, will change when the US Air Force takes over the whole UAV operation. They are quite large beasts as you have just seen, with a length of 27 feet and a wingspan of 48. They fly high and slow, cruising up to 25,000 feet above sea level, at just over 100 knots, although they can go faster. Amazingly, their Rotax 914 F turbocharged, four-cylinder engine, if you need to know," Slavić grinned and shook his head but there was no stopping the American, proud of his latest toy, "gives them an endurance of nearly twenty four hours."

Slavić turned to ask a question but his words were drowned by a low piercing alarm. Anxiously he turned to look at Anderson whose face was already losing its colour. "A test alarm I have no doubt?" the Croat queried without conviction as the PA system barked:

Intruders have been detected. This is not a drill. All personnel to their emergency stations. I say again. Intruders have been detected. This is not a drill. All personnel to their emergency stations.

Anderson stood as though in a trance. "No way!" he spat. "No way," and would have said more had he not been interrupted by the distant sound of a semi-automatic weapon being fired in long bursts. "The only sensible thing to do," he said more calmly, "is to remain where we are and wait for the incident report."

Ten minutes later the base commander appeared at the hanger door clutching a single sheet of paper which he handed to his country's Defense Attaché. Reading the hastily compiled account Anderson's pale face now turned puce, his eyes closed to little more than narrow slits and his hands began to shake.

"Those dumb bastards!" He forced the words through a clenched jaw then turned to the major to repeat his accusation. "Those dumb Croat bastards of yours. They've gone and shot up some bloody goat hunters. Outside the God-dammed wire for Chrisssake! Now every Croat will know there is something going on here. The police will need statements and God knows what else."

"In their defence, colonel," the major was not going to take this criticism of his men without attempting a repost, "the soldiers may be in the Croatian army but they were chosen, on your orders, from among the large pool of American mercenaries available and," he spoke softer now, "it was you that authorised the notice at the entrance saying that all trespassers will be shot."

"You son of a bitch," the Colonel shouted again, "They weren't bloody trespassing were they?"

"Not exactly but they must have seen what was happening if they were on the west side of the airfield. Which comes to the same thing."

Anderson, knowing this could only be true, now spoke more steadily, "Well, we'll see. Report to me at first light when they have brought the bodies in. And I want to know exactly where they were found and if they left any tracks that would help us establish where they came from and the route they took."

"Right away, colonel," the major replied, saluted and left the hanger.

Anderson turned to face Slavić, "Most unfortunate, Ante, two innocent Croat lives lost just because they stumbled upon something they shouldn't have done."

But Slavić, to Anderson's surprise, remained unmoved. Certainly the good news of the evening – of his career – was the unsolicited arrival of the most modern intelligence gathering system imaginable and one that had even been authorised by the President of the United States himself. Now, to cap that wonderful stroke of good fortune, a couple of mouflon hunters had been killed, but… mouflon hunters do not climb to the top of the escarpment late at night to seek their quarry. He grinned maliciously to himself at the thought of a more likely possibility: an ECMM monitor with a special forces background might well use the night-time hunting of wild mountain goats to the top of the hill – and beyond – as a convenient cover story.

"You're smiling Ante," Anderson was holding out a cup of fresh coffee. "There has to be a reason."

"Do you believe that good news comes in threes?"

"Rubbish," was Dwight Anderson's uncompromising reply… but then, Slavić thought, that was only to be expected from a senior Defense Intelligence Agency officer to whom good news seldom came at all, let alone in triplicate.

"Well I do, and I am already wondering what will happen next!"

CHAPTER TWENTY-FIVE

Tuesday 8th March 1994
Villa Perunika, Šetalište Ivana Meštrovica,
Split, Croatia.

James locked Villa Perunika's front door and turned to deal with the task uppermost in his mind: Matea's left thigh. Huddled in blankets, ashen-faced, she was reclining against an arm of a sofa, clutching a water bottle from which she was taking sips.

"I need the number of your friendly doctor. I know it is the middle of the night but if he is the friend you say he is that won't bother him."

Matea pointed to a desk. "That red address book. Under Nowak."

James dialled the number. Once it began to ring he handed the telephone to Matea. The conversation was short and, to James's limited knowledge of Croatian, to the point.

"He'll be here in half an hour," Matea said, handing back the telephone. "He speaks English so you will understand his prognosis. All I said was that I had been shot. He asked no questions but will come to his own conclusions."

Doctor Nowak was punctual. He and James were still shaking hands as they walked into the sitting room. "That's the trouble these days..." Nowak was a talker and did not stop as he pulled aside the tear in Matea's trousers and inspected the blood stained gauze, "...too many young men with weapons. Where did this happen, Matea?"

"In the woods near Bol. We were out for a stroll after dinner."

"I expect some lads were also out, hunting the wild mouflon."

"Yes, that's what we thought."

Nowak bent over his task, thought for a few seconds and then explained what he was planning, "I shall give you a local anaesthetic so I can clean the wound. Then I will leave it open for a day to make sure that there is no dead tissue. The gash is about five inches long, not too deep and has only grazed the flesh beneath but these high-velocity rounds can cause shock-wave damage that might not be immediately obvious. I'll also give you a shot of antibiotics in case any infection was carried across by the scarf you said you used. And a tetanus jab. When I am satisfied, I'll stitch the underlying tissue with cat gut sutures to bring the flesh together, before closing the skin with silk stitches." Nowak stopped, thinking before changing his mind. "No I won't," he corrected himself, "I haven't dealt with a gunshot wound for many years so I'll seek advice but I remember now that it must heal by itself once I've packed it with a dressing. Then it can be allowed to granulate from the base."

He looked down at Matea, "Happy with all that?" he asked.

Matea nodded thoughtfully.

"Good, now I need you to take your trousers off." Matea smiled at the doctor, then at James who excused himself saying, "I'll make you both some coffee then walk and collect Matea's car from the quayside. I'll be about half an hour."

Later, with clean bandages, pain killers and having been lifted up the stairs by James and the doctor, Matea lay in her double bed, propped up by three pillows. Nowak re-checked her pulse, temperature and blood pressure.

"Nasty wound, slight shock but insignificant loss of blood," he said to James, standing by his side looking down at the patient. "I'll be back tomorrow to change the dressings and check for dead tissue then, with any luck, it will start healing without infection. Meanwhile, keep her warm and well lubricated" – James smiled at the doctor's use of English – "and stop her walking on that leg as we do not want the wound to start bleeding again. When I am satisfied that the healing is going well she will be able to hobble for short distances."

Nowak had no idea of James's status and did not ask. The Markovićs and Nowaks, on both sides of the Confrontation Line, were well-established family friends who did not need to pry into a stranger's affairs. "You may have to start learning a few domestic skills," he advised James as he closed his bag and stooped to give Matea a farewell kiss on her cheek, "And you, my dear friend," he said to her with a theatrical wink, "No more mouflon hunting for a while!"

Matea smiled up at the doctor, "Of course not. How silly of me!"

"So, I'll say *doviđenja* and order you to sleep."

With the doctor's departure James sat on Matea's bed stroking her head while, inside his own, a jumble of possible future decisions were vying for supremacy. For many long minutes neither said a word, both realising that they were at a cross-roads not only in their personal relationship but also with that of James and the European Community Monitoring Mission.

"It's nowhere near dawn," James observed, looking at his watch, then the window, "I suggest we sleep so we can start the day with clear heads."

"Aren't you supposed to be taking the shuttle to Zagreb on Wednesday?"

"Let's talk about that when we wake."

"I must collect Dino as well. He's staying with friends who will take him to school but after that he is expecting to come home."

"Let's talk about that, too. In the morning. Right now I must find a bed."

"You won't have to look far," Matea patted the blanket alongside her. "I need you close."

"That close?" James queried, purposefully reticent.

"I was terrified, James and I'm still frightened. Not for my leg but for us. As individuals not as a couple. So, yes," she patted the bed again, "This close." Matea looked directly into his eyes. Pleading silently before saying, "Please James. Just be near me. Right now I need reassurance. Nothing more."

As there was nothing he wanted to do more than give that reassurance, James turned out the light, undressed and slipped into Matea's bed. Almost before his head dented the pillow he was asleep, and so was she.

Later that morning, well towards lunchtime, James showered, dressed in clothes still spattered with Matea's blood before taking her a mug of tea. Unshaven, he then sat at her desk writing notes and drafting signals. He had a number of issues to resolve and the first were plans for Matea and Dino's immediate safety. Without her injury they might, just, be able to bluff their way out of any accusation that they were on Brač but the gunshot wound was a telling piece of hard evidence, if Slavić was to hear of it.

James was also conscious that his status within the ECMM was uncertain. Any prolonged absence from Team Split would not help his case if he wanted to remain under his own terms:

terms that would be more honourable than those proposed by Pagonis. Top of his monitoring priorities, if not his personal priorities, was the need to telephone Colin Cooper: contacting Patrick O'Hara was second. Then he needed to polish the report he had begun in draft form for Magnus in London.

Matea surfaced naturally. She had been woken on several occasions in the night by her throbbing leg then, satisfied each time that James was still beside her, had slept again. Needing to wash she called out, *"Duša!"*

James, in the kitchen watching the electric toaster, answered as he walked up the stairs, "You called me that before. What does it mean?"

"Soulmate, or even darling if you wish."

"It's a lovely word. Thank you." He sat beside her, took a hand and asked, "How are you?"

"Much better for knowing that you are still here."

With his help Matea hopped to the bathroom and while she was occupied there James dialled the first of his telephone calls.

"Colin? James here. I'm on a private, civilian number so unlikely to be tapped," then he added, "Yet!"

Over the next five minutes James explained why he would not now be taking the shuttle to Zagreb on the morrow but would instead be nursing his 'lady interpreter'.

"Shot, you say. How? Where?" CC hesitated before asking, "Why?"

James elaborated, including a summary of what he had seen, ending with the observation, "I now have proof that the UN embargo is being broken by the Americans. I am of course assuming that supplying military intelligence is covered by the embargo and if it is then the UN should be informed. That way it might even be able to prevent the re-arming of Croatia and thus the inevitable war."

"Don't count on it James. As you yourself once told me, the US treats the UN with contempt and will pay no heed to calls for further sanctions or even the enforcement of the current ones."

"In which case the public at large should be told."

"I don't think many will listen to one man's version of events. Especially if that one man has been sacked as a monitor."

James remained silent, collecting his thoughts. He knew that the Predator issue was best discussed direct with Magnus Sixsmith who had his own avenues into the corridors of real power: avenues with tentacles that reached far and wide into that secret world he inhabited. James knew, too, that such information that he now had – M-84 tanks unloaded into Ploče, Predator spy planes landing on Brač, fighter aircraft being unloaded at Pula – might not get beyond Zagreb if passed through the ECMM network. That would simply be rocking the Mission's already unstable and duplicitous boat too hard for its own comfort.

CC hadn't finished and broke James's silence, "So precisely why were you sacked? Or should I ask, why did you resign?"

"Once I knew that Ploče was being used to import main battle tanks coupled to a suspicion that something irregular was happening on Brač I was ordered by Sublette to cease all coastal monitoring and concentrate instead on the confrontation line. At the same time Pagonis ordered me to continue monitoring both Ploče and Brač but, and I use the precise word that he used, I was to falsify my daily reports so that Sublette would believe that I was doing what he wanted. In practice I was to send a second daily report, but only to Pagonis, that reflected what was going on at the port and on the island."

"I see," CC said slowly. "In which case I endorse your decision but sadly Sublette got his dismissal in first."

"Sacked. Resigned. I'm not sure that it makes much difference either way now. Especially as I have all the proof I need to expose the circumvention of the UN embargo by two sovereign governments."

"Outside the ECMM it will be difficult for you to find a sympathetic recipient."

"I may have to take that risk." James was thinking of Magnus and his more-than-receptive ears.

There was silence at the Zagreb end of the line while it was CC's turn to think.

"James," he said at last. "This is too serious an accusation for you to walk away from. Although hamstrung, because of my position *vis-à-vis* that of the other Heads of Delegation, I need to discuss the problem with them and even take it as far as the Head of Mission himself if I get negative responses. I'll call back later if you give me your number."

James read out the telephone number and confirmed that it was his intention to remain in situ until his interpreter was fit enough to leave the house.

"Don't get too close, James," CC advised. "You will know even better than I from your earlier experiences that that sort of thing is frowned upon, if not actually disallowed."

"Ah, but if I am not a member of the ECMM…?"

"Touché," CC interrupted before saying goodbye.

Matea was helped back to bed to where James brought toast, fresh fruit and coffee.

"You may not recall but Augustin gave me a rather soggy parcel which I put in the fridge. He said it was a get-well present and that you would know how to deal with it. I had a look. It seems to be two small shoulders of lamb."

"How wonderful. The Brač spring lambs are a famous delicacy and can only be sold as such while the whole animal is under," Matea converted the weight in her head, "twenty four pounds."

"Sounds good."

"Sounds even better as you will be cooking it!"

James kissed her on her forehead and returned to the sitting room knowing that his next telephone call would be easier.

"Paddy?"

"James, where the hell are you?"

"Best discussed over a gin. If you are free later I have a few favours to ask."

After lunch Doctor Nowak banged on the bolted front door. James, suspicious of unexpected callers, checked from an upstairs window before letting him in. "How's my patient," he began.

"Peaceful night's sleep followed by a late breakfast. See for yourself."

Satisfied that no dead tissue would be entombed and that the high-velocity round had not caused deeper damage, Nowak re-packed the gash, administered another injection of antibiotics, placed a pack of oral antibiotics and analgesic tablets by Matea's bed and wished them both a good afternoon. Following a promise that he would be back again on the morrow to check the wound, the doctor was gone.

Shortly afterwards a violent knocking on the front door revealed Patrick, James's suitcase and Dino, who fled instantly to his mother's bedroom from where shrieks of joy and laughter flowed.

"Sorry the door was locked," James apologised, "I'll explain. In the meantime let's leave them to it. Did you bring the gin and wine?"

Settled in the sitting room's deep arm chairs, facing the setting sun through the wall-wide window, James recounted every detail of the Brač adventure. When he had finished he waved a hand towards the interior of the house. "So," he summed up, "I feel a great deal of compassion for Matea, coupled with a very real desire to protect her. And, perhaps a little guilt as she needn't have come with me. I could have refused but..." he paused to study his glass, "Now I cannot leave her. Not only will she be immobile for a few more days but I also have a deep down sense of unease for her safety. She's a soft target if Slavić or his henchmen ever get to know that she is involved; and they know already that we are aware of the helicopter's true nationality."

Patrick's smile was cynical for he, too, had news. "I received a call from Jean-Claud this morning telling me that I was now the Team Split leader and that a monitor will be sent in due course as my number two.

James grinned, "Good luck," he said, "As for my future I am waiting to hear. Sacked or resigned."

"And if neither happens?"

"I guess I will have to sit out the last two months of my contract in Zagreb, sifting through your Daily Reports and deciding what should be forwarded to Brussels."

"With your record I doubt they will let you do that."

James lent back in his chair. The sun had now sunk beyond Šolta and, apart from the unease surrounding Matea's safety, he felt surprisingly mellow. "Stay, Paddy, and enjoy some Brač spring lamb. It's my turn to cook!"

"Thanks I would love to but…"

Impatient knocking on the front door was answered by Dino shouting in Croat from the first floor, "I'll get it, Mama!" There was a brief silence as the boy ran down the stairs followed by an hysterical scream as the front door was slammed open against the inside wall throwing his tiny figure violently backwards across the wooden floor. Ante Slavić, scarlet in the face, wine on his breath and a pistol in his hand was pointing his weapon into every corner of the room yelling, "Where's that bitch of a traitor?" Behind him two armed military policemen stood, their hands hovering over their own firearms. Instinctively James and Patrick leapt to their feet.

"My God, she's not alone," Slavić blustered, staring, horrified. He slowly lowered his pistol. "Oh! And O'Hara too," he slurred. "I might have guessed the tart would have many visitors."

James squared up to the colonel. Speaking calmly and deliberately he said, "We are more than just visitors, Slavić, we are also witnesses. This is a private house and you have no right or business to be in here."

The Croat yelled an obscenity and made a grab for the boy but James was quicker. Sweeping Dino to his feet he was thrust behind Patrick for protection.

Slavić, gulping now, undecided how to react in front of such an unexpected audience, knew he was defeated. For the moment. Then the five-year old Dino broke the brief silence, "Mama! Mama!" he cried running towards the stairs. The colonel's pistol following every step.

"And while you're on your way, boy, you can take this to your mother." With his left hand Slavić pulled out Matea's bloodstained, paisley-pattern scarf from a pocket of his combat jacket and flung it at Dino's feet. "She left it behind on the hill." The pistol still followed Dino as he raced, terrified, up to his mother.

James, now with Patrick alongside him, advanced towards the over-heated colonel. "Put that gun away, Slavić, and get out. You've made your point and I have made mine to Headquarters of the ECMM. Your secret, if it was ever your secret, is now on its way to the United Nations."

"They'll do nothing. Neither you nor your allies can do anything to stop us taking back our land from the Serbs. The words of one flawed Brit is hardly going to make any difference."

James feared that he was right but it was not up to him to pre-empt international reactions.

Resentfully, Slavić turned to leave, sneering over his shoulder, "As you have been dismissed as a monitor I will be applying for your deportation and the girl with you. Until that moment comes," his smirk was more pronounced, "I advise neither of you to appear in public. I won't answer for the consequences." He pointed to the scarf lying on the floor. "Which ever one of you it was that was bleeding you deserve it for meddling in affairs that are beyond your comprehension."

"Go!" James commanded. Then emphasising each word he spoke with more than a trace of malice, "I will not be cowed by you and I will not allow the Marković family to be intimidated either so let me tell you this, Slavić…"

The colonel turned for the door but stopped as James persisted, facing the back of the Croat's head, "…if you try to harm her you will have me to deal with as well for I do not intend leaving her side as long as I am in this Godforsaken country of yours…"

Slavić laughed, a low menacing growl of a laugh.

"Of course," James continued speaking to the back of Slavić's scarlet-blotched, flabby neck, "If you murder one of your own folk you will only have to answer to your corrupt police but if you kill me then you will face a far less crooked, international judiciary. I would consider your options very carefully next time you pull a gun on me."

Slavić slammed the door behind him. From outside the noise of hollow, nervous, laughter faded into the dusk.

Thankful that Slavić had gone, James looked up at the first

floor landing. Matea, supported by Dino, was standing in her dressing gown, looking down with silent tears spilling across her cheeks; her son desperately trying to reach them with a handkerchief.

James ran up the stairs to hug both. "At least we now know where we stand. And so does Slavić."

Matea, though grateful, was not convinced, "James, you are not armed and anyway, one man can not face the whole of the Croat army."

"I won't have to if I am deported…"

"And then what about me, James? Will you just leave me?"

"Good God, of course not. If I go, you and Dino will be coming with me! I had already decided that." Matea wasn't sure if she was relieved at this news or hurt, horrified even, that such a fundamental decision had been made without her involvement.

Downstairs the telephone rang.

James returned to the sitting room to answer it, waving at Patrick, as he did so, to pour Matea a gin.

As CC's distinctive voice brought him back to reality James sank into an arm chair listening intently, saying nothing, every so often nodding his head in silent agreement.

When at last the Head of the British Delegation had finished it was James's turn to describe what had just occurred. He finished by saying, "Thank you CC. You have just made my life rather easier. I won't let you down."

The ECMM's Headquarters may have meant well but it was populated by too many representatives of too many countries with too many opposing desires. Slavić was, though, an immediate threat – an immediate and very dangerous threat – but James knew as well as anyone that bullies tend to crumble at the first hint of resistance.

"What was all that about?" Patrick asked.

"I'll tell you while I cook supper which we'll eat in Matea's bedroom. Before that I need a bath, a shave and clean clothes."

Refreshed, James sought advice on how to cook the spring lamb. Matea, too, was hungry for, as she complained, she was not ill, merely a little bent and certainly able to sit up to eat. The sight of Slavić's threatening behaviour in her own house had been an intimidating experience but, with James's reassurance, plus the added presence of Patrick, she felt relaxed enough to pass culinary instructions while sipping her drink. As it would take two hours to spit-roast the lamb in the traditional manner Patrick, in his own words 'jump-started' the process by cooking the shoulders in the oven for the first hour. Meanwhile both men, with Dino's enthusiastic help, prepared the vegetables.

"So what's your future?" Patrick began again.

James explained that CC had spent a long and tiring day for no one in Hotel Betonska had, at first, accepted that the United States was preparing to supply real time intelligence from a non-existent airfield with equipment that had not been invented. Neither could any of the other Heads of Delegation accept that ships loaded with cargoes from Germany, were somehow managing to by-pass the Standing NATO flotilla. The consensus, fuelled by reports from Pagonis and Sublette, was that James Laidlaw was a 'bloody nuisance' intent on rocking the boat for his own self-aggrandisement. Sublette's sacking of Team Split's leader was seen as a good thing 'and not before time'.

James had listened with a wry smile as CC continued. Having failed to canvas support for James's retention as a monitor from among his fellow Heads of Delegations he had demanded a meeting with the Head of Mission himself.

"Ah," the Greek diplomat had said, "Laidlaw. The man who

saved lives during the shelling of the Hotel Adriatica and who was so insulting to one of our generals?"

"The very same," CC had had to agree, fearful that this might be the end of his plan.

"I like his style. We need more monitors like him. Not frightened to expose the truth. Tell me more of his background."

CC had outlined both James's personal life – widowed, no children – with as much of his professional life as he thought it was safe to divulge – submariner, commando trained, decorated for a special forces action against the IRA.

As the result of the Ambassador's heavily-solicited intervention, James, if he agreed, was to be appointed a monitor at large while remaining subject to the ECMM's *modus operandi* and Terms of Employment. In that unusual capacity he was to observe the adherence to, or the contravention of, United Nations Embargo 713. Additionally, CC had received Camille's agreement – "for some reason she had smiled broadly when giving it" – that it would be more secure if James had his own interpreter.

"You've been busy, CC and I am most grateful."

"You will answer direct to the Ambassador but copy all reports to me. In July we might meet a problem when Germany takes over the Presidency. You've been out here long enough to know that in any future conflict Greece will take the Serbian side while Germany, inevitably, will support Croatia."

CC had ended the call with a question, "When do you think you will be ready to start?"

James looked at Patrick, "So, now you know."

"When did you say you will start?"

"I said that it would depend on Matea's leg," James explained, "and whether or not she is happy to be involved further."

"And if not?"

"Then I am not sure if I would want to take on the job."

"Are you falling for her?"

James did not answer directly, instead he inspected the vegetables and checked the lamb. Although he had known the answer for some time it was still a question that occupied his mind. When he returned from the kitchen he explained, "The problem is that I came out here to forget and not to be reminded of what might have been. I certainly was not looking for a replacement for Caroline."

James was thinking aloud for these were observations he had yet to explore himself, "It all started when I rescued Matea and Dino from Hotel Adriatica. I couldn't help noticing that Dino was the same age as my son would have been..." He stopped for a moment. These feelings hadn't crossed his mind for weeks, now they were back with all their attendant sadness, "...if Caroline had not died, taking the boy with her. So now I'm hesitant in case Matea thinks I will regard her as a substitute."

"You've never mentioned any of this before. I knew you were a widower but reckoned that if you wanted to tell me the details you would do so in your own time."

"Thanks, Paddy. I was never going to because, as I said, I came out here to forget."

"Don't blame you," the Irishman replied kindly, "and don't go on if you don't want to. Stupid of me to have asked."

"No, Paddy," James reassured his friend, "You were right to do so. I am a touch shy, if that is the right word, about admitting my feelings, for the reasons I have just explained. But the desire to look after Matea and Dino have intensified over the last day or so. I feel honour bound to protect her, but also I believe I have a duty to do so as well."

"And she knows none of this?"

"No."

"Any idea how she feels towards you?"

"Yes," James replied quickly, "and that doesn't help. I don't want her to think any feelings I have might be out of sympathy." He looked deep into his glass, "They are far, far more profound than that."

"Do you know what, James," Patrick advised, taking their empty glasses to the sideboard, "The sooner you tell her the sooner the more secure she will feel and the sooner she will get better. She will do anything to stop her country re-arming in order to prevent yet more bloodshed, yet more ethnic cleansing and, as she sees it, you are the key to achieving that."

"Is that treachery? As that bastard Slavić accuses her of committing."

"Another time. Another place maybe. Not here."

"You're right, Paddy. Now, how much longer before we can eat?"

There was time for James to make what he hoped would be the last call of the day.

"Augustin?"

In the next few minutes James briefed the British Consul on Doctor Nowak's positive prognosis; described Slavić's untimely appearance; confirmed that he could not leave the house while Matea was immobile and ended by stating, for the benefit of any phone-tappers that might now have been alerted by the Croatian colonel, that he needed to send a message to his 'non-existent' brother in London.

"I'll be with you in twenty minutes, "Augustin replied.

"Then you must stay for supper. Guess what it is!" They hung up.

With Augustin's arrival came his secure, Secret Intelligence Service-issue, mobile telephone and while the British Consul guided Patrick through the finishing touches of the lamb's preparation, James dialled Magnus Sixsmith's number from a spare bedroom.

"James?" Magnus questioned, "On Augustin's line and this late in the day. Must be serious."

"Both serious and time sensitive," James replied, "At least we think so." He followed this introduction with a full brief of the conflicting orders that led to his resignation, culminating with the events at Brač and Ploče. Summing up he added, "So, I have proof that the US is breaking the arms embargo. I'm pretty sure Germany is. I've been told not to monitor the coast by the French and yet to monitor the coast, covertly, by the Greeks. Then falsify my reports. As far as the ECMM is concerned I am now required, formally, to learn more about the Predator's operations and any other cargoes through the sea ports while I, in turn, will be monitored like a hawk by Slavić's men."

"All in a days' work, James." Magnus's sardonic laughter was not improved by the reception.

"Of course," James agreed, "but I can't do much till Matea is better."

"Let me stop you there," Magnus interrupted. "While you've been talking I've been thinking. The last of the British Oberon class submarines, HMS *Orion*, is still in service. Only just, as she is about to be brought home from the Med to pay off at the end of the summer. You may know her?"

"I do indeed…"

"We have a Royal Marines Special Boat Service team on board off Cyprus having finished a task for us further east." Magnus stopped and said no more on the subject. "Tell Augustin I need to speak to him, then I'll come back to you within twenty four hours."

"He has a roll of film that I took on Brač. He'll fax the prints, plus those of the tanks at Ploče, in the morning."

"Thanks," Magnus acknowledged, "Sadly, though, I don't suppose we have a snowball's chance in hell of stopping either the Krauts or the Yanks breaking the embargo but we can give it a damn good try."

James said goodbye and called Augustin to the 'phone.

The meal was a success, the lamb cooked, thanks to Augustin's late involvement, to perfection while the wine was... Croatian.

Before the two visitors left Augustin handed James the mobile telephone, "Magnus asked me to leave this with you so maybe you won't need me to send your reports. I will, though fax the photographs to him once I have them back. I've asked for two copies of each."

Patrick asked, "Are you sure you will be safe, James?"

"How the hell do I know, Paddy, with that idiot on the loose! But I think it might be safer, when Matea can walk, for us all to move into the hotel."

Alone at last and with Dino tucked up in his own bedroom James helped Matea to the bathroom.

With her teeth cleaned and standing on one leg, wearing a light cotton dressing gown, Matea watched James pull back the sheets on his side of the bed. "Oh good," she laughed aloud, "Tonight I don't have to ask you!"

During the short journey from the bathroom, with his arm around Matea's waist while hers held on to his shoulders, James's body was subconsciously – although becoming increasingly obvious – reminded of what, apart from Camille's experienced hands and tongue, it had been missing for six long years.

James had always known that one day a physical boundary would be crossed, properly, but he did not want it to occur without love and affection. Certainly he had not expected it to happen in Croatia, a phase of his life he regarded as a watershed which, once endured, would have cleared the emotional path for the future back in St Mawes. He knew, too, since that first night in Hotel Adriatica that Matea and Dino had seldom been far from his conscious thoughts: their helplessness when confronted with military weapons and international hatred and their vulnerability to the indiscriminate dangers of modern warfare had been forcibly imprinted on his memory. Memories reinforced when Matea's childhood friend, Miljana, had died in his arms as he read the letter amid the rubble that had, moments before, been Karin Plaza's primary school.

Now he wanted Matea, emotionally and physically, and he wanted her more than anything else he could possible think off. James reached for her hand. Holding it tightly he pulled it gently across his stomach, then he rolled towards her to kiss the back of her neck slowly and delicately. Matea sighed with the same pleasure that a cat might stretch and purr in front of a log fire, revelling in a man's touch for the first time since… she could not remember the last time she and her husband had made love before he was killed. It had been a more-than-frequent event, with each orgasm as superbly, lovingly-satisfying as the last. Over time all memories had slowly tumbled into one great kaleidoscopic pot-pourri of recalled desire…

Now it was happening again: and of that Matea was convinced.

James turned her face to meet his until, quite unexpectedly for both, they were kissing with a passion neither had known since the beginning of widowhood: lips explored lips, tongue explored tongue as hands began their own exciting searches.

Somehow James managed to take a deep breath and whisper, "Life will never be the same. Are you sure you want that?"

"I don't want it ever to be the same again," she answered,

"Let's take our time, there's no hurry now."

They took their time…

James woke early, slid silently from the bed, looked down at Matea's sleeping body, her face framed by her hair, and smiled with a well-remembered pleasure. Excited once more, as though the night had not been long enough to satiate a physical and emotional longing, he admired the full length of her naked body, recalling the words her lips had uttered in the darkness. Not for the first time an all-consuming sensation of tenderness swept over him. He knew, as he had known all along, that nothing now mattered, not Croatia, not Serbia, not the ECMM nor even the United Nations embargo mattered one jot when balanced against her safety and happiness. He tiptoed out of the room to fill the kettle.

The day, a Wednesday, was ordained by outside events rather than through any effort on James's part: Dino was being collected for breakfast and school by friends; the doctor was expected to call to change Matea's dressings and James was waiting for Magnus's call. All the while he was half expecting Slavić to make a second visit… but this time James would be prepared. As he had no intention of leaving the house, even for one minute, he could concentrate on writing his report, whether Magnus would need it or not. It was also the ideal time to study maps, charts, phases of the moon to plan his new monitoring routine. An even more ideal use of his time would be talking to Matea and discussing their future together.

She called from the top of the stairs, "*Duša*. You have left me already!"

"Not far and not for long," James shouted back, "I'm bringing some tea."

With Dino collected James sat on Matea's bed, running his fingers through her hair, caressing the back of her neck and asking questions. "Apart from your name I hardly know you," he began. "I suppose it's the same for you too."

For the next hour they behaved as young lovers do, talking, teasing, stroking, caressing, asking and answering questions.

"Thank you for last night," Matea eventually said, leaning back against James's chest. "I didn't want dawn to come. It was like being a teenager again."

"I hope your thigh didn't hurt?"

"That wasn't the bit that concerned me!"

"My inclination is to take you away from all this..."

"And my inclination is to go willingly with you," Matea replied hurriedly, before a serious frown wrinkled her brow, "I'm fed up with all the bloodshed, no matter on which side. Is it treachery to only want love and peace?"

"You have my love. You know that don't you?"

"And I love you too *duša* but what about the peace?"

"The peace will only come if the United Nations takes action and I am unsure that it will. We could argue that we've done our bit by alerting both the ECMM and the wider international community and so we can leave, if we must, with a clear conscience." James thought for a moment, "Perhaps not such a clear conscience as long as your parents remain in certain danger."

"Do you really believe that James?" Matea remained serious, "Is that what you want?"

"What I want is for you and Dino to be safe. Nothing more and certainly nothing less. And if you want to stay until we reach the point that we really can do nothing more then that is fine with me."

"We must stay, James. Even if we know we can never stop the bloodshed. We could never forgive ourselves if we go before we are forced to. Nor would my parents."

"It will become even more dangerous…"

"That's no reason to give in!" Matea retorted, "Or am I being selfish? It is my country and not yours. I have no right to ask you."

"If you want to stay then that is the end of the matter. We stay. But I think it would be best if we leave your house until things settle down."

Matea leant back and kissed James full on his lips. When she let go and James had caught his breath he said, "I'll get your breakfast."

"I would rather have you…"

Later that morning the mobile telephone rang. James lifted the hand piece and walked into the sitting room. "Laidlaw," he said.

"Can you speak?" asked Magnus.

"I'm alone."

"I've got the films. Firm evidence that Slavić and Anderson are working together. Good shots of them watching the Predator being unloaded. I can tell you that a second UAV will arrive in Brač. Probably over the weekend of the 26/27th March. The full moon period. I can't tell you what to do as an ECMM monitor but as we have all the evidence that we need for the British Ambassador in the UN to put before the Security Council, I have no reason to ask you to do anything more."

"That's a relief," James laughed, "but we have no idea what the Predator is here for, although Slavic's presence probably answers that."

"Do you remember that I said HMS *Orion* was doing some work for us, based in Cyprus?"

"With an SBS team. Yes."

"I've just come from a meeting with the Commander in Chief of the Fleet and both the Defence and Foreign Secretaries.

They have agreed that the submarine will position herself off the south coast of Brač in a week's time. She will be able to monitor the heading of UAV flights into and out of the island if you can give me the latitude and longitude of the centre of the runway and its alignment. If that doesn't work we will send the SBS team ashore. To do that I shall need guidance on where they can land unobserved and the best place from where to watch the airfield."

"I'll study the charts and maps as soon as we end this call."

"How's your lady interpreter?"

"Getting better. Her thigh isn't bothering her quite so much now." James nearly added that it was him that was bothering her thighs but, wisely, thought better of it. More sensibly he said, "As soon as she is mobile I'll be moving back to Hotel Split for safety reasons and will be taking her and her son with me."

"You'll know what is best. Meanwhile the sooner you can get that information to me the better."

"Give me an hour."

Making sure that Matea was comfortable James again laid out his charts on the dining room table where his calculations took no more than a few minutes. As a submariner he assessed the water depths close to Brač's south coast and the approaches from the westward, both of which were suitable for underwater operations. There was even plenty of water to within half a mile of the shore should the boat's commanding officer prefer to remain submerged. From there the total distance to the runway's south western threshold was a mile and a half. James had no idea of the rate of climb of a Predator, that was for someone else to assess, but he believed that the UAV's sensors would be active from before take-off to after landing and thus a submarine on the bearing of the take-off run, assuming a south-westerly wind, would have no difficulty observing the aircraft's ultimate course. A north-easterly wind, though, could be a problem as the aircraft climbed up over the land. He knew, too, that following the defection of most of Croatia's armed forces to Yugoslavia, Croatia had no anti-submarine capability. He telephoned Magnus.

"The runway's south-western threshold is at 43 degrees 16'.5 north and 16 degrees 40'.9 east and runs for, I would guess, between 4,000 and 6,000 feet on a bearing of 034 degrees true."

"Got it. Any idea for landing and observation points?"

James explained that anywhere to the east of Bol would be suitable as there was no coast road from which a landing could be spotted. Heading north to the position he had just given would mean crossing the only road out of the village which would not present an obstruction in the very light, night-time traffic. From his own observations he knew that to gain any high ground that overlooked the airfield without crossing the electrified fence would mean moving into the olive groves that cover Baljenik hill to the west. Here, he elaborated, the land was uninhabited and isolated while offering a good view of the whole airfield.

"Thanks, James. Keep me up to date if you discover anything more." Magnus finished by asking that the secure mobile telephone be returned to Augustin as soon as possible.

Having discharged the only planned task of the day and still under his self-imposed house-arrest, as he laughingly called it, he returned to Matea's bed. When Doctor Nowak changed Matea's dressings that evening he declared that she could now move around the house and, in three days, could drive. James made his second call of the day and the first on the house telephone.

"Patrick," he said, "We're free! Would you tell the hotel that we'll both be back in Room 519 on Monday and ask them to make up the room opposite for Dino."

As he stretched to replace the receiver there was a double click on the line before it went dead.

CHAPTER TWENTY-SIX

Monday 13th March 1994
Villa Perunika, Šetalište Ivana Meštrovica,
Split, Croatia

With Dino due to be returned direct to Hotel Split at the end of the day James and Matea packed their suitcases, secured the house, ensuring that each window and outside doors' security catches were closed and locked. James then drove Matea in her Fiat Spider the three miles to the hotel where Patrick was in the foyer waiting with the room keys, ready to help carry the luggage upstairs – via the lift.

As the doors pulled open Matea wished the two bored guards a good morning while the monitors humped the cases along the corridor to Room 519. James opened the French windows and looked out across the entrance to beyond Split harbour, imagining that he could see Villa Perunika's bedroom window through the haze on the far horizon. He stood for a moment, remembering, while Matea, behind him, began to unpack.

Villa Perunika – Villa Iris – was named, Matea had explained, after Croatia's national flower by her uncle and aunt when they had it built fifty years before and was now the house where James had first made love to their niece and where he promised her an undying devotion coupled with a continual search for peace for her country. The former, he had assured her, was set in stone but the latter... well, they both appreciated the obstacles that lay ahead.

James turned from the balcony and picked up Dino's small case. "I'll check his room," he said, "then you will probably want to unpack his things yourself."

Taking the key he crossed the corridor, unlocked the door, stepped inside... he stopped, sniffing. Puzzled. He sniffed more deeply. His first reaction was that the cleaning ladies had overdone – as he knew was their habit – their deodorant that morning. His second reaction was to freeze, enveloped by a sudden, powerful sense of foreboding. The last time he had smelt Old Spice aftershave was when it was wafting around Viktor and Bruno, Slavić's two deckhands, on board the yacht *Helena*.

Behind him, across the corridor, Matea watched James stand still as though he had instantly been cast in bronze. Something was wrong for he was usually imperturbable. Limping silently across the carpeted passage she placed a hand gently on his shoulder. Without turning he said very slowly and quietly, "Don't come in, darling." Then, in case she had not gathered the importance of his order, he repeated it, emphasising the urgency, "For God's sake don't come in. Something's very wrong."

He whispered harshly, "Get Patrick."

With Patrick's arrival James turned his head but kept his feet still, "Paddy," he said, "I'm certain those two deckhands of Slavić have been in the room. They will have been here for a reason and an unpleasantly dangerous one at that."

"An IED?"

"What's that," asked Matea from the passage, her voice already raised in fear.

"Improvised explosive device," answered Patrick. "But... probably not. Too sophisticated for them and kills indiscriminately..." Matea gulped audibly, her hand clasped to her mouth, "...and I doubt that would be Slavić's aim. Has to be more personal."

"You're right Paddy. There is something in this room aimed to do individual harm."

"Tread cautiously, James. Be very, very careful."

"Paddy," James was not certain what to look for nor how to look for it, "Why don't you take the right side, I'll search the left of the room. Look, don't feel. Behind everything. On top of everything. Beneath everything. Inside everything."

As Patrick inched towards the dressing table and wardrobe an uneasy sensation crept coldly down his back. His heart was beating. His hands were sweating. He took a few cautious steps forwards.

On the opposite side of the room James was experiencing a similar anxiety. The unknown, in his own milieu, was one thing but the unidentifiable among such banal, familiar, everyday surroundings was different.

"Stop, Paddy. Stop!" James was not happy. They needed to be armed. He had no idea what against but he was naked with nothing with which to prod, to prise, to explore hidden corners... to defend. He needed protection, no matter how primitive. "Matea, darling. In the office you'll find a couple of brooms."

Patrick was standing now by the shower door. It was shut. No noise came from the far side other than the slow, rhythmic drip, drip, drip of a leaking shower head, that added to the suspense. The room itself seemed, but only seemed, empty of hazards. What ever the boys had been up to had to be behind the closed door, or under the bed, or on the east-facing balcony:

the three areas yet to be investigated.

The two monitors stood statue-still, assessing the unfamiliar dread until each was armed with a broom, then, as Matea turned away, a slight movement caught her eye. It was not natural. Bed clothes do not move on their own unless, unless...

She stood still, slowly raising her hand and pointing. *"Duša,"* she said in a whisper, fearful of antagonising what ever it was that she had seen twitch. Her voice trembled as she murmured, softer than before. "Don't move but I think..." she was not finding it easy to describe what she thought. Her words were difficult to form as she struggled to articulate them through her terror, "...I think... I am certain... that the duvet just moved."

James swung round. Patrick leapt to his side with the bed in front of them, the length of a broom handle away. In the centre, beneath the quilt, a movement was obvious. The monitors looked at each other, slowly nodding their unspoken agreement. Neither had any idea what was between the sheets, only that if Slavić was involved, what was lying in wait had to be evil.

With all the strength each could muster James and Patrick swung their brooms downwards with the absolute, unbridled vigour of Olympian athletes. Matea turned her face away while the ferocious beating continued. Dust rose. Feathers floated free. Blood seeped upwards through the white cotton. Then the assault ceased. Whatever was beneath the deadly blows that had rained upon it could not have survived. If it had, James and Patrick remained prepared.

"Paddy," James suggested, "why don't you stand opposite me. When I give the word we'll pull the duvet back together. Fast."

In place, either side of the head, James commanded, "Now!"

Beneath the bedclothes, the bloodied remains of two adult,

male Croatian horned vipers, recently disturbed from their hibernation, lay entwined, twitching delicately in their death throes. Their brown, dark-zig-zagged bodies were immersed in a widening pool of gore as the fetid contents of their ruptured intestines oozed into the mattress.

Matea, clutching her mouth, rushed to James's room, reaching the lavatory bowl just as violent spasms of involuntary retching began to empty her stomach.

James and Patrick, both grim-faced and flushed with anger, stood back from their distasteful but necessary handiwork. Guessing that James, now in deep thought, would feel this latest attack more personally than himself, Patrick was the first to speak, "To know that it was a fellow human being that did this, not to a grown up but to a five-year old really suspends all my belief."

James, controlling his anger, replied more calmly than he felt, "Paddy, we've got to confront the bastard. Apart from that, I know Matea cannot go on under such sustained threats. She only has to be unlucky once and that will be that. I can't guard her or Dino that closely, not for twenty four hours in every twenty four. I had hoped we would be safer here but apparently not. I'll have to think again."

Dwelling on the negatives Patrick added, "And it will be too easy for Slavić to find out where Dino goes to school," before offering advice, "I'm not sure that a face to face with Slavić will do much good. He might draw his gun on you for he doesn't seem to have any qualms about using it."

"I hate to think what other tricks he has up his sleeve but whatever they are we must be seriously vigilant. I'm not sure how long I can continue to outsmart him as he has all the advantages."

Patrick studied the vipers. Dead or alive, he hated snakes.

Being an Irishman he had never had contact with them as a child: a dead snake was the only snake he had ever wanted to meet. "How poisonous are these," he asked prodding one with the handle of his broom.

"Dangerous to young people, the elderly and dogs."

"Know much about them?"

"Only what I can remember from some survival course. Either way, bad news."

Inspecting the carnage Patrick said, "This is a task for the hotel manager. The room between yours and the office is free. I suggest that Dino uses that one."

"Good idea, Paddy. And not a word to the lad."

"I'll also speak to the guards. My reckoning is that they will have been well bribed by Slavić so I doubt they will offer any plausible reason why or how the two lads not only had access to a key but were also allowed to roam the fifth floor."

"Bastard!" was all James could repeat. "Now I'd better look after Matea. What a terrifying thing to have witnessed."

"One thing, James?" Patrick queried, "What made you suspicious in the first place?"

"Old Spice aftershave. And I'll tell you something else. I bet it was supplied to Slavić by Dwight Anderson from the US Embassy in Zagreb. Can't buy it here in Split."

"You seem pretty certain. How do you know that?"

"No idea," replied James. Then he turned and strode across the corridor shutting the door to Room 519 behind him. Once more, and in quick succession, he was facing a crisis point. He would have to confront Matea with his solution: while knowing that she would not find it easy to accept.

"Matea, darling Matea," he consoled, an arm around her shoulders. Sitting on the edge of the bed she was wiping her mouth with a handkerchief. "I got you into this mess. It is up to me to get you out of it."

Between sniffles she asked, "How do you mean?"

"If you had not been with me, Slavić would never have been able to accuse you of anything."

"He wants me out of the way. He knows what I have seen." While James fetched a glass of water, Matea blew her nose. Her hand was shaking, her body shivering. "James," she said on his return, "I'm more frightened than when we were being fired at. That was instant fear. But this is a deep, deep terror that I know won't go away."

"You have to face up to the fact that you are one of the very few who thinks that negotiations are the answer, not a military invasion of the RSK. People will not take your side and Slavić will be bargaining on that." James was laying the groundwork for his proposal.

"We can't fight Slavić on our own."

"Which is why I want you to agree my plan."

"Whatever it is, it is Dino's safety that counts far more."

James, comforting in his reaction, was building up slowly to his suggestion. "I have not fallen in love with you only to watch you being scared when we should be celebrating our new-found happiness."

"How kind."

"Not kind. Realistic," explained James, "and that realism says that we cannot stay here any longer especially as we can't stop what is happening…"

"That would be a terrible admission of defeat," Matea countered. "and is what I would call treachery. Very different from Slavić's idea of treason."

James, knowing that he faced an uphill struggle, offered his only trump card, "Any invasion will need more than American intelligence. It will need a considerable increase in the fighting power of the Croatian army and that will take time. Maybe a year. We have got time to get away, then return to somehow rescue your parents when even Slavić will be pre-occupied with operational planning."

"Can we be of any influence if we leave?"

"I have an entrée into various organisations in London plus, now, the very top of the ECMM."

"Where are you suggesting?"

"Well," James took the plunge. "If you marry me we will go to my house in England, monitor events very carefully through my contacts then return when it makes a tiny bit more sense." He thought a little deeper, "And if you don't marry me…" he tailed off.

Matea sat immobile. She was in love with James. She had probably known that since he had saved her life and that of Dino but she also knew that there was nothing rational about her feelings. They were just her feelings. You don't fall in love with someone just because he saves your life. Or do you? She knew the answer.

"Did you just ask me to marry you?"

"Yes, I think I did!"

Matea lay back across the bed. "Hold me, James. Hold me very tight."

James did as commanded. Feeling her lips nuzzling his ear he knew her answer before she gave it.

"Yes," Matea whispered, "Yes please."

"It would mean leaving Croatia."

"Then we must leave… but not for ever. I have my parents… I'm desperate for their safety… and desperate to see them again."

"Not for ever. I promise."

They lay together for an hour, not daring to move. Each

needing to assimilate two momentous decisions: each deciding in their own idiosyncratic way how to come to terms with them.

Not wishing to break the spell, James gently removed his arm from beneath Matea's head and crept to Team Split's office and its insecure telephone. He dialled the Head of the British Delegation's number in Hotel Betonska.

Later he telephoned Magnus on his 'open' line and explained the situation. "I'll keep you in touch while you are in the UK. It's beginning to hot up from the intelligence perspective so, after your marriage, I will need you to come to London."

That evening over dinner, with Dino tucked safely up in his new room and the guards having been sternly lectured by Matea on their duties, the three discussed the day's prime event. It was agreed that Slavić needed confronting, not by James but by the ECMM itself.

As a valedictory observation James summed up the current position, "We have established almost beyond doubt that America is about to supply Croatia with intelligence on Serb troop strengths, dispositions and movements. We won't know that for certain of course, until we see a Predator flying eastwards but it has to be a pretty good guess.

"We are equally sure that Ukraine, with German help, is also breaking the embargo by importing M-84 main battle tanks into the country. We know too that the Croatian army is being boosted by a large influx of American mercenaries and with them, from what one sees on the streets, are coming American small arms. Closer to home, have you noticed that some soldiers are quite openly displaying swastika arm bands?"

Matea and Patrick nodded for the Nazi symbols had been the subject of much comment in the local news papers, and particularly in the radical *Slobodan Dalmatia*.

"Even closer to home," James continued, "We now

understand that Sublette does not want to know anything at all about the embargo contravention because if he does he will have to include it in his daily reports and thus open up the possibility that someone will take action to stop it.

"Conversely, Pagonis is keen to know what is going on, not as the Head of the Zadar Coordinating Centre but as a Greek special forces officer. Whatever he finds out will not go via HQ ECMM but direct to his Navy headquarters in Athens.

"Finally, in four months time Germany will assume the European Union presidency for the following six months. I will lay you a hefty bet that no action against the RSK will take place then, it would be too obvious, but during the six months that follow, when France holds the Presidency. So, if we assume that the RSK is to be invaded, it will happen next summer."

"That's convincing, James."

"And now I come to Ante Slavić. A known Serb hater. Chief of Staff of the 4th Guards Brigade which if I'm right will spearhead any invasion against Knin, the seat of the RSK government, as it's primary target."

The discussion continued late until at last James stood to face Patrick. "Paddy, my friend," he stated, "I'm afraid that this has to be goodbye but, I hope, a temporary one."

"Where are you going?" Patrick enquired, "It's a bit late!"

"I don't know why we've kept this from you till the last moment," James confessed, "but Matea and I are flying to England in the morning to get…" James could not bring himself to admit the reason… he couldn't say the word.

"Married?" Patrick prompted loudly, "Married?" James and Matea nodded. "Well I'm buggered," he said.

"We'll be back, but while Slavić is in this murderous mood we think it best to keep out of his way and we could think of no better excuse than to," he hesitated, the enormity of the decision had yet to sink in… "to… to…"

"Marry, James," Matea encouraged, "the word is marry. Or had you already forgotten!"

Grinning broadly James continued, "While I am away I'll keep you up-to-date with what I can glean from my London friends. I've discussed this with my Head of Delegation who has agreed to pass any messages direct to you."

"Well I'm buggered," Patrick repeated. "I'll miss you both, James and Matea."

"That may be so," James laughed, "but I have a final request."

"The answer's yes. What's the question?"

"Will you be my best man."

During the flight home James described life in England to Matea and Dino. He spoke of the house in the far south-west, of the formidable but lovely Mrs B, of his yacht *Sea Vixen*, of the capricious weather and that everyone drove on the left.

At Heathrow James made a number of telephone calls. Five hours out of Paddington – during which time Dino had gazed spellbound out of the train's window at the early spring countryside, wakening after the winter's drizzle and frosts – Jake was as good as his word and was waiting with the Bristol at Truro railway station.

Arriving in the dark Mrs B greeted the trio at Percuil House's front door. "This is such a lovely surprise," she exclaimed loudly with arms outstretched to welcome each in turn as they stepped from the car.

Matea's journey-long trepidation at meeting James's housekeeper was instantly dispelled by a warm, wet kiss on each cheek.

"You are most welcome. Most welcome," Mrs B repeated, "and about time too I kept on telling the commander."

Matea giggled, already feeling at home while Dino ran past

into the house happily knowing that no men with guns – he still did not know about the snakes – would come looking for his mother, or him.

"Mama has promised," he said seriously to Mrs B, leaving her unaware of the details of the promise.

Mrs B, hoping she knew James well enough and having read between the lines of the recent telephone calls, had made up the double bed in the main bedroom and was grinning broadly as she helped carry the suitcases upstairs. Everything was returning to normal and, an added bonus, a young child's laughter would, once more, reverberate through the house.

It had been a long day of contrasting emotions for Matea: joy at leaving the dangers behind; sadness at leaving Split knowing that they were running away and the belief that she had failed her country and, maybe, were about to fail her parents. Every time her feelings overwhelmed her – on the plane and in the train – she had taken James's hand and asked him the same question, "Are you sure we can help from this far away?"

"Not only is the answer still yes," he had reassured her but, each time, he also reminded her of, to him, the more important reason why they had 'escaped'. As soon as Matea and Dino had found their feet James would make an appointment to meet the vicar of St Just in Roseland church.

"Don't forget I am a Catholic," Matea had reminded him.

James had thought for a moment. "Well," he said, "as the church was founded in 550 AD I am sure it too was once catholic so I don't see a problem, especially as it was actually named after a catholic saint. We are both widowed so that won't be a difficulty either."

As they slipped into bed that first night at St Mawes James hugged Matea to him, making sure that their bodies touched at every possible point from their cheeks to their toes. "I feel safe now, *duša*. Properly safe. Thank you," she murmured into an ear. "It's rather sudden and I will relax soon but right now to know that no one will burst through the door is comforting. Knowing that if anyone does, having you beside me is even more soothing."

Their love-making was long, electrifying and, eventually, calming. Then, as a gentle mellowness swamped them they slept soundly without 'losing touch'. As he drifted to sleep James knew that Caroline would have approved that he was, once more, happy. Mrs B certainly did and that mattered almost as much.

In the morning Dino rushed into their room shouting in Croatian, "Mama, look. Out of the window." He hurled back the curtains, "The sea. Just like home but with so many boats."

Alarmed, momentarily frightened by the sudden intrusion, Matea, chided softly, "Dino, thank goodness it is you."

For the rest of the week James introduced Matea – and Dino when he was not at home under Mrs B's watchful care – to St Mawes's small, picturesque harbour, to the Rising Sun and the Idle Rocks hotels. They walked around King Henry VIII's coastal artillery fortress; they took the ferry to Falmouth on a shopping expedition; they drove round to Mylor and *Sea Vixen* to check that all was well in her winter state and, when Dino was resting and Mrs B had left for the day, they made love with the evening sun flooding through the bedroom windows. For Matea, memories of the dangers associated with Split, if not her native country, were slipping into the past while for James the almost seamless transition back to his previous life was satisfying. Snippets of news, when they came via Patrick, reminded him that the transition was... transitory and that one day they had an inescapable task to complete.

Locked away in a safe James knew that the Lennox family

had kept a collection of rings so while Matea was chatting to Mrs B in the garden he went delving until he found what he did not know he was looking for: a single, large diamond surrounded by a circle of smaller stones. If it did not fit then the jeweller in St Mawes would alter it: they may well have sold it to the family in the first place.

That evening, overlooking Carrick Roads, the darkness dotted with the lights of passing ships and the intermittent flashing of the navigational buoys, James took Matea's hands. He looked into her face, lit by two steady candles on the dining table. She guessed, she certainly hoped, that their engagement would, at some point, be marked in a more practical manner than a spoken promise and while she knew she had no right to expect anything more from this down-to earth Englishman... "Darling Matea," James began, then faltered. He had already asked her to marry him and she had agreed. Why ask again...? His left hand felt in a pocket. Slowly and purposefully he slipped the diamond ring onto Matea's finger, "I want you to have this permanent reminder of my love for you," he said simply.

Matea looked down. She had never seen anything so beautiful. She wanted to say thank you. She wanted to leap up and kiss him. She wanted to say that she would wear it for ever as a reminder of that love for her. Instead she burst into tears.

In bed she wanted to tell James what she had failed to say at dinner but, over the next two hours showed him in her own, practical manner. No words were needed.

That weekend the trio attended matins in St Just in Roseland church after which they invited the vicar to lunch. A date for a summer wedding was agreed, the banns would be read and a guest list drawn up. James, conscious that the ceremony should, by convention, take place from the bride's home, finally asked a question to which he had never known the answer. Only now did he discover that Matea's sole close relatives were Dino and her parents in Drniš. Her uncle and aunt, who had built and owned Villa Perunika, had died years ago leaving her, their one niece, the house. Hers had once been a large family that fate, and the war with Serbia, had slowly thinned out.

By chance Patrick, due a spell of mid tour leave, telephoned to ask if he could come to stay on his way to his native Cork via Newquay airport. "Better than that, Paddy," James retorted with a laugh, "You will be in time to carry out that little task I once asked!"

James and Matea were married in June with Patrick the best man, Dino the page and the reception in Percuil House. For their honeymoon, Dino stayed with Mrs B, whom he adored, while James and Matea cruised the local waters for a fortnight.

A favourite anchorage lay under the western cliffs of Rame Head, the distinctive promontory that marks the Atlantic approach to Plymouth, and the tiny shell of a chapel at its peak, a touch over 330 feet above the calm channel waters. In the hazy afternoon James rowed his bride of ten days ashore where they left the dinghy on the beach. "Race you to the top," he challenged, laying the oars across the thwarts.

"I'd rather we walked up together."

Holding hands, taking time to stop and kiss they slowly covered the circuitous mile to the peak where, stretching themselves across the summit's rocks by the small, stone building, James pulled Matea towards him. He whispered in an ear,

'Breathless we flung us on the windy hill.

Laughed in the sun and kissed the lovely grass.'

"Let me guess," she said, "An English poet?"

"Rupert Brooke."

"Is there any more?"

"Lots but the rest is quite sad and ends with the words, 'And then you suddenly cried and turned away.'"

"I'm not sad, though I might have been. No I'm not sad. Very far from it, *duša*. You have made me so happy. I know we have unfinished business and I can't stop worrying about that but here, right now, and for ever I hope, I am happy, happy, happy!" She rolled against James and snuggled her face into his neck.

The idyllic summer wore on: Dino was becoming proficient around *Sea Vixen* with James calling him proudly 'my unpaid, paid hand': in practice this was a misnomer for he was compensated handsomely with pocket money to cover his on-board duties. He began learning knots, splices and how to identify and name the different sea birds. His English improved following his enrolment in the local primary school.

On Christmas Day Matea, sitting on the floor beneath the decorated tree, surrounded by presents and torn wrapping paper tugged James down beside her. "*Duša*," she began holding tightly on to a hand as they knelt, facing each other, "you have already had your present from me but I have something even more special to give you."

James, unsuspecting, reached towards the nearby table for a glass of champagne. "I'm going to have a baby," Matea said.

The flute stopped on the way to his lips, the wine slopped, fizzing, onto the carpet. Unable, on the spur of the moment, to think of anything that wasn't trite, he leaned forwards to kiss her until she stopped him, "These are very early days but if I am right it will be due in mid to late August."

James's happiness was complete and Matea shared that happiness.

The idyll was balanced over the New Year when the news from Croatia began taking on a less savoury note with every telephone call from Patrick, Magnus and Augustin. The increasing number of soldiers sporting swastika armbands, the painting of huge 'U's for Ustaše on prominent buildings, the proliferation of troop movements supported by an increasing number of main battle tanks, and fighter aircraft – replacing those that Croatia had lost when it gained its independence from Yugoslavia – screaming low overhead, were all worrying signs. The completion of the transfer from the Croatian dinar to the old Nazi currency of the kuna added to the general despondency.

In the late spring of 1995, Augustin telephoned. "James," he began, "I think you should know that Slavić has been seen prowling around the gardens of Matea's house. I took a look myself and there is no sign of any break-in but the fact that he is still interested in her continues to justify your absence."

"She misses her earlier life," James explained, "although I have to say that since we have been back she has looked younger each day. I don't think it was until she was here that she realised just how on edge she always was."

"Sadly," Augustin said, hesitantly and with some circumspection, "I think that things are taking a most marked turn for the worse. I have been briefed by Magnus who, as you know, is privy to all manner of information."

"I'll give him a call." James suggested, "then visit him so he can speak openly?"

"I don't want anything to happen without you being warned. Especially as Matea's parents are still in Drniš and not likely to move on their own accord."

It was her parent's welfare that gave Matea most concern. She knew that she and James had failed to prevent the build up of Croatian arms and intelligence. All she could do now, when the time was right, was to rescue – by force if that became necessary – her mother and father from the inevitable and in that task she simply could not fail.

"James?" Magnus answered his telephone. "You must be psychic as I was about to call. Can you meet me at the same place as before. Same time." He offered a date.

The Lyndsay House was unchanged from James's first lunch in October 1993. He was shown to the same table as before and, as before, Magnus was precisely ten minutes late.

"If you hadn't seen what you saw at the Brač airstrip we would probably still be in the dark, so well done on that score." Magnus, by-passing all small talk, was heading straight to the point. "Now let me tell you the story so far. As a result of signal intelligence relayed to me daily from the Government Communications Headquarters – GCHQ – at Cheltenham we know the following," Magnus began counting facts off on his fingers, "The Croatian army is now 150,000 strong thanks to a large percentage of American mercenaries; the army has 350 tanks and we know where many of those came from; it is supported by 800 heavy artillery pieces and possibly as many as 18 Mig-21 fighters as well as a number of Russian-built – but not supplied – transport and attack helicopters. A United States contracting firm called Military Professional Resources Incorporated has, in collusion with the French Foreign Legion," James smiled at the open acceptance of French involvement, "supplied training, especially for Croatian non-commissioned officers. Although nominally based in Alexandria, Virginia, it has established a camp at Šepurine near Zadar."

"That's quite an army. No prizes for guessing why it is needed."

"Not when you see that the RSK has only 55,000 men under arms and a good number of those are not front line soldiers or are stationed in eastern Slovenia. Which leaves about 30,000 to guard the border with Croatia of 730 miles."

"No contest," observed James, beginning to make up his mind over his next course of action.

"GCHQ have also intercepted transmissions between the US intelligence team at your Brač airfield and the US Defense Attaché, Anderson, in Zagreb. The Predator is clearly doing its stuff and doing it rather well. Anderson is passing to the Croatian army the total dispositions and movements, in real time, of all Serbian ground forces."

"Did you use the SBS?"

"Invaluable. Saved a lot of time initially as they could confirm the departure and return of each mission and its heading, thus the time over any specific target could be worked out. Once we understood that then GCHQ knew what to listen to. The Predators are covering every corner of the Krajina regions; the whole of Bosnia Herzegovina as far as the Sava River, the border with Serbia proper."

"How imminent is the invasion?" James asked, "I need to know as I must return to complete an outstanding task."

"It is now June. Our assessment is that the build up is complete. The Croats will wait for the French presidency of the EU to be established..." Magnus paused for a sip of wine while he calculated silently in his head, "...so let's say early August."

As they said goodbye in Romilly Street Magnus promised that he would send a coded message indicating the date of the invasion that he knew would reach him in London from Zagreb – via Cheltenham – almost before it would reach Slavić in Split.

On the train home it was James's turn to calculate. To have any chance of persuading Mr and Mrs Tomić to leave Drniš willingly it would have to be done at the last moment. There could be no misunderstanding by the stubborn and proud couple of what the Croatian army was up to. Any later than the invasion and it would be too late: earlier and Matea's arrival in Split would soon reach Slavic's ears and the consequences of that were too terrible to consider.

It would be a fine judgement and contained in that judgement was the expected date of Matea's confinement.

CHAPTER TWENTY-SEVEN

Friday 28th July 1995
Percuil House, Tredenhum Road,
St Mawes, Cornwall.

The call came in Magnus's pre-arranged code. The Croatian invasion of the Republic of Serbian Krajina – code-named *Operation Storm* – would begin at 0500 on Friday the 4th August. "In just a week's time," James said hugging Matea close as he gave her the news.

He had never heard her swear before and he tried, not always successfully, to avoid doing so in front of her. This time it was different, "The bastards," she said vehemently, "the utter, utter bastards." Then she sagged into his arms, all strength flooding from her legs.

James guided her to a sofa.

"We failed," she said, struggling to control her anger. "We failed. The United Nations failed because it is frightened of America. Hundreds of people will now lose their homes and probably their lives. All because my country goaded the Krajinas into declaring a state of illegal independence with their provocative actions and stupid symbols. No wonder the RSK refused all requests to re-join Croatia."

She stopped, calm again, then asked quietly, "Why, James? Why do we have to still keep on fighting?"

He had no answer.

Hiding Matea's advanced pregnancy with a voluminous coat they checked in for the Lufthansa flight to Split that left Heathrow at midday on the Tuesday. Three and a half hours later they had collected their luggage from the untidy jumble that had been dumped in the customs hall and were walking towards a smiling Patrick in the arrivals terminal.

Dino was staying with Mrs B and had been promised fishing trips with Jake out into Carrick Roads and, if the weather was fair, round Anthony Head to Portscatho. Dino enjoyed staying with Mrs B!

In the Land Rover for the fifteen mile drive from the airport Patrick gave a running commentary, bringing his passengers up-to-date. The bulk of the Croatian army had manoeuvred to face the RSK across the confrontation line. Swooping overhead in a final proof that any pretence of non-involvement in the coming war had long evaporated, were American Grumman F-14A Tomcat fighter and EA-6B Prowler electronic counter-measures aircraft.

"You probably haven't heard that Sublette panicked the other day and sent everyone in Knin to Split when he heard that NATO – and for NATO read America – was threatening Gorazde. A town over one hundred miles away in Bosnia Herzegovina for heaven's sake! When the crisis subsided the Serbs refused to let any of the monitors return."

"So now the ECMM has no monitoring team in Knin at the precise time that they are needed most?"

"Got it in one, James."

Although Matea had arranged for friends to keep Villa Perunika clean and aired a feeling of trepidation swept over her as they turned into Šetalište Ivana Meštrovica. Who knew what hideous surprise might lie in wait if Slavić had learned of her return.

As they neared the house they stopped to buy food and wine, although Patrick had offered their old rooms in Hotel Split. "Thanks, Paddy," Matea replied, "I will feel safer in my own home as I rather imagine Slavić will be too busy to bother about me right now," she paused before adding hopefully, "although I pray that he doesn't know I'm back."

With Patrick's departure, and having assured himself and Matea that all was well at the villa, James spread a road map of Dalmatia across the dining room table. He telephoned Augustin, hoping that he would be in Split and not at his family house in Milna.

Twenty minutes later the British Consul was banging on the front door. With a bottle of Prošek between them the trio sat around the table and map.

"Here are a handful of classified Telexes that Magnus sent earlier today with instructions that I was to hand them to you as soon as possible." Augustin felt inside his brief case and placed three envelopes on the table.

While James tore them open and read their contents Augustin kissed Matea fondly on both cheeks, able to congratulate her in person on becoming Mrs Laidlaw, "And expecting a baby too," he observed before declaring with a further hug, "Will wonderful things never cease happening to you!"

James intervened, "Sorry to bring you two back to earth but it seems that I now have the Croatian army's complete order of battle."

Augustin showed no surprise for he had read the Telexes but Matea looked stunned. "Apparently the US President, Clinton, has himself agreed the plan of the ground attack personally with President Tuđman before authorising American air operations."

"I knew our own president was unreliable but I had no idea that Clinton was personally involved." Matea was appalled then, remembering, she answered her own unasked question, "Which is why the Predators were deployed in the first place. Nobody else could have sanctioned that."

"Sadly, you are right," Augustin confirmed. "He has a re-election to fight next year. This is one way of currying favour with his electorate."

"It's sick making," Matea blurted, close to tears.

James had to support Matea but, if the morrow was to be a success, he also had to summon the facts, "The main thrust in the south will be towards Knin. When that is in Croat hands, the army will spread out, backwards from whence it came, as well as forwards towards the Bosnia Herzegovina border. They have been ordered to burn houses, destroy crops and herd all civilians together who will then be forced to walk towards Serbia proper, carrying their possessions. Those that refuse to move will be shot.

"As we know the attack will begin at 0500 but prior to that, between midnight and 0400 the Americans will destroy, electronically, all Serb communications while their fighter aircraft will engage the anti-aircraft batteries defending Knin. All with the help of the Predator's sensors. The Croats will then have exactly one hour to coordinate their final radio instructions for the attack.

"The ground attack against Knin will involve the 4th and 7th Guards Brigade. Also at 0500 a small armoured thrust will be landed at Karin Plaza using their two Silba class tank landing craft carrying, in total, six main battle tanks. A smaller Type 21 landing craft will land one infantry company in support." James stopped. It was depressing and it was alarming. He looked at

Matea.

"The bastards," she repeated.

"Sweetheart," he replied, his hands following the roads along the map, "It's a little over forty miles to Drniš. Say two hours by car but it is also the other side of the mine fields. We can't move ahead of the army so we shall have to follow them. I suggest we drive as far as we can to be in position by five on Friday morning."

"If they let us."

"Do you know any short cuts?"

"I spent many years exploring all round the countryside. We'll need a four-wheel drive car though. My little Fiat won't make it."

"We'll sort that out in the morning," then, turning to Augustin, James offered supper.

"You've had a long day and you have work to do tomorrow. So thanks, but no," he replied, "However, do let me know how you get on." Augustin rose from the table, turned to Matea and said, "I am so pleased for you. By Friday evening, all being well, you'll have your parents back. And that too will be good news for them." He stopped before adding, "But the Croatian government is making a great mistake not only in the short term but for generations of," he used the former name deliberately, "Yugoslavians to come."

Augustin kissed Matea then, turning for the door, stopped, "Here, James," he said, "I nearly forgot. You might need these." He placed a pair of small night vision goggles into his hands. "Good luck," he said and was gone.

While James studied the countryside surrounding Drniš on the map, Matea made up two beds in the largest spare room, explaining, "I want mother and father to feel at home from the moment they arrive back here."

The following day, James and Matea – he refused to leave her alone in the villa and, anyway, he needed an interpreter – scoured the second-hand car garages until they found a Land Rover of the same model as that used by the ECMM. It was light grey, which, James laughingly remarked, was the same colour as the monitors' vehicles after a day's driving. Glad to have money in any form the dealer took a Lloyds Bank cheque.

On Thursday evening, with the Rover packed with warm clothes, sandwiches and a flask of coffee, James and Matea drove to Split's northern outskirts. It was not an easy drive. The roads were clogged with stationary military vehicles surrounded by scores of men lolling about, smoking, drinking, chatting. Relaxed. Off the roads, M-84 tanks lay partially concealed beneath rough camouflage netting and foliage.

Surprisingly they were not stopped until a quarter of a mile from the border where the minefields began, here an officer waved them to a halt. James, dressed in white and, for the first time, wearing the ECMM blue baseball hat with the 12 gold stars as a badge, was accepted as a monitor. Further luck manifested itself when the officer, after a close look, stood back. Holding out both arms he shouted, "Matea Tomić. Remember me from university? Juraj Capan."

"How could I ever forget," Matea blushed. Juraj had been an ardent suitor for much of the time they were studying together and she had liked him immensely – but not as a lover. "Now you are a major and about to go to war." It was as close as she could get to an accusation.

Major Capan who, seeing an ECMM monitor with Matea, had spoken English from the outset, waved them to the edge of the road, away from his soldiers. "I know your views Matea, at least I knew your views from way back and I don't suppose they have changed. Do you still have relatives on the other side?"

"Yes," she replied carefully for she could not remember Juraj's opinions, especially as he had read for a degree in politics. "My parents."

Unexpectedly he gave them now, "We are about to go to war and I must obey my orders but I had hoped it would never come to this. A test of Croatian arrogance and Serb stubbornness. As soon as it is over I'm quitting..."

Thinking she had been alone in her views Matea was heartened by what she was hearing as the major went on, "...but if Colonel Slavić hears anyone talking like this he has them court martialled or, at the very least, removed from their appointment."

"No freedom of expression in the 4th Guards Brigade?"

"Not unless you hate Serbs, are a homosexual and a friend of the colonel's then you can say what you like."

Matea and James said nothing. The major asked a question. "Why are you here, Matea? It is not a safe place."

She explained that they were anxious to rescue her parents before the war overtook Drniš. "I am pretty certain what will happen to Croats who stayed behind and I must stop that." She held onto the major's arm, "I must reach them before your soldiers do."

"I would hope they will be safe with my men but once Slavić takes charge there is no knowing what will happen."

"Is he here?" Matea asked looking around her, suddenly furtive.

"He won't appear until the danger is over then he'll supervise the removal of the Serbs along with what he describes as the Croatian traitors."

"Let me show you where they are." Matea turned to James, "Have you got the map?"

With the map spread across the Land Rover's bonnet Matea

pointed to her parents' house, stabbing a finger on the spot. "There," she emphasised, "four kilometres along the tracks west of Drniš."

"Well," the major thought for a moment, "you are in luck. I have been ordered to plan my axis of advance to by-pass that very hamlet. Odd, but I was told that it's too far out on a limb to be of any tactical importance so it will remain untouched until Slavić orders the mopping up. Probably towards the end of tomorrow. And we all know what that means. You should have plenty of time but my orders to my men to spare civilians are already being countermanded from higher up."

James asked, "Obviously we can't go there before the attack but could we follow behind and peel-off as we pass?"

"For Matea. Anything! Just keep at a safe distance. We don't expect much opposition but you never know."

Matea leapt at the major and kissed him on the lips.

"Wow," he said, "It's a long time since you did that. And by the way who's your friend? Most monitors from Knin have been frightened off."

"Oh!" she said, "I really should have told you. This is James. My new husband. He was a monitor but…."

Before she could think of a plausible reason why he was still dressed in ECMM uniform the major thrust out his arm and shook James's hand vigorously, "You are a lucky man so why don't you regard our protection as a wedding present."

Matea kissed the major again, this time on his cheek.

"I had better go now for my final orders but I must issue a warning. If Slavić finds out he'll roast you both. And me too. Not that that matters as I've already offered my resignation. He's a slimy bugger and could turn up at any time and anywhere."

James reversed the Land Rover down the road and parked by a deserted, stone barn whose wooden floors and red-tiled roof had long since been destroyed by fire.

As they settled down, watching the setting sun, they clung to each other with few words necessary. As unarmed civilians they both knew the risks they were about to face, especially as those who most wished them harm were on the Croatian side of the confrontation line.

Precisely at five o'clock the following morning and as James was screwing the top back on to the coffee flask their Land Rover was rocked by violent explosions. It was difficult to tell if they were distant artillery or air strikes: either way *Operation Storm*, ordered by Croatian President Franjo Tuđman and endorsed by the Clinton Administration, had begun. The geopolitical map covering this part of the Former Republic of Yugoslavia was about to be changed for ever: as were the lives of over 200,000 Krajina Serbs.

Through his night vision goggles James watched the troops ahead move off towards no-mans'-land and the RSK's border, fanning out as they did so in an orderly manner. American and French training had paid off for these were not the ill-disciplined Croatian soldiers he had encountered on his first arrival in the country.

To begin with the men advanced cautiously on foot until they reached the frontier itself, marked by an increase in the number of minefield warning notices. Here, scouting parties were sent forwards supported by M-84 tanks, the distinctive, eerie clanking of their tracks echoing across the still countryside.

Sunrise was at 5.45 and as nautical twilight surrendered to the first shafts of sunlight radiating outwards from beyond the eastern hills James packed away his goggles and started the engine. Through cleared sections of the minefields and across the border opposition was negligible, allowing most men of the 4th Guards Brigade to remain in their transport, flanked by the tanks. The eighteen mile journey towards Drniš, the only town on the route to Knin, was covered quickly.

A slight bottle neck at the town's southern outskirts, where a bridge crosses a shallow ravine, caused a short delay while the soldiers, now on foot, spread out either side for fear of being ambushed. James, watching through his binoculars, described the battle to Matea. Drniš offered the first resistance for Major Capan's troops where, in accordance with the orders from 'higher up', they fought easily through the town showing little pity for any civilian and even less for any hapless Serb soldier minded to resist. Bodies lay where they fell: old men, young girls, even domestic animals were ruthlessly slaughtered. Slavić's murderous malignancy had taken hold.

At the far side of the bridge Matea, revolted by what she was witnessing, asked James to stop. Composing herself she gave instructions towards her parent's house, "From here," she said, "I know a short cut across country that will bypass the western edge of the town before meeting up with the road that leads out of it to towards the coast."

Leaving behind the carnage, the noise and the terror, James followed Matea's directions along the rough sheep tracks that led towards the east-west road. Turning left onto the tarmac they were, at last, grateful to head away from the growing palls of smoke that were beginning to hover above Drniš, beyond their left shoulders.

Under a mile later Matea ordered, "Take the second right..." She paused then pointed, "There. That gravel track." James manoeuvred the Land Rover as directed. He had been here before, as a passenger, but let Matea navigate to help keep her mind away from the earlier sights. "About half a mile to the house," she announced in a matter of fact manner, thrilled that their journey was nearly over and that she would soon be reunited with her parents. It had been a long wait. The complicated part, persuading her mother and father whom she had not seen since 1991, to leave, lay ahead but for this brief moment she was glad they had made it thus far.

Peering forwards through the dusty windscreen, Matea suddenly screeched, "My God. Oh my God, we may be too late."

Beyond a line of mature olive trees thick black smoke was beginning to curl up into the post-dawn sky. This was not the smoke of a stubble fire, nor of household rubbish but the dark angry billows of a house fire forced vertically skywards by an intense heat below.

James stamped the accelerator to the floor, taking the final curves almost on two wheels, driving ferociously forwards. He didn't need Matea to shout, "Turn left!" where the road forked. The Tomić's bungalow was ablaze with no sign of life. In their panic neither noticed the jeep parked off the track to the left.

James leapt from the driver's seat and ran to the front of the house, which the fire had yet to reach.

"James! Don't!" Matea screamed after him but he had already charged the door with his shoulder and disappeared inside. Billows of black, acrid smoke, released from the interior, curled out and upwards from beneath the door's lintel.

"Too late, traitor." The voice from behind Matea was chillingly familiar and familiarly menacing. She dared not turn but stood motionless, scared at what was happening in front of her and petrified beyond reason at what she knew was approaching from behind.

"I heard you were back and guessed you would come here. Of course I could have stopped you in Split," Slavić addressed her back and quaking shoulders, every word filled with hatred and evil, "but this is a more secluded place to do what I have to do."

Without turning, Matea watched as, miraculously, James appeared at the open front door, his white 'uniform' burned and blackened with smoke, carrying her mother while her father, clutching to his saviour's belt, stumbled by his side. The parents she had not seen for four years were, finally, coming home.

But something wasn't right and the look on James's grimy face confirmed her worst fears. Matea lurched forwards screaming, arms reaching for her parents, "Mama, tata! Oh my God! James help them! Oh God please help them!"

James's wide-eyed horror made her stop, then, despite the personal drama playing out in front of her, Matea turned in the direction towards which James was staring. She spun round in time to watch, with undiluted terror, as Slavić aimed his pistol beyond her and squeezed the trigger.

CHAPTER TWENTY-EIGHT

Wednesday 9th August 1995
Royal Cornwall Hospital, Treliske, Truro,
Cornwall, England

Through the mists of his mind James knew that someone was holding his right hand, stroking it gently.

"Hello, James," a voice said. "Remember me? Maureen Thompson, the midwife."

Half drugged and wholly puzzled, James began muttering incoherently, unable to articulate any formed words.

Maureen waited patiently.

As his brain slowly cleared he eventually managed to croak, "What the hell are you doing in Croatia?"

"We're not in Croatia. We're in the Royal Cornwall Hospital at Treliske."

Still bewildered, James rasped once more, "So what the hell am I doing in Treliske?"

Maureen thought it best that Matea, whom she had only met at their wedding, answered the question herself. There was, though, a snag, Matea was in the first stages of labour, a few corridors away.

With the anaesthetic wearing off James began to take in his surroundings and, allied to them, his own circumstances. The left side of his head stung like buggery but he couldn't nurse it as, for some reason, his left arm was strapped tightly across his chest.

Glancing hazily around the room James began to experience a sensation of encroaching dread. "Where's Matea," he asked his voice rising sharply in pitch. "Was she shot? For Christ's sake tell me."

"She's fine, you'll see her shortly."

Not satisfied he asked abruptly, "Where's Dino?"

"With Mrs B."

James's dread now reached an even higher level. He asked again, "Where's Matea? Why isn't she with Dino?"

"We're going to wheel you down to see her as soon as you have come round properly."

"Why can't she come here?" Treliske Hospital was where terrible things happened. He had to know what was going on.

"James," Maureen said kindly. "She's having a baby."

The news took a moment to sink in. At last James relaxed. Got it. Of course. Wonderful things also happen in Treliske Hospital and he wanted to be part of them.

"Can I see her or is there some other bloody complication?"

"Everything is really fine. When you feel up to it we'll take you to maternity."

"I'm up to it right now. All I have to do is just lie here in bed while some other poor bugger does the work."

"I'm so glad Matea hasn't changed you!"

Alicia Marković Laidlaw was born at six thirty that evening, "Arrived in time for a gin," James joked to his wife as his bed was pushed closer to hers. "Now let's have a look at the latest beautiful lass in my life."

Mother and daughter were allowed home the next morning but James's shoulder and chest wound needed reconstructive surgery, prolonging his stay. Rested and with Alicia in the temporary care of one of Mrs B's nieces Matea sat by James's bed recounting what had happened for his own recollection had ceased the moment he had entered the Tomić's house. "Hardly surprising," Matea explained, "Not only were you shot in the shoulder…"

"…and the head," he corrected her.

"…and the head," agreed Matea, "but the UN team then pumped you full of morphine until the doctors in Split took charge. Then you were knocked out properly for the flight home."

"Thank goodness I came-to in time to greet Alicia."

"It was lovely seeing you before I went into the final stages."

Matea described the story further. Although hesitant to relive the memories of her parents' murder – memories that distressed her immensely – she knew, too, that James, while equally distraught at having failed to save them, had to know. From Split the British Government had chartered a medical evacuation aircraft that flew Matea, James and a number of others with the United Nations Protection Force to RAF Brize Norton from where ambulances ferried the wounded to their own local hospitals. The bodies of Alicia and Jusuf Tomić were buried by the International Red Cross at the back of the house, their graves marked with simple wooden crosses.

The same sad tableaux was being repeated across the 6,500 square miles of the now destroyed Republic of Serbian Krajina while 200,000 refuges were, even as she was talking, fleeing on foot to Serbia, Bosnia and Slavonia: all the while harried, molested, jeered and attacked by Croatian soldiers and police along every mile of their tortuous and tragic journey. After over 500 years of co-existence, the Krajina area of the Former Republic of Yugoslavia had been ethnically cleansed with practical and political support supplied by the United States,

Germany, France and Ukraine.

"I don't suppose you have any idea what happened to Slavić?" James eventually asked.

"When he left Drniš he was not seen again. Augustin told me that his yacht was also missing. While you were in Split hospital Paddy came to the house to help me shut it up. He said that there had been no word of Sublette either since he ordered all the Knin monitors, including himself, across the border."

"Either way I hope they both rot in hell! And what about that duplicitous bastard Pagonis?"

"Apparently he married Karla – you remember she was his private interpretress – but was then ordered back to Greece."

By September, James's shoulder, although stiff but with increasing mobility, was healed enough to allow him to row his family, steadily, out to *Sea Vixen*. Jake had kept the cutter shipshape since James had last been able to look after her himself, apart from their brief honeymoon, from nearly two years back.

With the vessel riding peacefully on her moorings Dino would rush excitedly around the deck and up the mast, until his little arms forced a controlled descent while James slowly gained the strength he needed for longer voyages than one day at a time.

Over the months and years life at Percuil House returned to normal. Dino was developing into a fine young lad while Alicia, now five, was beginning to display her mother's features and characteristics: and James loved his daughter even more for that. The family cruises at weekends and during the schools' Easter and summer holidays began to increase in length and navigational adventure. Dino continued to learn to splice, knot – which Alicia took delight in untangling – as well as the rudiments of navigation.

Matea loved St Mawes and James loved having her with him for she had fitted seamlessly into the life. Her own country, despite its treatment of the Serbs in Krajina, was at peace and with the death of President Tuđman in December 1999 she felt that the final break with the dishonest events of four years earlier had, at last, been achieved.

She also believed that her promise to Slavić, made to him on that terrible day at Drniš had, too, come to fruition when she was interviewed by Scotland Yard detectives acting on behalf of the International Criminal Tribunal for the Former Republic of Yugoslavia at the Hague. Evidence was being sought in order to indict Colonel Ante Slavić, late of the Croatian Army, with war crime offences, murder and crimes against humanity. Eventually he was charged, *in absentia*, along with other alleged war criminals, including Ratko Mladič, Goran Hadžič and Radovan Karadžić: all of whom were also 'on the run'. Matea would never understand why Tuđman – although now dead – and Clinton had not, too, been on the list but kept her thoughts to herself.

Athough it had given her no personal pleasure to give evidence, recounted under oath, of the terrible events of August 1995, Matea had fulfilled her undertaking to assist having her nemesis brought to justice. It was someone else's problem now and she could relax. There were many magical moments in Matea's new life and while nothing would ever erase the memory of how her parents had met their deaths she was content.

James and Matea's love grew, they were seldom apart and sailed as often with the children as they did alone. Her happiness was cemented in her own mind – and not for the first time – one typical morning as she held *Sea Vixen*'s long tiller. They were heading seawards down the Fal estuary from one of their favourite river anchorages with James standing behind her, his arms around her waist.

"Would you like some more Rupert Brooke," he asked.

"I'd rather have you."

"Not very practical at the moment. You'll have to put up with poetry."

"Go on."

"Is it the hour?" he quoted, "We leave this resting place.

Made fair by one another for a while.

Now for a god-speed, one last mad embrace..."

"That's lovely," Matea interrupted, resting her head back against James's shoulder.

"Do you want the rest of the poem or the embrace? I promise it won't be the last but it might be mad!"

"I might not be able to steer properly."

"I'll take that risk.

"...Do you think there's a far border town, somewhere,

The desert's edge, last of the lands we know,

Some gaunt eventual limit of our light,

In which I'll find you waiting; and we'll go

Together, hand in hand again, out there,

Into the waste we know not, into the night."

James paused to ask, "Do you want to go into that night?"

"Only with you." Matea replied then stopped, a frown creasing her forehead, "But let us both pray for no more waste, no more night."

"I promise." James said and as the months rolled on memories of the horrors of *Operation Storm* became less vivid and further apart.

Until...

...during lunch on Friday 28 July, 2000, James noticed the colour draining from Matea's face.

"What's up?" he asked kindly.

Pushing *The Daily Telegraph* across the table she said, "Read that and tell me if you think the same."

The news item she pointed to announced that the French police in the north-west of the country were following up reports that an indicted Croatian war criminal and his male partner, who was harbouring him – respectively a Mr Ante Slavić and a Mr Jean-Claude Sublette – had been spotted leaving Camaret village in a yacht and heading north through the Chenal du Four between the island of Ushant and the mainland. It was understood from interviews with local shops and chandlers, the article continued, that the crew of two men had embarked stores for a lengthy stay afloat and had bought charts of the south-west coasts of England. Descriptions of the crew, but not of the yacht, had been circulated via Interpol to British police forces.

"It's nearly five years since those two went on the run," James observed, "No doubt hiding out in some of the less salubrious of the Mediterranean's north African ports. Safe from prying eyes."

"Now, *duša*, I feel they are closing in on us. After all this time of peace we are back where we started and this time I'm not sure I can cope anymore. I've become too used to being safe…" Matea was scared and the look in her eyes had James, instinctively protective, rushing to her chair and hugging her from behind but he was too late to prevent her declaring, "Why should we have to relive the crimes of others so long after the event."

"They don't know where we are," James encouraged, "Here, we exist within the law and if Slavić comes looking for us then I am sure he will be spotted before he can do any harm."

"James," Matea was not convinced, "I don't know why, as I am sure you are right, but I am afraid. All over again, I am really afraid."

James, lifting her in his arms, whispered in an ear. "My darling Matea," he consoled, "Nobody is coming to get you and supposing they did they would have me to contend with. Anyway, St Mawes is a million miles from such evil. It's unthinkable."

He may well have said that it was unthinkable but he, too, was beginning to feel uneasy. It could not be a coincidence that Slavić was approaching their area. Searching. Matea had honoured her promise to expose him as a war criminal. Slavić had yet to honour his side of the uneven bargain.

Not wishing to frighten his wife further James, following his instinct, decided that this was not a time for risk taking. If the newspaper report was only half true then Slavić, almost certainly armed, had to be closing in for the kill. Once more – and finally – he needed to be outwitted.

James knew the local waters and estuaries well and the places to hide. He also knew the popular anchorages. Not even Slavić, away from his corrupt colleagues, would dare commit murder in front of the British public and hope to get away with it in order to continue, with impunity, his debauched existence. Or would he? Slavić was a desperate man; a man intent on revenge and the extermination of witnesses: a man desperate enough to commit one last murder before justice finally and inevitably caught up with him. He had nothing to lose.

James and Matea knew all of this. They knew, too, that in *Sea Vixen*, they had the ideal vessel for hiding in shallow waters if they raised the heavy, iron keel. And yet a distant memory troubled James... Of course... in *Helena*'s saloon had he not mentioned *Sea Vixen*'s name and his moorings at St Mawes? Had he not shown Slavić a picture and explained how deep her draught was. Matea, on deck during that journey back from Brač, had not heard the conversation and he had never repeated it.

"Come on," he said cheerily, "Let's push off earlier than planned. It's neap tides right now. The weather's good..." He looked at the barograph, "...and the glass is high and steady. The children are at home all day. Perfect conditions in every respect so why are we delaying?"

Matea, knowing James's enthusiasm for any nautical adventure, thought that, this time, she could detect a trace of more than his normal eagerness to get afloat. "James," she said with a mock serious expression, "are you sure you are not just a tiny, teeny bit worried too? If not what is the real reason for the sudden haste?"

"The weather's fine, the children..." he tailed off. "I've just explained."

"You're right. Who knows, the weather may break earlier than usual this year."

"That's settled then. We'll pack up tonight and push off in the morning."

On the morrow, James ferried Matea and the children out to *Sea Vixen* in the dinghy then returned to the beach to collect their kit bags and boxes of food. He planned to fill the water tanks while lying alongside St Mawes's harbour wall at the top of the tide: an evolution that always amused the children while giving Matea a last chance to walk the few yards for fresh meat, fruit and vegetables.

Later that afternoon, fully stored for at least three weeks, they slipped *Sea Vixen*'s mooring lines from the quay and motored gently into Carrick Roads. With Matea at the helm James, helped by Dino, hoisted the mains'l, followed by the jib then the stays'l. Once the three fair-weather sails were set Dino asked, "Where are we going tata?"

"Well," his adopted father replied, "Let me see now. You're old enough to read an English chart, you know where the wind is blowing from and the direction the tide is flowing in and if I tell you that we've got about four hours before we must anchor so that your mother can cook without the boat heeling over and that Alicia has to eat quite early... so... why don't you decide..."

Before James had finished listing all the factors that Dino's excited brain had to consider the boy was gone, shouting over his shoulder, disappearing below, "Don't you worry, tata. I'll find somewhere."

Dino loved being asked to make these 'complicated' decisions. Soon he was leaning on tip toe across the chart table, calculating. He knew that James would go nowhere near a marina while he, too, much preferred to anchor off beaches because... he did not need to think too hard... because of the beachcombing... and the crab collecting... and the shrimping... and the seaweed popping... and the driftwood gathering... and the campfire building... and the barbecuing... and, eventually, the star gazing. He selected a chart to chose somewhere where he could teach Alicia how to do all these wonderful and thrilling things.

Dino's little fingers did their sums, measuring out distances, searching for the ideal beach. He knew many that would be suitable, depending on the prevailing wind; and he had already experienced most of them between the river Yealm in the east and the Isles of Scilly to the west.

After twenty minutes of concentration he shouted up through the companion hatch, "Tata can we go to the little beach just north of Mevagissey? Not the big one further on with all the caravans? Please, tata."

James, from sneaking glimpses through the skylight, knew how much young thought had gone into this momentous decision and answered encouragingly, "The perfect place, Dino. The most perfect place."

Dino was happy. He didn't always get things right with his pilotage plans but when James used the word 'perfect', which he didn't do all that often either, then it was… perfect!

There were many yachts, speed boats, fishing vessels, merchant ships and ferries criss-crossing Carrick Roads that Tuesday in July; so many that no one on board *Sea Vixen* took any notice of a ketch with a varnished hull, hove-to to the east of the Black Rock beacon, half a nautical mile off the entrance to St Mawes harbour. Nor, as James's gaff-cutter bore away down-wind towards St Anthony Head, did anyone on board notice the two men manning the ketch, each with a pair of binoculars hung around their neck.

Later, safely anchored under the lee of the cliffs, off Dino's chosen beach, Matea cooked an early supper. With Alicia and Dino tucked up in sleeping bags their parents sat in the cockpit as the light faded, each clutching a glass of whisky.

"I'm so happy again," Matea said, almost shyly, as though she had no right to be contented, "And so lucky," she added. "Thank you James."

"Me too," he replied. "Isn't it odd that we have a war to thank for this."

"But not much else," Matea replied, wishing to talk no further about that phase of her life. "We've done with all that and now that you have brought me to this wonderful place please let us have no more talk of war. It's over. We didn't win our own battle but my country won its fight. Sadly, at the expense of others. Now there's nothing more to be said."

"Quite so," James said, glancing over her shoulder and out to sea. "I can see the light of another yacht. I hope he's not going to anchor here."

"You don't like company?"

"Not afloat. The whole point of going to sea is to get away from people!"

The distant yacht's red port-hand navigation light shone brightly as she ghosted northwards in the darkness. Half an hour later, as they were finishing their night caps, the same yacht, James presumed it was the same yacht and now showing her green light, was retracing her course in the gentle breeze.

"How peaceful this all is," he said before making the final decision of the day, "It's getting cold. Let's turn in."

Matea needed no persuasion.

As he lay in their bunk starring at the deck-head above he knew that, while they might have left St Mawes and now had the whole of the south coast in which to hide, Slavić remained a desperate man who would stop at nothing and certainly not rest till his deed was done. The final game of cat and mouse had only just begun... and of that James was certain.

An hour after dawn, James climbed on deck to check the rigging and anchor cable. They had had the anchorage to themselves all night, indeed it was so small that no other yacht would have had swinging room if it, too, had decided to drop a 'hook'. The wind remained westerly and although it had increased by a few knots it still offered the prospect of a pleasant day's sailing further to the east. With any luck, if the anti-cyclone eventually drifted north, they might eventually have a good run back with a following wind towards St Mawes before the food ran out. But, James smiled to himself, things never work out quite like that at sea.

They were in no hurry. If the wind did not change they could explore the upper reaches of the River Tamar until it did. *Sea Vixen* enjoyed a good thrash to windward but if it could be avoided for the sake of a day or two then a following wind would suit her young crew better. Anyway, that was in the future and not a concern for their first full day at sea.

After breakfast James rowed the children ashore, Matea remained to tidy bunks and prepare sandwiches should they decide to picnic on the deserted beach: and if it wasn't this one then it would certainly be another, farther along the coast. Making plans in advance, beyond the next beach, was not their style.

James had taken a hand-held, walkie-talkie with him in the dinghy: a precaution that he insisted on for he hated being out of touch with Matea. While Dino scoured the rock pools for shrimps and 'hidden flotsam' as Alicia dutifully held a small plastic bucket for the spoils, James collected drift wood to store on board for a later barbecue. The sun was warm, the temperature slowly rising beneath a sky dotted, only occasionally, by startlingly white cumulous clouds or, as Dino called them, 'fair weather fluffies'.

"Look, tata," it was Alicia who attracted James attention with her happy-sounding shout. James turned from his small pile of bleached wood to see his daughter pointing excitedly towards the low, rocky headland that marked the southern extremity of their tiny haven. Alicia enjoyed the company of others of her age, her limited experience teaching her that the arrival of another yacht meant new friends. Dino was fun but other girls were more fun.

James now watched the masts of a ketch-rigged vessel with sails furled, moving slowly, almost ghost like, beyond the rocks. Then, with a sickening realisation he knew that what he was watching in slow motion, as the varnished hull came into full view past the point, was *Helena*. The sedate speed of her way through the water, the lack of sails despite the useful breeze and her course, now straight for *Sea Vixen*, all suggesting a dreadful malevolence of intention.

James waved to Dino and Alicia to join him sitting on the sand, behind the beached dinghy then he pressed the 'transmit' button on the small radio.

Matea answered the loud squawk in the cabin. "*Duša*, is all well?" James only used the two-way radio in an emergency.

"No!" James answered sharply. "Stay where you are," he commanded. "Keep below and out of sight. If you can, lock the cabin hatch but only if you can do so without showing yourself."

"James, I know there is something wrong?"

"Slavić's boat is entering the bay so, please darling, do as I ask."

"I can see it now through the skylight."

"I'll distract him. Draw him away. It'll work if he thinks *Sea Vixen* is un-manned."

"Tata," Dino asked, "is mama in trouble?"

"Not as long as you are around to protect her." Despite suspecting that James was not quite telling the truth Dino offered more support, "I will help you help mama if she is in trouble."

"Thank you Dino, mama will be safe thanks to you."

Helena was less than one hundred yards from *Sea Vixen* with both crew on her upper deck, peering through binoculars at the anchored British cutter. The man at the helm slowed the ketch even further to a walking pace.

"Stay below, Matea. Stay below. That's the most important thing."

As he released the 'send' button a raucous screaming reached him from the cliff path behind. James looked back. Twenty, possibly twice that number of teenagers accompanied by an uncountable number of barking, excited dogs, were zig-zagging their way down the steep bramble-bound track.

Dino muttered disapprovingly, "They will steal all the shrimps."

Alicia, not keen on their arrival either, agreed with her brother, "And pop all the seaweed."

James looked seaward once more. *Helena* was already turning sharply away from the beach to head, at what had to be her maximum speed under power, towards the anonymity of the English Channel.

James called Matea, "I never thought I would thank a gang of half-drunk teenagers," he said.

"What do you mean!"

"I'll explain in a moment. The important thing is that Slavić has been frightened off. For the moment. But still keep out of sight. He's a wounded animal and will take any number of risks."

James stood to greet the first arrivals. "You'll probably want the beach to yourselves," he smiled.

Gathering children, driftwood, buckets overflowing with intertidal detritus and seaweed to be 'popped' later, James rowed as fast as his shoulder would allow back to *Sea Vixen*.

Approaching the vessel, he rested on the oars, handed Dino the radio and instructed, "Here, Dino. You've seen me using it. Press the red button and tell mama that we are nearly alongside."

Proud to be part of the adventure, for adventure it was in his young eyes, Dino pressed the button. "Hello Mama. It's Dino here. Tata says we will be alongside very soon."

"Thank you darling," Matea's reply crackled through the ether, "I'm so pleased."

With the dinghy secured on deck and Dino and Alicia in the fore-cabin sifting through their latest possessions, James guided Matea into the cockpit, away from young ears.

"It is bad news, I'm afraid." Matea said nothing. Her worst

fear had been confirmed just when she had found peace and happiness. She reached for his hands as James summed up their situation in the only manner he knew. Directly.

"Oh God, will this nightmare never end..." With uncontrollable tears saturating her cheeks Matea clung tight to her husband. "What can we do? The police. Call the coastguard. The lifeboats. Call someone. Please *duša*. Please."

James knew she was being rational but he was a fighter and, in those few moments, could foresee months of untold misery if Slavić lived.

Matea was right but James insisted, "Not yet. We'll lead him into a trap. If we confront him at sea it will be us that comes off worst. He might then be caught but it will still be us that will lose."

"A trap. How?"

"No idea." James was thinking fast. He had to come up with a workable plan. A plan that had to be fool proof. "*Helena* is faster than *Sea Vixen* but if we can gain a head start we could be somewhere safe, surrounded by others, before he catches up."

As he was speaking the cutter began to rock gently; enough to make James look up at the western sky then, down through the companion hatch, at the barometer above the chart table.

"The glass," he said, "Look at the glass!"

"That means wind. Plenty of it."

"A short-lived channel depression that can spring up from nowhere. It also means a cracking sail providing you want to run before it."

"James!" Matea admonished him, appalled that he could think of a 'cracking sail' when their lives, and those of their children, were at stake. "This is serious. It is not the time to think of having a good sail."

"Oh, but it is," he argued with a broad smile, "It most

certainly is!"

Matea was horrified that James could even smile let alone revel in the thought of sailing when there was a danger to be faced. A danger that, guided by Slavić's evil hands, had shown its face far too often. She wanted to hit James. She wanted to hit him as hard as she could to shock him back to reality. Instead she listened to him because she trusted him and she knew he trusted her. She knew his love for her and the children was, beyond any other consideration, overpowering. She knew, of course she knew, that he would have a plan. A workable plan the outline of which he would explain in his own time. She sat in silence, waiting.

Instead James said, "Tell the children that I promise them fish and chips in Looe for supper this evening."

"Is that your plan. Is that the best you can come up with? Fish and chips in Looe. Here we are facing..."

James held up his hands, "It may work," he said softly, "especially as I know I can trust you to help. I dare not tell you more because it will depend on the sea conditions and Slavić's reactions and I may have to change my mind."

Half an hour later, with Matea, Dino and Alicia in their safety harnesses and the mainsail hoisted with two reefs, James hauled in the dripping anchor cable. As he hoisted the jib the flapping and flailing sail was soon under Matea's control as she secured the port sheet on its cleat.

Walking aft, coiling ropes and checking that all was ready for sea, James shouted, "Dino, go below and tell me the course we need for Looe Island. Fifteen miles to the north-east."

As *Sea Vixen* cleared the southern headland the true wind filled the sails. Dino's face appeared in the hatchway, "Seventy five degrees, tata," he called.

"Well done, but a true seaman will call it zero seven five."

"Sorry tata."

"Not vital. It's the accuracy that counts."

Having added five degrees of magnetic variation to Dino's figure – the lad hadn't quite mastered the intricacies of a compass's peculiarities – James settled *Sea Vixen* on her course and looked around.

Helena was lying at anchor outside Mevagissey's walled harbour: out of sight from the anchorage *Sea Vixen* had just left. Ready to pounce. As James watched through his binoculars he could make out Sublette – it would never have been Slavić – struggling with the cable's windlass and calculated that they probably had a forty-five minute lead over the Croat. It wasn't much but as the time to cover the thirteen miles to Looe Island in the strengthening breeze, would be under two hours it might, just, be enough. The two yachts were roughly compatible in size but Slavić's Bermudian-rigged ketch would be faster... and then what? If Slavić could catch them offshore there was no doubt that he would use firearms. Close in, within sight and sound of people, James wasn't so sure.

The wind was rising, noticeably, with spindrift starting to blow off the increasing number of low white horses as they, too, began to chase *Sea Vixen*. Every so often a larger wave broke under the vessel's counter, lifting her stern, accelerating her down its leading edge. It was becoming exhilarating and if it had not been for their pursuer slowly gaining on them, it would have been thrilling. For all the physical delights of a 'cracking sail' James knew that the adrenaline flowing through his veins was not caused by the pleasure of the chase, the excitement of a race even – which it had become – but by the far greater fear of not reaching safety in time.

He assessed his decision: they could not have stayed at anchor for, during the night, they would have been at Slavić's mercy nor could they have sailed offshore for he would have followed them to his perfect killing ground. Out of sight of land. Their only chance was to run downhill, in as fast a headlong rush as they dared in the rising wind, towards the nearest port, and only then inform the authorities that an armed vessel was in pursuit. James had considered Fowey as a suitable destination until a more subtle plan, a more deadly scheme, formed in his mind and for that to happen he needed an area with the necessary hydrographic features.

It might work. It might not work. Almost anything had to be worth the risk to be rid of Colonel Ante Slavić once and for ever; and if he took Jean-Claude Sublette with him then that would be a most welcome bonus.

James asked Matea to take the helm. She was calm and experienced and they would need those very strengths of hers if the plan was to succeed. Happy that in the increasingly testing conditions she had the vessel under control James ducked below to study the chart in minute detail through a magnifying glass. As his strategy had only an outside chance of succeeding, and wanting to involve Dino as much as made sense for someone of his young age, James tossed him the tide tables. "You can be a real help Dino if you can tell me the time of high-water at Plymouth for today. The thirtieth of July."

Dino eagerly turned the pages, "Half past five this afternoon."

"Good lad. Its going to get even more bumpy before it gets better so you look after Alicia down here."

"Is it dangerous, tata?"

"Not a bit of it." James reassured him.

"Will we still have fish and chips for supper?"

"I promise."

In the cockpit, the lively tiller secure in her hands, Matea asked again, "Why can't we just call the coastguard on the VHF radio. Then Slavić can be arrested and we will finally be rid of him."

James had considered this most sensible of all the options open to him. He had considered it very carefully indeed, but he knew that that would entail years of painful cross-examinations, visits to the Hague and the perpetual reliving of that terrifying day at Drniš, all coupled to the possibility that one day Slavić might be free again or even be found not-guilty. Against those odds he accepted that his solution was not ideal but he would never forgive himself for not trying. He knew, too, that his plan might not work and, worse still, he knew that it might backfire, spectacularly, in Slavić's favour. He kept the radio call as an option but as an option of last resort and one only to be activated when he was certain Slavić was close enough to civilisation to be apprehended.

He relayed none of this to Matea but said instead, "It may come to that but he'll hear our radio call and then take even more desperate measures to destroy us or," James was thinking hard, evaluating all the possibilities, "perhaps, even worse, back off for as long as he likes, playing on our fears. Possibly for months…"

As the nautical miles beneath *Sea Vixen*'s keel were reeled off, the weather deteriorated markedly as Dino's fair weather cumulus 'fluffies' gave way to lowering, hard-edged cumulonimbus, darkening all the time, laden with moisture.

"Look beyond the skylight, Dino," James ordered through the main hatch, "See how the clouds have changed?"

"This is not the time for a meteorology lesson, *duša*," Matea interjected angrily. "Please!"

"'Fraid so," James called back, "Rupert Brooke can sum such things up so perfectly.

"Rank upon rank, unbridled, unforgiving,

Thundered the black battalions of the gods.

"Now, thanks to those black battalions I would like to put the third reef in the mains'l," James shouted above the wind, "to make her easier to handle but the bugger will certainly catch us then. As it is he has closed the gap to less than a mile. If he gets any closer we'll be within rifle range so we've got to make the harbour before he does. Once in sight and sound of people on the shore he won't dare."

James ducked beneath the boom to check the fast-closing coast, now three quarters of a mile to leeward, fringed with bursting spray. They had passed Fowey, they had passed Polperro, if they did not make it safely into Looe and were forced to run to Plymouth then Slavić would catch them before they were half-way across the nine-mile width of Whitsand Bay and James knew that that, most emphatically, was not an option. His first plan, the only plan now remaining, simply had to work. It would be a close run thing but he was determined to see it through for he had no other choice. It was not only imperative that all four of them escaped Slavić's murderous intentions – which they could have done in the earlier ports – but, of far more importance for Matea's final peace, it was vital that the Croat was destroyed, utterly and finally... Fowey and Polperro might have offered sensible, safe havens but, for his strategy to succeed, only Looe's underwater reef could bring about the ultimate, satisfying conclusion.

"Are we still aiming for Looe?" The tone in Matea's voice betrayed her fast-rising concerns.

James did not answer directly but said instead, "They pass very quickly, these summer blows in the channel." He tried to reassure her further, "If, together, we can get it right ..." then he stopped. He had no right to make promises he was unsure he could honour.

Matea's love for James was not always matched by her confidence, not in his decision-making but in her own ability to match up to his expectations. Now, though, was not the time to let him down. She said more calmly than she felt, "Just tell me what to do and when to do it."

"I love you," was James's unhelpful reply. "The next few minutes will be tricky as we meet the ground swell off the cliffs. Better double check that the children's lifejackets are tightly fastened. Not loose, how Dino likes his to be. Tell them to stay below, to hold on tight and do nothing unless I say so. I'll take the helm."

While Matea did as he asked James took another look beneath the boom. He knew well the passage between Looe Island and the mainland although he only ever attempted it at high water and on calm days when he could see the bottom. This time was different and, although expecting it, he did not like what he saw ahead. The half-mile passage between Hannafore Point and the island was a continuous line of breaking seas that made it hard to gauge where the less shallow passage was... but he had sailed through often enough and, as luck had it, they were approaching the reef at high water.

Checking astern James saw that, tenacious as expected, *Helena* was being guided directly down the track that *Sea Vixen* was carving through the foam and as the seas reached shallower water they were growing in height and increasing in gradient. With her long, heavy, lifting-keel *Sea Vixen* remained stable but the downwards rush on the face of each racing wave, with the rudder rock-solid in his hands, was still unnerving. Any deviation from this mad, impetuous charge and they would be rolled sideways by a breaking sea and... James shuddered.

His plan also depended, crucially, on Matea having the

strength to hoist the keel. If she failed they would all fail.

Nearing the bar and with the crests of breaking seas stretching uninterrupted from shore to shore, James lined *Sea Vixen* up with a well-remembered transit on the far cliffs. It was not quite the deepest section of the reef which made it even more suitable for the task. With half a cable to go, he shouted down to Matea.

"Darling. Stand by. Get Dino to help. It's got to happen first go… and fast." He looked at the breakers piling up ahead then added, "Shut the hatch but leave a small gap so you can hear my commands."

If James had worried about any aspect of his plan it was this moment. With the keel lifted *Sea Vixen* would lose much of her directional stability. Controlling her for the crucial transit of the reef in the waves that were building steeper as the sea bed shoaled would require every ounce of his strength on the tiller and the quickest of reactions. His left shoulder simply had to cope.

"Mama and me are ready, tata." Dino's little face was pressed to the gap in the hatch, his eyes wide with innocent excitement.

James shouted below, "Bravo," he encouraged. "When I scream, 'now' hoist away for all you are worth."

With the tiller gripped in both hands and the rudder humming and vibrating as each overtaking breaker accelerated the vessel to the point of instability, there was no turning back even had *Helena* not been astern. James knew that he would not be able to control the cutter with so much sail set if she lay across both wind and sea and he was relying on Slavić's belief that he, James, knew a passage to safety. So far, the Croat had behaved according to the rules.

It was, literally, now or never. With a last minute check that their adversary was still directly astern James judged the moment.

As a heavy, breaking sea burst green and white across the cockpit James yelled, "Now!" towards the companion hatch.

In the saloon, Matea and Dino hauled on the rope purchase that raised the keel. Dino's eyes bulged and his immature muscles strained but he knew he was playing a vital part in this unknown escapade. He didn't know why it was vital, he just knew that if James asked for something to be done at sea in a hurry then he had to help. One day he would be told.

As the monstrous iron weight was raised *Sea Vixen* responded. Slewing to starboard, her round bilges lost all grip as another sea foamed across the deck. James tried to pull the rudder hard up to windward, his arm and back muscles working at the utmost limit of their strength, but it was solid in his hands. The cutter skidded sideways to port, broaching, close to being rolled… close to annihilation… but drawing one more foot less… one foot further from the deadly reef beneath.

Fifteen seconds was all it took to cross the bar with the cutter out of control in a mass of tumbling breaking surf, the rocks not four feet beneath her bilges. For those long, fifteen terrifying seconds she heeled to 45 degrees, the lathering seas reaching to her mast. Then, just as suddenly and just as violently, she rolled upright as the weight of water on her upper decks sluiced overboard to port. The bar was astern. They had made it.

"Lower the keel!" James shouted, and as stability returned and the rudder regained its grip *Sea Vixen* swung wildly back to her original course in the lee of the reef.

The transition to peace was one of the most pleasant physical sensations James would recall: though he would never admit that to his wife.

He looked astern. The picture of a beautiful yacht – or even an unattractive motor vessel – running at speed onto rocks is not a pleasant one. For a split second James was appalled at the sight of *Helena* in her death throes… but sometimes a single bereavement is necessary for the many to survive.

In the very spot that *Sea Vixen's* keel had been raised *Helena's* varnished hull reared up as though lifted on the back of some vast oceanic leviathan. Then it stopped dead in the water, listing sharply and wallowing erratically as heavy seas swept, unimpeded across her now-stationary deck. The main mast snapped at the cross-trees and crashed forwards. A terrible crunching sound reached James's ears, audible even above the roar of the breakers. *Helena's* keel, grinding itself on the rocks below, was ripping her lower planks apart.

In calmer water now James ran forward to lower the mains'l while Matea furled the jib.

"We must go back and try to save their lives," James shouted in her ear.

Appalled at this sudden and inexplicable reversal of James's strategy – from killing Slavić to saving the man who murdered her parents – Matea swung round shouting, "Must we *duša*? Must we? What crazy thing are you now suggesting."

"Yes! We must. It's a brotherhood of the sea thing. All seaman are obliged to help those in distress. We must check if he is all right."

Matea looked more closely at James and saw that he was grinning broadly.

"Yes," she smiled back, "of course we must."

With the engine running sweetly, James headed towards the bar where two yellow life jackets were bobbing among the flotsam. One of *Helena's* crew, arms flailing and shouting loudly, was trying desperately to struggle free of the floating detritus, the other appeared lifeless. Ropes and torn sails grabbed at both bodies as they drifted clear of the reef and into deeper water.

James stopped *Sea Vixen* alongside the nearest head. Recognising the flabby, waterlogged features of Ante Slavić, his bulging lifejacket framing his obese face as it struggled to support his immense body, James was astonished that he could feel no compassion for a fellow seafarer. Matea climbed out of the cockpit to clutch his arm, both of them swaying together as the vessel rolled in the spent swell on the lee side of the reef. White faced, she stared down at the man who, for so long, had been her archenemy, her nemesis, yet even at this defining moment she could feel no emotion as she watched, impassively, Slavić snatching and clawing in vain at the smooth sides of *Sea Vixen*'s gently rolling hull.

Without taking her eyes off the drowning man Matea made her confession and, in that moment, all fear left her. "*Duša*," she said, surprisingly gently, "I don't want to see him live," James had lowered the boathook to within Slavić's reach but Matea pulled it aside adding, "but I can't watch him die." Fighting back what she would later call her 'tears of liberation' she swayed back to the cockpit and went below to comfort her children.

Wielding the boat hook James shouted at the Croat. "Grab hold of this," he ordered.

Slavić retched and spluttered, pausing for breath between each word. "Thank – you," he coughed hopefully, "I – thought – you – said – your – boat – drew – nine – feet."

"That's right, she does," James replied coolly, "but only four feet with the keel raised."

The look on Slavić's face would remain another source of pleasure for the rest of James's life, but... there was one final task to perform. One final promise to be honoured.

As the Croat's finger nails scratched uselessly at *Sea Vixen*'s high sides and the slippery-wet, boat hook's varnished pole

James could not avoid a final taunt, "Don't be afraid of dying, Slavić. You've caused and seen enough deaths for it to hold no fear for you."

"*Pomoć,* James. *Pomoć.* Please."

"Too late Slavić. Far, far too late to ask for mercy," and with these final words James thrust the metal boat hook hard into Slavić's inflated life jacket, giving it a violent twist as he did so to make quite sure. The sound of escaping air was another satisfying memory that, too, would last him well in to old age.

Realising that James had no intention of 'helping those in distress at sea' Slavić screamed, his face puce, his eyes wide with panic, his mouth opening and shutting, "You – bastard! You..." but his words turned to bubbles as his head sank through the foam until all that remained were blood and vomit rising slowly to the surface in one last, obscene image.

Calmly James stowed the boathook before manoeuvring *Sea Vixen* away from the immediate area of debris, then he grabbed the radio microphone, "Mayday relay. Mayday relay. Mayday relay. This is yacht *Sea Vixen, Sea Vixen* reporting the foundering of an unidentified sailing vessel off Looe harbour. Two men in the water. Am attempting a rescue. *Sea Vixen*, out!"

The coastguard answered immediately, asking James to stand by until Looe's inshore lifeboat, was 'on scene'. They requested more details. James was circumspect with his answers.

The arrival of the RNLI's 'rigid-inflatable' allowed *Sea Vixen* to continue her voyage until, with Dino, Alicia and Matea on the upper deck handling warps and fenders, they brought the cutter alongside Looe Harbour's western quay.

Safely secured, Dino took James's hand, "Tata," he asked looking trustingly up into his step father's eyes, "where's the boat that was following us?"

"Very sadly it hit the rocks."

"Why did it do that?"

"It's what happens when you get your sums wrong."

"You didn't get your sums wrong, did you tata?"

"Thanks to you and mama, Dino, we all got everything right. Especially your sums."

"Was anybody hurt?" Dino's anxious face was still looking up at James.

"We tried to save them but unfortunately we were too late."

Dino thought for a long time. "Are we still going to have fish and chips?" he eventually asked.

"Of course, a double helping. Tell mama and Alicia that we are waiting."

The following morning a police officer and the lifeboat secretary stood on the quay looking down at James. "We would like to thank you for your help yesterday," one of them shouted, "Pity it ended in tragedy."

"Tragedy?" James affected curiosity.

"We found two bodies on the rocks at first light. One had suffered a head wound, possibly caused when the mainmast collapsed and the other's life jacket was ripped open. Must have snagged in the rigging as the yacht foundered. Just so much dead weight. Helped to pull him down."

"Poor buggers," James said.

"We can't work out why they tried to cross the bar in such a strong onshore wind."

"Damned fools if you ask me."

"Why did you?"

"I knew the way," James replied a touch flippantly, knowing that from the shore it would have looked irresponsible.

"Oh well," the constable replied, "Every skipper must answer for his own actions." He pulled out a notebook, "Interestingly," he consulted the pages, "among the effects washed ashore there was a plastic wallet containing the details of your own vessel. Plus a number of firearms in a waterproof container, including a sniper rifle with telescopic sights. The deceased was also wearing a pistol in a shoulder holster. Would you know why any of that would be?"

"Not a clue, officer. Not a clue."

"Judging by other papers we have identified one of the crew as a wanted Croatian war criminal."

"His death will save the lawyers a lot of work."

"You don't seem too concerned?"

"War criminals deserve all they get."

"They also deserve a fair trial."

James thought for some time before replying, very deliberately, "No, not always."

EPILOGUE

Tuesday 4th May 2015
20th anniversary of *Operation Storm*
Croatian Airlines Flight OU491, Heathrow to Split Airport

From the aisle seat of the Airbus A319 James leant across Matea to watch the approaching Dalmatian Coast, 20,000 feet below. With the offshore islands beautiful in the evening's sun, reflecting off the calm sea below, he detected a mistiness in his wife's eyes as she gazed down at her old home. As he inclined back she kissed his cheek. "Thank you, *duša*, for bringing me here," she murmured. "It's been a long time and now I don't know whether I am happy or sad."

The visit to Matea's home country had been planned numerous times over the intervening years but each time the proposal had been delayed and then cancelled. Matea, happy in her new life and with no close relatives alive in Croatia, had been hesitant to resurrect hosts of bad memories. Dino and Alicia had completed their English schooling. Alicia, now at Newcastle University reading modern languages, and Dino, a veterinary surgeon with a fiancée and a practice in Cornwall, had returned at regular intervals to ensure that the leasing agent was keeping Villa Perunika in good shape as a 'holiday let': one of many along the popular Dalmatian coast. James had often considered accompanying them during their bi-annual

421

visits but felt that any return, and especially the first since 1995, had to be with Matea.

Now the moment had come. The children were waiting to meet their parents at the airport. "We've arranged a little tour for you, mama," Dino began as they loaded their luggage into his car, "but first of all we'll have a family dinner in Villa Perunika tonight with spring lamb from Brač," James and Matea looked at each other and smiled, "then tomorrow we'll drive to Drniš and show you where grandpa and grandma are buried."

"They are in a very beautiful garden where the house used to be," Alicia continued, "and well looked after by the local farmer. Miljana is now also buried with them."

"How lovely. You are so kind," Matea answered, "and I would like to see Augustin too."

"That's fixed. We fly on a day trip to the modern Brač airfield on Wednesday. Augustine is elderly now and wants to see you too so Filip will drive us to Milna for lunch."

"Perhaps, for old times sake, we should have a drink in Hotel Split's Riva Bar," James suggested, "and maybe ask if I can visit Room 519."

"All arranged as well, except that the hotel is now called the Radisson Blu Resort."

"I wonder if they've replaced the carpet in the foyer?"

Everywhere they travelled the shops were full of goods, food was on sale, and the people looked happy. Those crowds that they did encounter were no longer exhausted-looking refugees wandering aimlessly but contented tourists spending money. It was a different country to the one that Matea had left and she was pleased. It was a country with a bright future but also a country with a dark past.

On Thursday evening, standing at the villa's sitting room window, overlooking the Splitski Kanal smiling towards the islands and the setting sun, Matea took James's hand. Leaning her head on his shoulder she whispered, "I'm ready to go home now, *duša.*"

"Home?"

"St Mawes. Always will be," she replied with a wide grin and a squeeze of James's waist. She thought further, "It is lovely to see a happy Croatia again and for that I am grateful but we did bad things to gain this peace. And that is why I still worry about the future. You can't wipe out over 500 years of history and displace 200,000 people in one day then not expect some form of retribution..." She stopped to think before adding, "Eventually."

AUTHOR'S NOTES

Following the ethnic cleansing of an estimated 200,000 Serbs civilians from the Krajina region during *Operation Storm* in August 1995, of whom upwards of 2,000 were probably murdered as they fled east, a United Nations official commented that, 'Almost the only [Serb] people remaining were the dead and the dying, notwithstanding that the Krajinas had been their homeland for over 500 years.'

Despite these cruel statistics the number of prosecutions and permanent convictions for war crimes has been, and remains, lamentably low.

Mladen Markač, the Croatian Commander of Police Special Forces during *Operation Storm*, was indicted by the International Criminal Tribunal for the Former Yugoslavia (ICTY) for war crimes in the Republic of Serbian Krajina (RSK). In April 2011, he was found guilty and sentenced to 18 years imprisonment. On 16 November 2012, the ICTY Appeals Panel found him not guilty on all charges. On his return to Croatia he received a hero's welcome.

Ante Gotovina, also of the French Foreign Legion, served during *Operation Storm* as a major-general commanding the Croatian forces that attacked Knin. In 2001, the ICTY indicted him on war crimes and crimes against humanity in connection with that operation and its aftermath, from which date he spent four years on the run until captured in the Canary Islands in

December 2005. Gotovina's convictions were overturned by the ICTY Appeals Panel on 16 November 2012 and he was released from custody

Ivan Čermak, Croatia's one-time Assistant Defence Minister, commanded the Croatian Army's Knin Corps during *Operation Storm*. In February 2004 he was indicted by the ICTY on charges of conducting criminal operations to remove, by force and permanently, the civilian Serb population from the Krajina region. In April 2011 he was acquitted of all charges and released.

Gojko Šušak, was the Croatian Defence Minister in 1995 and a prime architect of *Operation Storm*. Croatian judges declared that he too had been implicit in the same 'joint criminal enterprise' as Gotovina but he was never charged and died in 1998.

In September 2002, the ICTY indicted the former Croat Chief of the General Staff, Janko Bobetko, with war crimes following *Operation Storm*: he refused to surrender to the court and died in 2003 before a decision could be reached regarding his extradition.

Emilio Bungur, who was convicted of war crimes against Serb civilian prisoners, was arrested on 22 August 2015 near Sibenik after ten years on the run. The Croatian supreme court had, in 2007, sentenced Bungur to six years in prison, *in absentia*, for crimes against Serb civilians at the Lora military prison camp in Split between March and September 1992.

In 2014 Croatia sentenced Bozo Bacelić to seven years for killing two civilians and one prisoner of war in Prokljan, near Sibenik.

Radovan Karadžić, a former Serbian President, was arrested in Belgrade on 21 July 2008 and extradited to the ICTY while Ratko Mladić, a former Bosnia Serb general, was extradited to the ICTY on 31 May 2011 after nearly sixteen years on the run. By 2015, both Karadžić and Mladić remained on trial for charges of genocide, crimes against humanity and war crimes committed in Srebrenica, Prijedor, Ključ, and other districts of Bosnia. On 24 March 2016 Karadžić was found guilty of ten out of eleven counts of genocide, war crimes and crimes against humanity. He was sentenced to 40 years imprisonment. In October 2016 Mladić awaited trial while in March 2016 Vojislav Šešelj, a former deputy Serbian prime minister was cleared of all charges of crimes against humanity, causing the current (2016) Croatian prime minister, Tihomir Orešković, to describe the acquittal as 'shameful'.

Dragan Vasiljković, nicknamed Captain Dragan and known to the Secret Intelligence Service as Daniel Sneddon, was the founder of a Serbian paramilitary unit, *Knindže* (*Knin ninjas* or Red Berets). Accused by Croatia of war crimes a warrant for his arrest was issued by Interpol. It was not until January 2006 that he was detained in Australia and imprisoned on the orders of the High Court of Australia in anticipation of extradition to Croatia. He was extradited on 8 July 2015 after losing his thirteenth appeal and, in October 2016, awaited trial. The author, as part of his ECMM monitoring duties, met him on a number of occasions in his training camp in the RSK.

Milan Babić was elected the first president of the Republic of Serbian Krajina. In 2004 he was indicted for war crimes by the ICTY and became the first to admit guilt and make a plea bargain with the prosecution. He was sentenced to 13 years in prison but was found dead in his prison cell in The Hague in March 2006. The author, as part of his monitoring duties, met him in Knin in 1993.

Milan Martić is a former president of the Republic of Serbian Krajina and convicted war criminal. He was a senior commander of RSK forces during the Croatian War of Independence. Martić was convicted of war crimes by the ICTY on 12 June 2007 and sentenced to 35 years in prison.

Goran Hadžić, also a former RSK president was, in 1995 and *in absentia* sentenced to 20 years for launching rocket attacks on Šibenik and Vodice. In 1999 he was sentenced to an additional 20 years for war crimes, then in 2002 Croatia accused him of the murder of almost 1,300 Croats in Vukovar, Osijek, Vinkovci, Županja and elsewhere. On 4 June 2004, the ICTY indicted him on 14 counts of war crimes and crimes against humanity. In 2011 he was arrested and extradited to The Hague. In November 2014 Hadžić was diagnosed with terminal brain cancer. His trial was delayed until April 2015 when the court ordered his release. He died in July 2016.

Four further war crime cases came before the Zagreb courts in 2014, including that of a former Croatian soldier, Rajko Kricković. His was the first case relating to *Operation Storm* in which Serbia and Croatia worked together on the basis of a war crimes cooperation protocol.

Subsequently, some 40 other war crimes, involving 200 victims connected to *Operation Storm*, were investigated by Serbian and Croatian prosecutors. Several former Croatian troops were convicted of aggravated murder during *Operation Storm* rather than war crimes. Jelena Djokić Jović, a war crime trials monitor with the Zagreb-based, Non Government Organisation Documenta, described this as 'a poor criminal proceedings statistic [for crimes that were undoubtedly committed]'.

While Croat President Franjo Tuđman was still alive the ICTY's chief prosecutors decided against indicting him for war crimes. However, in 2002 a new chief prosecutor, Carla del Ponte, indicated that she would have indicted him had he not died in 1999. Graham Blewitt, a senior ICTY prosecutor, was also quoted by the AFP wire service as saying that 'There would have been sufficient evidence to indict President Tuđman had he still been alive'.

It is of note that, in 1995, Germany and the United States refused to condemn *Operation Storm*. The US President, Bill Clinton, allegedly stated that he was 'hopeful that Croatia's (August 1995) offensive will turn out to be something that will give us an avenue to a quick diplomatic solution.' The US Secretary of State, Christopher Warren, also stated that 'events of summer 1995 could work to our advantage.' Bearing in mind, *inter alia*, the breaking of United Nations Arms Embargo 713 by both Germany and the United States, coupled with the air support provided by the US during *Operation Storm* these might be considered duplicitous statements. Tuđman's forces were partially armed and supported by the US thus making it obligatory for him to receive the 'green light' from the Clinton Administration before embarking on *Operation Storm*. Therefore a question must be asked: why were no indictments considered for those responsible for approving and ordering these illegal actions?

For the Russian part it is useful to quote *Time Magazine* of 14 August 1995:

The Russians, who have close ties with the Serbs, expressed particular anger at the German and US responses. The Russian Foreign Ministry declared that 'unnamed' western governments (Germany and the United States) *'showed solidarity with the military action of the Croat side.'*

On the 20th anniversary of *Operation Storm* – in 2015 – the then Croatian Prime Minister, Zoran Milanović, described the war as 'just, defensive and humane' while, conversely and unsurprisingly, the Serbian Prime Minister, Aleksandar Vučić, described *Operation Storm* as 'the biggest [example of] ethnic cleansing since World War II.'

A report by the Croatian Helsinki Committee for Human Rights is worth reading for further information on events that led up to *Operation Storm* and its aftermath. One passage from 1993 states:

Since 1991 the Croatian authorities have blown up or razed ten thousand houses mostly of Serbs but also houses of Croats. In some cases they dynamited homes with the families inside.

A later Wikipedia report states:

The International Criminal Tribunal for the Former Yugoslavia later tried three Croatian generals charged with war crimes and partaking in a joint criminal enterprise designed to force the Serb population out of Croatia, although all three were ultimately acquitted and the tribunal refuted charges of a criminal enterprise. In 2010, Serbia sued Croatia before the International Court of Justice claiming that the offensive was an example of genocide. In 2015, the court ruled that it was not genocidal, though it affirmed that the Serb population fled as a direct result of the offensive and that serious crimes against civilians had been committed by Croatian forces. Up to November 2012, the Croatian judiciary had convicted 2,380 persons for various crimes committed during Operation Storm.

A report titled *US Role in Storm* by Ivo Pukanic dated 24 May 2005 will be of interest and can be found on the internet.

A penultimate note: as early as 20 November 1991 Lord

Carrington, presiding over negotiations to ensure independence for individual nations following the break up of Yugoslavia, posed the question: 'Does the Serbian population in Croatia and Bosnia and Herzegovina, as one of the constituent peoples of Yugoslavia, have the right to self-determination?' Then, on 11 January 1992, it was concluded by the commission

that the Serbian population in Bosnia and Herzegovina and Croatia is entitled to all the rights concerned to minorities and ethnic groups...'

and

that the Republics must afford the members of those minorities and ethnic groups all the human rights and fundamental freedoms recognized in international law, including, where appropriate, the right to choose their nationality.

Several of the major players in the 1995 Balkans conflict are still involved in world politics having suffered little damage to their reputations... and yet there is no Statute of Limitations for war crimes.